When the Whippoorwill Calls

A novel by

Peggy Poe Stern

Moody Valley
Boone, North Carolina

Published by
Moody Valley
475 Church Hollow Road
Boone, N C 28607
moodyvalley@skybest.com

Cover painting by Peggy Poe Stern
Cover design by David K. Stern
First edit 11/ 25/ 2020 by DKS
Edited 2/07/2021 by PB
Edited 2/16/21 by PPS

Published 2020
ISBN: 978-1-59513-071-6

Dedicated to
Appalachian Friends and Family
Past, Present, and Future

Chapter 1

Tally sat humped up in a chair by the edge of the bed where Momma lay. Momma's coughing wasn't as strong or as often as it had been. Tally hoped it was a sign she was getting better, but she'd learned hoping was a useless thing. Her momma had lain in bed fighting for each breath so long she'd not been able to talk above a whisper. This morning she was too weak to put words together.

"Doc Ro..." she managed to get that much out of her cracked lips, causing another gasping fit to hit her as her body convulsed in pain.

Tally knew who she was talking about. Dr. Robinson lived two ridges over and down in the valley from their place. Momma had asked for him several times in the past week, but her dad refused to go after the doctor. Not that there was a chance he'd do it to begin with. He said the doctor did nothing more than cheat honest folks out of their hard-gotten earnings. He wasn't about to hand over what little he'd worked so hard for to get a no-account sawbones to see a woman that didn't need seeing to.

"Hur--ee," Momma managed to whisper as her body contorted in worse pain.

Tally didn't know where her dad was or when he'd return. He'd gotten up at the crack of dawn from sleeping next to Momma's sweat-soaked body and left. From her pallet in the loft, she'd heard him cursing Momma and saying that a man

1

couldn't get a good night's sleep no matter how much he needed it.

Tally jumped up from the wooden chair and leaned closer Momma so she could hear her whispered words better.

"Doc Robinson?" Tally questioned. "You want me to go atter' him?"

"Hur--ree," she whispered again in a pain-filled voice as fresh tears rolled down her cheeks.

Tally knew her dad would give her a whipping for going after the doctor when he had forbidden it, but she was so scared for Momma that a whipping offered little deterrent. Her mother's lips had taken on a shade of blue in her pale face. Sweat oozed from her forehead and upper lip, dripping onto the lumpy pillow. Just seeing the way she looked was enough to make Tally willing to do anything to help her – even going against her dad.

"I aim to go get him, Momma. You'll be all right till I get back, okay?"

Tally's words were a mixture of begging and praying. She thought Momma's head nodded, but she couldn't be sure. Tally's heart was pounding in her chest with worry and fright as she raised up from leaning over Momma, crossed the room, opened, and closed the shack door. Her dad had forbidden the door to ever be left open. He claimed no-account critters would sneak in through an open door. He never worried about the cracks in the walls and floor. Dad acted like the cabin was a mansion when it was only one room with a loft and a leaky roof that barely kept the rain out. Momma wouldn't let anybody criticize or say a bad word against her dad. "He does the best he can with what he'd got to work with," she'd say. Tally concluded her mother was either blind or loved Dobb Simmons so much she refused to see how arrogant and lazy he actually was. Tally wanted to love her dad, but she couldn't. She wasn't blind or stupid, nor did she like being afraid.

~~~~

The chilly morning dew wet Tally's legs and feet as she ran through the tall weeds in the yard. She didn't have shoes on, but it didn't matter. She wouldn't have taken time to put shoes on even if she'd wanted to. Besides, she had to save what pitiful shoes she had until snow was on the ground. She'd gone barefoot until hard calluses had formed on the bottom of her feet. Momma was more important than the sharp rocks her feet would hit or the briars that tore streaks on her bare legs. There was no doubt how bad off Momma was. She thought about going to the witch woman, but she had a fear of her. The only person who could help her was the doctor. She believed deep down in her heart if she could get him to Momma in time, he would be able to make her well. Doctors were rumored to be able to work miracles. If she didn't . . . she didn't want to think about that, not now, now ever.

She needed her momma in the worst sort of way. She had three older half-brothers, but they were long gone from home. She also had a half-sister, Mary, who was the oldest of Momma's children. Mary was born two months after Momma turned sixteen. Mary had slipped off and got married when Tally was a baby. Mary had married Frank Lang. He was twenty years older than her, a widower with five motherless children. The last Momma heard from Mary, Frank had moved them somewhere up north in the Kennett Square, Pennsylvania area. As for her three half-brothers, only the good Lord knew where they were. Momma prayed and cried over them often, but she never mentioned their names in front of Tally's dad.

Momma didn't blame the boys or Mary for leaving home. In a way, she encouraged it. Tally suspected Momma would have left a long time ago if it hadn't been for her young'uns. Momma put great store in her young'uns having a roof over their heads and food in their bellies no matter what she had to endure. A woman might be able to disappear from a cruel husband if she was alone. Momma knew a mother with a bunch of children had no hope of providing for them when they were on the run. Not only that, but not even the good Lord could protect them if Dobb Simmons ever caught up with them.

By the time Tally came along, Momma was worn out and broke down. Still, Tally would often catch her standing statue-still on the highest part of the look-out rock cliff gazing down in the valley.

"What're you doin', Momma?" Tally asked when she came upon her standing her that way.

"Daydreamin'," she'd said.

"'Bout what?" Tally wanted to know.

"Where my young'uns are, and if they're happy. I don't hold it against 'em for taking off the way they done. It's not like they had a choice other than to make a run for it. Life was mighty hard on 'em livin' here with Dobb Simmons. I know that only too well."

Life was hard on Momma and Tally, but neither of them could do a thing about it. Tally was too young and Momma was too old to put up a fight against a man such as Dobb Simmons. Time had her momma set on the mountain as solid as locust tree roots were set in the ground. Tally figured she was still young enough for her roots not to get set, but time would set her roots too, unless she ran off with some old man the way her sister did.

"You'll have to go, too, when the time comes," Momma would tell Tally. "I don't 'pect you to stay on this mountain once you've growed enough to get away."

A different kind of sadness would come to her momma's face when she said that.

"I wonder what it's like in places other than on this mountain," Momma would say with a longing sound. "Once folks leave here they don't come back. I figure if things weren't better where they're at than here, they'd return," she reasoned.

Tally figured her momma's reasoning was about right on most everything other than on her dad. Tally remembered what Jimmy, her youngest half-brother, had said about her dad. "He hain't worth a pile of hog shit, Tally. Momma made a bad mistake when she married up with the likes of him."

He might be Tally's very own dad, but she agreed with Jimmy. Momma hadn't bettered hers or her children's lives by marrying Dobb Simmons – the way she had intended. All she bettered was his lazy, no-account existence.

"Lord, what can I do to get us out of this predicament?" Tally had heard her whisper in prayer. "I jumped right outta the frying pan into the fire. I need to rectify it. Please God, show me a way out."

Tally tried to make herself stop thinking about Momma marrying a man like Dobb Simmons as she ran through the woods. But then, if Momma hadn't married up for a second time, she wouldn't be alive, but none of that made a lick of difference. What was done, was done. Right now she had to concentrate on running fast without tripping over rocks and tree roots, while not getting lost. She'd never been to the doctor's place before, but she'd been near when she went with Momma to pick berries. When folks were as poor as Job's turkey, they had to gather everything God provided just to be able to keep flesh on bones.

Tally had no idea how she'd pay for the doctor seeing Momma. She had no hard-earned coins and neither did Momma, but she would pay him some way sooner or later. Perhaps she could gather herbs like the old witch woman did. She ought to have plenty of years ahead of her to work enough to pay one doctor, if her dad didn't kill her once he found out what she had done.

Odd how trees, rocks, and brambles could look alike in the deep woods. Nothing was familiar. Tally wasn't sure if she was running in the right direction, or if she had become completely lost and was running in circles. She tried to remember the direction Momma had gone when they picked berries, but they were going from field to field instead of traveling in the deep woods. She was trying to run along the top of the ridges, staying on the high point of the mountain. It would slow her down if she went down into a valley where cleared fields were and then had to climb up steep hills. She found herself sobbing with bewildered tears when she came upon a huge laurel hell she'd have to crawl through or turn around and retrace her steps.

"You lost?" a voice asked, causing her to let out a screech as she jumped about a foot. She whirled around to see a boy who was a right smart bigger than her. He had on ragged bibbed overalls, but not nearly as ragged as the feed sack dress she wore. His hair was long, brown, and his face and body were as skinny as a reed. It was easy to tell that she had been fed more than he had.

"Who are you?" she asked, trying to stop herself from crying, ashamed that he would see her weakness.

"I'm Clancy," he said. "What's wrong with you? Why are you crying? You lost or hurt?"

"Momma needs the doctor," she told him as she wiped her runny nose on her arm.

"That where you're headed right now?"

Tally nodded.

"Then I best show you which way to go. You got turned around a right smart. Follow me."

Tally had never set eyes on the boy before, but it didn't matter. She had no choice other than trust him if she wanted to get to the doctor's place. Her dad had warned her often to never trust a boy or a man, but her momma was counting on her. She took out after him as hard as she could run. He stayed well ahead. Not only was he skinny, his legs were bony and a lot longer than hers, plus they work a sight faster. Sometimes he slowed down to wait on her to catch up.

Tally's lungs were heaving in pain, and she had just about run out of breath when he suddenly quit running.

"There it is," he said as he stopped on top of the ridge and pointed down the hill to one of the houses in the valley.

Tally stood still as she stared at the square, white house with a tin roof. She turned toward Clancy, but he wasn't there. He had disappeared as if he had never existed.

She wished he would have gone down to the doctor's place with her. His presence had helped with her fear, plus he'd gotten her to the right place before he had left her on her own. She gritted her teeth to keep her chin from trembling and took out running down the steep hill as fast as her shaky legs could go.

A woman with a white straw hat on her head and gloves on her hands was working in a patch of pretty blooming flowers. Tally had never seen the likes of her or the flowers before.

"Good grief," the woman said as she stood straight up, when she saw the child running toward her. "What in the world?"

"The doctor! Momma needs the doctor bad," Tally yelled at the top of her aching lungs as she bent double, hands clutching her side, heaving for breath.

The woman's eyebrows raised until they disappeared underneath the band of her hat. Her mouth opened. She didn't say another word as she stared at the dirty, ragged girl.

"Where is your momma?" A man's voice ask from an open door.

"Home. Momma can't get out of bed. Hurry! She's in a bad way," Tally managed to get out in a rush of breathless words.

"What's wrong with her?" asked the man with salt and pepper hair sticking out in all directions as he came outside to stand on the porch, while looking Tally over with disapproval. "What's your Momma's name, child?" he then asked.

"Sally Simmons. Please hurry. I think Momma's dying. She's in a bad way," she rattled in a frightened, high pitched voice.

"She Dobb Simmons wife?" the frown on the man's face deepened as he asked the question.

Tally nodded. She hadn't wanted to answer him in case he knew her dad.

He clenched his teeth together but the word, "Shit" slipped out.

She feared he wasn't going to help Momma as she sank to the ground with crying sobs taking their toll.

"Poor little thing," the woman said making sure she didn't get too close to the smelly, dirty child huddled before her. "I'll get her a glass of sweet tea while you get your medical bag."

"I took an oath to help those in need, but there are people and places I won't tread upon," the doctor said more to himself than to the woman and Tally.

"Dear," the woman said in a condescending way, "Look at this child. Someone needs to help her and her mother regardless of who her father happens to be."

"You don't know Dobb Simmons," the doctor told her. "He's not the kind to mess with. Mean as a striped snake. Won't let a doctor or anybody else near his place."

"Dear," she said again with a slight uplift of her lips, "I attend church on a regular basis along with most ever lady far and near, not to mention attending other worthwhile ladies' groups here in this valley. There is little gossip my ears have not been subjected to, and that includes the goings on of Dobb Simmons and how he treats his pitiful wife."

"A bunch of gossiping women," the doctor grumbled as though he didn't hold them in great esteem, which he didn't. "Tell-a-woman something and you inform the world."

The woman patted him on the arm as she rushed past him. He stood there looking down at the girl with a disapproving frown on his leathery, worn face.

"Hurry, Dear," she said as she came back outside. "I have a feeling this really is urgent. Here, honey, stand up straight and drink this. We'll help your mother," she assured Tally as she handed her the glass.

"We?" the doctor sounded displeased.

"Yes, we. I intend to put this pitiful child in the back seat of your car and go with you."

"No, you're not," he told her as his eyes widened and his brows shot up.

"Don't argue with me, Dear. I have no intention of sending you into a volatile situation alone."

"I certainly don't intend putting you in a dangerous situation either; and believe me, anything to do with Dobb Simmons is dangerous. The man is a crazy fool. He beats his wife to a pulp."

"Hush now. Stop arguing with me. God will be with us. Hurry, now."

"God doesn't stop bad things from happening," he told her firmly as he turned his back on them and went back inside the house.

The woman took hold of Tally's arm with her gloved hand. Tally wiped at her eyes and nose on the dirty sleeve of her other arm. The woman let out a sigh, took a clean handkerchief from her apron pocket and thoroughly wiped the child's face. When she finished wiping, she stuck the handkerchief in the girl's ripped pocket.

"Water for cleanliness comes free. From now on, make a habit of using it," she told Tally with a gentle firmness.

The doctor came back outside, stalked past them to the black car. The woman kept her hold on Tally's arm and practically dragged her to the car, opened the door and pushed her into the back seat, then closed the door. She got in front beside the doctor.

Tally hunched up, shaking, even though she was trying to be brave. Never before had she been put inside a car, much less rode in one.

"Foolish woman," the doctor accused.

"You're not the only one called to assist those in need," the woman informed him.

"Humph," he grunted. "I'm not the only one who needs you to stay alive and healthy," he said as though it was an ongoing statement he made often.

"Yes, you do need me," she told him firmly. "More so than most doctors need a nurse."

He grunted and argued no more.

They rode in silence for what seemed like forever. The silence had Tally going over in her mind what her dad was going to do to her when the doctor showed up with her riding in the car. She recalled the only time she had screamed at Dad when he had knocked Momma down onto the floor. He'd grabbed her by the hair, slapping both sides of her face several times with his big hand and then used his booted foot to knock her down beside Momma.

"Don't move," Momma had whispered low enough so he couldn't hear her above his raging yells.

"Damn spawns of the devil. All I ever asked you for was a son and you gave me that rag-bone gal. She ain't no-account and neither are you. Ought to throw you both in the big river and find me a good woman. One who'll give me my boy."

Much to their surprise, Dobb Simmons stomped out of the house and left them alone.

"Are you alright?" Momma whispered, lying still.

"Uh, hum," Tally sniffled.

"Stay put a while longer. Make sure he don't come back."

They laid there until Momma decided it was safe for them to get up off the plank floor. Momma was hurt more than Tally was, but she didn't complain.

"Dad will kill me for getting you," her mouth opened, and she dared tell the doctor.

"He doesn't have to know," the woman said as though it would be simple to keep it from him.

They would show up at their place to doctor Momma, and her dad wouldn't have to know? She didn't know anything about men like her dad if she thought he was going to swallow that.

"We'll tell him measles are spreading among the children, and we are on a mission to vaccinate every child," the woman said as though it was only logic.

The doctor let out a disbelieving breath of air but didn't go against what the woman said.

"We'll let you out of the car close home and you can run ahead and hide from us. We'll accidently find your mother in need of medical attention," the woman continued.

Tally thought the woman was as foolish as the doctor evidently thought, but neither of them was coming up with a better idea. Tally had no choice other than take what was offered.

"Take your time getting back to the house," she told Tally. "We should arrive before you in order to fool your father."

~~~~

The doctor stopped the car before they reached the narrow, rough path that served as a road. The path ended part way up the mountain below their shack. Tally got out and ran just as fast as she could to get back to Momma. A horrible feeling had taken hold of her. The closer she got to the cabin, the worse the feeling became. It was as though something horrible was hovering over her like a black cloud reaching down to encompass her, causing her to run as fast as she could to get back to Momma like she'd run to fetch the doctor.

She stopped behind a big maple tree, heaving great breaths of air into her lungs, while determining if her dad had returned to the cabin. Seeing no sign of him, she slipped to the shack and peeked in the single window Momma was always washing. There was no sign of her dad. Momma was still a lump lying under the ragged bed quilt. Tally eased to the door, opened it, and left it open for the doctor as she slipped inside as silently as possible.

Momma didn't move as Tally leaned over her. She appeared to be sleeping peacefully, which was something she hadn't done in a long while.

"Momma," Tally said a little above a whisper. "The doctor will be here any minute." She thought Momma's eyes flickered open. They appeared to be looking right into hers. Her momma's parched lips moved open slightly.

"Momma?" Tally called again, a bit louder. "You're gonna be alright. I brought the doctor. He's gonna cure you."

Momma's eyes opened a little wider and her lips parted farther. Tally put her hand on her mother's forehead to check her temperature the way Momma always did with her when she was sick. Her flesh felt cool and dry. There was no longer the burning fever that brought a cold sweat Momma had for the last few days. Tally hoped that was a sign Momma had gotten better while she was gone after the doctor. Tally sat down on the edge of the bed and stared at her momma's face. Her momma's mouth kept creeping open further, but her eyes remained as they were.

A few minutes later Tally heard the sound of twigs snapping and heavy breathing. The doctor and woman had arrived. Her dad never made a sound when he walked in the woods. "Only a fool makes noise," her dad claimed.

Tally stood up and rushed to the door, feeling something sticky on the bottoms of her feet. She looked down to see the red of blood in the dim confine of the cabin. She must have torn up her feet without realizing it to have blood on them. She took the handkerchief out of her pocket with the intent of wiping away the blood. She'd need more than one handkerchief because she was standing in a pool of blood. There was even a streak covering the feed sack material Momma had used to make a sheet. Momma used a mixture of pine needles and chicken feathers to make a mattress and pillows. She had plenty of pine needles, but few feathers.

The doctor and woman reached the open door.

"Damn," the doctor said as he rushed to the bed, trying not to step in the blood that had pooled on the wooden boards.

The woman's breath caught in a gasp. "Come here, honey," she managed to say after she had taken in the scene.

Tally walked across the wooden slab floor leaving bloody footprints behind. The woman put her arm around Tally's shoulders and led her outside.

"Let's find some water and wash your feet. Is there a creek nearby?"

Tally nodded and led her behind the house where a spring ran from under a rock. The woman put her hands on the little girl's shoulders and eased her into the water. She took off her gloves and used her bare hands to rub Tally's feet until they were clean. It made Tally think of the last time Momma had washed her feet. It had been a while.

"What happened?" Tally asked, seeing her feet hadn't been shredded or even had a tiny cut. "Where did all that blood come from?"

"I used to take baths in a spring branch much like this when I was a little girl. Sometimes I'd stay in the cold water so long my lips would turn blue. My body would be shaking from the invigorating chill," the woman told her as though it was a pleasant memory. "I liked it when I was your age."

"I don't like being cold," Tally told her.

"Right. You're a sunshine girl. I can tell by your tan. I bet you stay outside a lot."

Tally looked at her legs and arms. Her tan was more browned by dirt than by the sun. She hadn't washed herself since Momma took to her bed. Momma used to heat a wash pan of water every night for her and Tally to wash themselves before they went to bed. She'd have to wash up fast before the doctor cured Momma. Momma would be sure to fuss at her if she wasn't clean.

"Give me the handkerchief I put in your pocket and I'll help you with a bath if you'll take off your clothes off."

It was those words that brought Tally to her senses. She wasn't about to take off her clothes or let that strange woman wash her. Tally took a closer look at the woman's face and knew something awful was wrong. If the blood hadn't come from her feet, it had to come from her Momma. Tally surprised the woman by leaping out of the water and making a run for the cabin where her Momma was. The doctor grabbed her as she ran through the door. He was coming outside. Tally beat at the hands holding her, but it did no good. He was a sight stronger than she was.

"You can't go back in there," he said as he pushed her backward and closed the door.

"I want my momma," she yelled at him.

"I know you do," he said. "I know you do."

Tally broke loose from the doctor and ran into the woods. Realization hit her hard. She hadn't gotten the doctor to Momma in time to save her.

~~~~

Tally hid in the woods watching from the undergrowth as the woman sat on a block of wood in front of the door to keep her from going back inside. The woman stayed even after the doctor left. The sun was going down before the doctor returned. Four women were sweating and trailing along behind him, each carrying things in her hands. Two men were walking by his side. All three of them were carrying shovels and some sort of thick, folded material.

"Where is the girl?" the doctor asked the woman.

"She hasn't returned," she told him.

"I'm not surprised. It's the way of these mountain people. It's their nature to hide when things turn bad."

"Where do we dig?" one of the men asked the doctor.

"In the softest ground you can find," another man answered him. "These mountains are filled with rocks and roots making digging a deep grave difficult."

"Come with me to the spring branch. We'll need a lot of soap and water to get things cleaned up and her prepared for burial," one of the church women said. "Lord knows Dobb Simmons will let her lay right where she is until the maggots eat her. Us Christian women can't allow that to happen. Even Dobb Simmons' wife deserves a Christian burial. Lord knows she never got a decent moment living with him."

"I don't want to think about being Dobb Simmons' wife," another woman said.

"What happened to her?" one of the women asked.

"Looked to me like she bled to death from a miscarriage. There's blood everywhere."

"Did Simmons show up?" another woman asked.

"No."

"It's just as well," said the questioning woman. "Let's hope we get the job done before he comes back. It'll be easier on us. I've heard mighty bad things about the man."

Tally jumped about a foot and almost squealed when a hand took hold of her shoulder. It was Clancy, the boy who had shown her how to get to the doctor's place. He was quick to put his fingers to his lips to make sure she wouldn't make a sound that would give her hiding place away. He motioned for her to follow him, and she did – all the way to the top of another ridge.

"They can't hear us from here," he finally spoke. "If they get hold of you, they'll take you to that orphanage place and lock you up where you can't get out. That's what those church women did to me when my momma died. I pried out a loose board that was nailed over a coal chute and left that place they had shut me in."

"My momma isn't dead," Tally told him, hoping what she said was true. "She's only resting. The doctor will cure her."

Clancy heard the pleading sound in her voice, but he knew the truth was better than a lie.

"Yeah, she is. Might as well face it," he told her. "You've still got a dad and a cabin to live in. In a way you're luckier than I was. Then again, knowing what a rascal your dad is, he'll have them lock you up in that home the same as they did me."

The cold chill of fear run through Tally. Her own safety interrupting the memory of all the blood on her feet that came from Momma.

"You'll have to hide out until they've given up and gone away," he informed her.

She just looked at him, trying to find words to express how she was feeling, but not one sound came out of her mouth.

"Can't take you to my cave," he said. "Can't chance nobody knowing where it is, especially a girl, but I'll keep you hid while they're on the mountain. They'll leave come the gloaming. God-fearing, church going people all like their comfort and this mountain atter dark ain't one of 'em."

Tally sat there with Clancy until she grew tired and laid down in the leaves, waiting. It turned dark and then light again.

"Is it morning?" she asked him.

"Yeah," he nodded. "Wondered how long it was gonna take for you to come around and talk again."

"Momma?" she said.

"Sorry, but it's real. She's gone and there's not a thing you can do to change things. They've already buried her."

"Buried her?" his words didn't make good sense. How could her mother be buried?

"Yep, you might as well buck up and face it now than later. Those do-gooding church men dug a hole out behind the cabin and put your momma in the ground."

His words were like pouring cold water over her on a winter day. *Dug a hole. Put Momma in the ground.* Tally remembered a little robin she'd tried to save. She'd dug worms for two days trying to get it to eat. All her determination and care did no good. The baby bird died. Momma dug a hole, and they buried the baby bird – never to be seen again.

"Come on. Stand up. I might as well show you her grave while you're still in shock. Pain of reality will hit you afore long. When it does, it will hurt like hell and you'll scream a blue streak. I did when my momma died and left me alone. You'll get over it though, same as I did. Like I said, you've got a dad regardless of how sorry-assed he is. We best hurry. Some of those church folks will most likely come back to find you after they've eaten their good breakfast and drunk a pot of coffee."

Clancy took Tally by the arm and pulled her to her feet. She followed him even when she didn't want to see anyone's grave, especially her mother's. He took her to a place not far from the spring branch where Momma always grew her garden.

"Look at that. Buried her right smack in the middle of her garden place. Figures. Too lazy to dig where's there's rocks and tree roots," Clancy said with disapproval.

Sally had readied the garden to plant. She always started shoveling it up in late March. It took her until the first of May to turn it all over. Dobb could have done it in hardly any time, but physical work of any kind never suited him.

"He married me for what he could get outta me," Momma had told Tally not so long ago. "Reckon I ought not complain. I done the same thing with him. Didn't work out on my behalf. Done dandy fine for the likes of him."

"Ought not complain," Tally repeated Momma's words as she looked at the mound of dirt that was now her mother's forever resting place. She couldn't believe her momma was really under all that garden dirt. Suddenly, she turned and ran toward the cabin as fast as she could. There was a ragged quilt and the mattress cover hanging on the clothesline along with the empty mattress sack. On the ground, in the edge of the woods, was a cleared spot where the pine needles and feathers had burned. A few of the needles and feathers had escaped the fire and were blowing about with the breeze. She turned away from the sight and went inside the cabin. The bedframe stood against the wall where it had always been. The plank floor beneath the bed had been scrubbed clean, as had the planks where she had left bloody footprints.

"Those do-gooders were too lazy to scrub the whole floor," Clancy said from behind her. "Surprised they did what they did."

Tally looked up toward the loft where she always slept. If she climbed the ladder and went to sleep, she'd be sure to wake up and find Momma cooking their breakfast. She was certain of it.

"No way," Clancy interrupted her hopeful thoughts as if he was reading her mind. "You can't stay here for a while. Somebody will show up soon trying to find you. We best put a get-on away from here."

"I want my Momma," Tally told him with a trembling chin.

"Yeah, and I want a mansion filled with ham hocks and honey."

She'd almost gotten used to him taking hold of her arm to pull her into the woods. It was easier to let him tell her what she should do than doing things on her own.

~~~~

Clancy kept her hiding in the woods for three days. They ate the things he was able to glean from the woods. Thank goodness he was good with a slingshot. He called it a gravel shooter. He could kill squirrels and rabbits with it if he got close enough to them, which didn't happen as often as was necessary to ease two people's hunger.

They slipped close enough to the cabin to hide in the undergrowth to watch as the church folks came looking for her. On the third day the preacher and one other man were confronted by Dobb Simmons stepping out of the woods with a loaded shotgun aimed at them. They hadn't heard him coming. Dobb had always been able to move as silent as a snake in wet grass.

"What have you heathens done with Sally?" he demanded.

"Mr. Simmons, we regret having to tell you your wife died. She is buried out back near the spring branch."

"You're a bunch of lying assholes," he yelled. "You've been trying to get her away from me since the day I married her."

From where they hid, Tally could see the fury burning on his leathery face. She expected to hear the shotgun roar and see the church folks drop to the ground.

"Again, you have our deepest condolences," the preacher said. "We'll show you her grave and say another prayer for your peace of mind along with her heavenly resurrection."

Dobb didn't seem to move a muscle as he pulled the trigger on the shotgun. A huge clump of dirt and weeds shot up into the air between the two men. Tally never knew grown men could run faster than a deer.

Clancy didn't have to put his finger to his lips or hold onto Tally to keep her silent. She knew her dad was both mad and drunk. The only thing that surprised her was that he didn't shoot both men. Tally had an idea the only reason he didn't was because he no longer had hogs to get rid of the bodies. He's sold all of their hogs a few weeks back when Momma started getting sick and wasn't able to take care of them. Tally knew her momma was tearing rags to fasten between her legs, but she didn't know why.

Tally remembered her dad yelling at her mother best not be losing his boy now that she finally got one to stick. "If it's another damned girl, you'll sure enough regret it," he threatened as though it would make a difference to the outcome.

Momma once said Dobb Simmons wanted him a boy to train up to be as mean as he was. God saw fit to make Tally a girl. And she wasn't one bit mean.

"The good Lord knows a man like Dobb Simmons would sure enough turn his son into his own image or kill him trying. Run all my other young'uns off, he did. I'd take you and run away too, but he'd never stop until he found us. He threatened to kill my other children if I ever tried to leave him. I knew we'd be worse off than we are now. At least you'll be able to leave here someday," Momma would tell her.

Tally watched as her dad grabbed a shovel and went out back. Didn't take a minute for him to find the grave and start digging. She was surprised to see him actually digging. He'd never done it before. It didn't take as long as Tally thought it would to dig down to Momma. Three days in the cold ground had kept Momma from total decay. Still, she was hardly recognizable as the strong odor of rot reached where Tally was hiding. Much to her horror Dad swung the shovel into Momma's bloated belly.

"Damn!" Clancy mumbled as he clamped his hand over Tally's mouth to silence her scream. "Close your eyes. Don't look," he whispered.

Tally wanted to close her eyes and not look, but her eyes refused to obey. She had to see what happened next. Dad dropped the shovel, bent over the grave and pulled something up. Even from her distance away, Tally recognized it as the tiny form of a naked baby.

The words that came out of her dad's mouth were not fit for human ears – or any ears. He was calling Momma names and cursing that she had killed his only begotten son. He dropped the remains of the pitiful baby boy, picked up the shovel and started swinging it into the grave with a fury, hitting Momma over and over.

It was then Clancy put his other hand over Tally's eyes.

~~~~

Clancy took her deeper into the woods than ever before. She lay down in the leaves and cried herself to sleep. When she opened her eyes, it was dark, and she was alone. Panic filled her as she stood up.

"Lay back down. I'm back. Everything is okay now," he assured her.

Tally lay back down and slept again. She woke up to the smell of meat cooking. Clancy was roasting a rabbit.

"What's the chance you'll be able to survive in your cabin alone?" he asked.

"I don't know. When Dad has one of his crazy spells, I'm not safe."

"Without your Dad," he added.

"I'd be okay, I guess. I can do most of what Momma did," she told him, trying hard to keep her chin from trembling.

"You've got a milk goat and chickens. I've been going back to your place to feed 'em most nights while you sleep. Hain't milked the goat. Never learned how. She'll be about to pop. Can you plant the garden on your own?" His questions had Tally puzzled, but she answered the best she could.

"I think I can. I always helped Momma."

"Good."

"Why do you ask?"

"Cause it's time for you to go back to the cabin and get things done. Best to start now before it's too late. You can't take life easy if you want to survive and not go to that orphanage."

"But Dad..."

"He left out during the night. Won't be coming back. It's a good thing Preacher Hadley and that snoopy bunch of women don't know he's gone."

Tally didn't want to go back to the cabin with Momma gone. She was afraid of being alone with her dad. She didn't believe he left out and wouldn't be coming back. He had made a habit of disappearing for a few days at a time, but he always came back. Momma and Tally had it good during those few days he was gone. They paid dearly for their good days when he returned.

"Will you stay with me?" she asked Clancy, hopefully.

"Nope."

"Why not?"

"I've got my own life and you've got yours."

"I'm only seven," she told him.

"I know that already. I'm twice your age, but you've got a place to live and your momma trained you good enough to survive on your own. The only thing that might bother you is Preacher Hadley and those church women, but I'm guessing your dad put the fear of meeting God Almighty into that bunch. Don't think they'll be climbing up this mountain again for a mighty long time. I'll be able to see 'em at the foot of the mountain if they do. Probably can hear 'em too. Ain't learned to keep their mouths shut. Won't take much for me to scare them off. They don't know your dad left out. If you do meet up with somebody, which ain't likely, tell 'em he'll be back shortly. Got that."

"Got it," she said, but she hadn't. Nothing was making sense.

Clancy sent her to walk back to the shack all by herself. She dragged her feet and looked over her shoulder all the way. She had become accustomed to having Clancy with her and didn't like being alone. She thought she felt Clancy's eyes watching her every step of the way, but when she looked back, she was alone. When she reached the cabin, there were no mattress cover and mattress sack hanging on the clothesline. She thought it odd Dad would take them down. She found it even more odd when she went inside to find the mattress sack filled with pine needles and put back on the bed. The mattress cover and ragged quilt were on the bed, dry and smelled clean. There was a good stack of wood behind the stove. The entire floor was scrubbed clean, but she thought she could still make out the places where her mother's blood had been. Those church folks had been busy. The thing that puzzled her the most, and twisted her guts with fear, was seeing her dad's shotgun leaning up behind the front door.

Her dad never went anywhere without his shotgun and sack of shells. Both were there. Dad always kept them near the bed in case there was need of them during the night. Something mighty fearful was going on. Momma was gone, Dad was gone, but his gun wasn't. Tally ran outside to hide in the underbrush, but neither dad nor Clancy showed up.

After a while, Tally got brave enough to crawl out of the underbrush and go to the garden. She couldn't stand the thought of what Dad had done to Momma and the pitiful, unborn baby that had been inside Momma. Dad might have dug her up, but he'd never put out the effort of filling her grave back in. He'd be sure to leave her for the wild animals to get at.

Much to her surprise, Momma's grave was filled in and rounded up as it had been before her dad had at it. In the soft garden dirt were footprints of Clancy's bare feet.

Chapter 2

~~Clancy~~

Clancy learned early on how to be almost invisible as he roamed through the woods, over the rocky mountain terrain, and down in the gullies. Sudden movement was sure to catch the eye, as were bright colors. The color of dirt was the best concealer. He'd learned to wallow in the mud if he was around somebody when he didn't want to be seen. He blended in with the underbrush like an owl in an oak tree as he watched the girl take hesitant steps toward the cabin. She tugged at his heartstrings, but there was no way he could keep her with him, even if he had wanted to, which he didn't. It was a heady feeling to have someone need him instead of always being the one who needed. Still, he realized she would be better off in the cabin than running the woods with him. He had no life – only the most meager of existence, but it was his life. During the lean times, he had to go down in the valley to scrounge from farm to farm gleaning anything the farmers might have missed in order to feed himself. Keeping her with him would mean both of them would starve. As it was, it took just about all his time to feed and shelter himself. Winters were a trying time – a time of hardship and starvation. So far, he had survived them, but just barely. There was no chance he could make it through a winter with the girl.

He followed her to the clearing where the cabin had been built many years before. The clearing was in a saddle near the top of a high mountain. He knew Dobb Simmons had never cleared an inch of the land. It was Billy Gray, Sally's first husband, who did the clearing and built the little log cabin for his wife and children. The cabin was nothing to brag about, but at least it kept out most of the wind and rain.

It was no secret that Dobb Simmons took advantage of the helpless. After Billy Gray died from a logging accident, Sally and her children were desperate and unlucky. The rains didn't come, and Sally's garden dried up instead of producing much needed food. Her milk cow stepped in a groundhog hole causing the cow to lose her balance and tumble down the highest rock cliff on the mountain. Sally had not even gotten to salvage her for meat. The walls of the rock cliff were solid rock worn slick by thousands of years of brutal mountain weather. There was no way to get down the sheer rock of the cliff to where the cow had landed. The buzzards got to enjoy her.

Sally and her children's lives went from bad to worse when Sally came down with some sort of sickness. She thought Dobb Simmons would be an answer to her prayers. It turned out she was the answer to his.

Dobb Simmons brought a preacher to the mountain while Sally was still sick. The man said marriage words over them and then signed papers. Dobb paid the preacher two dollars and claimed ownership of everything Billy Gray had worked so hard to provide for his family.

Miles of wooded, steep, rocky land surrounded the clearing and rough log cabin. Cliffs of solid rock, like fingers sticking up from a cupped hand, reached toward the clouds. The clearing was the cupped palm of the hand. Over thousands of years vegetation debris had been blown into the cup until there was enough soil to support a garden and a few farm animals. There was also a small spring branch drizzling up from the rocky basin. Good soil and water were the means of survival – be it meager at best. Inside the cup was slim pickings. It was the only place within miles Clancy hadn't pilfered from.

~~~~

Poor land made poor folks. Clancy knew that for a fact. His momma had been as poor as Job's turkey. High uncharitable mountains all too often had a way of slowly starving its inhabitants to death or made them as stringy and tough as a thin strip of whet-leather. He had turned out to be the thin strip of whet leather.

It was the rich and privileged who lived in the fertile bottom land. The more impoverished a person was, the higher up on the mountain he lived. After his parents died, Clancy climbed higher up the mountain. He had found a hard-to-reach cave in one of those tall fingers. Inside the cave were signs of bobcats, mountain lions and bears, but it didn't bother Clancy. It actually gave him comfort. Wild animals didn't stick around where people trod. He had to make sure he was never seen, or he would never find any peace. Oddly enough, he didn't consider himself as being a part of the human race. After years surviving in the high mountains, he considered himself more connected to wild animals than to his own kind.

Clancy huddled in the underbrush and watched the girl feed the chickens and milk the nanny goat. When he did the feeding, he hadn't so much as taken one egg, although the temptation was great. He knew the girl would need all the eggs and milk if she were to survive. She was younger than him and not nearly as capable. That was why he intended to watch over her the best he could whenever he could.

Looking after her was why he did what he had done.

Clancy had followed Dobb Simmons as he made his way to the rock cliff where the cow had fallen to her death.

Clancy knew Dobb wanted to make sure those church folks had left the mountain. It was well known Dobb hated church people who were determined to mind his business instead of their own. They had set foot on his property once before trying to get his wife and stepchildren away from him. He'd put a stop to it then just as he put a stop to it now. Clancy had no doubt they would be fair game to Dobb if they returned.

Dobb would find a way to get away with whatever he chose to do to those who trespassed on his land.

Dobb stood on the topmost rock as he gazed into the valley below. He watched the car that brought them there and now wound its way along the twisting road taking them away. A cloud of dust lifted into the air behind the car. Seeing that dust made him mad all over again. He should have shot every last one of them. There were only two things that stopped him. He wouldn't be able to hide their car for long, and he'd have to dig their graves, being he no longer had hogs. Looked like he'd have to get a few hogs right soon. He laid his gun down at his feet so he could use both hands to unscrew the lid on his jar of shine.

Clancy watched as Dobb's Adam's apple bobbed up and down as he swallowed.

Clancy silently put a round rock into the pouch of his slingshot, squeezed it between thumb and fore finger, pulled back on the rubber, took aim, and turned loose of the pouch. There was a hollow thump of sound as the rock hit Dobb in the back of the head. The jar fell to the rock and broke, splattering the shine. Dobb let out a screech as he pitched face forward, unable to catch himself. He tumbled down the steep rock cliff much as the cow had done.

Slowly, and silently, Clancy crept forward until he could see the body of Dobb Simmons sprawled on the rocks below. Satisfied, Clancy picked up the gun and took it back to the cabin.

Tally would be safer without Dobb Simmons than she would be with him. He was certain of that much.

Chapter 3

"That poor child," Nurse Whitley bemoaned the girl's fate to the doctor as she slipped off her sun hat and went inside to fix his breakfast, leaving her beautiful flowers outside. "Something has to be done for her."

"Now, now, my dear. It's best not to get involved with a Simmons. Nothing good could possibly come of it."

"But that poor child," she said again.

"All high mountain children are poor in more ways than one. I learned long ago there is no way to help the children regardless of where they come from, especially if the parents live in the isolated high mountains. They're nothing more than small slivers off their parents. You'd have to give them different parents to help them. To change their parents, you'd have to change the mountains and a way of life that was set in stone centuries ago. In other words, my dear, it is impossible to alter the impossible."

Nurse Whitley gave him a disgusted look. She believed it was possible to better any situation regardless of where they lived and who they were. "Doctor," she said with raised chin and determined tone of voice. "You of all people know God works miracles in the most impossible ways"

"Not always."

"Yes, always. He hovers over these mountains. All that's needed is to climb to the top of that mountain and lift your hands upward to connect with him."

The doctor all but rolled his eyes in disbelief, but he used a gentle hand where Nurse Whitley was concerned. "That may or may not be true, my dear, but God doesn't work miracles all the time. He allows free will so his children can do whatever they please, be it good or evil."

"Tell me, Doctor, what will become of that poor child if she doesn't get assistance from someone?"

"The same thing that happens to other backwoods children. They survive or they don't. Only the strong make it. And that's how it should be," he made a point of adding.

She reached out and laid her hand gently on the doctor's arm. "If you believed that, I wouldn't be here."

"I do believe it, and you are here," he told her firmly. "Unfortunately, what I believe has nothing to do with reality, the same as what you believe has nothing to do with reality."

"Doctor, are you really such a pessimist?"

Dr. Robinson shook his head sadly, "When one sees what I've seen there's little to be optimistic about."

"That's not true and you know it," she insisted stubbornly.

He only looked at her and shook his head again. He'd learned early on that a tender heart broke easier than a hardened one. A doctor was subjected to things others never had the misfortune to witness. He was once called to the shack of a somewhat retarded man who had hung his wife to a tree limb. When asked why he did such a thing, he replied. "A woman what can't stand a mite of hangin' ain't worth havin'," the man had told him. Or there was the six-year-old girl who had been sexually molested by her drunken father and two of his drunken buddies until she died. "That's what they's made for," the father said to justify their actions. Those two incidents weren't the worst of it. There were other things that bothered him to think about much less tell – and people liked to condemn him because he sometimes sought the aid of mind-numbing drink that was as strong and powerful as the mountains it was made in.

"How's she doing this morning?" the doctor asked.

It was the same question he asked every morning and every night. "Slightly more restless than usual," she told him.

"Does she need more medication?"

"No," Nurse Whitley told him. She had always insisted that less medicine was for the best.

"Restful sleep helps heal," he assured her. His words contained his usual touch of hope.

She had heard those same words, with the same touch of hope, since the day she arrived. Sleep wasn't going to improve Elouise's problems. Nothing was going to help, but the doctor refused to accept the hard truth. He had to pretend, even when he knew better.

Nurse Whitley was convinced the doctor was the best man she had ever met. That was one of the reasons why she stayed when she knew it would be best if she left.

"Sit down, Doctor, and I'll have your breakfast in a jiffy. I only have to warm it up."

The doctor saw his breakfast sitting on the back of the stove and lifted his brows.

"Do you think feeding me will butter me up in order to get me to do what you want concerning that little mountain girl?"

"I feed you every morning," she told him. "It's what you pay me to do."

"I don't pay you to cook for me. I pay you to take care of Elouise."

She smiled at him with her normal show of tolerance. "All three of us have to eat, and you're a lousy cook."

The doctor looked at her and let out a long-suffering sigh.

Chapter 4

The air was lifting upward from the low valley, bringing a wave of warmth with it. Time was best for him to fire his still when the air was rising instead of settling down in the valley. A man learned to do his work on a warm night when smoke from his fire was carried into the sky instead of blowing down toward the valley where folks lived. Caution and temperature were the keys to success. A man could never use too much caution when he was running liquor. He also had to choose a time when the temperature was between 50 degrees and 90 degrees. Too cold and the yeast in the mash wouldn't work. Too hot and it would be killed. The good thing was that the high mountains never got to 90 degrees even on the hottest day of summer. As for 50 degrees, the temperature could drop below that just about any day. During the winter months the mountains froze over. Twenty degrees below zero happened often.

He had considered building an underground basement in his house where he could control the temperature enough to make his brew, but the aroma of brewing grain would surely give him away. He'd most likely get busted on his first run. Wasn't worth the chance. He'd make his liquor during the warm months and rest his heels during cold weather.

Tucker wiped sweat from his brow with his stained handkerchief, then returned it to his back overall pocket. He'd been hauling deadfall all day long and wished he could use his donkey to drag it in, but that would leave too much of a trail. He'd best do it on foot. It took a pile a-plenty of deadfall to keep the fire going long enough and hot enough, but he'd been

doing the same thing ever since he'd been knee high to a
grasshopper, just as his dad and granddad did before him.
Thing was, he couldn't use a chain saw or even an ax. Sound
carried far and echoed down in the valley, so he had to rely on
deadfall of a usable size. Fortunately, in the heavy wooded
areas, there seemed to be a never-ending supply. It was second
nature for him to get making liquor right every time – unless
something unexpected and terrible went wrong.

In life, as well as in making liquor, a body never knew
what was coming next, so it was always best to be prepared
for the worst. It was a lesson he'd learned long ago, but it was
awfully hard to figure out what the worst was going to be.

He already had his corn mash heated and cooling in the
creek. When it reached eighty degrees, he would add sugar,
yeast, and rye, let it ferment for ten days, strain it and put the
liquid back in the still to heat and distill the alcohol from the
water.

One of the good things about going about his business in
the rugged mountain was that nobody bothered him, which
was a wise decision. Even the law knew better than to go into
the highest part of the mountains. Lawmen and revenuers had
a way of getting themselves lost and never finding their way
out. Tucker didn't believe in harming anybody, including law
men and revenuers, but he didn't believe in helping them
either. Folks had the responsibility of taking care of their own
selves. Yet, there were times when a man had to do what was
unpleasant in order to save himself.

There were a few wayward individuals who were
determined to plant their roots in the rocky, inhospitable high
mountains. Admittedly, some were never-do-wells – people
who wouldn't be safe anywhere else. People who were
running away from something or someone and needed a place
to hide. There were also people who needed to live an isolated
life. People who were trying to escape something horrible, be
it of their making or not. There were also a few of a rarer kind.
Those humans who wanted solitude and hated life with other

people. In other words, the rugged mountain range was the place folks went to be left alone.

Tucker considered himself having all those reasons, plus he also considered himself as being a kind of go-between. The mountain dwellers overlooked each other's existence the same way they overlooked timber rattle snakes.

As long as the snakes didn't have the misfortune of crossing their paths, they were allowed to continue living.

The low-landers and town folks ignored him and his business profession as long as he provided them with what they wanted at a price they were willing to pay. As for the few law men who tread into the mountains, he sometimes aided in giving them a Christian burial the same as his father and grandfather had done. He knew what had happened to those unfortunate revenuers. They had come too close to the big liquor operation several mountains over in Wilkes county. They used any means to brew liquor faster and more plentiful. Folks called it rot-gut liquor because that was exactly what it did. Rot the gut from the inside out – if it didn't out-and-out kill a man first. Tucker knew the man who was head of the operation. His name was Grubb Claxton. Folks were wise to stay clear of him and his.

Once Tucker had gathered enough deadfall to fire the night's work, he needed to make sure there were no so-called do-gooders making their way into the high mountains. It always puzzled him why do-gooders insisted on interrupting the lives of people who wanted nothing more than to be left alone. Not one of the mountain folks ever hoofed it down the mountain in an attempt to change the way those people managed to survive. Not that he always agreed with the kind of behavior folks exhibited, but he did believe each person had the right to survive the best way they could. Even the little boy, Clancy, had a right to live his own life.

Tucker moved away from his stack of firewood, picked up a mason jar, dipped it into the stream of pure, cold water and drank long and hard. He believed water was the liquid of life as were many of the plants that God saw fit to grow. Tucker knew where the best branch lettuce was located and in the fertile places where ramps, wild ginger, and sang grew. The old granny witch visited the sites often and harvested the herbs sparingly. Regardless of her oddities, she was one of the few people he respected.

During winter months he wondered how the old witch woman managed to survive. Her shack was little more than a lean-to with a tin stove pipe sticking through the roof – certainly not enough of a stove to keep old bones warm. It was best to prepare for a long winter during the warm months. If not, it became the time of root hog or die.

Tucker put the jar back with the others and started the long trek through the laurel hells and over rock cliffs to the lookout point where he had a better view of the valley below. He made sure he never took the same route enough to leave a path. A man couldn't be too careful especially during times he was feeling confident. He had learned that truism the hard way.

Tucker had no need to rush, concealing darkness was several hours away. At least the do-gooders never ventured into the high mountains during the hours of darkness. They knew better. Things prowled freely after the light went out – and that included him. The only times he was in the mountains during daylight hours were when he gathered deadfall and when he hauled his produce out. Those were the critical times when he depended on the lookout point to keep him informed if someone was entering the mountains. A man never knew when somebody would have it in for him – be it the law, a disgruntled customer, or an inferior competitor.

He hadn't expected to see Dobb Simmons standing on the topmost rock of the lookout gazing down into the valley, but the sight didn't surprise him. Dobb was the man who helped distribute the shine Tucker brewed. The man who was willing to take all the blame and heat if something went wrong, and yes, Dobb also took the credit for making the best shine in the whole entire state, although he never lifted a finger in the making. Let Dobb have at it, was Tucker's motto. All he wanted was the profit from his hard work, not the credit.

He knew Dobb's wife had died and been buried by the church folks. He also knew the church women, headed by Mrs. Gidley, were planning a way to get the little girl away from Dobb. He didn't blame the women. Dobb was the scum of the earth, but Tucker wasn't taking sides one way or the other. It was hard enough for a man to mind his own business without trying to mind someone else's.

What surprised Tucker were the faint sounds coming from nearby. For years, he'd trained his ears to pick up the slightest sound. That's how he kept doing what he was doing. Tucker quickly leaned against the concealing trunk of a huge oak tree with a thick cover of undergrowth surrounding it. He made sure his moccasin covered boots didn't crunch a leaf or snap a twig as he tried to make himself disappear. He always wore his hand-made moccasins over his boots when he came into the mountains to work.

Moccasins didn't leave much of a footprint, plus they had a way of padding the noise walking made – kind of the way a cat did when it drew it's claws into its soft foot pads. Heavy work boots left heel prints, but boots protected from snake bites.

He slowed his breathing and tried not make the slightest movement. His eyes narrowed as he peered into the shadows where he picked out where young Clancy Ledford was hiding.

He'd known both of Clancy's parents before they'd died within days of each other. Nobody knew exactly the name of the disease that took them, along with dozens of others, away from their loved ones. Whatever it was hit fast and deadly. Even Dr. Robinson was puzzled, which wasn't exactly surprising. He also knew Clancy's uncle, Fred Ledford. Fred was a crook and a scoundrel. He put the boy in the locally run orphanage in order to get the pitiful possessions of his brother. The boy knew little about possessions, but he did learn about abuse while with his uncle, as well as in the orphanage. Clancy was smart enough to escape and head into the high mountains. Tucker figured the boy was a goner for certain. He'd made a vague attempt at finding the boy, wanting to help him out any way he could, but the boy disappeared like mist rising toward the hot sun. He spotted the boy later on, pleasantly surprised the boy had survived.

Tucker watched as Dobb took his liquor flask from his back pocket, lifted it to his mouth, and took a long draw. The boy put a rock in the saddle of his handmade slingshot and let fly straight at the back of Dobb's head. The rock made a clunking sound when it came into contact with Dobb's greasy, black-hatted head. Dobb's body jerked. He dropped the flask he was drinking from, along with the gun he always carried with him, took a stumbling step forward, lost his balance, and tumbled down the rock cliff. Clancy rushed to the cliff, looked over the rim for a few moments as though he was considering what he should do next. The boy drew in a heavy breath, let it out slowly, bent down and picked up the shotgun Dobb had dropped and left at a run.

Tucker stayed hidden for a spell, making sure the boy didn't change his mind and return. Deciding the boy was long gone, Tucker made his way to the cliff and looked over the edge much like the boy had done. Sure enough, Dobb was laying sprawled on the rock filled bottom of the cliff. Branches of the scrub brush, protruding from the rocky crags, had been broken off all the way down the steep side of the rock cliff. A few scrub brush had been pulled away roots and all from where they clung to the shallow crags. Dobb wasn't moving. He was either dead or knocked out cold. Either way Tucker turned his back and walked back into the shadows of the woods. None of what he'd witnessed was his doing. Best a man minds his own business, or he'd sure enough end up regretting it.

"Hell-fire," he finally mumbled before he had gone far.

Dobb wasn't worth a plug nickel. The boy had popped him in the head with a rock, but it was Dobb's own fault he had fallen. He shouldn't have been guzzling liquor while standing near the edge of a cliff. Tucker longed to walk away and leave Dobb where he lay, but the image of what would happen next became clear. The weather was hot enough to bloat Dobb's body if he was dead. Insects, buzzards, and a number of flesh-eating animals would gather. Folks down in the valley would see the buzzards circling. The do-gooders would also see the buzzards and think they circled over the body of the little girl – or that Sally's body could have been unearthed. Those church women commiserated with Sally and her unendurable plight of being the wife of an abusive man. There was a chance some of them would be brave enough to return. Tucker let out a disgusted grunt. It was best he made his way down into that hole and do what any decent man ought to do.

Bury the dead.

There weren't many folks who knew how to climb down into that hell hole without killing themselves. To Tucker's knowledge, he was the only person still alive who could do it – not counting the old witch woman. She'd been in every crook and cranny that existed. She had become part of the mountain's hidey-holes.

His granddad knew how, but he hadn't divulged the secret to a living soul, not even to Tucker. It was a gray fox that had shown Tucker the way when he was still a boy. Now that Tucker was a man, the openings through the cracks and crevices had become much more difficult to squeeze his body through, but still manageable when a man was bone-thin as bailing wire.

Again, Tucker considered leaving Dobb to his own fate, but Dobb never divulged Tucker's business location to anyone as far as Tucker knew. For that alone, Tucker figured he owed Dobb a decent burial. More than that, the little girl and the boy had the right to live their lives however they wanted – be it stay where they were or make their way off the mountain to receive the eager ministrations of the do-gooders, which would most likely be adding the girl to the orphans in the local orphan home. If word got out that Dobb was dead, the do-gooder-vultures would start circling in search of the girl. Personally, he considered living on top of a mountain far better than being enclosed in what the do-gooders claimed to be their charitable-run orphanage.

Tucker made his way through the tight cracks in the rocks and crossed the basin to where Dobb lay. He kneeled down and touched the pulse in his throat with two fingers.

"Shit," Tucker mumbled. Dobb had a pulse. It would be much easier to bury him between two of the rocks than to drag him through the narrow cave-like cracks in the rocks, but a man had to do what his conscience told him was the right thing. It wasn't easy maneuvering Dobb's thick body through the narrow openings of the rocks. Dobb lost clothing and skin, but Tucker finally managed. Now, what was he going to do with Dobb? It was obvious he needed care if he was to live. Care that Tucker neither had expertise or time to give him. Dobb's little daughter wouldn't be able to look after him if he took him to the cabin. His only choice was to go to the granny witch.

~~~~

Granny Witcher crossed her arms in front of her skinny chest and reared her spine back until the top of her chin reached as high as Tucker's chest. She looked upward staring Tucker in the eyes. "No," she repeated again. "Ain't gonna do it."

"Please."

"No. You toted him outta that hole. That makes him your problem, not mine."

That was a fact. Tucker had to agree with the wizened old woman. It wasn't her place to take care of Dobb. "You know I can't take him off the mountain to the doctor."

"Can if you want."

For one thing, Dobb might tell about the location of his still. He might tell about Clancy shooting him with a rock if he knew who and what hit him. Even worse, he might blame it on Tucker. Plus, those church women would go after Dobb's girl like a duck after a June bug.

"What can I do other than ask you for help?"

"He's your row to hoe, ain't mine. Don't like him. Never have. Best to let him live or die on his own power."

"I'm desperate, here," Tucker pleaded. This old woman was one of those granny witches who had special insight into the use of herbal medicine, along with a kind of witchcraft still possessed by a few rare mountain women. Such women were a mystery as old as the mountains they thrived in. No one seemed to know where they came from, or where they went when their time on earth came to an end. They appeared in mystery and disappeared in mystery. Folks condemned such women until they had need of one – as he now did.

"He has a place. Take him there," she told him.

"His girl is there."

"So?" She did her best to sound like she didn't care.

"She can't take care of him. As you already know, she's a young child, plus she's been through enough already. We both know some of what went on in the cabin."

"Not my fault," Granny Witcher told him again.

"You know about Sally and the little girl, don't you?"

"Not my place to butt my nose into other folk's business. Dobb Simmons told me sech a long time ago."

Tucker had to force himself not to laugh out loud at her remark. It might not be obvious, but in his opinion, she was always butting her nose in everybody's business.

"Her mother just died from a sickness that caused her to miscarry. Bled to death while the little girl went after Dr. Robinson," Tucker told her the gossip he'd overheard while at his house down in the valley. One thing was for certain, where there were people, there was a running stream of gossip.

"So," Granny said as though she didn't care, but Tucker knew different. He also knew Dobb refused to let Granny Witcher treat his wife the same as he refused to let Dr. Robinson treat her. Dobb had once told Tucker he'd learned Sally a lesson for seeking the granny witch out. He figured it was only one of the many beatings Dobb doled out to his wife.

"So, you know good and well that little girl has already had enough heartache in her life. It'll be difficult enough for her to survive without having to take care of a grown man with a broken leg and two broken arms, not to mention all the other injuries he got from the fall."

"Same for me," she told him firmly.

"No, Granny, it's not the same for you. You're a capable adult who can work miracles. That girl is nothing more than a fledging baby," Tucker said what he knew to be true.

"I'm a feeble old woman. Like I just told you, he ain't my doin'. Ought to of let him perish in the hole he fell in. Been best for all if you had."

"Granny," Tucker's voice took on a pleading tone. "You're the only one I trust enough to ask for help. If I take him to the Doc's place, those church women will have his girl before she knows what's happened to her. You know what that means. The orphanage."

Her eyes narrowed. "I've been confronted by Dobb 'afore. It's a far sight better if he's dead rather than alive. Can't befriend a timber rattler. Can't stop 'em from biting you," she told him firmly. I'm sure you've heard the old tale about the tender-hearted woman and the snake."

"I have he told her," even though he hadn't.

"Don't matter if you have, I'm gonna tell it to you again."

"Down by the river on a snowy day a woman saw a half-frozen snake.

"Oh, take me in, tender-hearted woman, or I'll surely die out here in this icy cold snow."

"Oh, you poor, pretty thing," she cried, "I'll warm you up and take care of you. I surely will."

That tender-hearted woman picked up the snake and held it to her warm breast and took it home with her. She wrapped the snake in her warmest blanket and laid it by her fire. Right soon, the snake revived. She clutched it to her bosom again, delighted that the snake had come back to life.

"If I hadn't brought you in, by now you would surely be dead," she said.

In repayment for her loving care, the ungrateful snake gave her breast a vicious bite.

"Why did you bite me? I saved your life," she cried out in anguish. "From your poison, I'm surely to die."

"Shut up, you stupid-hearted woman. You got what you deserve. You knew damn well I was a vicious snake before you took me in."

"Dobb Simmons is that poison snake you're asking me to take in."

Tucker let out a sigh. "Okay. I understand that, and I agree. He's a poisonous snake. Still yet, I can't leave a man to die just because I don't like him, and neither can you. So, let's dicker on your price. It's not like I expect you to do it for the love of Dobb Simmons. I expect to pay you to look after him. What's your price?"

"Ain't no price high enough to make me take care of that snake. I've seen what his bite does to folks. Tender-hearted Sally is dead, and her children are scattered only the good Lord knows where. I know better than to bring that snake into my little shack."

Tucker couldn't argue with what she said. He knew there was hardly room for her, although he'd only seen the inside of her little shack through the open door. Every square inch of the place had something in it, including the ceiling where herbs were hanging as thick as cobwebs in an old, deserted barn.

"Give you four free jars of liquor each month until he's well if you'll look after him." Tucker knew it was all she could do to afford enough liquor to make her herbal brews and salves. He often gave her liquor in trade for concoctions he had little to no use for, but other folks and the doctor might buy from him.

"Look after him?" she questioned.

"Yeah, look after. There's a deep rock overhang about halfway between here and the rocky lookout. I've got him under the overhang right now. I've already set his leg and arms knowing you could have done a better job of it. Still, he'll need your concoctions to keep down infection, along with food and water. Chances are he won't last long regardless of what kind of care he gets."

"Take him to that fool who claims to be a doctor."

"Can't do that. Like I already told you, those church-going do-gooders will haul that little girl to the orphanage as soon as they find out about Dobb's accident. You of all people should understand how they can't keep their noses out of other folks' business."

Tucker knew those women made a point of condemning Granny Witcher every chance they got. They tried to run her off once for giving one of their husbands the herbal medicine that cured him when the doctor couldn't. They called her a heathen witch and a disgrace. Accused her of being a charlatan. Actually, Tucker thought folks were afraid of her and what powers she just might possess. That was why they pretty much left her alone.

"Humph," she grunted as the situation became clear. "Might consider checkin' on him once in a while, but it'll cost eight jars a month. In advance," she added.

"Six."

"Nope," she told him with a final shake of her snowy-haired head.

"You run a hard bargain," he told her.

"He ain't worth one jar of shine, but my time is. At my age I've not got much time left. That makes every hour precious to me," she informed him. "Bring my eight jars as soon as it's run off."

"Only if you start caring for him now. I gotta get the mash started."

She nodded her agreement, but she wasn't much happy about it. Looking after a man such as Dobb Simmons caught her with indecision between what was right and what was best.

Chapter 5

Tally got through each day in a daze. She did the things that had to be done and then sat on the packed dirt of her mother's grave for hours. There seemed to be nothing she could do to keep the pain and fear down. Her mother was gone, and she would never come back, regardless how much Tally wanted and needed her. As for her dad, Tally wasn't sure if she wanted him to come back or not. Being alone was scary, but so was the hurt her dad dealt out.

Fear that she couldn't survive on her own haunted her every moment. How could she possible do all the things needed to stay alive – all the things her mother did. Without help she would surely die. Part of her wished she could live with Clancy, wherever that was, until she remembered how hungry she had gotten during the time she was with him. She didn't like being hungry any more than she liked being hurt. He mother had made sure she was never hungry. What she really wished could happen was for Clancy to move in the cabin with her, but she knew that could never happen. She hadn't seen Clancy since he sent her to the cabin.

"Get up from there and stop feeling sorry for yourself," her mother's voice sounded in her head. *"You're a big girl now. You're capable."*

Chills crept over Tally. She jumped up from the dirt and looked about. Her mother's voice had been so real she expected to see her standing near, but she wasn't anywhere to be seen.

"Plant the garden," her mother's voice sounded again. *"Right now."*

Tally ran to cabin to find her momma's seeds. She and her mother had worked for weeks at turning over the garden ground. They'd been at it as soon as the ground had thawed from the winter freeze. It was easier to turn over at first thawing. Her momma had planned on planting the seeds the day she got sick but was unable to get out of bed even to cook breakfast – something Tally had never known her mother not to do. "We've got to eat no matter what," her mother would say.

A garden made the difference between surviving and starving. "Plant what ought to be planted, when it is time to plant it," her mother would say. Food was the second most important thing next to shelter. At least she had the cabin, animals, and sacks of dried beans and potatoes, which Clancy didn't have. She wondered where Clancy was and if he'd come back again.

When Tally got to the cabin, she climbed into the loft where Momma kept her seeds hidden under Tally's pine needle mattress. Momma had never trusted Dobb not to go into a fit of rage and destroy them. Her dad never needed a reason for the things he did. He was always on the edge and looking for an excuse to punish her Momma for anything even when she wasn't responsible. There were times when Tally thought he intended to kill her mother, but he always stopped short of doing the deed. As for her, she was ignored as long as she stayed out of his sight and never crossed his path – which wasn't always possible.

How the church women down in the valley knew what was going on, she didn't know. Perhaps one or more of her brothers told someone when they left the mountain. She was too young to remember much about Mary, or the two older half-brothers leaving. She did remember when Jimmy left. She also remembered her mother crying because she feared her boy was hurt so bad, he wouldn't be able to make it out of the mountains. Tally had hidden in the thick growth of ragweeds and stinking Jimson weeds out behind the barn as her dad dragged Jimmy to the hog lot. He lifted Jimmy by an arm and leg and threw him into the mud and manure of the lot as easily as if Jimmy was a sack of acorns Jimmy was always picking up to feed the hogs. Momma had tried to stop Dobb, but his big fist hit her in the face, knocking her flat, breaking her nose and addling her. Dobb didn't dare go into the hog lot. He knew better. A passel of hogs was a dangerous thing especially where they were hungry.

The half-dozen hungry grown hogs rushed Jimmy, each hog wanting to be the first at getting a meal. Jimmy was flailing about in the muck, trying to get to his feet but couldn't. He ended up burying himself deeper in the stinking mud wallow. It was the muddy manure that saved him, along with the hungry hogs turning on each other. The biggest sow had her hip ripped open by the huge boar's tusk, blood flowing down her hip and legs. The smell of her blood drove the other hogs crazy. They turned on one of their own with squealing. blood-lust fury.

Dobb saw what was happening and went bat-shit wild with cussing and yelling as he threw everything he could get his hands on at the hogs, but it did no good. Even he knew better than to get into a lot of blood-lust crazed hogs. The hogs were ripping at the sow, tearing off snouts full of flesh and running with their prize. As horrible as the scene playing out before Tally's frightened eyes, it was a blessing for Jimmy. He was able to climb out of the hog lot and make a run for it while Dobb was focused on the loss of his sow.

Tally never saw Jimmy again, but the sheriff and preacher showed up a few days later. Fortunately, for them, Dobb wasn't there.

Momma met them in the yard.

"We came about your son," the preacher told her.

"Sons," Momma corrected him. "I have three sons."

"Your youngest son," the preacher told her.

"What about him?" Momma asked sweetly.

"We need to talk to him."

"Why?" Momma's eyes narrowed in her bruised face. Her nose was crooked and both eyes were as black as stove soot.

The preacher didn't hesitate. "We think he was involved in stealing from several different people."

"What?" Momma demanded, not the least bit surprised. If anything went missing down in the valley, the mountain folks always got the blame. "When?"

"Two days ago."

Momma's back went ramrod straight and she grinned right in the sheriff's face. "Weren't none of my boys," she told them. "They left here a long time ago. Ain't seen hide nor hair of 'em in years. Don't even know where they be at. They shore enough ain't around these parts – that I know for a fact."

"Care if we take a look around?" the sheriff asked as sweet as you please.

"I do," Momma said. "This here is private land. You've no call to be trespassing on it."

The sheriff's jaws tightened, and his shoulders reared back. The expression on his face hardened. The preacher put his hand on the sheriff's bony arm before the sheriff got words to come out of his thin lips.

"She's right, Sheriff," the preacher said. "I did hear her boys left some time back. Her girl left before they did. Sorry we bothered you, Mrs. Simmons. If you don't mind me asking, what happened to you face?"

"My business," Momma said. "Be on your way. Don't come back."

The sheriff wanted to resist, but the preacher patted him on his narrow back. The preacher knew they didn't have anything on Simmons. It was known far and wide the sheriff was a mortal enemy of Dobb Simmons. "We best be going. Mrs. Simmons knows where we're at if she should need us."

It was easy to tell the sheriff didn't like the preacher taking over. Even Tally knew the sheriff wouldn't forget it.

"Sheriff's a vengeful sort," Momma mumbled as she watched them leave, heard the sound of the car engine start up and fade away.

"Thank the good Lord," Momma mumbled again. "Jimmy made it."

~~~~

Granny Witcher gathered supplies and put them in a hemp sack. She knew exactly where the deep, overhanging rock was located. It was cave-like without being a cave. It was about twenty feet deep with a tree growing on top of the rock. What she didn't know was how much tending to Dobb Simmons would need. However, much it was, she figured it would be more than even she was prepared to handle. She would do the best she could and that was all she would do. During her lifetime she'd put back together a lot of busted-up, no-account men, but none she despised as much as she despised Dobb Simmons. No meaner man existed in the mountains. In her opinion, he was the resurrection of the devil himself.

Dobb had come around and was moaning by the time Granny Witcher reached him. She stood at his head, looking him over, judging what injuries he had sustained. Tucker had indeed set and bound both arms and one leg. He hadn't done a thing for all the cuts and scraped-off skin on his head, face, hands, and body. Neither had he done anything about Dobb's bodily functions. He stunk worse than week-old carrion in hot sun. She didn't hesitate to take out her butcher knife. Dobb squinted an eye and let out a weak squeal as she came at him with the knife. She ignored him, bent down, swung the knife, and cut the nasty britches off him, tossing them as far away as her bony arm could.

Relief came to Dobb's face, but it didn't last long. Granny Witcher lifted the jar of her precious shine and poured it directly on the blade of her knife, letting it dribble onto his hind end. The liquid burned its way over scrapes and abrasions as it washed some of the stink away. She didn't stop there. She poured it on his body, his good leg, his head, and face. His tongue came out between parched lips to lick at the trickle of shine running into the corners of his mouth.

"More," he whispered, his cracked lips forming the word almost soundlessly.

"No," she told him firmly, "I'll give you a drop of water directly." She had no intention of using her precious shine to ease his pain. All Dobb's life he had caused other people an unmeasurable amount of pain. It was time he knew what it felt like.

"Hurt," he mumbled.

"I'd reckon so," Granny Witcher said. "What goes about, comes about."

"Home," he whimpered.

"You ain't got no home." She wasn't about to take him back to Sally Gray's little cabin. He'd run all her other children off; he wasn't running the little one off too. She opened her hemp sack, took out a tin cup and poured a little water in it. She mixed in several different powdered herbs and used the spoon to dripple the liquid into his mouth. He swallowed eagerly, disregarding the bitter taste.

"Burned your taste buds out, ain't you," she said. "Guzzling liquor does that to a body." She let out a disappointed sigh. "Looks to me like you're gonna live unless I decide to rid this rock of vermin. Reckon I'll have to mosey off a while and think on it some. A body ought not to do things without a lot of thinkin' on it, regardless of how much they want to."

Granny Witcher didn't consider her place a cabin or a shack. She thought of it as a hut – a temporary place to hold her herbal medicines along with her. Someday, when her dying time came, she'd drink some of her special elixir, strike one of her hoarded matches and that would be it. Every sign of her existence would be gone. And that was the way she wanted her time on earth to end.

She hadn't always been considered a granny witch. She'd been married once, lived in a southern mansion with a maid, a gardener and a husband who had family connections in high places. She could still close her eyes and smell the hot summer aroma of roses growing in her garden as she sat on the veranda drinking sweet tea. There were herbs – all kind of herbs, growing alongside a variety of vegetables. There was green grass along with fields of livestock – cattle, horses, chickens, geese, and Jersey milk cows. She was thrilled to be the loving wife of Clarence Witcher. He was everything she dreamed of in a husband. It was a fact that she and her husband were living the good-life – until the unimaginable happened.

She hadn't gotten with child.

Her husband and his family needed a male heir, which she hadn't provided. Divorce was considered almost as bad a horror as being infertile. The solution? Kill her off and make it look like an accident.

~~~~

Tucker was placing the last jar of shine in front of Granny Witcher's closed door when she got back from checking on Dobb.

"How is he?" Tucker asked.

"Alive."

"Will he stay alive?"

"Could, if fever don't set in."

"Will it set in?" he asked as though she was able to give him an answer.

"Can't say. You gonna leave him under that rock?"

"Got a better idea?"

"Nope. Just thinkin' wild animals might get at him. Saw big bear tracks on yonder mountain this morning."

"Humm," Tucker grunted. "Could save you and me both a lot of problems."

"Would at that," she agreed.

"Say, don't reckon you'd look in on his girl, would you?"

"Mighty far for a crippled old woman to walk," she grumbled as though she wasn't able to walk all over the mountains in search of herbs, not telling him she'd already took to the woods to check on the girl. She'd seldom gone on that side of the mountain. The farther she stayed away from Dobb Simmons' territory the better. The man was as despicable as her first husband.

Sometimes she grinned when she thought of the man she was still married to by paper and law. He was an adulterer living in sin and didn't know it. The woman he now called his wife was an adulteress. She also knew the son his adulteress claimed belonged to Clarence Witcher wasn't his son. She felt a bit of satisfaction at that knowledge, even if Clarence Witcher didn't know she was alive.

As for her and Gray Leaf, their marriage didn't come from paper and law the way the white mans did. Their union came from God himself. Their union was something only God could dissolve.

Sally's girl was tall for her age, bone thin, with dirty-brown hair that would most likely darken as she aged. Odd how light-haired young'uns hair darkened and dark-haired young'uns hair lightened with age. Even now, after all the years, being considered barren by her husband and his parents caused the old ache to return. Try as she might, she'd never been able to purge all the trauma that had brought her to the high mountains to live a more desolate life than a beggar in the street – and yet it was the life she refused to change.

"Her being alone worries me, but I reckon it's better than the orphanage as long as she don't starve to death," Tucker said.

"Living is not easy no matter where you're at," Granny Wicker repeated what she knew all too well. "You spending the night on the mountain?" she asked, wanting to turn the talk away from her. She knew Tucker was the secretive type, had to be.

"No other choice," he answered.

"Reckon you'll have to haul your own brew out now that no-good has disabled himself."

"Reckon so," he said.

"Best keep your eyes open. There's marauders about."

He nodded. She didn't have to be telling him such as that. There'd been a lot of rumbling going on. Men claiming to be the law were going about trying to bust up stills. Talk had it they weren't the law at all, but competitors trying to stop other mountain men from producing high quality liquor, while they were selling liquor that was just short of poisonous. They didn't even skim off the head before selling it. The first that comes out of the still was called the head. A man ought to throw that away, if he didn't, whoever drank that stuff wished they were dead. Then comes the hearts, which is the best stuff and what he sold. Next was the tails, which was low proof stuff. A good distiller ought to throw that away, or at the very least, pour it into the next run for a little added alcohol.

Tucker knew his still's location would be nigh impossible for someone who wasn't from the mountains to find, but he kept his eyes open just the same. There was always the chance someone might luck up and stumble onto the impossible. Having a man like Dobb Simmons around kept locals away. It was best for folks to think Dobbs was the moonshiner instead of him when possible, but some folks down in the valley knew better. Dobb liked that idea. In payment, Dobb got some cash, liquor, and all the waste mash he was willing to tote home to feed his hog. If there had been anyone else willing to help him, Dobb would never have been hired. Oddly enough, and to Tucker's surprise, Dobb had worked out well enough.

Now, Tucker wasn't sure what he was going to do for much-needed help. A man couldn't stay awake day and night doing everything it took two men to do.

"Want a job?" he surprised himself by saying those words out loud to Granny Witcher.

She actually laughed. "Exactly what could you expect of an old woman, other than miracles?"

"Yeah. I want a few miracles for a change."

"Then you'll have to look somewhere else, cause I'm fresh out of those things."

"And all this time I thought you were capable of doing the impossible, being a witch woman and all," he spoke what was on his mind.

She looked him in the eyes. "If I was a witch, would I be here?"

Tucker lifted a brow. She had a point. "Now that you mentioned it, why are you here?"

"Got no other place to go," she told him. "Why are you?"

He thought about an answer to that question. What else was there for him to do that he could make a living at? All he'd ever known was liquor plus a slight amount of farming. He grew corn at his place down in the valley. So far, nobody questioned where all the bushels of corn went that his donkey wasn't able to eat – although most folks knew without ever putting it into words. He knew his profession remained safe as long as the men retained a degree of control regardless of their do-gooder wives' intentions.

He gathered strawberries, blackberries, plums, apples, grapes, and any other kinds of fruit he could use to make his brew. Most of the men preferred pure corn liquor with as high a proof as he could manage. There were a few of what some called pansy-assed men who liked sweet and flavored brews. Granny Witcher wanted the high alcohol content corn liquor.

Chapter 6

Nurse Whitley couldn't rest. She kept seeing the little Simmons girl's frightened eyes as she stood among her beautiful flowers. Even worse was seeing the broken little girl who had stood in a pool of blood as she looked at her mother's dead body. She couldn't possibly survive in that shack of a cabin with a father such as Dobb Simmons. It was known all over the county that Dobb was abusive to his wife and her children. She had seen the oldest boy when Dr. Robinson had treated him after he escaped into the valley. What Dobb Simmons did to him was barbaric. The Good Lord only knew what he would do to that little girl now that Sally was dead. Unless her instincts were wrong, Simmons had more to do with his wife's death than anyone would ever know.

"Doctor," she said one morning while he was eating his bowl of oatmeal. "I'm worried about that little Simmons girl."

"Don't start that again," Doc Robinson told her as he raked the bowl with his spoon for the last bit of oatmeal. "People living in those mountains, including children, have to survive the best way they can. Some make it, some don't."

"How can you say such a thing? You saw the condition that little girl was in, not to mention her poor, dead mother."

"If we interfered in everyone's lives we feel sorry for, we'd be at it every moment of every day."

"I'm not concerned about everyone. It's one little girl who can't take care of herself that has me concerned."

Doc Robinson pushed his chair back, got up, and headed for the door. "You've got your hands full taking care of Elouise. Other folks have to learn to take care of their own."

"How can you be so heartless," she demanded.

"I've spent my adult life taking care of people twenty-four seven, my dear. I can only patch up their injuries. I have nothing at all to do with their souls. I'm not God," he added. "As far as how they live, I'm not the man who controls such as that, and you're not either. Leave Dobb Simmons and that little girl alone or you'll end up regretting it. Listen to me for once."

Nurse Whitley glared at his back as he left. She had no intention of doing nothing. Once she had done the dishes and seen to Elouise, she would take a little walk.

"Would you like a back rub?" Nurse Whitley asked Elouise.

"Need you ask? I don't want to get bed sores like I did the last time you ignored me. I asked Joseph to fire you, but he has too soft a heart to toss you in the big road."

Nurse Whitley ignored her harsh words – as she always did. She gently folded the bed clothes down and rolled Elouise onto her side.

"Don't be so rough," Elouise told her harshly.

"Sorry, I'll do my best to be gentler," Nurse Whitley said the same thing she always told her. Her hands touched her gently as possible, but it did little good. Elouise simply liked to complain. She did her best to understand what Elouise was going through. It had to be horrible to have little to no use of your own body. She would probably be even more bitter than Elouise if she were in the same predicament.

"Where is Joseph?" Elouise demanded.

"He's making his rounds like he always does each morning."

"Like he always does each morning," Elouise mocked. "He never spends time with me. It's always his patients. His obligations to others. It's never about his wife."

Nurse Whitley knew that wasn't true. The doctor thought about his wife most all the time. He had no choice and neither did she. If left to Elouise, she would demand every minute of her husband's time. The good doctor was right when he said his wife had always been spoiled and selfish. Nurse Whitley opened the back of Elouise's gown and warmed the lotion in her hands before touching her back. It took a lot of lotion and massages to keep down bed sores and degeneration of what little muscle mass Elouise still had. Daily exercise of her limbs was something else that put Elouise into a foul mood.

"That stuff is cold. You're trying to freeze me to death."

"It's not cold. It only feels cold because it's tingling stimulates the tissue of your back."

"That stuff stinks to high heaven."

"It has a refreshing minty smell. You've always liked it."

"No, I've not. I hate that smell."

"I'll ask the doctor for a different cream if you like."

"He won't give it to me. He doesn't care what I like or what I don't like. He hates me and wants me dead."

"That's not true and you know it. He does everything in his power to keep you happy and healthy."

"If he cared anything about me, he'd have cured me by now," she said, warming up to her usual rantings about anything and everything.

Nurse Whitley closed her ears to the continuous stream of complaints as she finished rubbing her back, retied the gown and eased her onto her back. She lifted her up and propped two pillows behind her back to make her more comfortable,

"I don't want to sit up. I'm not strong enough. Can't you see you're causing my back to go into spasms. You don't care how much I hurt. You take pleasure in my pain."

"If you don't want to sit up, you can lie back down as soon as you swallow your medicine and drink a little water."

"I'm sick and tired of drinking water, and I certainly don't want to swallow that so-called medicine. You're trying to poison me. I know you are."

"This is what the doctor prescribes for you."

"No, it's not. He would never have me drink that horrible tasting stuff. It's poison. You're trying to kill me. I know you are," she ranted on and on.

"Don't talk silliness. Without you I wouldn't have a job," Nurse Whitley told her with a tired smile on her lips.

Nurse Whitley poured a spoonful of medicine and tipped it into her mouth before Elouise could clamp her lips closed. The woman never learned to keep her mouth shut even when the spoon was coming toward her – as it did several times a day. She removed the pillows from behind Elouise's back and eased her down, making her as comfortable as possible. Soon, she would be sound asleep, and Nurse Whitley would have a much needed few hours to herself.

Nurse Whitley packed everything back into her satchel and left the room, paying no attention to Elouise's complaining and calling for her to come back. Such complaining had become a ritual for Elouise every morning. She seemed to get pleasure out of such carrying on. The good Lord knew the poor woman needed all the pleasure she could get. Nurse Whitley's heart broke for Elouise every single day, but there wasn't one thing she could do to alter her condition. Once someone severed the spinal cord, that was it. Elouise was paralyzed from her chest down. Nurse Whitley was thankful Elouise still had some movement in her arms, enabling her to feed herself to a degree, although, most of the time, she insisted on being spoon-fed like a baby. Nurse Whitley considered Elouise a very lucky woman because the man a woman married affected everything in her life. Her mental health, her peace of mind, the love inside her, her happiness, her success, her health, her children, how she lived, how tragedies were handled, and many other things in her existence. Elouise had suffered a tragic accident, but she was fortunate enough to have a husband who went far beyond every single obligation a husband had. *For better or worse,* he took his vow seriously.

Nurse Whitley never argued or complained. It was her job to take care of Elouise and that was what she had done for the past ten years. She had been in her late twenties when she interviewed for the job with the doctor. He talked to her for a short while and then hired her on the spot, disregarding several more qualified ladies. He never asked about her life before she showed up at his house, and she never volunteered information about her past. All she had told him was that she had been raised by her grandmother.

And that was why she was overly concerned about the little Simmons girl. She knew all too well what it was like to be raised without a mother. A girl needed her mother's protection from birth to adulthood – and sometimes even longer than that. She had no intention of taking the doctor's advice and leaving well enough alone.

She hurriedly washed up after feeding and caring for Elouise, tiptoed to the bedroom and cracked the door open enough to be sure the medicine had affected Elouise enough for her to fall asleep. She left Elouise and headed out the door, hesitating slightly to look at her beloved flower garden. Pretty flowers made her happy. Their beauty eased the hurt of what she'd never had – her own home, a loving husband, and much wanted children.

It took only a few minutes of fast walking to reach Beatrice Gidley's house. Beatrice thought she ran the church because she was the head of The Women's Program for a Better World. The preacher and most of the men ignored her and the rest of the women as best they could, which was difficult considering most of the men were married to the women in the group.

Nurse Whitley knocked on the door impatiently. She didn't want to leave Elouise alone for too long without the doctor's knowledge. She heard noise inside that sounded like a groan, and then the sound of footsteps. A curtain was pulled back as someone peered out. The door was finally opened. Beatrice stood there in regal superiority.

"If it isn't Valarie Whitley. You sure it's safe to leave Elouise Robinson alone?"

"She's sleeping. Actually, I have an urgent concern I wanted to talk with you about."

Nurse Whitley saw Beatrice's eyes go from irritation to interest.

"Well, in that case come in."

Nurse Whitley followed Beatrice into the parlor. She was surprised to see three other women seated there.

"Oh, I'm sorry. I didn't intend to interrupt anything," she said as the three women showed irritation on their faces, along with curiosity.

"We can continue our meeting after you tell us what you're concerned about," Beatrice told her as she sat down at the head of the table with the three other women.

Nurse Whitley sat down in a vacant chair without being asked to do so. She came with a mission and intended to be listened to.

"I'll get right to my concern. It's about the little Simmons girl. I believe she is in danger."

"In what kind of danger," Beatrice asked.

"As you know, since all of you were there to bury her mother, she has been left alone with her father."

"And?" Beatrice questioned.

"He isn't the kind of man a child should be left with. Some of you were a witness to what he did to Sally Gray and her children."

"They were his stepsons. There are usually conflicts between a stepfather and stepsons," Beatrice argued.

"She has a point," Ellie James said. "But we all know what kind of man Dobb Simmons is. I wouldn't trust him with my dog, much less a child."

"The girl is his own daughter – not his stepchild," Beatrice pointed out.

"And Sally was his own wife," Ellie told her. "We all saw the bruises on her body, both old and new, when we readied her for burial."

"Fine," Beatrice said. "If that's your opinion, let's have a vote on whether or not the girl should be forcefully taken from her father and put in the orphanage."

The other two women agreed the girl should be taken away from her father and put in the orphanage.

Nurse Whitley had gotten the conclusion she'd come after, but she still was not satisfied. Thing was, she didn't have a better suggestion.

"Is that all that brought you here?" Beatrice questioned her.

"Yes, that is all."

"Good. Then we'll continue our meeting." Beatrice stood indicating Nurse Whitley should leave.

Nurse Whitley stood and followed her to the door. Beatrice opened and then closed the door firmly behind her without saying one courteous word of good-by. Nurse Whitley knew it was an intended insult, but she was used to women trying to insult her. She did what she thought was best while ignoring women such as these.

*

"I didn't know Valarie Whitley was a friend of yours," Ellie James said to Beatrice in her too sweet tone of voice.

"She's not," Beatrice told her firmly. "She does have a lot of inside information I want to be kept informed of since she works for Dr. Robinson. He is an important man with a lot of influence. We can't exactly blackball her."

"I imagine he does a lot of pillow talking," Ellie said pointedly.

"There is no proof of that," Beatrice told her, although she believed it herself. However, as the leader of The Women's Program for a Better World, she was supposed to keep her own opinions to herself.

"You don't have to pull a goody-two-shoes in front of us," Inez Williams told Beatrice. "Dr. Robinson is a man whose wife has been bedridden for years. Valarie Whitley was young and pretty when he hired her. We all know what happens in such a situation."

"That's old news," Beatrice said with irritation. She didn't like being called a goody-two-shoes. She considered herself a woman with other people's best interests in mind. "It's good we are having a meeting. We can determine what needs to be done with the Simmons girl. Does anyone have a suggestion?"

"It's not our responsibility to take care of her. She's not an orphan. She has a daddy," Inez Williams told her. "We've got enough decent children to look after. We don't need to start taking in mountain trash. Our orphanage would be overrun with kids the parents want to get rid of. We all know how mountain trash breed like a bunch of rats."

"Sally Gray was a good woman," Ellie said.

"That's a matter of opinion," Inez was quick to say.

"We're not here to discuss Sally Gray or Valarie Whitley. The question right now is do we put the Simmons girl in the orphanage and rescue her from a horrible life?"

"We have to remember who her daddy is. A nasty piece of work, that one," Beatrice told them.

"And that's only one of the reasons we ought to have the church rescue her," Ellie said.

Chapter 7

~~Tally~~Tucker~~

Tally's breakfast was some of the first cornbread she'd ever baked by herself. She had done something wrong because it didn't taste good, but eating it anyway helped to ease her hunger. She couldn't believe how easy her mother had made cooking look when Tally found it almost impossible. Momma made every task look easy. It didn't matter if it was inside or outside work. The only thing Tally did effortlessly was continuous crying. Hardly an hour passed without Tally breaking into a fit of tears. Even at night, during sleep, she would wake up to find her pillow soaking wet. The sight of her momma's dead body haunted every minute of her days and nights.

She gathered her mother's seeds and took them to the garden. She tried not to look at her momma's grave but was drawn to it. She walked over it with bare feet. The dirt was warming up every single day, but Tally still felt frozen inside and out. She shivered as she looked about the now barren garden. She had to plant if she wanted to survive.

Clancy's mention of the orphan home came to her. According to Clancy, living there was much worse than the hardships of surviving in the mountains. She wondered if she would have food to eat if she was there. Would she be warm on a cold night? Would she be alone and afraid every moment of her life?

Here, on the mountain, even planting a garden seemed beyond her. She couldn't believe how difficult it was to plant all by herself. She'd always been the one who dropped the seeds, while her mother did everything else. Now, mother wasn't there to tell her what to do next, and it made her feel even more helpless.

"You're a big girl now," her mother's voice kept sounding in her ears. *"You can do what you have to do, child. Don't let nobody tell you that you can't – even if it's yourself."*

She wiped the tears from her eyes with dirt-stained hands. "I'm afraid, Momma. So very afraid," she whispered out loud and then lifted her head and strained to catch more of her mother's voice.

Instead, she heard the snapping of brush coming from in front of the cabin. For a moment, her heart soared thinking it was coming from her mother's footsteps. Suddenly, the soaring took a nosedive. It couldn't be her mother. Her mother's grave was in the middle of the garden only a few feet from where she stood. She knew it couldn't be Clancy. He never made a sound. It had to be her dad, and most likely, he would be drunk and mean. She didn't take time to drop her mother's hoe as she ran toward the woods where dense underbrush grew. She eased into the edge of a heavy growth of weeds and lay flat on her belly the way Clancy had shown her to do. Breathe deep and slow. Don't move a muscle, she repeated to herself what Clancy had told her. If she moved, her dad would be sure to see her. He had a sharp eye.

"Anybody home?" She heard a man's voice say. "Dobb, are you in there? We've come to have a talk with you. It's important."

It wasn't her dad after all. It was worse if that was possible. It was the preacher's voice she heard.

"He's not answering. Tally, honey, are you in there? Can we come inside?" A woman's voice called out.

Tally cringed. They had come after her just as Clancy had warned they might. She didn't know what to do other than stay as silent as possible. If by chance they spotted her, she would have to outrun them. Suddenly, a new fear hit her. She'd left her dad's gun and ammunition behind the door. What if they took the gun and shells? She would be punished for allowing them to take them when her dad returned.

She started to tremble even though she was trying to stay still. She was sure they would hear her heart pounding in her chest even though she was a fair distance away.

"Nobody is in here," said the woman after she cracked the door open. "It's warm inside and there's a smell of food having been cooked. I think I'll go inside and have a look around."

"No, Ida, we best not do that. Dobb can't be far away. His heavy coat is hanging on the back of the chair. If he returns to find us in his house, there's no telling what he'll do."

"Don't be silly. Now's our chance to see how that poor girl lives here with her dad. Everybody talks about how abusive he is."

"Even more reason for him not to find us in his house. I agreed to bring Bob and you here to ask Dobb's permission to take the girl against my better judgement, but I'm not trespassing in his house. Besides, this place is as neat as a pin. There's no sign of a struggle or anything such as that. Actually, it appears much the same way we left it, except for the warm stove and the smell of food having been cooked."

"I'm not goin' in there," the man who must have been Bob spoke up. "I'm not willing to get shot and fed to the hogs."

"I heard he sold all his hogs," the woman said.

"Smells like they're still here, and I'm not willing to be shot and buried either. Let's get away from here. I've got the heebie geebies," Bob insisted.

"No," the woman said firmly. "We're here. I don't intend to leave without that girl."

"You can't take her with you when she's not here," the preacher tried to reason with her.

"Then we'll have to wait inside until she returns."

"Not me," Bob said. "I'm leaving this place if I have to walk off the mountain by myself. I'm gettin' a strange kinda feeling like we're being watched. Look at my arms. I got goose bumps the size of chinquapins. Feels like a cold wind is blowin' over me."

"Me too," the preacher admitted. "And I'm not a man who gets the heebie jeebies. I don't believe it's Dobb watching us. If he was, chances are he'd either show himself or shoot us from ambush. Don't know why I let you harass me into bringing you all the way here," Preacher Hadley told Ida.

"You came because you didn't want me to come by myself, and you've lived with me long enough to know I'd do it. It's your mission in life to save souls. It's my mission in life to save children."

Bob didn't comment on her statement. He didn't want to make Ida mad at him. He did question children being saved by that so-called orphanage home that bunch of women had come up with.

"Right. Now, I'm taking you away from here before one of us gets hurt or killed," the preacher told his wife.

"I'm not afraid of Dobb Simmons or any other man," Ida said bravely.

"I'm afraid of him," Bob admitted.

"Me too," said the preacher. "The last time he shot at us, he missed intentionally. Don't think he'll waste a shell a second time."

"Then you shouldn't have come if you're so afraid," Ida said with foolish bravado.

"Right," the preacher agreed. "I agreed to bring you up here. Now, I'm taking you away."

"Turn my arm loose. If you drag me away from here, I'll just come back. I intend to put that girl in our orphanage where she belongs. We don't need the likes of her living on this mountain without proper supervision. You know what girls like her turn into. No woman wants her husband or sons running up here getting no telling what kind of diseases."

There was more arguing as the sound of their voices faded. Still, Tally stayed hidden until the sun started to drop behind the tree line. The wind had brought the sound of a gun being fired before she heard a car engine winding down the rough mountain. Was that her dad shooting at them? Had he come back and gotten his gun while she was in the garden. She dreaded his return almost as much as she dreaded going to the orphanage. She stayed hunkered down for a while longer. She didn't trust all of them to be gone. The woman could come back or still be there, waiting – so could her dad.

Finally, she crawled from her hiding place and slipped through the woods circling the house trying to determine if there was any sign of someone still being there. Little by little she eased toward the cabin until she gathered enough courage to open the door and peak inside. The place was empty, and her dad's gun and shells were still behind the door exactly as they had been. He hadn't been the one who shot the gun. A shiver from not knowing who was on the mountain ran over her. She turned the wooden buttons to keep them out, sat down on her mother's bed and gripped the ragged quilt in her hands until her shaking eased up.

~~~~

Tucker had heard the car groaning its way up the mountain and hurried to see what was going on. A man in his business couldn't be too careful. He'd been readying his load to haul down the rough mountain road. Thank goodness he hadn't started out or he would have needed to find a place to pull his donkey and sled off the road to hide. The so-called road was narrow with steep rocky sides making it difficult to find a place where a man could drive anything into the woods. His donkey and sled could maneuver through the woods, but it was much easier and faster to drive down the rough road. Plus, the rough road didn't leave a trail back to his still.

He had hidden in the woods and watched them until they got out of the car. He then followed behind the preacher and the other two as they hoofed it the rest of the way on foot to the cabin. He was relieved to discover the little girl was nowhere to be seen. At least she was smart enough to hide when somebody showed up. He had no idea what he'd do if she'd been there and they had gotten hold of her. That orphan home wasn't a fit place for children. It was more like a jail for the children that the woman didn't see as fit to live among the more important folks. Among those women were the preache'sr wife, the sheriff's wife, the banker's wife, and Beatrice Gidley.

Tucker watched until they left. The preacher was all but dragging his wife every step of the way to the car regardless of how angry she got.

Tucker knew Ida believed she ruled her husband along with everybody else she came into contact with. Her husband making her leave was more than she could comprehend. How dare he treat her in such a way. She was used to getting what she wanted. After all, she was not only his wife but the head of the committee for Women for a Better World.

It was well known Ida Hadley and Beatrice Gidley were in competition with each other to see who had the most control over the orphanage, along with everyone else's lives. No wonder he had to keep their husbands in a supply of his shine. Actually, he kept a lot of the men in supply. Life might be more tranquil if the women indulged as well.

As soon as they were in seeing distance of the car, he lifted the shotgun he always carried and shot it into the tree limbs over their heads. They needed to think Dobb was still alive and watching for them. The preacher knew Dobb Simmons sometimes gave one warning shot – two warning shots was highly unusual – there was never a third warning from Dobb Simmons.

Tucker leaned against a tree trunk and grinned at their hasty retreat. Preacher Hadley didn't have to drag Ida into the car. She jerked loose from his hold and took cover faster than both men. Ah well, as soon as they were gone, he might as well go toward the rock overhang and check on Dobb.

He found Dobb laid out in a bed of leaves far enough back under the crevice to be sheltered from most of the weather. Wooden stobs had been driven in a semi-circle around him with some kind of herbs tied to them. Granny Witcher was obviously trying to counter his smell while keeping wild animals away from him. He was sound asleep. She must have given him a sleeping draught to keep him silent along with keeping him from thrashing about while his bones knitted back together.

Such a useless piece of human flesh, Tucker thought. Why was it God allowed such men be born, much less survive? If Dobb Simmons had a purpose in life, it had to be to father the little girl. As far as Tucker knew, there was no other good that ever came out of the man.

Again, he wondered about his decision in saving Dobb Simmons' life.

Oh, well. Things happened and folks got along the best way they could. Right now, he had to gather his shine and make his own deliveries. He didn't think he'd be delivering any at the drop-offs Dobb usually made. They were too dangerous for his comfort.

~~~~

Tucker's last stop was at the doctor's house. He saved the best stop for last. He needed something good to end his day with. Seeing Valarie Whitley did his soul good, and at the same time seeing her broke his heart. Everyone knew she belonged to the doctor, but he could pretend she might someday belong to him.

Ten years he had loved her. He never believed in love at first sight until he set eyes on Valarie Whitley. What he felt for Valarie Whitley wasn't a pleasing thing. Instead, it was more like a burning pain hurting uncontrollably inside his chest that nothing was going to cure. Even he knew she had eyes for no one other than the doctor who was tied to a bedridden wife. Folks declared it was the guilt Valarie Whitley felt that caused her to take such good care of the doctor's hateful wife. Even during her healthy years Elouise Robinson was said to be a royal bitch with a lashing tongue that cut like a razor blade. Folks never could figure out why a good man such as the doctor married such an obnoxious woman.

He knocked on the kitchen door instead of going to the doctor's small office next door. Nurse Whitley was seldom in the doctor's office. He was all but holding his breath as he waited for the door to open.

It felt like having ice cold water poured over him when the doctor opened the door instead of Valarie Whitley.

"You're late," Doc Robinson said. "Expected you yesterday. Meet me at my office," he said as he shut the door in Tucker's face.

Tucker turned and walked away. He ought to be used to disappointment by now, but he wasn't. Odd how a man could have eternal hope.

Chapter 8

~~Granny Witcher~~

Granny Witcher forced her stiff joints to move her off her herb-filled mattress as soon as she heard the first sound of a morning bird's call. She believed the aroma of pine needles, ginger root, rosemary, sage, and mint helped her both mentally and physically. It also countered musty odors when it was too cold to take her morning dip in the freezing water of the creek, which was all but a short time during summer. During those times a wash pan and rag had to do good enough. Weather in the high mountains was something she had trouble adjusting to, even after all these years.

The warmth of the low-land suddenly haunted her memory.

She could feel the heat of the sun on her young flesh, feel the vibrancy of muscle and mind as she ran barefoot in the green grass of the yard the gardener maintained to perfection. She could smell the wonderful scent of azalea blossoms, daffodils, hyacinth, and other early blooming plants. She recalled the joy of using shears to clip flowers for bouquets for every room in the house. Oh, how she had loved her life as a privileged daughter, and then the privileged wife of Clarence Witcher.

Her life had still been good even though her marriage wasn't the kind that was made in heaven. It wasn't even the kind of marriage that came from love at first sight – maybe not even love at all in the usual sense. Her marriage came about from the love of power, a marriage made for prosperity, an arranged marriage, a business deal between two high society ruling families. The offspring of such a union would be the future holder of great wealth and control from the two families combined.

After a year into the marriage, it became obvious there were no offspring in the making. Loraine Carter Witcher had not lived up to the Witchers' or the Carters' expectations. Clarence and his father had gotten together privately to discuss the problem. Loraine Carter had been the first choice in a business transaction, but not the only choice. Luck was with the Witchers. The second choice was still single and available. The second choice's family wasn't as powerful or as wealthy as the Carter family, but would do well enough. A plan was decided between her husband and his father – one that could allow them another chance at a legitimate heir while still saving their reputation as well as maintaining the Carter's goodwill.

Unfortunately, Loraine had no clue what they were up too. She should have known Clarence Witcher had a reason for showing her special attention during mealtimes when he'd never done that before.

"Eat all your food," he'd say. "Drink all of that herbal tea you like so well. I'm concerned about you. You've been looking pale lately. I fear you're not well. You need to stay inside and get more rest."

She ate her food, drank her tea, and went upstairs to look in the mirror. She didn't look at all pale, but a short time later she was not only pale, she was vomiting in a waste basket. The tea had not agreed with her. Quickly, she disposed of the contents of the waste basket. She wanted no one to know about her queasy spell. Hope spiraled. Was it possible she was finally with child? A few days later, she knew that was not the case, even though the vomiting continued every time she drank the herbal tea her husband encouraged her to consume.

She tried to stop drinking the tea, but her husband insisted and got mad when she didn't drink it. So, she forced herself to drink it while trying not to gag, but as soon as she was alone, she would make sure she stuck her finger down her throat to rid her stomach of its contents. Still, she would feel the troubling effects of what she concluded her husband was surely putting into her tea.

"The tea is making me sick," she confided to the colored cook when she caught Loraine emptying her stomach behind the house.

Cooky, as the cook was referred to by the Witchers, frowned. She always tasted the tea before she served it to little Miss Loraine to make sure it was brewed just right. It was, and it never affected her in any way.

"Is you with child?" Cooky asked hopefully.

"No," Loraine assured her. "My stomach feels a little better after I vomit the tea up, but a weakness remains."

Cooky took her chin in her hand and turned her face until she could get a good look at the pupils of her eyes.

"You's been feeling right dizzy-headed lately, ain't you?"

"I, uh, yes, kinda," she admitted in a rather slurred voice.

"You's got any runnin' off?"

She nodded. Her bowels had been mighty loose. She had to use the chamber pot several times during the night as well as during the daytime.

"Humph," Cooky grunted thoughtfully. "From now on, leave a few drops of that tea in your glass."

The very next day as they were eating their dinner, there was a disturbance outside. Clarence's favorite riding horse had managed to open the gate and was running through the manicured lawn. Clarence took it upon himself to rush outside and verbally chastise the groom who was trying to calm the excited horse enough to be caught.

Cooky wasted no time rushing into the dining room and replacing the glass of tea with another. Loraine was wise enough to drink the tea slowly and without comment after her husband returned, fuming with anger at the neglectful groom allowing his horse to escape the paddock and kick up tuffs of grass in his prized, green lawn.

As soon as the meal was over, Clarence left the house to check on his horse and browbeat the groom some more. Cooky wasted no time in drawing Loraine aside before she could go upstairs.

"Let me smell your breath," Cooky said.

Loraine opened her mouth and breathed out.

"Just as I though. There's the faintest sweet scent and a slight smell of garlic. I didn't cook with no garlic."

The next day Cooky made sure she encountered Loraine while she was alone in the flower garden gathering her bouquets of flowers.

"I's got bad news. Awful, awful news fur ye," Cooky whispered. "Ye ain't gonna' believe what Mast'r Witcher doin'. He's an evil man I tell you. Evil to the core of his rotten soul."

Loraine didn't wait for her to say the words she had feared hearing. "He's poisoning me," she said before Cooky could.

"I's sorry – bad sorry, but that's 'xactly what he's a doin'."

"What is he putting in the tea?"

"Arsenic. Me and Buck rummaged through Mist'r Witcher's thangs. Buck found a bottle of it with fresh drips runnin' down the outside. Arsenic don't leave no strong smell no taste in you's tea. They's a somewhat smell of garlic if a person has a mighty good smeller."

"I should have known," she admitted. His reputation would suffer if he divorced her. Divorce was looked down on. It showed a man made a bad decision in choosing his wife. The Witchers could not take a chance on harming their reputation. So, Clarence and his father decided to kill her instead.

"What can I do? I don't want to die," she told Cooky as a tremor took hold of her.

"Do no-account tellin' the law. 'Sides, you'd never prove nary a thing' against them high and mighty Witchers."

"The law and everyone else is controlled by his family," Loraine agreed with trembling chin. "I don't want to die," she said again.

"Ye ain't gonna' die of his pizen. Stayed up all night figurin' on it. Ye's gonna' drown instead."

"What?" Loraine choked out.

"You's knows how my boy loves to fish. He's gonna' fall in the river. You's gonna' try to save him."

Loraine shook her head. The plan was absurd, but what was the alternative? Clarence would kill her one way or another. She was sure of that much. The more she thought about it, the more Cooky's plan made sense, but how would it all happen? How would she disappear? Where could she hide? It wasn't like she had distant relatives she could run to for escape.

"Ain't gonna take a chance. We's gonna to do it right now. Bo goin' fishing today, do it every week at this time a day. Ever'body knows it. Can't wait nary bit longer, fer he'll get ye fo' certain if we do, be it with poison or some other way."

She pulled a small wad of money from between her massive breasts. "This here's my savin's. Buck has you's a change of clothes, a pair of sturdy boots, and a sack of food. I done give Buck a change of step-in for you and some torn rags to put in your sack. Expect you'll be needing 'em afore you get settled. Bo's waitin' fer you's in the woods. Hurry now."

Cooky stuck the money in her hand and gave her a slight push toward the path through the woods that led to the river. Her feet moved, but her mind had almost stopped working. All she could think about was arsenic. He'd been giving her arsenic. She'd be dead by now if it hadn't made her so sick, she vomited it up. It was too much for her to believe, yet she did believe it. She'd never been important to Clarence. Didn't he come home smelling of different perfumes several times a week? She knew he spent more time with other women than he did with her. She was nothing more to him than a broodmare – one he had to service regularly in order to beget an heir.

"Hurry, Miz Loraine. Ain't no time to waste. Bo's awaitin' on ye. Go, you'll be taken care of right proper."

Once Bo and she reached a spot in the river where there was a swift undercurrent, she found out why. Buck was waiting in the undergrowth with a plow mule that was as old as he was. He had her take off her fancy shoes. He ripped several pieces of material from her dress tail and handed the pieces to Bo.

"Go behind that there bresh and put these here things on. You's can stuff you's dress in the sack to take wif' you," Bo told her once they were out of sight of the house. They certainly didn't want anyone to see what they were doing.

He took a pair of worn britches and a flannel shirt along with a pair of worn boots and a sweat-stained cap from a hemp sack and handed them to her.

"Best ta' be fast," he told her. "Laggin' gets ye seen. Pull the cap's bill down over your face. Make sure all yer hair's under the cap. Don't want it's prettiness to be seen."

It was man's clothes, hanging loosely over her body. Obviously, the clothes had belonged to someone smaller than Buck and larger than Bo. They were well worn and had a lye soap smell clinging to them. When she returned from the brush, he told her Bo would put on her shoes and leave footprint leading into the water. He'd then toss her shoes in the water and leave bits of the torn cloth from her skirt on a few rocks and brambles growing in the middle of the river. When he had finished, and given them enough time to get far away, he'd run to the house and tell Cooky he'd seen Miz Loraine fall in the river instead of sticking to the story that she'd jumped in to save him. White folks wouldn't take too kindly to a white woman drowning from trying to save a darkie, even when the darkie was a child. Not only that; everybody knew Bo could swim like a fish when Loraine couldn't swim at all.

Loraine felt dumbstruck as she took off her dress and put the pants and shirt on. Oddly enough they were too big and yet fit well enough. The boots and wool socks Buck had given her were big enough to slip up and down on her feet. He put her on the mule and walked beside her through the deep piney woods, away from the river as well as the life she'd always known. Bo followed for a long way, using a pine branch to wipe away their tracks. After a mile or so, she looked over her shoulder to see Bo heading in the opposite direction wiping out his own footprints.

"Why can't we go by car?" Loraine asked Buck as she felt the discomfort of the mule beneath her.

"Don't have nary 'un. Don't trust any of 'em who do."

They stayed in the cover of the woods as much as possible. Always trying to travel over land the colored folks owned, where no one would think anything about a man and a mule leaving tracks in the soil.

Buck had stayed with her for days as he led her away from flat land into the rolling hills. It was obvious she had been pampered all her life causing her to be unable to travel as fast as Cooky had expected. Most of the time she found herself in tears brought on from dissolution as well as exhaustion. She and Buck both tried not to eat much, but the food Cooky had packed ran out after three days. They drank water out of the creeks and ate whatever greens, roots and berries they could find. Buck didn't take time to kill anything, not that he would have built a fire to cook it. Time and concealment were of importance. She had to be far away without anyone getting a glimpse of her or Buck. A black man with a white person on a mule would signal trouble regardless of the reason. If that white person was recognized as a woman, Buck would be in a deadly situation – and so could she.

Finally, after what seemed like forever, they saw tall, blue mountains looming in front of them. "I's aim to leave you dirct'ly," he told her. "They's folks what'll take you to a place where you can hide out for a spell, from there you's be on your own."

She feared she wouldn't be capable of being on her own for a long while. She was a pampered white woman without the smallest survival skills. Loraine Carter had done almost nothing for herself. There were always servants paid to jump to accommodate her every wish. She didn't even know how to prepare food. All she'd ever grown were her flowers. Her hands, body, and mind were soft and tender.

She had learned, though. Oh, how she had learned. She tried to count the years since she had been that soft, naive girl. It had been nigh onto fifty years give or take a few.

She drew in a deep breath saddened by memory. She still had that hemp sack and her torn dress. The dress she had brought with her, with the pieces torn out, was under the mattress. She had kept the dress as a reminder of her past life, but she'd never worn it again. She used the hemp sack most every day.

Granny Witcher looked down on the man sleeping in the bed of leaves. He'd lost weight and his straggly beard clung to his sunken cheeks. His hair was long and greasy, He smelled, even though he was naked from his waist down. She raked away the soiled leaves from near his body and replaced them with clean ones, only to need to do it again the next day. Maybe it was time to stop giving him the sleeping draught. His arms and legs were healing. They moved about rather well, but they were weak. She ought to let him move about more, but movement could also hamper healing bones. Not only was she tired of looking after him, Tucker had stopped making shine for some reason or other. He usually ran off a batch at least once a month. It had been over a month since he brought her jugs of liquor.

Dobb continued to stink like rotted carrion even though she used some of her precious liquor to pour over him, The weather was starting to heat up enough for blow flies to gather and lay eggs all over him. She wasn't a fan of flesh-eating maggots, even on a man like Dobb Simmons.

And then, there was the question of what would happen if she did stop drugging him? Most likely he'd go back to the cabin where the little girl would have to take care of him. That poor little girl was having enough trouble taking care of herself. She checked on the girl several times a week just to make sure nothing bad had happened to her, but she never let the girl know of her observation. Sally Gray had come to her often, bringing vegetables or herbs in trade for different kinds of medications. After the little girl was born, Sally did her best never to get with child again by coming to her for herbs that would help keep her barren. Sally never wanted to give Dobb a son who would be raised up to be like his daddy. As the girl child got older, Sally came less often. It seemed to her that Sally did not want the little girl to know she existed, but even a small child remembered more than folks thought.

Granny Witcher put her bottle of medicine back in her pocket without giving any to Dobb. Instead of spoon feeding him as she often did, she left a pint jar of soup and a quart jar of water within his reach and left. It would be easier on the girl if a crippled man came home rather than one who was healed.

Chapter 9 Tally

~~Tucker~~Dobb~~

Weeks passed before Tally got somewhat over being scared of being caught and taken to the orphanage. Every time the wind blew leaves, every time she heard a twig snap, she'd run for the woods to hide. She had been afraid to sleep in the house during the night, and yet she was afraid not to. There were wild animals maundering in the high mountains. Bears, mountain lions, bob cats, and even smaller animals were always a danger. Her momma had once killed a timber rattler with a hoe. It was curled up in the path that led from the house to the garden. There was sure to be more poisonous snakes. "There are many things you don't expect that would kill you, but they will" Momma had warned her. "Best to keep your ears and eyes open all the time. Don't blindly trust nothing."

Tally tried to stay observant, but she feared she was nearly deaf and blind to the dangers. But not any longer. Now, without her mother to protect her, she saw danger lurking everywhere. There was so much she didn't know – so much she couldn't do. Chopping wood with an ax, getting a fire started with her mother's tinder box brought her to frustrated tears. Sometimes she tried to strike the flint and steel to get a spark for what seemed like hours. Momma often used the fluff from cat tails to catch the spark, but there was no fluff in Spring. She found that feathers, leaves, and dried straw sometimes worked. She needed heat to cook food she couldn't eat raw. Sometimes she needed heat to warm her chilled body when she started shivering from cold or fear.

She did her best never to cry. Her dad always whipped her when she cried. Her mother never whipped her. "You don't need a whippin'. You're a good girl," her mother would assure her.

She came to realize her dad did not whip her because she was bad. He whipped her because he was bad. He liked whipping those who were weaker than him. Her mother was weaker than him, just as her brothers and sister were.

~~~~

It took some time for Dobb to come to himself. He was puzzled at the sticks that were fastened to his arms and leg. He found a sharp rock and sawed at the material that held the sticks fastened to his limbs until he had them off. He tried to sit up and found he could do it. There was pain. He didn't like pain. He wasn't surprised to discover he was naked from the waist down. He'd been all but buried in leaves under a rock overhang. He looked about and spotted the soup and water in the jars, eagerly grabbed both jars and drank all of the soupy broth. Damned if he wasn't hungry and thirsty. Worse than hunger and thirst was his craving for liquor. He wanted it in the worst sort of way. He looked about and saw his britches hanging from a rhododendron limb where the sun and rain had been able to get at them.

He moved his arms and good leg as he tried to stand. Damned, if everything about him didn't hurt like he was in hell's fire. To make the hurting worse, was the weakness that had a hold on his entire body. His arms, legs, his whole body were nothing more than skin over bone. He figured he must have been mighty bad off for a mighty long time to put him in such a pitiful shape as this, but he didn't know for how long.

He sat back down and tried to remember what had happened to him. He kind of remembered something hitting him in the head and him falling down the rock cliff into the basin where the cow had died. Snippets of Tucker dragging him through narrow, rocky openings came to him. Intense pain had caused him to open his eyes long enough to see Tucker for brief moments before the terrible pain blacked him out again.

The next time he opened his eyes an image of the witch woman standing over him with a knife was vivid. She'd cut his britches off him. She'd also fed him stuff from a spoon. Most of all he remembered pain.

As he sat there, he concluded Tucker had tried to kill him. Had the witch woman saved him? Somebody had to of done it. It had to be the witch woman. He must have been under the rock for a long time. The weather had warmed up. The trees had put out leaves. Things had happened to him during that time. Things he wasn't certain about, but those things made him mad and revengeful.

But, before he got even with anybody, he needed food and more strength. He also needed Sally to feed and care for him the way a wife ought to do. He crawled his weak body to his britches. He couldn't allow Sally to see him butt-naked. She would get too much pleasure from him being too weak to pull his britches on. It took a while to get his cut britches back on. Sally would have to do some sewing on them. It took longer for him to find two sticks to serve as crutches. It also took unbelievable determination for him to keep moving toward home. His arms and leg were on fire with pain. Every few minutes he'd have to stop, drop to the ground, and rest up a while. Getting back on his feet was nothing short of torture. He needed liquor. Plenty of it.

It took the rest of the day, the night, and part of the next day to make his way through the woods to get within sight of his cabin. His strength gave out before he reached it, and he sank to the ground.

"Sally!" he yelled to the top of his lungs. "Come help me, Sally."

Sally didn't come. She didn't call back or show up in the open door of the cabin. He'd beat her half to death with his sticks for not coming to help him when he called for her.

Suddenly, before his eyes could focus, a streak of something came out of the open door like a bullet shot out of a gun and disappeared into the woods.

"Who the hell was that?" he mumbled as he looked toward the spot in the woods where she had disappeared.

"Sally!" he yelled out again, but all he got in answer was silence.

He was tired, exhausted, and in need of water and food in the worst sort of way. He tried to stand but was too shaky to get to his feet even with the help of the sticks. His arms were too weak, and his good leg couldn't do it all by itself. He tried to crawl the rest of the way to the open cabin door, but he couldn't do it. He only got a few feet in the rocky ground before his body started to tremble. His bad leg wouldn't bend right, and his arms. Ah, mercy, how his arms ached.

The thing he wanted more than water and food was liquor. He craved it as much as he craved his next breath of air. He closed his eyes. Breathed through his mouth to calm himself. It seemed to work, at least enough to remember he always kept a jug or two of liquor in the cabin hid in the old flour bin. He opened his mouth to yell for Sally again, but snapped it shut. He was smelling a foul odor. It didn't occur to him that it could be himself. Instead, his depraved mind saw the remains of a baby boy that he'd cut out of that no-account woman's belly. His boy. The one he'd wanted, waited for all these years.

The memory of his dead boy made him fly into enough of a rage to get to his feet and crabwalk the rest of the way to the cabin. His want of his jug of liquor was stronger than all the pain he was suffering.

~~~~

Tally heard the yelling of her dad from where she was hiding in the woods. Fear washed over her. It was bad enough to face him when her mother was alive to try protecting her. There was no way she could face him on her own. She gathered enough courage to peep through an opening in the undergrowth to see him on his hands and knees. He got up and was struggling toward the house. Drunk again, she thought. Even if he passed out from being dead drunk, she wasn't about to go back to the house while he was there.

But what was she to do?

Was it possible for her to live in the woods all by herself? She didn't think so. Maybe she could find Clancy's cave – go live with him. But she hadn't seen him since he sent her home alone. She'd roamed the woods for hours without Clancy showing up. She feared those orphanage people had captured him even though he was fast and woods smart. He could have gotten hurt or sick. He could even be dead, eaten by wild animals, but she wasn't going to let her mind think about such as that. She wanted to think there had to be a reason he didn't show up to check on her during the past weeks. At least, she hoped there was a reason other than he simply didn't want all the hard work of looking out for her welfare.

She hid in the woods all night long. Didn't even come out to milk the goat or feed her mother's chickens. The goat was starting to bleat to be milked by the next morning, but she was too afraid to take a chance on being out in the open long enough to milk her.

By the time the sun started going down, she gathered enough determination to slip close enough to the cabin to see through the open door. There was enough light left in the cabin to see her dad lying on the floor with a jug lying on its side and another one sitting upright only inches from his hand. She could hear his snoring from where she hid.

He didn't look anything like the dad she feared. The man she was looking at was no longer the broad, powerful man she remembered. His body had shrunk, his beard was white, and thin hair that hung in greasy clumps on his round head. She could smell an odor coming from him even from the long distance from the cabin to where she hid. Hurriedly, she rushed from her hiding place through the woods to the shelter where the goat and chickens were. She fed and milked the goat, fed the chickens, and gathered the eggs. She drank every drop of the warm milk, but she didn't want to eat slimy, raw eggs. She hid the eggs in a hollow stump where she could get them later.

She went back to her hiding place in the woods as the gloaming of night set in. All she had to comfort her was the call of a whippoorwill coming from high on a tall, rugged mountain. She wondered if Clancy was able to listen to the mournful sound, and if he felt desperate the way she did.

~~~~

Tucker had finally delivered all the jugs he had, and needed to think about heading up into the mountains. Business was so good he was thinking about going up on the price some. The supplies he needed were sure enough going up in cost every time he bought a load, but a man had no choice other than to pay the price when he had a business to run. He packed sugar, yeast, and cracked corn on his donkey and headed into the woods in the middle of the night as usual. Everyone knew he made liquor, but they ignored his business endevors as long as he didn't flaunt it in their faces, and sold them what they wanted at a cheap enough price. It had been a while since he ran off a batch. He didn't need as much shine since he didn't care about supplying the customers Dobb delivered to. Dobb's customers were a mean bunch of no-accounts who'd just as soon kill a man as look at him. The only thing that stopped them from killing Dobb was their fear of being without plenty of good liquor to drink at a price they could afford. They would be right heated up when they discovered Dobbs wasn't going to show up. Of course, there was also the fact that most of Dobb's customers didn't think Dobb was worth killing.

He went in the opposite direction to where his still was located. He took his strategy from mother birds who faked being injured as they drew the predator away from their nests. A body couldn't be too careful when it came to what he made a living at. Each time he headed into the mountains he tried to go a different route, which proved to be difficult at times. The mountain was rugged, rocky, and dangerously steep in places. So far, Dobb was the only one who knew where his still was located, plus there was the possibility the old woman Granny Witcher knew, although he'd never seen any evidence of her snooping about. She'd been in those mountains so long she knew where every herb, berry, rock, and tree limb were located. One thing about the old woman, she minded her own business and let everyone else mind theirs. He did have a sort of business going on with her. He traded her liquor for herbs and such. He could double his money by trading liquor for sang roots and other herbs, not to mention the salves and concoctions he traded to the doctor. It was a fact that her medicines were good stuff. They worked the way she claimed they'd work.

As for Dobb Simmons, he didn't trust that pitiful excuse of a man as far as he could pick up and throw his donkey, but he had hired him and kept him in a supply of liquor for his own use and mash for his hogs. Dobb had sold his hogs some time back and hadn't bought any to replace them yet. Tucker feared the mash might be piling up too much. He'd have to haul it off and pour it in ravines in hopes wild animals would eat it before hunters found it. He ought to climb down into the ravine and check it out after he dumped the next load.

One benefit was that the mountain land where his still was hidden was in such steep and rough terrain it was almost impenetrable except for those with real determination. Most hunters took the easy trails. The downside was the exact same thing. It took him most of a night to meander his way over the mountains until he decided he wasn't being followed. Tucker knew it paid to be paranoid.

There was little daylight left between the setting of the sun and darkness especially when the threatening storm took away most of the light and left an ominous gloom in the deep woods. The massive mountains cast dark shadows even during high noon that gave a man the feeling of dread, if not actual causing fear in the soul of the bravest of men. The sinister feeling got a hold on Tucker as he led his donkey over the moss-covered tree roots even though he had walked the same way many a time. To make things worse, the wind had picked up and was blowing hard enough to lift the damp, moss covered roots of the tall trees upward several inches before the roots settled back down. It seemed the ground itself was taking huge breaths of air and then letting its breath out only to repeat it over and over again. His donkey tended to balk, but Tucker encouraged the donkey and himself to keep trudging onward.

Tucker assured himself those trees he was walking over had not uprooted during the worst of storms and high winds, which were many. Most likely they wouldn't uproot while he and his donkey were walking on those heaving roots. He half grinned as he mumbled soothing encouragement to his donkey in an attempt to keep up his own courage. Still, a shudder crept over him at the weird movement of the roots beneath his feet. The place had an eerie strangeness that got to a man during the best of times. It was a place where the sun never shined, and the air was always cold – a perfect place for bad omens to roam. A place where a man just might not be safe maundering about especially during a bad storm such as was brewing right now.

Tucker had a feeling he was being watched, but he couldn't imagine who might be watching him in a place like this. As far as knew, Granny Witcher had never set foot anywhere near his still, even when she needed the alcohol for her brews. Other than her, the Grays, and Dobb Simmons, no other people tried to survive on this side of the mountain where the unforgiving land was too rocky for a man to make a decent living on. It was where the poor, criminals, and the insane had been relegated to hide out. It took a mighty crazy man to go into this mountain – a man like him.

Then there was the boy. To the best of Tucker's knowledge, he was hiding out on a different side of the mountain where there were huge boulders and winding caves for him to hide in. Not that the boy didn't come down out of those caves and go into the valley to plunder food and other things he needed or wanted. Folks had blamed things they missed on Sally Gray's boys until they realized they had all left out. Some blamed Dobb Simmons. Now, one or two of the valley dwellers were looking at him with accusing eyes. He'd heard comments and warnings during his deliveries.

"Tucker," preacher Hadley had said when Tucker slipped him a full jug. "Old man Gidley claims his brand new double-bitted ax has gone missing. Wouldn't know anything about it, would you?"

"I wouldn't," Tucker told him firmly. "I've got my daddy's and my granddaddy's axes. They're the best kind ever made. Wouldn't need or want one of those they pass off on folks these days."

"That's what I told Gidley and the sheriff," Preacher Hadley said. "Just thought I'd mention it in case you needed to know. Just thought you might know somebody in need of an ax. By the way, the sheriff happened to mosey by your place and found you gone. He didn't find any sign of a new ax."

Tucker bristled. "Don't got nothing what don't belong to me fair and square. You can pass that information on to old man Gidley, his wife, the sheriff and anybody else gossiping enough to want to know."

"I'll do it," the preacher assured him.

Just thinking about old man Gidley accusing him of stealing raised his hackles all the way down his back. Gidley was another customer he wouldn't be delivering shine to even when the old man needed it as badly as the preacher and the doctor. Afterall, Gidley was married to Bernice.

Tucker thought about the time when he'd been married as he climbed toward his still. Marriage was good for some folks and pure hell for others. It all depended on who you married up with and that was a fact. It could be a union that put you in heaven or hell – sometimes both, depending. To him hell had

been his lot while married. His marriage had left him a sad and
bitter man who couldn't get himself back on track. When a
wife did what his wife had done, it did damage to a body's
manhood until he couldn't get over it no matter how much he
wanted to.

There had been a time when he thought every man was
meant to marry young and populate the earth. Now, he knew
better. A man was better off alone than to tie himself to a no-
account woman. He'd found out that bit of wisdom the hard
way. He forced himself to stop remembering and pulled his
mind away from the mistakes he'd made in the past to the
things that had to be done right now.

A storm was brewing both beneath his feet and in the
heaven above his head. He had to hurry if he got to his shelter
before the storm hit or he'd be in a terrible fix if his supplies
got wet.

Tucker finally got the surefooted donkey and himself over
the bucking tree roots to a rocky outcropping where it would
give them some shelter if he didn't make it to his shed before
the storm hit. One good thing about a mountain made of rock
was it had plenty of outcroppings that could offer some sort of
protection during a storm. And this storm felt like it was going
to be a doozy. Tucker scolded himself for becoming so
distracted he had not realized the storm was on its way sooner.
He should have been more careful when he set out with his
supplies strapped to his donkey. Cracked corn might be able
to survive a storm, but sugar and yeast couldn't. He had
allowed his want-to of heading into the mountain to overcome
his caution in realizing there was a storm in the making.

Tucker tried to take his concern away from the threating
storm by thinking about the doctor's nurse. He might as well
admit his attitude about women didn't stop him from getting
his want-to for Valarie Whitley up in the worse sort of way.
His little place down in the valley was much too close the
doctor's house for his comfort. It was pure hell for a man to
see the woman who kept him in a state of rut being with

another man – a man who was already married to a different woman. Every time he saw Nurse Whitley, he imagined her lying in bed with the doctor, while the doctor's disabled wife slept in another room. He wanted to grab hold of Nurse Whitley and drag her away from that sinful house and the man who claimed to be a doctor, but he sure to hell didn't want to marry a woman such as she was. A woman who screwed a man she wasn't married to would screw with another man. He wanted that man to be him.

All that was left for Tucker to do was run as far as he could into the high mountains in an effort to ease the unrelenting want he was always feeling for Valarie Whitley.

Chapter 10

~~Tally~~Dobb~~

Thunder rumbled until the earth shook after giant streaks of lightning flashed through the sky as a warning of the fury of the storm to come. Wind had picked up until it whipped the trees back and forth with enough force to cause their new leaves to lose their life-giving hold and blow through the air until it looked like a green rain was falling. Tally put her hands over her ears and whimpered with fear. Where could she possibly go to find protection? She couldn't go to the cabin for shelter with her dad there. Her fear of him was greater than her fear of the storm that was whipping about her. The tiny little enclosure where the goat and chicken huddled was the only place she knew to go, but it wouldn't provide as much shelter as the outcropping of rock she was now hiding under. She pressed herself against the hard rock and curled into a tight ball against the ground. Her small body was shaking almost as desperately as the leaves on the trees.

Sobs were shaking her body as a hand touched her back causing her to let out a squeal of fright.

"Don't be afraid, child. It's okay. Nothing is going to hurt you. Granny will see to that. Now, calm yourself and come along with me. I aim to keep you dry and safe."

Tally opened her eyes to see Granny Witcher bending over her. She was almost as afraid of the old witch woman as she was her dad.

"It's okay, child," she repeated. "I won't let nary a thing harm you. Not your dad and not the storm either."

Tally didn't believe her.

"Don't you remember how your momma used to bring you to my place?" Granny's voice was soft and cajoling as she tried to put a memory into the girl's mind. Surely, you've not forgotten all those times," she spoke softly, trying to ease the girl's fear away.

Tally did remember. She was afraid of the woman back then too. Momma went there when she was sick or hurting. Momma claimed the old woman was a blessing straight from heaven. Her dad called her a witch and threatened to take his gun and get rid of the crazy witch woman once and for all if Momma ever went to her again. Momma told Tally not to concern herself about the old woman because her dad was too afraid to get within shooting distance of the old woman. Now the granny witch was standing over her – taking her by the arm – pulling her to her feet.

"No need to be afraid of me, child. There's a bad storm arising. Not safe being out in the woods. Trees are going to uproot. Limbs will be falling on your head. There will be hail and rain cold enough to chill you to the bone."

Tally wanted to fight, to run away, but she didn't. There was no place for her to go. She allowed the witch woman to hold onto her arm and followed beside her as though the old woman had cast a spell on her. Tally's heart was pounding top speed, and her bones were turning more to rubber with each step she took. She knew her time had come. She was doomed, and yet she couldn't do a thing other than let the witch woman lead her through the woods. Lightning struck overhead lighting up the sky to be followed by a clap of thunder that shook the ground beneath their feet.

"Don't fret, child. I done led your nanny goat to shelter and carried your chickens home in a sack before I come after you. I owe you that much for keeping your daddy alive when I ought not to have done it. Been best if he'd a perished, but I countered what mother nature would have done. Kept him alive, I did. Blame myself for that."

Her words were spoken soft and comforting, much like Momma's had been. Somehow, the overwhelming fear Tally felt was starting to drain away. The woman made her remember Momma and her gentle ways.

Tally hadn't realized how cold she was until she felt the warmth of being inside the witch woman's tiny shack. Still, she shivered. The storm had brought an early darkness, but there was light coming from a wick in a glass jar. The jar gave off a minty smell along with the mingled aroma of hundreds of herbs tied in bunches and hanging from the ceiling. After being out in the open the aroma was almost too powerful, and at the same time, it had a soothing effect.

"Sit down on my bed, child. I've already brewed you some warm broth. It'll warm up your insides and help ease your shivering."

As Granny Witcher dipped up the broth, a wonderful smell reached Tally, making her mouth water. She hadn't smelled anything that good since Momma took to her bed.

"Drink up," Granny Witcher told her as she held out the bowl. "I'll go check on your goat and chickens. I've got them in the pen I just got through building for 'em."

Tally watched the old woman go out the door, closing it behind her. She didn't hesitate to put the bowl to her lips and gulp the warming liquid down. It had a rich meaty flavor seasoned with herbs Tally had never tasted before. She wanted more and considered getting off the narrow bed to dip up another bowl, but decided it wouldn't be right. The old woman would need some for herself and there seemed to be no other food on the stove.

Tally occupied herself looking about the tiny room. There wasn't an inch of wasted space. Against one wall was the narrow bed with shelves all the way to the narrow ceiling. On the other walls were shelves containing jars filled with dark liquids. Some of the shelves contained dark colored jars of what she thought were dried herbs. Other jars contained roots and bark. They were also jars wrapped in cloths to protect them from the dim light inside the tiny room. Some of the jars had labels on them, others didn't. There was only a narrow foot-wide walkway between door, stove, and bed.

A person taller than her and the bent-over stature of Granny Witcher would not be able to stand upright without bumping their heads against all the bunches of herbs hanging down from the ceiling. Yet, it didn't feel cramped. Instead, it felt like being enclosed in a wonderful green garden.

Tears came to Tally's eyes as a long-ago memory returned of her momma bringing her to this same place. There had been the same kind of wonderful smell as she and her mother slipped through the door into the room.

"I'm in need, but I have no money or nary a thing to give you in return," Momma told the witch woman with her head hanging in embarrassment.

"I ask nothing in return," Granny Witcher told Momma. "I help whoever I can, whenever I can."

Tears came to her Momma's eyes as she quickly turned away. "I'll make it up to you somehow," Momma whispered.

"You already have," Granny Witcher told her. "I've not forgotten a thing. I still owe you."

Tally puzzled over those words back then, and she puzzled over them now. How was it possible that Granny Witcher owed her momma?

The door opened and Granny Witcher entered carrying a pint of milk and two eggs. "For your breakfast," Granny Witcher told her above the roar of the storm that was blowing above the tightly enclosed hut. "Lay down and sleep now. Your eyes are drooping. Don't fear, child. You will be safe with me."

Tally believed her.

~~~~

The smell of hot grease and frying eggs brought Tally from a peaceful sleep. For a wonderful moment, she thought she was back home, and Momma was cooking breakfast. It was the tiny flicker of the mint-scented candle that brought reality back to her. The letdown brought stinging tears to her eyes along with a fearful feeling of desperation. Momma was still under the garden dirt. Never again would she cook Tally breakfast. Never again would she feel her momma's loving hands comforting her. Never again would her mother be there when she was afraid.

Tally wasn't home – without her momma she no longer had a home. She was in the witch woman's shack hiding from a world that was too cruel for a little girl to survive in.

"Dad hurt Momma," she said into the darkness of the room. There was something about the smell of eggs frying in grease, the way Momma used to do, that loosened her tongue. "He hit Momma and wouldn't stop. He made Momma cough and get sick. I didn't get the doctor in time to save her."

The girl was silent for a few moments as images of what happened rushed her. She had to tell somebody what happened, and the only person there was the old woman. Like a boil her mother had lanced for her some time back, she had to get out the puss of what her dad had done before her pain could start to ease.

"Dad dug Momma out of the ground," she whispered. Telling the witch woman about the nightmare that kept replaying in her head. "He hit her in the belly with the shovel. Took what looked like a baby out."

Tally said no more, leaving Granny Witcher to imagine what the little girl had witnessed.

"You're safe," she assured her. "No need for you to be going back to the cabin while he's there. You ought to be hungry. I've got eggs, corn grits, and goat milk. Did you know all suckling animals can live on goat's milk including human babies?"

She shook her head and cringed when Granny said the word babies.

"It's a fact. I got honey for your grits. Wouldn't hurt to put a few pounds on your bones."

~~~~

It had taken a great deal of effort for Dobbs to get himself the rest of the way to the cabin, but his need of liquor had a strong enough pull to keep him moving regardless of his pain. Everything about him felt weak and hurtful. He was dizzy and the inside of his head didn't feel right. Tears of relief streamed down his sunken, beardy jaws when he found the jugs of liquor were still in the flour box where he had put them for safe keeping. He clutched one of the jars with both hands, forced the cork out with his thumbs, lifted the jar to his mouth, and guzzled.

A wicked headache woke Dobb. Hair-of-the-dog was what he needed. He forced his aching body to roll over and managed to sit up and reach for his jugs with painful arms. His leg hurt almost as much as his head and arms. He forced his eyes to focus, only to get a better look at his torn, dirt-caked britches. He remembered the witch woman cutting them off him. Damned if he wouldn't get even with her. With even greater anger he recalled flashes of Tucker pulling his body through tight, hurtful places. Tucker was trying to kill him just because Tucker owed him jars of liquor, the mangy coward. He reached for a comforting jar, and then the other. Both jars were on their sides, empty. Had he drunk both? Must have because there wasn't any left in either jar. Sally and that gal wouldn't dare touch his shine. Sally hid his jars once when they were first married, and he'd taught that no-account woman a lesson she hadn't forgotten. As for the girl, she was nothing but a sniveling coward. A no-account slit-tail girl. She ought to be in the cabin here taking care of him. He was hungry and bad off. He sat there, flat on his now bony rear end, staring at his dirt-caked, smelly, cut britches, shaking his head from side to side. Things started to clear slightly. The main anger bubbling inside him focused on Tucker - the man who had dragged him over, under, and through rocks. Tucker had tried to kill him. He hadn't succeeded, but he dang near came close.

Dobb thought about the old witch woman, tried to remember what she'd done to him. He peered out the open door. Confound, if there weren't grown leaves on the trees. He remembered seeing leaves and plants growing in the woods while he crawled toward the cabin, but he hadn't realized they were fully put out. Why hadn't he noticed them before? He looked down at his arms, body, and legs. Flesh had disappeared off his bones like a melting candle. He must have been in bad shape for a long time.

Another image of the old witch woman came to him. She was spooning what he thought was soup in his mouth and saying *"Swallow if you want to live."* Could it be that old witch woman was keeping him alive instead of trying to kill him? She had held water to his mouth and told him to drink slowly. No. There wasn't a good thing that woman had ever done. The mountains would be better off without her, and so would he.

Such thoughts reminded him that he was hungry and thirsty.

He grabbed hold of the bed and pulled himself to his feet and leaned against the wall, managing to hobble across the room

He found a half-bucket of water sitting on the table along with the remains of cornbread. He ate the tasteless, hard bread and washed it down with a dipper full of water. He needed to have a word with Sally. That was the worse cornbread she'd ever baked. It was rock hard on the outside while being pasty on the inside.

Where was that woman at? Must be out back wasting time in that garden of hers, It made him mad when she wasted a lot of time behind the house. She was supposed to be in here taking care of him. He looked about the cabin again. Sally had become damned slack cleaning the cabin. Mud had been tracked in at the door leaving muddy bare feet tracks, He looked at his own feet. Where th' hell was his shoes? Did that no-account Tucker steal his shoes when he left him for dead? Dobb's anger rose as a headache pounded in every inch of his skull like a continuously hitting sledgehammer. His pain and anger drove him to get up enough steam to limp out back of the cabin where the garden was. Damned if he wasn't going to find that no-account woman regardless of where she was hiding.

Spindly plants were growing in crooked rows. He recognized potato plants, beans, corn, squash, and tomatoes. Odd, there was a three by eight strip of dirt in the center of the garden where nothing was planted except a few straggly wildflowers. What th' hell was Sally thinking to leave a strip of good dirt unplanted? He'd learned that woman not to be wasteful. He hobbled to the bare spot and took a closer look. Th' hell if it didn't look like some kind of grave.

Suddenly, and without warning, he had the image of a tiny baby boy's body decomposing as he held it in his hands. His son! The male heir he had been desperate for Sally to give him. A sound, like a baby pig squealing, came out of his mouth. His good leg gave way and he fell to the ground. More images of what was in the ground beneath him rushed into his mind's vision. It was too overpowering for his weakened body. He did something he would never admit to doing. He cried.

Chapter 11

~~Education of Tally~~

Granny Witcher didn't believe in allowing anyone to sizzle in their own misery. It was best to keep the mind and body as busy as possible. She'd told Tally they would rise before dawn the next morning, eat a cold biscuit and jelly and head out into the high mountain to gather herbs. Tally didn't want to go anywhere. She felt safer lying in the little bed beside the old woman. There was something about feeling the warmth of another person beside her that gave her comfort along with a sense of safety. Never during her life had her dad allowed her to sleep beside her mother, even when she woke up crying from having nightmares. Her dad would whip her for crying and put her back in her own pallet of a bed in the loft.

Tally ate her biscuit and drank a glass of goat's milk while Granny Witcher gathered a large sack and a smaller one for Tally.

"Let's get going," Granny Witcher told her.

Tally set her glass down next to the wash pan and followed Granny Witcher outside. Granny Witcher closed the door without locking it. It was still pitch dark, but Granny Witcher seemed to be able to see where she was going. It took all of Tally's vision strength to see the faint form of the woman moving in front of her. The woman moved like a wisp in the dark. Tally followed as close as she could get to the old woman as she took an upward slant steep enough to strain the legs. At the same time Tally felt the life in mother earth beneath her bare feet. The soil she walked on had as much life as the twigs and leaves that brushed her skin.

"Mon-o-lah," Granny Witcher said. "That's what the Cherokee call mother earth. You do realize the earth beneath out feet is as alive in its own way as you and I are. Roots are her veins running under the soil, and water is her blood of life. Without our mother earth nothing would live. Not plants, animals, birds of the sky, or us humans. She deserves more respect than she gets. The Cherokee understand such things, while the white man only wants to take what they can get from Mon-o-lah."

"Are you Cherokee?" Tally asked as she stumbled along in the dark.

"No," Granny Witcher was quick to answer. "I was a prissy southern belle with lily-white complexion when I was your age. My tender hands had never known a callus or so much as an hour of hard work. My body had never known what it was like to be hungry or exhausted. I was a petted little thing, well loved by my parents – at least I had all that for a while."

Tally wasn't sure if she should believe her or not. She was wondering how this old woman could possibly have been her age. As for being a prissy southern belle with tender hands, that was too much for her mind to grasp. The old woman's hands were brown and crisscrossed with stains and dried-up skin like leather that had been left out in the weather too long. The skin on her face looked just as bad. As for ever being her age, Tally decided it was possible, but she couldn't envision her as being young.

"Did you have a mother?" Tally's chin quivered when she said the word mother. She made an effort to control her pain of loss. She knew all too well she'd never be able to replace what was lost.

"'Course I did."

"And a dad?"

"And a dad," Granny Witcher said.

"Did your dad hurt you the way my dad hurt me and Momma?"

"No. He was good to me except for one thing. He arranged my marriage," she said, and then wished she hadn't. She didn't want to go there, even after all these years it hurt when she thought about Clarence Witcher. She had wanted love between a husband and wife, wanted a real family with children. Instead, she found out how worthless she really was to the man she was supposed to matter the most.

Tally knew almost nothing about marriage, only that her mother regretted marrying her dad. To Tally marriage was a bad thing – a hurtful thing.

"He hurt Mary and my brothers. He hurt them bad. Momma said it was because they didn't belong to him like I did, but he hurt me too – just not as bad."

"What did he do to them?" Granny Witcher asked in a gentle voice filled with sympathy.

"He made Mary cry a lot. When the boys tried to help her, he hurt them worse than he hurt Mary."

"Didn't your momma stop him?"

"He hurt her more than the rest of us," she said in a whisper. "Momma cried a lot and said they'd have to leave or be killed. They tried to get her to take me and leave with them, but she knew he'd hunt us all down. They left one at a time until they were all gone."

Granny Witcher wasn't sure if it was best for Tally to talk about what happened or not. Would letting her talk lance the festering inside of her and give her ease, or would it make things worse? Sometimes it was best to leave things alone especially if the child was young enough to forget. Trouble was, she didn't think Tally would ever be able to forget anything.

"There are always bad things you can't escape. There will come a time when it is necessary for you put the bad behind you and make sure you find good to fill your days with. That is how good wins over the bad,"

Tally heard what Granny Witcher was saying, but she didn't understand the full meaning. To her good and bad were simply that. The bad was when hurt was being dumped on you by someone else. The good was when you were being left alone.

Not being able to see where she was going in the dark woods was also a bad thing that was dumped on her. Granny Witcher ambled along as though she was floating on air, while Tally stubbed her toes on rocks and roots. Twigs now slapped her in the face and undergrowth seemed to reach out on purpose to scratch her legs.

"It's too dark. Can we stop for a while?" she could not keep herself from whining even when she didn't want to.

"U-li-si-gi," Granny Witcher said. "That is the Cherokee word for dark. T-sa-la-gi is the word for light. There is always light after darkness. It is the way of nature. In nature animals see in the dark. Humans need to do the same. It takes a lot of practice to train the eyes to see what they're not accustomed to seeing. There will not always be equal amounts of light and darkness during a year's time. You need to learn how to see all things, child. Along with many other things."

Tally continued to follow, twisting, and turning through the narrow trail that led higher into the mountain. She could feel the upward slant of the narrow trail they were following, The air became colder, and there was the coolness of the earth beneath her feet, the aching of her muscles as her legs strained to keep up. She couldn't understand why they couldn't wait until there was enough light to see where they were going.

"Most herbs contain their most potency in early morning," Granny Witcher answered the question without Tally having to ask.

Tally thought of all the herbs hanging from the rafters along with others occupying every other available spot in Granny Witcher's little place. Surely there was already enough to last a lifetime. Why did they have to be going after more?

"I need many herbs, barks and roots," Granny Witcher told her. "Not only for medicines I use to help folks, I have to sell what is provided by mother nature down in the valley to buy supplies that we will need. I have nothing else to barter with. There is a rule God intended us to go by. That is to take only what is needed and not a bit more. One must never take the biggest and best for it is needed for reproduction. Survival of the fittest is powerful and necessary in all things. Including the human race. However, the human race is going in the wrong direction. It is no longer the fittest that are surviving. Those in power, namely the government, is forcing the fittest and most powerful to provide for the weakest and ill prepared. Therefore, the weakest and physically inferior are reproducing mentally and physically impaired humans. Then the government demands the fittest to take care of the inferior, even when it is detrimental to their own survival and reproduction."

Tally heard what she was saying. She wasn't sure she agreed with everything Granny Witcher was telling her. Her mother had been smart enough to know people in the valley thought she and her parents were among the unfit people, although none of them had offered to take care of them. They definitely thought Granny Witcher was unfit to live. Many of them went as far as wanting to be rid of the witch woman, as well as Tally, her parents, and her siblings. At least her siblings were long gone and hopeful safe. Now, she knew those down in the valley wanted to put her in an orphanage, but she didn't know why. Clancy had told her what their orphanage was like. She didn't want to be in a place like that anymore than Clancy did.

Thinking about Clancy made her wonder if he was alright. At least she had Granny Witcher who claimed she would look after her. Clancy had nobody. How was he surviving? Was he finding enough food to eat? What if he got hurt or got bit by a timber rattler? She wanted to ask Granny Witcher about him; but was hesitant. She wasn't sure if the old woman knew about Clancy. If she didn't, Clancy might not want her to tell on him.

Tally and her mother had been over the mountains hunting for berries and such, but she had never been that high on the trail where Granny Witcher was taking her. She trotted close behind the old woman and felt the steepness of the trail. Granny Witcher was climbing to the very top of the high mountain. The air became cooler and Tally shivered, making sure she stayed as close Granny Witcher as she could manage.

Finally, the old woman said, "We're here. Sit down for a spell afore we gather sang and wild ginger."

They sat down in a mossy spot near a grove of white pine trees as the first touch of dawn touched the top of the mountains. The sky went from a brooding gray to a pale bluish hue, to faint pink, and then to a startling orange as the sun arrived like an explosion. Slowly, the sparkling brilliance of the morning sun moved down the mountains lighting up their world from the top down.

"The silence of the night is waking up with song. Listen to the calls of the morning birds. They're welcoming the day regardless of yesterday's storm," Granny Witcher said. "It does the soul good to be a part of a new day – a new chance at living. It reaffirms there is always light after darkness," she repeated what she'd told Tally before. "I know that for a fact. I've been through enough darkness to tell you there is always light to come along with a new day."

Tally understood what Granny Witcher was trying to tell her but understanding did little to ease her fears.

"When we gather herbs," Granny continued telling Tally things she thought the girl should know. "We take only what we need, but we never take the best. On the contrary, we take the weakest, the imperfect. Again, remember to never take the best, although, admittedly, it is greatly tempting. Leave the best to reproduce itself that way the fittest shall survive It is best if the unfit never sows it seeds or lay its eggs. It takes more time and food to keep the inferior alive than it does to keep the fittest alive.

"God above is wise in all things. He figured that out at the beginning of time. That's why he gave everything predators. Take deer for instance. Panthers, bears, even dogs take down the weakest and the diseased. That way the strongest will survive and continue to provide meat. Even the birds of the air know this is true. Take the hawk and the quail. The hawk will catch the slow birds. Therefore, the slow will raise no offspring who would also be slow. In turn the hawk also allows the strong quail to survive by eating the ground rats, squirrels, snakes, and other rodents that eat the quail's eggs. It is the balance of nature, the survival of all things. It is the way," Granny Witcher pointed out. "I fear it is only humans that do not live by the way. The strong are forced to keep the weak and useless alive. In turn the weak humans produce weak young that the strong must also take care of. Soon there is more weak than strong. The survival of the fittest will no longer exist."

"You gather herbs to take care of the weak," Tally reasoned.

"Yes," she said. "I fear that I do that very thing. If I see I've done wrong, then it is my responsibility to remedy my mistake. My duty," she added with regret as she thought of Dobb Simmons.

~~~~

Granny Witcher sat on the softness of the moss as she watched the dawn creep over the mountains instead of gathering the herbs as she had intended. Having the girl with her caused her mind to keep going back to when she had to run away from her husband to keep him from killing her all because she hadn't given him an heir.

The most ironic part was that Clarence Witcher had been the infertile one. She had gotten with child on a warm spring day. It had been easy – so very easy with Gray Leaf. God had made them as one – and they were still as one.

*

The last day they traveled, Buck and she hid out during the daylight hours and traveled during the darkness of night. She was thankful for the time spent hiding. She was so exhausted she didn't think she would be able to ride the bony-backed mule one bit further. It was the first time she had known how painful riding a mule could be. She seldom rode in a saddle on her husband's fancy horses. Riding the mule had given her running sores in places she couldn't tell Buck about.

"I need to walk," she told him when he said it was dark enough for her to get on the mule.

"The mule is faster."

"I hurt too much," she objected. He'd had her sitting on her hemp sack of belongings in order to cushion her rear end slightly.

"It figures," Buck said. "It ain't much far now. Once I hand you over, you'll be on foot fur a powerful time. Gotta fetch the plow mule back home. There's a powerful lot of work fur a mule to be at."

Loraine wouldn't miss the smelly, razor-backed mule, but didn't know what she'd do without Buck. He had told her he'd turn her over to 'folks' who would take care of her. Now he was telling her she would be on foot for a long while.

"Will I be in a house?" she asked. She had been out in the weather for too long. She hadn't realized the miserable impact the weather had on people while she was safely secure in a mansion.

"Don't figure on it. Don't know 'xactly where they hide folks."

"What kind of people do they hide?" she wanted to know.

"Know nothin'," he was quick to say. Best you's don't." Buck clamped his mouth shut, an indication he wasn't going to say anything else.

She was on foot stumbling over roots and rocks in a night so black she couldn't see the mule in front of her. Buck had her by the hand dragging her behind him. She jumped at the sound of a terrifying noise.

"Screech owl," Buck whispered really low. "Sounds like a woman painin', don't it?"

Buck stopped, listened, and then let out a sound similar to what she'd heard. Minutes later a voice spoke near them.

"Brought another one, I see." The voice was low, but not a whisper.

"Yeap. This 'un's a woman."

"Woman," the voice said, sounding none too pleased.

"She's plum wore out from all that travelin'. She's a soft one. Go slow." Buck turned loose of her hand, gave her the hemp sack, stepped away from her and started to lead the mule away.

"Wait," she mumbled in a trembling voice. "You can't leave me like this."

Buck never said another word. All she heard of him was the faint sound of him and the mule leaving her behind.

"Let's go," the voice said. "We have to move fast."

"I can't," she whimpered.

"Got no choice," the voice told her.

She thought she saw a darker shadow move toward her through the darkness of the woods. A huge hand grabbed her by the arm and dragged her forward.

"No," she whimpered again, but the hand only tightened and dragged her onward.

She hadn't gone far when she fell to her knees. The hand pulled her to her feet and pulled her after him. She fell again and again until her legs buckled without her being able to stand on her blistered feet.

Much to her amazement, hands picked her up and tossed her over a shoulder as bony as the mule's razored back. The last thing she remembered was her head hanging down his back and his hands holding onto her legs.

She became aware of the loud sound of running water moments before she opened her eyes. She was laying on the hard ground in a dim place. She blinked a few times and tried to sit up.

"Let me give you a hand," said the voice as a big hand took her by the shoulder and lifted her into a sitting position.

"Where, who . . ." she mumbled before she realized what had taken place.

"We're in a kind of cave behind a waterfall. That's the noise you're hearing. I'm called Lee. What are you called?"

"Loraine," she said through a dry throat. "I'm thirsty."

"Good. Shows you're okay. I carried you for most of the night. I was thankful you don't weigh much, but you did get heavy after a while." He moved toward the light, rolled up his jacket sleeve to keep it from getting wet, and caught water in a cup, and brought it back to her. He held the cup to her lips. Both her hands gripped his as she tipped the cup to drink.

"Thank you," she told him.

"Are you hungry?"

"I'm not sure. I was at first, but there wasn't much food. After a while, I no longer got hungry."

"Here, chew on this. It's venison jerky."

She took what felt like a thin piece of cardboard in her hand. "What is venison jerky? How do I eat it?"

"It's dried meat. You have to chew it."

"It's hard."

"It's supposed to be hard. Keeps it from spoiling. Just put the edge of it in your mouth and chew on it until it softens enough to bite off a small piece. Then you chew on the piece until it softens enough to swallow it."

She did as he said, finding the meat both peppery and salty. She tried to see what he looked like in the dim light. "You've got a dirty face," she said between chews.

"I know. Mud on your face and hands keeps you from being seen as easily."

"Why don't you want to be seen?"

He chuckled slightly. "Because I'm helping you escape from something or someone."

"Oh," she said. "How did you know to meet me?" She had almost said meet Buck, but Buck had warned her not to say his name. He had helped her. She would protect him.

"Someone comes to that meeting place once a month when the moon is at its darkest. Sometimes there's someone to meet, sometimes not. Still, one of us will wait out the night."

"What if no one shows up?"

"Then we leave. Why are you running?" he asked. "Knowing helps us determine what kind of protection we give you, along with how careful we have to be."

"My husband tried to kill me."

"Why?"

"I can't have children," she felt her chin tremble and bit down harder on the jerky to keep him from seeing her weakness.

"Your husband tried to kill you because you are barren?"

"He wanted an heir."

"So, you ran away?"

"I had help faking my death."

"Okay," he said. "How did you die?"

"Drowned. They'll find my shoes and scraps of my clothing down by the river."

"How do you plan on surviving? Do you have money?"

"No," she told him. She was afraid to admit she had the small amount Cooky had given her in case he would take it from her.

"Do you have some place to go?"

"No. I was told there would be someone who would look after me." Her chin trembled again.

"Yeap, and I'm afraid it was my turn to be unfortunate enough to get the helpless woman who needs someone to take care of her," he mumbled. "Okay. If you've rested enough, we'll head out."

"How much farther do we have to travel."

"If I told you, you'd probably cry," he said with a touch of humor that she certainly wasn't feeling. He hadn't been the one forced to run away on the back of a mule to be handed over to a strange man.

"How far?" she tried to hide her fear by biting down harder on the jerky to keep from bursting into tears.

"We're going into the high mountains. How long it takes depends on how fast you can travel on foot. I won't be carrying you now that we're far enough into the wilderness not to be seen or matter that we leave tracks. By the way; if we should run into somebody, you're my wife, Janie Gray. I'm Lee Gray. Can you remember that?"

"Yes."

He took her by the hand, carrying her hemp sack in his other hand, and led her to the edge of the enclosure where the water was tumbling down. It wasn't a huge waterfall, but it wasn't tiny either. He said something to her, but she couldn't understand him because of the noise. He gripped her hand and indicated she was to follow him. He jumped on a rock and jerked her behind him. The cold water hit them both as he jumped again. He continued to jump them from rock to rock until they were on dry ground.

"Good," he said. "You didn't fall in."

"We're wet," she complained.

"Not bad. We'll dry off soon enough."

He didn't turn loose of her hand as he set a fast pace, although she knew he could have gone faster and was slowing his pace to match her shorter legs. She gritted her teeth and did her best to keep going.

Chapter 12

Tucker took his donkey into the shelter with him as the storm roared, whipping trees double moments before the rain hit. He'd beat the storm in the nick of time. Again, he chided himself for not paying more attention to the weather. He knew a storm could hit quick and hard without much warning. He'd even felt the unusual heat down in the valley, but he paid it little attention. He thought the heat felt extra warm because he'd been used to the coldness of the high mountains. Sometimes, when the weather was at its best, it was a set up to fool a man about a storm that was about to come. Oh, well, it wasn't the first storm he'd endured on the mountain, and he didn't expect it would be his last.

To Tucker life was a storm. Regardless of what he did, he couldn't find that comfortable place where his soul could rest. He hadn't exactly planned on being a moonshiner, but his pa and grandpa had been one, so it was easy to step into their shoes. He'd helped them at the still since the beginning of his memory. His grandpa and pa did things different back then than he did these days. He used sugar and yeast which his grandpa and pa hadn't. It wasn't that they took more pride in making liquor than he did. It was harder for them to get the sugar and yeast. Plus, buying large supplies of sugar was a giveaway as to what they were doing. He worried about the sugar and cracked corn he bought, but it was undercover. The man he got it from owned a store. He traded the sacks of sugar and cracked corn for liquor. From his grandpa's time until now, the sale of liquor had to be kept undercover.

When making moonshine was brought up, most folks got
their feathers in a ruffle. Folks were either for it or against it.
It appeared the majority of all city folks condemned it and gave
moonshining a bad name. At the same time, they went into
liquors stores and bought all the liquor they wanted at a higher
price than mountain moonshiners sold a better quality for. Fact
was moonshining was a welcomed profession as long as the
government got their cut. At the same time the moonshiners
were damned, the big city criminals were hiring mountain men
to run stills in the hills and hollows of the mountains, so they
could get a lot of liquor cheaper and without government
interference. It didn't matter to them if it was good liquor or
not. All they cared about was getting a lot of liquor cheap.

Unlike the liquor Tucker ran off, there was another still
over the backside of a far mountain where Grubb Claxton and
his men had a reputation of brewing bad liquor. They used lye
or potash to turn their mash fast, while giving liquor a good
bead. Often, they ran their liquid through sheets of tin or iron,
even old radiators were used, making poison liquor that could
kill a man, or at the least end up eating his insides out from his
swallow all the way down to his liver and guts. Tucker made
a point of staying away from that bunch. So far, they had left
him alone. Tucker knew it was because his still was too small
for them to worry about, plus Grubb Claxton bought Tucker's
liquor from Dobb for his own use.

Tucker's grandpa and pa would never put anything in the
liquor they made, even sugar. If they had used sugar, it would
have stretched the liquor and made more of it. His grandpa and
pa claimed it wasn't pure whiskey if sugar was used.

Their still, and now Tucker's, was a small one by
anybody's standard, but they hadn't needed a large one and
Tucker didn't either. He wasn't trying to get rich quick, which
would never happen. All he was trying to do was survive doing
the only trade he knew.

A lot of folks claimed moonshiners were a shiftless, lazy
bunch who didn't like hard work. Was that ever wrong.

Stilling, when done right, was mighty hard work. His grandpa used to shell the corn and put it in a hemp sack in the sun or by a fire if the weather was cold. He'd pour warm water over the sack, turning it two or three times a day, depending on the heat. The corn needed to be stirred up often. In four or five days the corn would have long sprouts on it. They would take their other corn and use their own mill stones they made themselves to make their cracked corn. Then they would put water in the pot until it was three quarters full. Then they poured the cracked corn in and built a fire under the pot.

Every moonshiner Tucker knew tried to use ash wood because it made little to no smokes as it burned. There was nothing like a trail of smoke rising up from the top of a mountain to tell the law or other no-accounts where a still was located. Heat waves from the hot fire was also a giveaway. Heatwaves and smoke were why men located their stills in heavy brush and trees. It didn't take long for the moonshiners to all start firing their stills at night. Not only did the darkness help conceal the smoke and heat waves, it hindered the revenuers. They might slip up on the moonshiners in the dark, but most likely the moonshiners would get them first.

After the mash was cooked, they drew it off through a slop arm in the bottom of the pot running it into a barrel. Then they added the sprouted corn they had ground up. The mash, ground corn, and sprouts in the barrel were covered up and let set for four or five days to *work*. It had been Tucker's job to stand on a stump and stir the mash while it was working. After about five days a cap would crust over the top. He or his dad would break up the cap until it was nearly gone. When their mash got to that point, they were ready to make a run.

The mash was poured out of the barrel and put into the pot with the lid on it. Fire was built under the pot to get the mash boiling, where the steam would rise up into an attached copper coil called the *worm*. The worm was put through a barrel that had cold water running in it. The cold water turned the steam back to liquid. The worm continued out of the barrel and emptied the liquor through hickory coals to strain off the *bardy grease*. If a person drank that, it would make them sicker than a puking dog.

The small amount of liquor they had run off, which Grandpa called *singles,* wasn't ready yet. It was somewhere around two hundred proof. Then they had to drain off what was called the *backings*, which hadn't turned into steam. Then came the job of scrubbing the pot. Once everything was scrubbed clean, the backings and the singles were put back into the pot with water added and a fire built all over again. When the process was finished, the liquor was ready to put into jars and sold.

Those who claimed moonshiners were a lazy bunch had never made good liquor, which some citified folks called corn whisky. Grandpa always claimed good liquor could be ruined in a lot more ways than it could be made good. The fire shouldn't be too hot or too cold. You had to run it off at exactly the right temperature and time. You didn't want the mash to scorch. If it was run off too early the liquor was too weak. If it was run off too late it turned vinegar like. A good moonshiner needed to be able to read the bead to judge what proof it had reached.

Tucker remembered how his grandpa or pa would lower him into the pot to clean it, because he was only six years old and still small enough to fit inside. It was hard work, but it was easier for him to clean the pot then than it was now that he was a grown man.

"Tucker, old man," he mumbled to himself. "You're getting' too old for such hard work."

It seemed like everything was against a hard-working man, including the weather and his impatient, stomping, old donkey who was doing his best to reach the sacks of cracked corn, tied to his back, with long, stained teeth. That old donkey wasn't a bit hungry. He was bored and so was Tucker. Crammed up with a gassy donkey in a narrow space was just about as potent as drinking shine.

All of a sudden that old donkey stuck his nose in the air and started snorting and braying like his life depended on it. His hind feet started kicking the flimsy walls of the shelter as he bucked straight up in the air. His head hitting the flimsy plank and tin roof. Tucker jumped to his feet to get out of the way, but a lot of the corn and sugar he had unloaded from the donkey's back and stored in a wooden container to help protect it from the elements was getting trampled.

Tucker grabbed hold of the donkey's halter in an attempt to stop his bucking. The donkey reared in the air, hitting his head on the ceiling again, then slammed Tucker against the door. The door flew open and Tucker hit the wet ground with a force that knocked the breath clean out of him.

The donkey had gone to his knees but was up again in a flash and running downhill at full speed. Unfortunately, or perhaps fortunately, Tucker's fingers had been caught in the halter in a way that made him unable to get loose. He was being dragged away from an angry mother bear, over roots, rocks, and brambles at great speed. His clothes were being ripped to shreds, while pain shot through every part of him.

At the same time, he was thankful in a most horrific way. He had a better chance of surviving being dragged by the donkey than he'd had laying on the ground in front of a hungry mother bear. It was obvious the mother bear and her cubs had taken shelter from the storm in the rocks near the shelter where she smelled the freshly cracked corn, sugar and yeast. The donkey had both heard and smelled the mother bear when Tucker couldn't. The donkey did what donkeys were supposed to do. It was hellbent on breaking free and running away from danger as fast as it four short legs could travel.

It didn't take long for Tucker to stop being thankful he'd gotten away from the mother bear. He started praying his fingers would come loose from the halter. They didn't. Neither did it take long for the pain to make him start praying death would come quickly if he was going to die anyway. It was the trunk of a tree in the way of his head that stopped him from having to endure more pain.

~~~~

"What in the name of the good Lord," Ida Hadley almost yelled as she saw the donkey run past the church house dragging something. "Preacher! Preacher, come here fast," she yelled this time at the top of her lungs.

"What in the world is wrong?" Preacher Hadley wanted to know as he came out the front door of their house.

"Did you see that?"

"See what?"

"That donkey went by here like the hounds of hell were after it. It was dragging something."

"What donkey?"

"The one that ran by here just a minute ago. It was dragging something," she repeated what she'd said the first time.

"So?"

"So, go see what it was all about. It was like a streak. I didn't get a good look, but something's not right."

"You go. I'm busy preparing my sermon."

"You want me to go after a run-away donkey?"

"Don't see why not."

"I told you it was dragging something."

"So?" he said again.

Ida huffed up in indignation, pushed her husband away with a snort, and started high stepping in the direction the donkey had disappeared.

The preacher decided something might be wrong if Ida was actually headed out to chase a donkey. He went outside to spot a patch of torn up grass and went over to it. He bent down and looked closer. There were hoof prints, bent over grass where something had been dragged, and spots of blood.

"Good Lord above," he mumbled. "She really did see something," He took off running in the direction his wife had taken.

Ida found the donkey in Tucker's old barn. When she got a closer look at what it had been dragging, she started screaming for help at the top of her lungs. Preacher Hadley showed up seconds behind her.

"Shut up," he ordered a moment before he checked the donkey and what it had been dragging. The blood-covered body of a man was holding onto the halter of the donkey. His arm had obviously been pulled out of joint at the shoulder allowing all but his head to drag the ground. His bloody head hung down, almost touching the ground. All semblance of clothing was missing from his bloody body.

"Get Doc Robinson quick," he told Ida as he slowly approached the donkey. "Easy boy, easy," he coached, as he tried to calm the frightened donkey. Slowly, he touched the donkey's back and gently eased his hand toward its head. The donkey was wet with sweat and shivering with fright, but it didn't pull away. It obviously wanted to be free of what it had been dragging.

The preacher unlatched the halter and slipped it over the donkey's head. The halter had been repaired many times with pieces of rope, wire, and bailing twine. The man's bloody fingers and hand were tangled in the repairs. The man's head and upper body had been mostly against the side of the donkey with his hips and legs on the ground. He dropped all the way to the ground of the stall once the halter was removed. The preacher carefully placed the man's arm on his naked chest. He figured the man was Tucker since it was his donkey, but the skinned and bruised face was covered in so much blood and dirt it was hard to tell, plus the light was mighty dim in the old barn stall. Preacher Hadley thought of moving the man from the stall; but decided against it. He'd either have to carry the bloody man or drag him. He figured the man had been dragged too far already, and he certainly didn't want to get blood on his clothes. Ida would have a fit if she had to get blood stains out.

The heaving and exhausted donkey huddled against the wall trembling, as Preacher Hadley took his handkerchief out of his hind pocket, bent down and wiped at the blood until he could get a better look at man's face.

"Shit, Tucker. It is you. What in the world happened? You've gotta be dead. You sure enough look like it."

Preacher Hadley then placed the handkerchief over Tucker's exposed mud, blood, and debris covered privates. Ida didn't need to see such as that when she returned with the doctor. Especially when the man wasn't a stranger. It just didn't seem a decent thing to see what was meant to be kept hidden from women's eyes. It wasn't decent. Not to mention she might find him better equipped than her husband.

It felt an eternity before Doc Robinson arrived wide-eyed, out of breath and carrying his worn black bag.

"Thank goodness you're here. It's Tucker, but I'm not sure if he's alive or not," Preacher Hadley told him.

"Know what happened?" the doctor asked as he kneeled down beside Tucker.

"His fingers and hand were caught in the donkey's halter. I had to take the halter off to get him loose."

"Dragged him a long-ways by the looks of him," the doctor said as he took out his stethoscope and held it to Tucker's chest. "His heart's still ticking strong. Don't know how he's still alive but he is. Looks to be skinned all over. We'll need a stretcher, or something to get him to my place. It'll take more than me and you to carry him. He's a right good-sized man. Can't hardly treat him proper in this stall, not that it'll matter much. It'll be a miracle if he lives long, but we'll have to give it a shot."

The doctor had hardly gotten the words spoken when Ida, Beatrice Gidley, Ellie James, and Inez Williams arrived, each one trying to be the first inside the door, filling the tiny space inside the stall. Old man Griff Gidley showed up behind the women, puffing and out of breath.

"Help has arrived," the doctor said. "Ida, Inez, you get him by the feet. Preacher, you, and Griff hold his middle up. Ellie and I will carry him by the shoulders. Ida you hold his head up to keep it from bobbing."

"He's dirty and bloody," Ida objected as the others made unpleasant sounds at having to carry the blood and dirt-covered man.

"That he is, but you'll wash. Now make yourselves useful since you're here. Hurry up, grab hold, and we'll carry him to my office. Right now!' he added with authority.

~~~~

Nurse Whitley had a clean sheet draped over the examination table and a variety of supplies ready. If the man was alive, he would be brought to the examining room. If he was not alive, he would be taken to the enclosed area that had been converted from a side porch. The doctor did not want a dead person in the examining room. A lot of time dead people could still carry diseases. Although there were folks with diseases in the examining room, there was no reason to take chances when it wasn't necessary. Considering the shine Ida Hadley was cutting, there was no way the man could be alive. It was also known that Ida was easily excited, causing her to exaggerate. Either the examining room or the death room was sure to be needed, and sometimes both rooms. She had both places ready by the time she heard the noise of their returning. She opened the door and looked out, saw them carrying the body and stepped back out of the way.

"Bring boiled water, wash cloths and towels," the doctor told her.

She rushed to the kitchen to bring what would be needed. She was shocked and surprised at what she saw. For one time, Ida hadn't exaggerated. She had never seen anything like what they were carrying in. Blood, dirt, leaves, and even sticks were plastered to every inch of a human body.

"Everybody out except the preacher. I might need someone to hold this poor man down if he should come around while I'm working on him."

Nurse Whitley gathered everything the doctor asked for. She felt slightly bad for not already having everything the doctor needed in his examining room, but she had taken time to prepare the death room also. By the looks of what she saw, the man was already in need of that room.

She carried a kettle of boiling water, the washcloths, and towel into the room and placed them on a small table near the larger examining table. She pulled out a washpan from a cabinet, lifted the kettle and poured the hot water.

"It's very hot," she warned the doctor.

"Cool it down with liquor. It'll serve as a disinfectant. You start washing his feet and I'll start at his head. We can't tell how badly he's hurt until we have this dirty mess washed off him."

"What happened?" Nurse Whitley asked.

"Got his hand caught in the donkey's halter and was dragged."

"Is he the . . . ?" she hesitated to say the man who delivered liquor in front of the preacher, although gossip was the preacher drank more of Tucker's brew than he drank water.

"Tucker, the moonshiner," the doctor supplied his identity.

"What's the chance he'll survive?" she asked as she dipped a washcloth in the mixture and started cleaning his feet.

"Don't know yet. Depends if he's just skinned all over or if his brain and internal organs were damaged. He's got a gash on his head along with a right big goose egg of a knot, but his face and head don't seem to be skinned up too badly. Chances are his lower body took the brunt of his injuries. I'll have to sew up the gash on his head after I check the rest of his body. Probably have more places to sew up considering all the blood covering him."

Nurse Whitley glanced at the preacher who was leaning against the wall. He was eagerly watching everything they did. while listening to every word they said. Ida, Beatrice, and the other women would surely wring everything that went on out of him. This was a big enough thing to wipe the little Simmons girl from their minds – at least for a little while. Nurse Whitley wasn't about to forget about that poor little girl. To her, the little girl was much more important than the man who made liquor.

Chapter 13

~~Clancy~~

Clancy had known a bad storm was on the way and figured he ought to get Tally's goat and chickens more feed before the storm hit. Wet mash was much heavier to carry than squeezed drier mash. Several times he'd sneaked near the cabin to check on Tally without her seeing him. He feared she would want him to stay with her if she saw him, and that was something he wouldn't do. He'd gotten used to the way he was surviving and wanted nothing to change. He'd learned invisible was safe. He was satisfied to know Tally was doing better than he'd expected. She was growing a garden and doing a fair job of it. In the meantime, she was living on goat milk and eggs. The only good thing Dobb Simmons had done in his entire life was siring that girl. Clancy figured she had to take back after her mother.

Clancy had gone to where Tucker dumped his mash twice since he'd sent Tally back to the cabin. He had filled a sack with mash as heavy as he could carry. He made sure he didn't drag the sack or have to set it down to rest. He didn't want to leave any kind of drag trail. Tally's goat and chickens needed something to eat, and he was making sure the feed barrel in the barn stayed full.

He was always careful to go when Tucker was not on the mountain, making sure he never left a footprint or anything that would indicate what he was doing. Tucker would never know he got the mash as wild animals were always eating what Tucker dumped. Clancy was glad Tucker dumped his mash, but he also thought Tucker was foolish in doing so. What he ought to do was put the mash a little at a time in the creek so

121

the water would wash it away. Dumping the mash on the ground drew bears and other animals like rabbits, squirrels, and even wild turkeys. Bobcats and mountain lions were attracted to rabbits and wild turkeys. He'd seen bobcat tracks but not the big mountain lions. He'd seen a lot of bear tracks and piles of bear crap. He'd even spotted a sow bear with two cubs, and was extremely careful to keep his ears and eyes peeled for sounds and signs. One thing he didn't want to do was get between a sow bear and her cubs.

Clancy had left the gully where Tucker dumped his mash. His sack was full and giving of a sweet, rancid smell as Clancy wound his way to the top of the mountain when what he feared happened. He heard the grunts of a sow bear right near him. She must have smelled the mash he carried in his sack. He knew better than try to make a run for it. The sow could easily overtake him. Climbing a tree wasn't an option either. Bears could climb better than he could. There wasn't even a rocky overhang narrow enough for him to crawl into where the cub bears couldn't follow him. His best bet was to drop his sack of mash and head to Tucker's shelter. The nearby shelter wasn't much, but most likely it would keep a bear out. He just hoped he didn't have enough of the mash's odor on him to make the sow follow him. Feeding two suckling cubs took a lot of food for her to produce milk.

His dropped sack slowed the sow bear down long enough for him to get into the shelter. It didn't take long for the sow and cubs to finish off the mash and follow him to the shelter. He could hear them circling the shelter, grunting, and snorting as the sow sniffed the air to see if there was more mash nearby to ease her hunger. Once the lightning flashed and the thunder roared, the sow and cubs seemed to wander off. Clancy decided he might as well stay put in the shelter of the shack until the storm hit and was over. That was until he heard the sound of Tucker quarreling at his donkey. Clancy eased out the door only moments before Tucker showed up. Thankfully,

Tucker was too busy trying to get the resisting donkey to move forward to see Clancy slip around the side of the shelter.

Clancy was skinny enough to crawl between the narrow rock overhang and the back of the shelter just as the rain hit. Tucker had managed to get the donkey inside the shack with him. It wasn't long until Clancy saw the sow bear and cubs snooping about the shack ignoring the storm that was upon them. The next minute the donkey was braying and kicking the planks of the shack. The door flew open and Tucker and the donkey disappeared. Clancy stayed put as the sow bear went inside the shack. She came back out, sniffing the air and following Tucker and the donkey straight down the mountain.

Clancy wasted no time crawling from his hiding place and making a run for it. The rain wouldn't harm him nearly as much as that blasted sow bear could. Thing was, he hadn't gotten any feed for Tally's animals. He figured he might as well check out the feed barrel since the animals' shelter was closer than his cave high on the other mountain. He was already wet through and through. A little more water wouldn't matter.

He had no fear of the bear following him. The donkey still had the sacks of cracked corn and sugar tied to its back. The freshly ground corn was what had attracted the hungry bears to trail Tucker and the donkey. For a moment, he had considered following behind Tucker and his donkey until good sense set in. During a bear attack, it was every man for himself. Most likely the donkey would pull free of Tucker's hold, and Tucker would try to hide, while the bear would continue after the donkey – at least for a little ways. Bears could run fast, but the donkey would be faster.

Clancy was surprised to find the goat and chickens were no longer in their shelter, nor were they anywhere in the fenced area. Not only that, but the barrel of mash used to feed the animals were gone. He tried to look for tracks, but the rain had already washed over the ground erasing any sign of hoofprints.

He looked toward the cabin. There was a thin trace of smoke rising from the rock chimney. It gave off the smell of fire built out of wet wood that was having trouble burning. The goats and chickens could have escaped. Tally could be building a fire to keep warm during the storm. He eased toward the cabin hiding behind ever tree and clump of brush he came to. He had learned from wild animals that it was best to never leave himself exposed in the open. A body never knew who could be watching – even during a rainstorm.

He eased up to the single window. Shutters had been closed over it, but there was a crack between them big enough for Clancy to peek through. There was little light inside the cabin. Clancy could only see shadows. The shadow he saw froze him to the spot. It wasn't Tally he was seeing, but the outline of a man. An ice-cold fear crept over him. There was no sign of Tally. The man went to the cook stove, lifted the stove eye, and poked wood into the slow burning flame. The flame gave enough light for Clancy to recognize the man.

His fists clinched and his eyes widened. Shit! No way. He'd seen Dobb Simmons laying at the bottom of the cliff with his own eyes. He'd been all busted up. His arms and leg were pointing in the wrong directions. He appeared to be as dead as a doornail. Not only that, he knew for a fact that Tally had been alone in the cabin for weeks. How was it possible for the man to be inside the cabin?

Clancy eased around the corner of the house and knocked on the door, loud, several times then ran like crazy to a nearby tree with a trunk thick enough for him to hide behind. He waited. Nothing happened. He picked up a rock and flung it hard. It hit the door with a loud thunk and bounced back into the yard. Again, nothing happened. Clancy threw another rock.

This time the door opened, and Clancy saw the face of the man he hated.

Dobb did a quick look about the yard, cursed a blue streak at the storm that was blowing rain in his face, pulled his head back inside, and closed the door.

Clancy was stunned. The man he thought he'd killed was still alive. A surge of confusion took hold of him. Being the cause of another person's death had bothered him, even when he convinced himself it was for the best. He tried to convince himself somebody had to protect that little girl, and he was the only one who would do it. He hadn't succeeded. Where was the little girl now? What had that no-account man done to her? She'd been there the last time he'd brought backings for the goat and chickens. Where could she be? What had he done with her?

Clancy longed to break into the cabin, grab the man by the throat and choke the truth of what he'd done with the girl out of him. What could a boy do to a man who was three times his size?

Chapter 14

~~Tucker~~

"Is he going to live?" Nurse Whitaker asked the doctor as she dipped the washcloth in the disinfectant water as she washed the size twelve feet. The feet were not as badly skinned as his legs, but it appeared some of his toes had been broken and the toenails ripped off.

"Depends," the doctor told her.

"On what?"

"How tough he is along with how well he's taken care of. He's skinned up right bad, and there's several places where he needs stitches, plus there's a knot on his head that's grown to the size of my fist. He'll need a lot of sulfa drugs along with care to keep his wounds clean."

"You expect me to take care of him?" she didn't sound nearly as disgusted at the idea as she felt. Just touching him was almost more than she could endure. There had always been something about the man that made her skin crawl. Part of it was the way he always looked at her, tried to get to close her.

"It'll most likely keep both of us busy for a while if he's to live."

"Would his death be much of a loss?" she couldn't resist asking.

"A lot of folks would miss his liquor. He makes the best and safest brew of anybody about. Folks aren't afraid to drink it, and I'm not afraid to use it on patients. I'm just thankful he delivered my supply before this happened. It'll be a while before we get any more, and that's if he lives. You do realize here in the mountain backwoods all the disinfectant we had for many years was liquor. Folks used it to get rid of skin infections, cuts, puncture wounds, sore throats, coughs, worms, pneumonia, lack of sleep, sorrow, and all sorts of pain."

He stopped washing and inspecting the injuries on Tucker's head and neck to look at her. Her nose was wrinkled in disgust. Her teeth gritted.

"Why do you dislike him?" the doctor asked.

"In a way he reminds me of my dearly departed husband. There doesn't need to be another of his kind," she said as she washed his legs and torso. If the doctor wanted the man's privates washed, he could do it himself. She wasn't about to touch that.

"I've doctored a lot of people who I don't like. My personal feeling for somebody doesn't stop me from doing my job. It shouldn't stop you from doing yours."

"Sometimes I wonder exactly what my job is."

"Your job as a nurse goes hand and hand with my job as a doctor. There are times when we do what we have to do, not what we want to do."

She chose not to comment on what he said. "Is he married?" She'd seen him around and was well aware of the contempt the women had toward him, but she knew very little about the man.

"Don't know. He had a wife once, but according to local gossip, she ran off with Tucker's brother. Don't know if either of them sought a divorce, but Tucker claims he got one. He lives entirely alone. Most of the time he hides out somewhere in those high mountains making his liquor. Get that big container of salve off the shelf. The one that came from the old witch woman."

"Why do you get those concoctions from that woman? It's not safe. No telling what she puts into that stuff."

"I see you've been listening to that *better-than-thou* bunch of women again. I've told you not to put much credit into what those women gossip about."

"It's not that I give them credit for anything. I have my own opinions."

"I hate to admit it, but that old woman comes up with some concoctions that work better than I can order from so-called scientific experts. She learned them from the Indians. I've heard she lived with them for a long while."

"There are no longer Indians," she made a point of informing him.

He grinned. "Sure, there are. They just don't go about scalping people – even when some people deserve to be scalped."

"Where?"

"All over. Most mountain people have Indian blood in them. It's no big deal. I've even got some in me."

"No, you don't," she told him firmly. "You've got blue eyes."

"Read your history. Get that black salve off the shelf."

"Why that salve?"

"It works and it's cheap. I save the expensive stuff for town folks and women who think medicine has to be expensive to work."

She got the salve and held it out to him.

"Go ahead and rub it all over his legs and body, while I put sutures in his head. Don't rub it on the deep cuts until I get them sewed up. I've got to hurry. He's showing signs of coming around. Putting sutures in is painful. He'll likely fight me if he wakes up. Oh, before you put the salve on him, get a jar of the liquor he brought the other day. Its proof is high enough to take the hair off a hog. Pour it all over him."

~~~~

"I can't believe he'll live regardless of how badly he's bruised and skinned up. He had to lose a lot of blood and taken a lot of hard knocks, but he has to be one of those tough, wiry men who survive everything that befalls them," Nurse Whitley commented.

"His clothes were made from wool and deer hide. It was tough enough to protect him for a time before it was torn off. Plus, he's as tough as whet-leather. He's never had anything easy in his entire life that I know of."

"Where did he get his clothes? Nobody wears such as that any longer."

"Who knows. Most likely traded for them."

"He ought to have plenty of money to buy decent things, considering what he does for a living."

"Doubt he has much money set aside," the doctor told her. "Men like him don't know the value of what they produce. He sells his stuff so cheap he's lucky to have enough to buy more supplies to make another run."

Nurse Whitley disagreed. "Why would he bother if he's not making a good living?"

"Some men have a low opinion of themselves. Therefore, what they produce has a low value."

Tucker's body jerked as the liquor ran over the most injured places. A low moan escaped from deep down in his throat.

"We best stop talking and hurry this job along, my dear," Doc Robinson told her. "He'll be coming around before long. After we're through, it will be up to God if he'll live or not.

~~~~

Tucker opened his eyes to what he thought was his favorite dream. Nurse Whitley was leaning over him, her hands touching his body in a way he'd always wanted – except there was too much pressure, too much pain. He tried to open his mouth and tell her to be a little gentler with her caresses, but he couldn't get the words out. "Hurts," he finally managed to force the one word out.

She jumped at the sound of his voice. She hadn't realized he was awake. "No doubt," she answered as she looked into his eyes, then away. "I see you finally came around." She didn't sound pleased.

Around to what? he wondered.

"Do you remembered what happened to you?"

"Dreaming," he said.

"Dreaming nothing. It's more like you've been in a living nightmare."

"Hurts," he mumbled again.

"No doubt. In case you're wondering, you're lucky to be alive. Your donkey dragged you home."

"Where am I?" he managed to get more than one word past his dry, chapped lips.

"At the doctor' place."

"You're real?"

"Of course, I'm real. The doctor has me looking after you."

She didn't sound nearly as pleased about taking care of him as he was. He was willing to suffer pain if she was really there with him, taking care of him, rubbing his body. He kind of remembered being caught in a storm with his donkey. He'd grabbed hold of the donkey's halter and couldn't turn loose.

"My donkey?" he asked.

"It's in the pasture. I'll tell the doctor you're awake."

Tucker listened to her leave the room. He closed his eyes and tried to remember exactly what happened. He did kind of remember getting a glimpse of what might have been a bear, but the donkey was dragging him so fast he couldn't be sure. He kind of remembered trying to stop the donkey from running by bracing his feet in the dirt. All it achieved was gouging his boots against rocks and roots. And then there was that little sapling right in front of him. He couldn't dodge it with his body or his head. And then from that moment until now, he remembered nothing.

~~~~

"I don't want to take care of that man," Nurse Whitley told the doctor again.

"Why not?"

"I simply don't like him."

"Liking someone has nothing to do with being a nurse."

"I have enough to do taking care of Elouise," she added.

"I'll tell Elouise she can't take up so much of your time. I've always told you not to baby her so much."

"She's pitiful," Nurse Whitley insisted.

"If that's how you want to describe her."

"How would you describe her," she wanted to hear how he would describe his wife. He made a point not to talk about his wife any more than necessary.

"Bitter," he was quick to say. "You and I both know she's angry with the world because of what happened to her. She's especially angry with me."

That was true. Elouise Robinson was a very bitter woman who was angry all the time. It appeared she wanted to blame her husband for her condition, even when he had nothing to do with it.

"Plus," the doctor continued. "You cater to her every whim not because you're a devoted nurse. You do it because of guilt."

Nurse Whitley didn't know how to respond to that comment. Of course, she felt guilty. She was guilty of falling in love with the woman's husband. She suspected a lot of women were in love with other wives' husbands, but not all of them slept with those husbands.

"A man has the right to get what little pleasure he can out of life," he told her as he placed a hand on her shoulder and squeezed gently.

It was true, she lived for the touch of his hand. It didn't happen often enough – couldn't happen often enough to satisfy the need within her.

"And so, does a woman. What we do together doesn't hurt Elouise. She has always been a self-centered woman. I was surely drunk the day I married her," he added, and took his hand away.

Nurse Whitley didn't argue with him further. It would be a waste of time. He didn't see things the way women saw them. There was no doubt in her mind that Elouise knew what was going on with her nurse and her husband. Nurse Whitley also knew that Elouise really was self-centered enough to use guilt to get everything she wanted from both the doctor and her. Still, the poor woman was bedfast. She had no way of getting up and going to her husband's bed during the middle of the night – the way her nurse did.

~~~~

Tucker lay on the hard, sheet-covered cot. There was a strip of wax paper under his body that crackled every time he moved. Nurse Whitley had placed it there, telling him it would keep his skinned body from sticking to the sheet. He hated the sound. What he didn't hate was the feel of her hands rubbing salve over his almost naked body, even when she did it with her teeth clinched and her nose wrinkled up. It was easy to tell she didn't like taking care of him. Never had he done anything to make her dislike him – unless getting skinned up counted.

"I hate to cause you extra work," he told her. "I wouldn't be here if I could get myself up. I really do want to go home."

"Hopefully, it won't be long."

"You're a good nurse. You have a gentle way about you."

"I do my job," she told him sharply. It was obvious she didn't want to talk to him or listen to him talk.

She finished the salving, turned, and walked out of the room with a straighter back than usual. Right there goes an unhappy woman, he thought.

~~~~

Doc Robinson came into the room where Tucker lay stretched out on his back. He didn't look too happy as he came to Tucker's cot.

"You sure enough got yourself in a fine fix this time," he told Tucker what they both already knew. "Took a fifth of your liquor to disinfect your body. I expect you to repay me for keeping you alive with a year's free supply."

"I'll do it as soon as I get out of here and run another batch."

"Might take a while."

"Tomorrow?"

"Nope. You'll be right there on that cot for a week or more depending if you become infected or not. Probably a month before you'll be able to get out and about, maybe longer."

"I'm tough."

"Matter of opinion. How far were you dragged?"

"Long ways," was Tucker's answer. He wasn't about to give any hint to where his still was located.

"Storm spook your donkey?"

"Bear."

"Feel like eating some soup?"

"Not much hungry. Would like a few swallows of my shine."

"You in pain?"

"What do you think? Feels like I've been tossed in hell and I'm being burned up alive."

Doc Robinson went to a cabinet on the wall took out a jar with a little liquid in it and poured half a finger in a glass.

"Might need more 'n that," Tucker told him.

"Nope. Just enough to take the edge off until you can sleep. You need the pain to keep you from moving about. Wouldn't want you to rip out all those stitches. Had to sew your tough hide up like it was a patchwork quilt."

Tucker tried to sit up, but the pain was too great. He gritted his teeth in an attempt not to cry out.

Doc Robinson put his hand under Tucker's head, making sure he didn't press on the big pump-knot where the stitches were. Tucker winced. There wasn't a square inch on him that wasn't hurting. Doc Robinson put the glass to Tucker's mouth and let him drink all that was in the glass without stopping.

"Got a gullet of steel," Doc Robinson told him as he eased his head back down.

"Raised on it. Drank it from a baby bottle," Tucker told him, which wasn't too far from the truth. If his ma ran out of paregoric, she would feed him liquor with sugar in it to make him sleep.

"I can believe it. Try to get some sleep. Nothing else you'll be doing for a while. You're in fair shape considering how far you were obviously dragged. Had to be for a lengthy distance considering you've been skinned as slick as a squirrel."

Tucker tried to sit up again, hoping the small amount of liquor would give him more determination. Not only was he too weak, the pain was too great for him to move. He longed to have a full jug of what he brewed. Liquor might not take away pain, but it would numb a man's brain until he no longer cared how much he was hurting.

The only good thing about what had happened was being cared for by Nurse Whitley. Valarie. He said her name over and over in his mind. How he would love to whisper that word in her ear during a time of passion. He was certain he was man enough to make her forget about the pudgy-bodied, soft handed, wimpy doctor. A woman like Valarie deserved a hard-bodied man – one who was tough enough to survive being dragged a few miles while hanging onto a donkey.

There was a cowbell near his cot to ring if he was in need. He looked at the cowbell and clinched his fists to keep from grabbing hold of it. If he rang it, would it bring Nurse Whitley back to him? He didn't think she would take too kindly to him ringing for her, especially if he didn't have a mighty believable excuse for doing so.

~~~~

When Nurse Whitley left Tucker, she went inside and washed her hands with soap and water before she went outside to her flower garden where she turned on her garden hose and scrubbed her hands again. One scrubbing wasn't enough to get the feel of touching that man off her hands.

She needed to spend time with her beautiful flowers to ease the repulsion that was surging through her. She didn't like rubbing the despicable man's naked body even though she was a nurse – especially when the man was Tucker Layman. She had a strong dislike for him that went beyond his moonshining and the resemblance to her husband. She had no answer as to why she was having such a strong reaction. It wasn't like she hadn't come across men she despised. She had only seen Tucker in passing, and every time he would stare at her as though he was taking her clothes off, while trying to pretend he wasn't doing it. There were some people who made other people dislike them on sight. That was her reaction to Tucker the first time she set eyes on the man, and it hadn't changed.

She'd had the opposite reaction the first time she saw the good doctor. Her heart started racing and her breath came faster. Her face flushed and her eyes sparkled. Doc Robinson had taken one look at her and hired her instantly. He hadn't even asked for her references, nor had she asked for his.

The questions that battled in her mind continuously were complex and without sufficient answers. Should a man have to give up his most treasured enjoyment in life? Should a woman give up hers in an attempt to avoid cruel gossip from a bunch of 'better-than-thou' women? Or the conjecturing looks of men who were wondering what she would be like in bed.

Nurse Whitley's solution was not to hang her head in shame, but to confront the lions and join their pride. Beatrice and Ida's bunch of women didn't welcome her, but they couldn't exactly shun Doc Robinson's nurse when there was always a chance they might need the only doctor available. They resolved to look down on her. At the same time, Nurse Whitley looked down on them. The doctor liked to delve into Tucker's brew before he went to bed at night. His tongue would be rather loose by the time Nurse Whitley joined him. He told her things about people that she would have never imagined. There was not one person in the entire community who didn't have secrets they wanted to keep hidden. He also told her things about his wife, Elouise.

The doctor confessed his wife hated making love with him. Elouise told him it was a disgusting, repulsive act. She claimed he was depraved and vulgar for thinking about doing such a thing. She wanted nothing to do with it, and if he forced her, it would be nothing other than forced raping of his wife. He was in the process of seeking a divorce when she had her accident. What kind of man divorced his disabled wife? Doc Robinson certainly wasn't going to be that kind of man then or now.

If she wanted to have any kind of relationship with this man, she had to take what was available. Elouise was bed-ridden, but she was extremely healthy in other ways. As for her mind, Nurse Whitley wasn't so sure. A vindictive psychopath came to mind. Elouise was charming when she chose to be, but it was only superficial. She tried to use it to get her way. When she wasn't getting her way, she was brutal and accusing.

There was no denying the woman was intelligent and manipulative. She was also incapable of love. She suffered from a lack of remorse or shame. She certainly had a grandiose sense of self-worth and a disregard for other people's feelings. Nurse Whitley knew Elouise lied much easier than she told the truth. She wasn't even sure Elouise knew the difference between her lies and what was truth.

The doctor was wise in bringing in outside doctors to diagnose his wife's condition. One of the doctors suggested she be institutionalized. Another pronounced her as a paraplegic for life. When the preacher and some of the women brought gifts of food to Elouise in an excuse to check her out, Elouise went ballistic. The fit she pitched was renowned as she screamed for them to get out of her bedroom and stop gawking at her.

After that, the doctor refused to allow his wife to have visitors, which included the preacher and the good women of the church. He told everyone Elouise was in such critical condition that getting the slightest upset could cause her death. Isolation, he claimed was the only way to keep his beloved wife alive. Nurse Whitley agreed with his logic and decision. To be honest, she was leery of the woman, although she couldn't exactly understand why. She was never sure of what the woman was capable of doing.

At first some of the people disapproved of Elouise's isolation, but as time crept onward, objections turned to acceptance. There was sympathy for the doctor until he hired Nurse Whitley as his wife's nurse and caretaker. She was too young and too attractive for a doctor with an invalid wife to have around. No one seemed to care if she was a qualified nurse or not. Age and looks were more important.

As time passed, Nurse Whitley wasn't exactly accepted. It was more like she was ignored, while being allowed to mingle freely with the other women. Nurse Whitley had no doubt their attitude would have been different if they hadn't feared their need of the doctor and perhaps his nurse.

Chapter 15

~~Clancy~~

Regardless of how upset Clancy was at seeing the man he thought was dead, there wasn't much he could do about it at this time. His only weapon was a slingshot. What had him toren up was the girl. What had Dobb Simmons done with Tally?

He headed through the woods, circling the cabin, ignoring the rain, hiding from tree trunk to tree trunk as his eyes searched for a fresh grave. He didn't see any evidence of disturbed dirt. A fresh grave could be seen even in the rain. Maybe Tally was hiding somewhere along with her goat and chickens. The missing goat and chickens were a key to her disappearance. He suspected she had left and taken them with her, but how had she managed?

He told himself to get his emotions under control and do some hard thinking. He went to the goat shed just to make sure the nanny and chickens were gone. They were. The fact that the barrel of food was also gone gave him some hope. Had Dobb hurt Tally and run the goat and chickens off. The barrel of feed would still be there. For Tally to move the animals along with the heavy barrel of feed was unlikely. Someone had taken them.

Had those orphanage folks come after Tally? Did they have her locked up in that horrible place? If so, she would be too little and too scared to escape. Why hadn't he checked on her more often – kept a closer eye on the poor little girl? In Clancy's mind there was only one thing he could do. He'd have to sneak down the mountain and get her out of that place. He wasn't exactly sure how to go about it without getting caught himself. Maybe if he had a weapon other than his gravel shooter, he'd feel safer going off the mountain.

Suddenly, it occurred to him that Tucker might have left his gun in the shelter when he was dragged off by the donkey. Now that he thought about it, he had no idea how far the donkey dragged Tucker. Couldn't say that he cared. In Clancy's opinion, Tucker was okay, but he wasn't one of his favorite people. At least Tucker never told anybody about seeing him on the mountain. If he had, Clancy figured somebody from the orphanage would have come looking from him, which they hadn't. He might ought to climb back up the mountain to Tucker's shelter and check things out regardless of the mother bear.

The only thing that made him hesitate was that blasted mother bear. There was a chance she was still hanging about the shelter. Once an animal got used to easy pickings it stopped foraging for itself. He figured the hungry mother bear had already consumed all the backings Tucker had dumped from his last run. Between the wild animals and him carting off feed for Tally's animals, the backings didn't last long, which was a good thing for Tucker.

Clancy paid no attention to the rainy weather. He was already wet to the bone. He was used to his clothes drying on him. It wasn't like he had clothes to change into whenever he wanted. When something wore slick out, he had to go off the mountain in the dead of night to steal something off a clothesline and hope nobody noticed.

He couldn't even dig herbs to take to the feed and seed store to trade for things he needed like the old witch woman did. He almost never saw her even when he sensed she was roaming about. Sometimes when he was in the woods or near the creek searching for food, he had the feeling he was being watched. He knew it was the old witch woman. She was like a mist – there one moment and gone the next.

He knew where her shack was located and made a point of never going near it. Not that he was afraid of her or anything like that. He wasn't, not really, but the thought of her gave him a queasy feeling deep down in his guts. A woman who roamed the woods all hours during the night was more than odd, and a whole lot lacking a full load. Suddenly, a thought struck him. Was it possible, Tally was with that witch woman? Surely not. That witch woman would never bother with a child, or would she? Lord knows what a woman like that would want with a little girl. His mother had read the story to him about Hansel and Gretel and the witch woman.

Maybe he would go check her place out, just in case, but first he wanted to see if Tucker had left his gun behind. It would be like finding a treasure if he had, especially if there were several shells to go with it.

He crept through the rain dripping woods, keeping a sharp lookout for the mother bear. One thing was for sure. He didn't want to come up on her and her cubs. He reached the shelter without seeing any sign of the bear. The door was hanging wide open on one hinge where Tucker and the donkey had hit and tore it loose. Still yet, he wasn't willing to take a chance of going through it without knowing what was inside. He'd learned at an early age never to presume anything. He slipped to the side and peeped through a crack between the boards. The place was empty. It was safe to go inside.

Sure enough, there lay Tucker's gun along with a leather pouch with shells in it. Clancy could have danced a gig. Some time had passed without Tucker coming back after the gun. Did that mean he'd been hurt or perhaps he was somewhere in the woods hurt bad, or dead. He picked up the gun and shells and left the shelter. Chances were, Tucker would never know what happened to the gun, Still, Clancy believed in sneaky caution along with knowing exactly what was going on when possible. He thought it best he followed the dragging trail the donkey and Tucker left through the woods.

The rain had done a fair job of washing the trail away, but Clancy had spent a lot of time tracking things, and he knew good trackers would have no problem following the drag trail

Tucker and the donkey left behind. There was broken
undergrowth, and places where Tucker's boots gouged out
rocks and dirt. There were also the hoof prints of the running
donkey. Clancy broke off a handful of brushy limbs and used
them to wipe out the tracks as best he could. Tucker wouldn't
want somebody backtracking him. His still wasn't too far from
the shelter.

Much to Clancy's surprise the drag trail went all the way
off the mountain. He stopped in the edge of the woods where
he still had cover from being seen. He'd found strips of
clothing, spots of blood, one moccasin and then the other one
as he followed the drag trail. Then he found Tuckers boots a
good ways from each other. Clancy made sure he picked up
every telltale article left behind and hid them in the underbrush
where he could get them on his way back up the mountain.
Evidently, Tucker had not been able to get loose from the
donkey. Looked like the donkey had headed straight for home.
That meant somebody had to find Tucker. To make sure his
thinking was right, he made his way through the woods,
making sure he kept out of sight, to Tucker's place. There in
the pasture was the donkey without his riggings.

Guess he'd get to keep the gun. If Tucker wasn't dead, he
had to be in mighty bad shape.

Part of Clancy wanted to head back up the mountain right
then, but another part wanted to save the girl if she was in the
orphanage home. He felt right safe carrying Tucker's gun even
when he hadn't ever shot one. He was sure he knew how. He
figured it didn't take much know-how to aim a gun, cock it
and pull the trigger.

It took him a while keeping out of sight as he made it all
the way to the other side of the little community to where the
old house was located. It wasn't much. Little money had gone
to the house's improvement. The bars on the windows were
loose and the locks on the doors were easily picked. The fence
around the place was easily jumped over by a determined boy,

especially at night when there were few watching the half-starved children.

He knew there were a lot of sponsors from off that donated to the orphanage. The preacher along with the good women of the church had gotten good at begging funding for the orphanage. They got money from churches as well as private donors. He'd even heard the government had a hand in funding the place, but he knew next to nothing about government kind of stuff. One of the biggest donations were clothing and shoes. Still the children were dressed in rags. The women used a room in the church to sell second-hand clothes with the pretense of getting much needed income for the orphanage. They convinced the people they were doing a good deed by buying and wearing secondhand clothes. The local store had just about stopped getting in clothes to sell. Clancy wasn't sure where all the money came from or where it went, but he was sure it never benefitted the children.

In Clancy's opinion, it was better to live in a cave than in that place, at least for him. He had to admit most all the children in that place wouldn't be able to live the way he was living. The nights got long and lonely. The days were spent trying to find enough food to eat.

In his opinion, the women who ran the orphanage ought to allow folks to adopt the children. He'd eavesdropped on two of the women and heard them saying if the children were adopted, the flow of funding would come to an end. He got good at keeping his eyes open as well as eavesdropping. There was a lot folks didn't want others to know about.

Those women also talked about begging those rich people from up north to send any kind of help they could offer for the poor, helpless, orphaned hillbilly children. The women would send a pitiful picture along with a so-called background letter to each person who sent them money each month for that specific child. Clancy figured someone was still sending money for him.

The children did all the work. The girls cooked, cleaned, and scrubbed laundry. The boys had to work in the fields to grow what little food they had to eat. Most everything they grew was hauled to market and sold.

The orphanage had guards and a mean dog to keep the children from running away.

Clancy had learned where the guards and dog were during certain times. He had chosen to make his run for freedom in the early hours after midnight during a hellacious rainstorm. Neither the guards nor the dog liked getting wet by a cold rain. He didn't try to leave by a door or a window. He went down in the basement and out the coal chute. He'd scaled a huge tree near the fence and climbed out on a limb until his weight bent the limb over the fence. Needless to say; he hit the ground running.

One thing was for certain, he wasn't going to climb back over that fence. The old wooden fence had a lot of cracks between the wooden planks. He saw several boys working in the garden. Four girls were hanging the washing out on the line. Their heads were hung, their dress sparse and ragged. None of the girls resembled Tally.

"Pssss, hey, girl," he called out little above whisper when one of the girls got to the end of the clothesline near the fence.

The girl stopped pinning the shirt onto the line and cocked her head sideways as though she might be hearing something that wasn't there.

"I need to ask you a question."

The girl downed her head even further as though she hadn't heard him. "What?" she finally questioned.

"Has a new girl been brought in lately, like in the past two weeks?"

"No. We've all been here forever. Nobody's new," the girl said, and moved away from the fence. It was obvious the girl didn't want to get caught talking to somebody. She would be punished if caught.

Clancy believed her.

If the girl wasn't in the orphanage, and there wasn't a fresh grave, she had to be hiding out in the woods somewhere, which didn't make sense. He would have been able to spot the girl, a goat, chickens, and a barrel with feed in it. That left one other place she might be. He'd have to check out the witch woman's place.

He reassured himself he didn't need to be afraid of the old woman. It wasn't exactly like he believed in witches. He reassured himself again that she didn't have the power to put some kind of hurting hex on him. All his reasoning didn't take away the queasy feeling he had or ease the want for heading in the opposite direction from the witch woman's place. Tally had to be someplace if she wasn't dead or in the orphanage home, and he was determined to find her.

Clancy was circling in the woods to get to the right place to climb back up the mountain when it occurred to him to check Tucker's place out. He'd seen the donkey in the field, but he hadn't seen Tucker. He didn't think Tucker could still be alive, much less be in the house, but it might pay him to make sure. He hid the gun in a thicket, and snuck to Tucker's window like a hungry dog that was slinking up on what he ought not be, and peeped in. Empty. He circled the house, peeking in each window. The place was deserted. He eased up a back window that would be the most difficult seen if someone passed by. He crawled in, looked about the bedroom, and laughed right out loud. There were clothes hanging on nails that had been driven into the wall. Warm looking clothes. Several quilts were on the unmade bed. He left the bedroom, paying no attention to the living room and went straight to the kitchen.

Again, he laughed with delight. There was a cabinet with tins of canned food, mainly pork and beans. He pulled out a drawer and found spoons, forks, and the best thing of all, sharp knives. He went back into the bedroom and took the dingy pillowcase off the pillow, went back to the kitchen and chose what found treasures he thought he might need, making sure he didn't take too much.

Back in the bedroom he stuffed two pairs of pants, two shirts, and a wool coat in the pillowcase. He took a quilt off the bed and folded it as small as possible. It was too big and bulky to stuff in the pillowcase, which was okay since the pillowcase was mostly full. Under the edge of the bed, he saw more shells for the gun and grabbed them with glee. He lifted the edge of the thin mattress and spotted another prize. A pistol with an almost full box of bullets. He quickly stuffed them in the pillowcase; and looked out the window to make sure there was still no one about, tossed the pillowcase and quilt out, eased out the window, closed it, and disappeared as fast as possible. Once he reached the shelter of the woods, he looked back to make sure he hadn't been seen. Satisfied, he retrieved the hidden gun, the rags, moccasins, and too large boots, wrapped them in the quilt, and headed back toward the mountains with his heavy load.

He was surprised at how slow he had to travel, as well as how many times he had to stop to set the heavy load down to rest. He'd never carried anything heavier than a double-bitted ax or hammer and nails. Instead of taking the long way through the mountain that led to the area the witch woman ranged in, he chose a beeline direction toward the higher mountain where his cave was hidden in huge boulders. Every time he left the cave, he rolled several large rocks into the opening, placing them just so. The rocks helped to keep large animals out, plus he would know if someone had rolled the rocks away to enter the cave. Most likely, if they left the cave, they wouldn't place the rocks exactly the way he had.

The sun had set, and the chill of night was setting in. He didn't want to be caught out in the open during the night if he could help it. Bears and other wild animals had young and were desperately searching for food. He might not be able to drop his load, aim and shoot the gun if he was attacked. Tucker and the mother bear were proof enough.

Chapter 16

Granny Witcher looked down on the sleeping girl. She had always wanted a daughter, even though she was thankful to have given birth to a son. She eased her thin bones onto the narrow cot beside the girl and covered them both with the thin quilt. Fortunately, she and the girl neither one had an ounce of fat on their bodies. They fit snuggly together on the narrow bed. Their bodies warmed each other during the chill of the night air.

Granny Witcher wanted to sleep, but sleep didn't come. Instead, she thought of the little son who once slept beside her – and the man who gave him to her. For many years, she had longed for both of them to return to warm her bed and her life. It was a lonesome thing to watch the years slip by. Just when she thought she was wise enough to make a difference in her own life, hard years of living had taken over and crippled her body until it was difficult to merely stay alive.

So is life, she thought – and so was death.

Her sleepless mind went flying back to Lee Gray. When she was her weakest and the most afraid, he had told her it didn't matter if he delivered her alive or dead – just so he delivered her.

He almost hadn't delivered her alive, or himself either. They had been walking through steep, wooded ground for what seemed like a lifetime when he had suddenly stopped walking, turned to her, and said in a low voice.

"I want you to keep up with me and not make a sound until I tell you it's okay to stop or talk. I don't care how tired you

146

get or how bad you need to take a piss; you are to keep following me and remain silent. You got that?"

"Why?" she asked as a stubborn streak came over her. Much to her surprise he answered her.

"Smell that scent that's carrying on the wind? I've gotten us closer to their still than I intended. They must have moved it. We're traveling over a mountain where some mighty rough young men are known to marauder about. The old man is blood kin to the devil himself, and his boy is not any better. Our folks have tangled with them before."

"Can't we go a different way?"

"Yeah, we could have, but it's too late now. Any other way would have taken us days longer. Didn't think you could walk that much farther. Hopefully, they won't be out and about, or at the least, be passed out from drinking their own rotgut liquor. Now, shut up, walk fast. Stay close to me until we're safely on the other side of the mountain."

She followed in his footsteps through unbelievable terrain she never realized existed. There were times when she was sure she couldn't take another step, but she did. Why? Because she had no other choice. He usually stayed as far ahead of her as he could and still remain in her sight. This time he didn't. There were times when he took hold of her arm to help her over a rough spot, while indicating for her to remain silent and keep up with him.

She was beginning to think he was deliberately trying to scare her with talk of rogue moonshiners when he suddenly came to a sudden stop.

"Well, well. Looky what I've found," said a man as he stepped from behind a tree with a long gun held across his arm. The gun was aimed at Lee's chest. The clothes he wore looked worse than those she had on. A greasy hat flopped on a head that was too small for his body. She was staring at the kind of man she'd been warned to stay away from all her life.

"We've got us a pretty one this time. Boss can't have her all to his self like he did the last one."

Lee Gray tensed, but he didn't say a word as he put an arm around her, pulling her in front of him and holding her there.

A second man stepped from behind another tree on the opposite side of them and leered at her from her head to her feet and back again. "I get a go at her first," he declared with a lopsided grin.

"No, you hain't. I saw her first."

"It's your turn to have your fun killing him. My turn to have a go at the girl afore you do," he insisted.

There was a blast of noise a moment before she hit the ground. She landed so hard breath was knocked out of her for a moment. She saw the long gun fall from the man's hands an instant before he pitched backward. The second man leaped at Lee Gray, knocking the pistol from his hand. Lee Gray had held her in front of him not as a shield, but to block the men from seeing him pull the pistol from his shirt. He'd shoved her to the ground out of the range of fire.

The man was broader and heavier than Lee. His weight took Lee down, but Lee was slender and quick to roll from under the man. She saw the flash of a knife as Lee pulled it from his boot with one swift movement as he sunk it into the man's belly, pulled it out and stabbed it across his throat. For the first time in her life, she saw the dark red of a man's blood spilling out of his body.

Lee Gray got to his feet, looked from one man to the other. He kicked the long gun from under the man he had shot, wiped the blood from his knife on the man's dirty clothes, and put the knife back in his boot. He looked about for his pistol and picked it up with his other hand. He turned to her. "Are you all right?"

No. She wanted to scream that she would never be alright again, but she couldn't make a sound.

"It had to be done," he told her. "They would have killed me and done worse to you. Get up. I've got to find a place to dispose of their bodies. We need to get away from here before the rest of that bunch finds out what happened. Hopefully, they didn't hear the pistol fire, but I'm not counting on it."

~~~~

She imagined he took a perverse kind of pleasure in her attempt to keep up. She was still in a state of shock at what happened. Never had she imagined; much less been subjected to what she'd been through in the last few days. She was raised to be timid and well cared for. Every well-bred southern girl had certain rules of correctness they were required to adhere to – rules they didn't make, rules that were made decades back. Doing anything else would have gone beyond the southern culture, and resulted in being excommunicated from polite society, as well as their parents and relatives being snubbed and cast out of the blue book of high society.

She had no idea what Lee Gray now expected from her. Most of her outdoor walking had been done on level ground under a parasol. There were no mountains for her to climb during her childhood and early marriage.

No men killed before her very eyes.

Until now nothing had been expected of her other than being beautiful and ladylike while doing what she was told to do. Never had she wore man's clothing, rode a mule, walked miles, been accosted by the dregs of humanity, and threatened to have the unspeakable done to her. Never had she seen men shot and stabbed before her eyes or watched in mute shock as a grave was dug with a flat rock in soft dirt beneath pine trees. Never had she tried to keep up with a longed-legged man, while she had blisters burst and oozing on her swollen feet.

She trudged onward at a limping rush, until she thought she was going to drop. She didn't. She kept on going a little bit slower, and then even slower. The sky turned dark and the wind grew icy cold as it whirled around her, shaking the leaves on the trees. A jazzed streak of blinding light flashed in the sky at the same time the light came to earth. A tree not fifty feet from her made a deafening sound as it exploded into thousands of splinters.

She stopped dead still as the ground shook beneath her feet. She dropped as though the bolt of lightning had struck her – or a gunshot had. In an instant, hands had a hold on her arms. She was being half lifted, half dragged, through the woods. He dived under a narrow rock overhang with her still clutched in his hands.

"You okay?" he asked. "Were you hurt, burned anywhere?"

She was speechless even though she didn't think she had been hurt. She had felt a strange tingling sensation go through her body that had not completely left her.

His rough hand rubbed the hair from her face until he could glare into her eyes. "Your pupils are even. Can you talk?"

She heard him, opened her mouth to speak, but nothing other than a whine came out. Another flash of lightning shot over their heads and the ground shook. Her arms went around him, and she held on for dear life.

"It's okay," he soothed as his arms tightened around her. "You're okay. I've got you. Nothing is going to hurt you. It's only a storm. It'll be over soon."

The last streak of lightning had torn the rain clouds open. Water came down in huge, determined torrents, beating the ground until water spewed upward with each pounding drop.

The determined resolve to be strong and brave left Loraine. Tears came as she buried her face in his shirt. Her shoulders shook. Her body trembled harder.

"Go ahead, cry it out. We shouldn't travel in this storm. It will be over soon. Such storms hit hard and leave quickly. The hard rain is a good thing. It'll wipe out our tracks."

He was right on that. The storm stopped almost as suddenly as it started. She had cried until her tears turned into sobs. He had held onto her during the storm, still was. The man who was in such a hurry was now giving her some time.

"Are you okay now," he asked.

"I'm ... okay," she managed to say.

He gave her a slight squeeze. "You were more scared than hurt."

"I ... felt it," she told him.

"Me too. It makes a body tingle all over. The shock of it can settle your nerves, calm you down a bit. We'll rest a while longer before we start, let the water run off a bit."

"What a...bout those bad ... men?" she questioned. The ones he hadn't killed.

"They don't like being out in this storm any more than we do. Most likely they're holed up somewhere funneling down liquor. Plus, they most likely don't know their two buddies are no longer on top of the good earth. It'll give us time to be gone before they discover the grave. I made a mistake in judgement. I shouldn't have taken the easy way to get over the mountain instead of traveling up the back side the way we usually bring people in. I knew you couldn't hold-up going the hard route. We have to go around rock cliffs."

Loraine said nothing more. The thought of the bad men started putting determination back into her. She wanted to get away from that place more than she wanted to rest.

"Let's ... go," she said.

He helped her to her feet and frowned when she wobbled, but said nothing. This time he walked slower and didn't get ahead of her. She had no idea how she made it the rest of the way to the top of the mountain. She was in some sort of stupor as she kept putting one foot in front of the other – one foot in front of the other. Once they reached the top of the mountain, going downhill wasn't much better, but she kept following the man in front of her. He moved forward only feet in front of her to enable her to see where they were going.

Clouds had filled the sky along with fog rising in the woods until there was a strange darkness that obliterated everything. Mud had stuck to her boots until it seemed she was walking with buckets on her feet. She was getting slower and slower.

Her knees buckled.

~~~~

She was dry and warm when she opened her eyes again. There was sunlight shining through a small window.

"I see you're awake," the man's voice said.

She looked from the window to the man who spoke. He looked different, but he was definitely Lee Gray.

"It's daylight," she said.

"You passed out. I had to carry you."

"Oh, I'm sorry."

"Why didn't you tell me about all the blisters?"

"Would it have done any good?"

"I might have been more sympathetic."

"I doubt that."

He grinned.

"Where are my clothes?" she asked as she looked at her arms and chest that were sticking out from under the cover.

"I washed them. They're drying."

"Whose clothes am I wearing?"

"Mine."

She looked at him again. He was clean, as were his clothes. Even his hair looked like it had been washed and re-braided. "Where are we?"

"At my cabin. It was closer than where I was supposed to drop you off. You got heavy after a-ways. You've slept for two days straight."

"No," she said with surprise.

"You were exhausted."

She tried to sit up in bed and finally managed. "How far is it to where I'm supposed to be dropped off."

"Miles."

"Hadn't we best get started?"

"Stand up," he told her.

She tried and gasped as her feet touched the rough plank floor. She looked down at her feet. They were discolored and swollen twice their normal size.

"Your blisters got infected. You're lucky they are healing instead of getting worse. It'll be at least a week or maybe more until you can walk far."

Her eyes widened as she glared at him and sank back down on the bed. "What will I do?" she said in a hopeless tone of voice.

"You'll stay here," he told her.

"But . . ."

"No buts. You and I haven't a choice in the matter. Besides, the group you were to leave with has already traveled to another location. They couldn't wait on us any longer."

"What others?"

"Let's just say those looking for a better life. Those who need help and protection."

She opened her mouth to ask more questions, but he held up his hand to silence her. "I've got soup on the stove. You'll need to eat. I could only dripple a little down you. I discovered you enjoy fighting me."

*

Tally moved in her sleep, and it brought Granny Witcher back to the present. How she wished she was able to go back and relive the time she had spent with the man who had told her to call him Lee Gray. His real name was Gray Leaf, and he was what was known as a breed. He was half Cherokee and half white. His father's people had never claimed him, but his mother's people had.

It was against the law for a white person to marry an Indian, punishable by both husband and wife being jailed. Gray Leaf's father had never married his mother. It wasn't against the law for a white man to ride an Indian woman whenever the notion struck them. Gray Leaf was the result.

Gray Leaf's father now lay in a white man's graveyard. His mother had also passed away. His grandmother lost her life while being driven away from her home on the trail of tears, leaving her small daughter behind to survive the long trip. He had no idea where his mother's remains were laid to rest, or if she'd had a proper burial. He could barely remember his parents and his Cherokee relatives. A man who was one fourth Cherokee and three fourths white took him in. He had told Loraine that he had a wonderful childhood running wild and free over the mountains and down in the glens.

Finally, she drifted off to sleep with a smile of memory on her withered face.

Tally woke her up as she got out of bed by crawling over the top of her. When Granny Witcher opened her eyes, Tally let out a long breath of relief.

"What is it, child?" Granny Witcher asked.

"I thought you were dead," Tally said with relief.

"What made you think that?" she asked as she sat up.

"It's daylight. You always get up before dawn."

Granny Witcher didn't tell her she lay awake reliving the horror as well as the love she had shared with a man his Indian relatives called Gray Leaf. It didn't matter how long she lived; she would always have those wonderful, happy years to hold deep in her heart.

"I'll start a fire and make breakfast," Granny Witcher told her. "Once we wash up, we'll go search for herbs again."

"Shouldn't we be working in the garden?" Tally liked gardening better than roaming through the rugged mountains in search of healing herbs.

"We've planted every inch of good ground. All we have to do now is let them grow. Besides, you need to learn about herbs and which ones cure what."

"Why? You know all that already."

"I do, but you don't. I won't be around forever. Once I'm gone, you'll be glad I taught you things I wish I'd known when I was your age."

Tally wrinkled her nose. She doubted that. She didn't want to be known as a granny witch who had no life other than to take care of sick people. She didn't like or trust people. She was afraid of them and what they were capable of doing.

We'll only be searching for herbs. I've been occupied in the morning hours causing me to dally too long in the daylight hours to dig them. As I told you before, they are more potent in the early morning when everything fills up with new life. I want to tell you about them and the powers they contain."

Tally washed the two bowls and two spoons and put them away on the narrow shelf. It was the only place that wasn't covered in herbs or some kind of concoction.

"Did you know that so-called doctors who are supposed to be in the know once believed in bleeding people when they were sick?"

"Bleeding people?" Tally questioned with her nose wrinkled.

"Yeap. They cut a vein and drained blood out. A good-sized man has about a gallon and a half of blood in them. A woman has less, as does a child. If you lose half the amount of blood in your body, you're dead. A man could survive by losing a quart or a little more if he's big. A child couldn't take losing a cup of blood."

Tally cringed. She didn't want to talk about losing blood. It reminded her too much of her mother. Again, she saw all the blood on the bed and on the floor. She felt the sticky wetness on her feet where she had stepped in her mother's blood.

Granny Witcher knew what her words brought to the child's mind. She decided long ago that it was better to face the truth than try to hide from it. If you faced the worse and lived through it, you became strong enough to get over the trauma and go on with living. If you tried to hide from the truth, it was always hiding in the shadow waiting to devastate you when you least expected.

She started to tell the child her mother might have lived if she had been there in time to stop her bleeding but thought better of it. The girl was still hurting too much to hear that truth. In time, she would instruct her how to remove an aborted baby and go about stopping the blood flow. She would tell her how to gather sage and yarrow to use as a bolus to pack inside the woman's vagina. She could also drink a tea made from shepherd's purse, red raspberry leaves, sage, and yarrow. Sometimes it worked, sometimes it didn't. But then her mother wasn't having a miscarriage because she couldn't carry a baby to full term. Tally had said her mother had been beaten by her father. The only herb that cured that was feeding Dobb Simmons a brew of wild hemlock. That stuff was deadly.

"I hate him," Tally had said. "I wish he was dead."

Granny Witcher saw Tally's face and knew the girl needed more time. She wasn't ready to talk about her mother or her dad.

There was one thing for certain. Granny Witcher regretted keeping Dobb Simmons alive. She'd have to do some thinking on that very thing. If she had the ability to save his life, did she also have the ability to take it?

Chapter 17

Tucker couldn't sleep, couldn't find any position to lay where he wasn't hurting a cut, bruise, or torn place. His body really did look like a skinned squirrel – skinless and hairless. He had stitches in more places than he knew where they were located. Doc Robinson gave him pain medication, along with drinks of his own liquor he had brewed. Nurse Whitley gave him nothing for pain. It was as though she took pleasure in seeing him suffer. To save him, he couldn't understand why.

"What did you do to get dragged?" she asked as she poured disinfectant on his skinned places.

It took him a few minutes of gritted teeth to get over the stinging pain enough to talk without cursing.

"A bear scared my donkey. I grabbed him by the halter and my hand got hung."

"You couldn't get your hand loose?"

"I wouldn't be laying here on my bare ass if I coulda done that, now would I?"

She tried not to be insulted by the way he talked, but she was. "Why didn't you take the halter off?"

He looked at her face to make sure she was serious in the question she asked. Did she think he'd hold on if there was any possibility of getting the halter off? It hurt when he rolled his eyes. "Hell woman, are you stupid? How the hell was I supposed to get the halter off that damn donkey that wouldn't whoa when I yelled for him to stop."

"Humph," she said. "Bet you regret that."

"You're damned right I do, and in the worse sort of way," he told her as she rubbed stinking salve on his body without taking time to be gentle. The salve just about set him on fire, and he suspected she was doing it deliberately. "Why don't you like me?" He didn't believe in beating around the bush with questions.

"Is there a reason I should like or dislike you?" She asked sharply.

He thought about it a moment and decided there wasn't one single reason that he could figure. "In case you haven't noticed, I'm a mighty fine fellow," he assured her.

"That's a matter of opinion."

"What you got against me?" he asked, surprised at her words.

"You lack . . ." she hesitated, searching for the right words. She saw no reason to lie to him, and yet she didn't want to be too insulting, "refinement, plus you make illegal liquor."

"Elixir," he told her. "I provide Doc with some mighty fine quality elixir. He needs that stuff in more ways than one if you ask me."

"Again, that's a matter of opinion."

He was irritated by her comment as well as her attitude. He considered himself more manly than the Doc, plus he didn't have an invalid wife. "What do you see in the Doc, anyway."

She gave him a look that should have let him know how disgusted she was with him. "He's a fine man," she informed him in her most haughty tone of voice.

"He's also a married man with a bedridden wife."

"I assure you, I'm well aware of that," she snapped.

"Do you also know you're the butt of a lot of jokes by both women and men alike?" he asked with sarcasm.

She made a point of pouring mercurochrome on his worst places and took pleasure as he squalled out in pain from the stinging.

"Hell-fire, woman! That monkey blood hurts like the devil," he said after the stinging eased off enough for him to squall out words.

"No pain, no gain," she told him.

"You ought to know," he snapped back at her. "You have to suffer a lot of pain knowing folks call you Doc Robinson's trollup."

She turned her back on him and stalked out of the room. Anger was clearly on her face. Shit, he thought. He wasn't exactly winning her over the way he'd hoped to do. Pain, along with a vulgar mouth, wasn't getting him very far with the woman he was attracted to. He'd have to work hard if he was to turn things around. His ex-wife had always complained about his crude ways. She claimed a woman needed a man who could be comforting, one who had gentle hands and gentle ways. He'd let her know in a hurry that he wasn't that kind of man.

At least he had a donkey who didn't care how crude he was. He also had one that was willing to drag him for miles without stopping when he was hollering whoa.

~~~~

"If I have to tolerate that man one more time, I'm going to kill him," she told Doc Robinson as she rushed into the room he used as an office.

"What happened this time?"

"He said I was your trollop. He said I was nothing more than a joke with men and women alike."

A flash of anger hit the doctor, followed closely by amusement. No one could accuse Tucker of being two-faced. He told what he thought when no one else would dare say such a thing, regardless of what they were thinking.

"My dear, since when do you care what a crude old moonshiner has to say about you?"

"Since you insisted, I have to endure his naked body while I try to keep his wounds from becoming infected. I'm telling you right now, he can up and die for all I care. I'll do nothing else for that horrible man."

"Any type of cloth sticks to his flesh because his skin has been scraped off. Besides that, I've cured a lot of people I'd preferred to have let die," he told her calmly. "I'm sworn to heal instead of harm and so are you."

"Oh, no you don't. You can't pull that crap on me. Just because I'm a nurse doesn't mean I have to take name calling and hurtful insults from a patient or anyone else."

"True," he told her. "I'll look in on him from now on. He'll be so heartbroken he'll most likely die. I guess you know he's struck on you."

New anger flashed over her face as she glared at the doctor. "Struck isn't the word I'd use for what he's feeling when I'm near him. Makes me want to give the man a left-handed castration," she spit out the words with intense disgust.

"My dear, don't go getting your panties in a wad. I meant it as a compliment to you and so does he. You do realize men can't always control what their body does when an attractive woman is close by. Why, most all the men around here have the hots for you. I don't think you realize what a beautiful woman you are – both outside and inside," he added. "You're a kind and caring lady as well as a nurse. I don't know what I'd do without you. You're the air I breathe and the reason my heart keeps beating. You know that don't you?"

She knew, but sometimes knowing it wasn't enough. Sometimes the truth about their relationship hurt too much to endure. When she looked at the reality of things, she really was his trollop. She had the choice of being a much-loved trollop or leave the man she loved to live a lonely, chaste life filled with emptiness. She had chosen the doctor and forever would.

But what was the future in it? What would happen to her if something happened to the doctor. She'd have to leave and try to find another job. Perhaps she'd even have to change her name to get a decent position, but then her name was on her nursing certificate. She couldn't get a job without it.

The doctor put his arms around her and drew her close. "Everything's all right, and it will stay that way."

She allowed him to make an attempt at soothing her hurt feelings, but deep down inside she wondered if he would be willing to make her his wife if Elouise were to die? For some reason, she had her doubts. Most men made sure a wife and a trollop always remained two separate people.

Chapter 18

~~Dobb Simmons~~Clancy~~

Dobb Simmons became aware of the knocks on the door along with what sounded like a firm kick. He let out a stream of curse words as he made his painful way off the bed and limped to the door, opened it, and looked outside. All he could see was the pouring down rain the storm had brought. The rain was so fierce it was coming down sideways beating against his face as he stood there. Water had puddled in every dip and ditch until it looked more like a river than solid ground. He slammed the door close and cursed the storm. He cursed whatever had blown against the door causing him to open it. There for a minute, he'd thought it was Sally trying to get out of the rain, but she wasn't there – no one was there.

An odd kind of shiver brought chill-bumps until every hair on his body stood up. Things were going on out there he didn't want to think about, bad omen things. He hadn't been in his right mind when he opened the door. He finally realized it couldn't be Sally knocking on the door. He knew for a fact that she was in a grave rotting. He'd dug her up and saw it was her with his own eyes. Not only that, but she'd also taken his son to the grave with her. He cursed Sally for dying and killing his only boy before it ever had a chance to live. He cursed her over again for all the trouble she was still causing him. A man had a right to live in comfort. Even the Bible read it was a man's God-given right, just as it was a woman's job to treat a man like a king while she took care of a man's every need. God knew men were superior to the animals on earth, the fowl of the sky, and especially to women. God had even taken a rib from a man to make a woman to serve his needs. That very fact said all a man needed to know. A woman wasn't a person. She was only a man's rib and worth no more than one bone.

As soon as he got to where he could walk a little better, he'd have to go down off that mountain and find him a young, healthy woman to give him a boy. Perhaps a lot of boys. There was a gob-plenty of women down there for him to pick from. He would be choosy this time. He wanted him a woman who knew her place – one who realized how lucky she would be to have a real man marry her.

A man needed sons for many reasons. Several boys could do enough work to make a man rich. He would be able to run his own still and put an amateur such as Tucker out of business. A man could always count on his sons to have his back. That was something Sally's bunch of boys never did. They were always against him regardless of how much sense he tried to beat into them. He was relieved when they slinked off that mountain like a bunch of no-account, mangy dogs with their tails between their legs. He'd give them what-for if they ever came crawling back.

As for that big ole Mary girl of Sally's, she'd best hope he'd never get his hands on her again. He'd had fine plans for her, but she didn't have the sense to know when she was well off. She was young and healthy enough to give him all the sons Sally hadn't given him. He had a right to her, being he married her mommy. A man owned his family, so he owned her as well as Sally. Hell, he owned every single one of that bunch, but they appreciated nothing he did for them.

He was fixing to hump that big ole girl up when the sorry snitch ran to her mommy. Sally was a selfish bitch. She wasn't willing to share him even with her daughter. She sent Mary away and claimed she'd married some man, but he didn't believe a thing Sally told him. All he got out of taking that sorry woman as his wife was a cabin and land. He reckoned that was something, but not nearly enough to pay him for all he'd done for that woman and her ungrateful bunch of Billy Gray's spawns.

As for that no-account girl Sally claimed belonged to him, he didn't know what happened to her and he didn't care. She was as worthless as a pile of animal scat. She couldn't cook worth a lick and knew nothing at all about taking care of a man. He assured himself he was better off without that midget of a slit-tail.

He cursed the storm again. The rain had brought cold air putting more pain into his broken bones than he'd been having. He needed liquor if he was to overcome his suffering. Thinking about liquor made him think about Tucker and all that good liquor stored in jugs up near the top of the mountain. If he could just get his bum leg working, he could have all the liquor he wanted to drink.

Thinking of Tucker caused another image to hit him. Again, he saw Tucker standing over him, felt horrible pain as Tucker pulled him through narrow, rocky spaces. Tucker had hurt him so badly he'd blacked out. Again, he remembered seeing the crazy old witch woman standing over him with a knife as she looked down on him. He had an inkling she'd allowed him to stay alive instead of killing him, but he wasn't too keen on that inkling. She'd left him naked in the dirt for who knew how long. He'd even been butt-naked when he'd come to himself. No telling what all that old witch woman had done to him while he was laying there passed out cold. He'd heard plenty of tales about what witch women did to men. He stuck his hand through the hole in his britches pocket and felt around right careful like.

"Damn her to hell!" he squalled louder than the roar of the storm that was raging over the mountain with enough force to shake the cabin.

~~~~

Clancy had never realized how far, or how steep, those mountains could be when a person was carrying a load. Never before did he have enough of anything heavy enough to need carrying. An ax or a hammer hadn't amounted to much weight, but they had been a matter of survival for Clancy. He'd left the orphanage home with only rags on his back. He now felt blessed with unexpected riches. The fact his riches came from Tucker didn't bother him in the least. A man who had been dragged as far as Tucker had been, most likely wouldn't be needing a thing ever again, other than a hole in the ground. Clancy needed the things he took in a mighty bad way else he wouldn't have taken them. His folks had taught him stealing was wrong. He rationalized that he wasn't stealing. He was merely surviving. He might as well take a little of what he needed to survive as to let someone who needed less than he did get them.

He did wonder about Tucker and what kind of shape he was in after he'd been dragged all the way down the mountain. He'd kinda like to know if he was in the graveyard or at the Doc's place, but he wasn't curious enough to take a chance on finding out. Somebody would be sure to see him if the left the cover of the woods. When he was little and his parents were alive, they tried to avoid Tucker. They'd shake their heads and say what that man did for a living wasn't Christian. He wondered what his parents would think knowing some of the things Tucker no longer needed would help their son survive.

Finally, with aching arms and straining legs, Clancy made the trek until he reached the entrance to his cave. He hid in a clump of undergrowth while he checked the placement of the rocks. Satisfied they hadn't been moved, he rolled the rocks aside and entered the cave. Clancy stored his treasure trove with a joy that surprised him. He'd been assuring himself that material things didn't matter. Nature provided him with everything he needed. He now hated to admit that wasn't entirely true as he looked over the things he'd laid out. Boots, moccasins, overalls, a coat to keep him warm meant more to him than he'd realized. Even the quilt was nothing short of extreme comfort. He grabbed a tin can of pork and beans and cut it open with his knife. He almost cried with pure pleasure as he ate the contents with a real spoon and drank what little liquid that was left in the can. He ached to open another can, but he knew to save the tin cans for hard times come winter. Material things were going to make his life a whole lot easier than it had been. Without them, a man had to spend every hour of every day trying to survive, and he hadn't been doing as good as he'd hoped.

He tried to figure out how long it had been since he'd escaped the orphanage home. How many winters had he almost frozen to death? How many times had he starved until he was almost too weak to find food? How many times had he huddled in some sort of hiding place to get away from a wild animal that would have made a meal out of him? What was it he had to do in order to change the way he was living? Steal, cheat, kill?

The answer hit him like a slap in the face. Dobb Simmons had an easier life than he and the old woman because he had a cabin. At least the witch woman had a shack that provided shelter from storms and warmth from the brutal winter snows. All he had was an empty cave. Dobb had a cabin with a stove and a real bed. If Dobb had died the way he was supposed to, he could have moved in with Tally when the winters became brutal instead of making her go it alone. Both of them together could have lived good, but he had been foolish by missing his chance – or had he? He had Tucker's gun and plenty of shells. The gun could do a job the gravel shooter could never do. It wouldn't be a bit of trouble to dig up the soft dirt Sally was buried under. The church folks had dug the grave. They'd have no reason to ever dig into it to see who was there. They already knew.

As for Tally, she'd sure enough be better off without a dad such as Dobb Simmons. Even if he never found Tally, his life could also be improved without Dobb Simmons in it. Nobody cared what happened to that sorry excuse of a man. Nobody would miss the likes of him.

The can of pork and beans filled up his shriveled stomach so full he became sleepy. He was exhausted from carrying the heavy load all the way up the mountain. He wrapped the quilt around himself and laid himself down. How good it felt to be full, warm, and comfortable in the dark, cold cave. He fell right to sleep.

Chapter 19

~~Nurse Whitley~~

"He's developed a high fever. Some of the deeper puncture wounds are becoming infected. Chances are there's still debris we didn't get out deep in those holes. Have you been pouring the alcohol in them the way I told you to?" Doc Robinson asked Nurse Whitley after he'd examined Tucker and left the room.

Nurse Whitley was in the kitchen preparing Elouise's breakfast and medication. Anger flared in the nurse. She did her best not to show it. She'd told him at least a dozen times she did not want to take care of the insolent, insulting man. He ignored her completely. He actually treated her objections as being childish and petty.

"Maybe he needs a doctor's magic touch instead of that of an ignorant nurse."

Doc Robinson shook his head in bewilderment. "My dear, don't go getting your bloomers in a wad. I know you dislike the man, but you're a nurse. Besides, I'm only asking you a question."

Nurse Whitley thought she deserved to reward herself for holding her temper in check as she answered him. "One of the puncture wounds oozed out puss along with what appeared to be tiny pieces of bark yesterday. I did my best to pour hydrogen peroxide in the wound. He wouldn't let me. When I tried to pour liquor on his wounds, he grabbed my arm and did his best to drink what little liquor was left in the cup. I have an idea there is more dirt and debris in some of the puncture wounds, which I had nothing to do with."

"I'll give him enough ether to put him out while I check his wounds more thoroughly," Doc Robinson told her.

Nurse Whitley didn't respond. Instead, she picked up the tray she had prepared and carried it into Elouise's bedroom. The bedroom door was wide open. It irritated her. There were times when the doctor and she discussed things that were best Elouise didn't listen in on. She'd closed the door after she had helped Elouise bathe and dress earlier. Nurse Whitley feared Elouise was starting to have one of her irate fits of stubbornness, which she did on a regular basis. The doctor had evidently checked on her and left the door open.

"Are you ready to eat breakfast?" Nurse Whitley said pleasantly, even when there was no feeling of pleasantness inside her. Elouise was becoming more difficult every day. She refused to eat breakfast at a regular time. She waited until Nurse Whitley was the busiest to ring her bell. Elouise always insisted Nurse Whitley cook her the most unusual and difficult to prepare breakfast. Lunch and dinner weren't any easier. Many times, Elouise insisted she was too weak to feed herself, wanting Nurse Whitley to spoon-feed her.

Elouise was sitting up in bed with a smug grin on her face. "Where is my husband?" she insisted in her most peevish voice.

"I believe he is still tending to a patient. Would you like for me to feed you?"

"No, I want Joseph to feed me. You always try to choke me to death. Go tell him I need him this instant."

"Very well. I'll tell him your wishes," she said as she set down the food on the nightstand and left the room, closing the door behind her, making sure it latched. If Elouise wanted to eat, she was perfectly capable of feeding herself. However, she would give the doctor his wife's request.

She found him holding a cloth over Tucker's nose and mouth as he trickled drops of ether into the cloth.

"Breathe slowly and stop fighting me."

"Want liquor. Stops the pain," Tucker mumbled. He was in more pain now than he had been the day he arrived.

"This will help the pain. I'll give you all the liquor you want later on. Right now, I need to clean your wounds again. There seems to be trash deeper in the puncture wounds than I thought."

"No, stop it," Tucker knocked at the doctor's hands causing him to drop the cloth.

"If you don't stop fighting me right now, I'll leave and let you die right where you lay. The only reason I'm fighting to keep you alive is so folks won't have to waste their time digging your grave." He turned toward Nurse Whitley. "What do you want?" he demanded with irritation.

"I want nothing. Your wife wants you to feed her breakfast."

"Can't you see I've got my hands full right here? It's your job to feed her."

"I tried, and now I have given you her message." She turned and walked out the door. It was time for her to tend to her flower garden. She had endured enough stress for one morning.

Her gardening soothed her better than all the anti-stress medication the doctor pumped down his wife's throat. She no longer gave Elouise any medicine at all. Elouise claimed she was trying to poison her and insisted her husband attend to her. Nurse Whitley was delighted, regardless of Elouise's reason for doing so. She suspected Elouise was trying to prove to her husband that she didn't need a nurse, at least not one who was young and attractive. She also wanted her husband's undivided attention.

Nurse Whitley could have assured her that would never happen. She was by the good doctor's side almost every minute of every day and part of most nights. It was only a few minutes during those nights she actually had his undivided attention.

Minutes later Elouise's bell started ringing rapidly without stopping. Nurse Whitley raised up from her bed of flowers, dusted off her apron, took off her gloves and went inside. She took time to wash her hands before she went into Elouise's bedroom.

"Where have you been? I've been ringing my bell forever."

That wasn't true. Nurse Whitley had been only feet from Elouise's bedroom window when the bell started ringing. "I took time to wash my hands. What can I do for you?"

"How dare you not to tell my husband I need him?" she ranted as soon as she saw Nurse Whitley.

"I went straight away and told him you wanted him immediately."

"You're a liar. He would have come to me if you'd told him. I demand you go tell him, right now," she ordered in a screeching, high-pitched voice.

"I told him before, but I'll tell him again," Nurse Whitley told her and walked out the room. She had taken offence at being called a liar. She went straight to the doctor.

"Your wife has become enraged again because you haven't rushed to do her bidding fast enough. She's accusing me of not giving you her message."

"Tell her I'll come as soon as I've finished here. I have to finish cleaning the infected places while the ether is still in effect."

Nurse Whitley didn't argue, instead she gritted her teeth together and tried not to clinch her fists. She had no intention of going back into that bedroom only to be yelled at. She considered offering to finish cleaning the infected places on the horrible man but changed her mind. If she jumped at every irate demand Elouise made, she would be jumping continuously. Elouise's bell was ringing nonstop as Nurse Whitley went back to the house. She went into the kitchen and put wood in the cookstove. A nice hot cup of coffee was what she needed along with a few minutes of silence. The bell kept ringing. There would be no silence in that house until the doctor came.

Lukewarm coffee would be good enough. She poured two cups and left the kitchen. She sipped on her cup as she went back to the doctor. She handed him the other cup of coffee.

"Thanks, I need that, but hold on. I have to wash my hands before I touch anything."

"Elouise is in a rage," she told him lightly. "I left her to it."

"Did you give her medicine?"

"No. You know good and well she claims I'm trying to poison her. She wouldn't even let me feed her."

"Shit," he said, wiped his hands on a towel, took the cup of cool coffee, and glanced toward Tucker. "Pour liquor on his entire body and cover him up. It'll probably sting enough to wake him up."

She finished drinking the sorry cup of coffee, set the cup down, and took a jar of liquor off the shelf. She turned up the jar and poured it over his body as the doctor had told her. She took a clean sheet and covered him up. She usually rubbed salve on his injuries to keep the sheet from sticking to his wounds. She had no intention of rubbing his body ever again.

She hurried to her garden and lingered near the window in time to hear Elouise screeching at her husband. She looked through the crack in the curtains where the fabric of the curtains didn't meet.

"She's trying to kill me, I'm telling you. I want her gone immediately."

"Want me to feed you?" he asked, ignoring her screeching.

"Feed me? Are you serious? That food is poisoned. I'll not eat a bite as long as she's in this house."

"Have it your way," he said as he turned his back to her. He flipped the cork from a small tube in one easy motion and squirted the liquid into her open mouth. "Swallow it," he told her. "Or so help me, I sit on top of you and pour it down your throat."

There was a minute of silence before Elouise spoke again.

"Why do you always do that to me?" she whined. "You can have your way with me without doping me up. I'm crippled so badly I can't get out of bed, but I can still screw your balls off and you know it."

"Don't be vulgar," he told her.

"You like dirty talk, always have."

"If you're not going to eat, I'm leaving. You've called me away from a man who's two breaths away from being dead. I'm not listening to your foul mouth."

"Don't you dare criticize me. I know you don't come to me anymore because you're screwing that woman like you're a randy billy goat. You think I don't know what's going on in my own house? I hear you moaning and groaning at night while I have to lay here crying my heart out."

"You're being hysterical. I've taken as good care of you as I possibly can, and so has your nurse."

"Nurse! She's not my nurse. I don't want her here. I want her gone, and I intend to scream my head off until someone hears and comes to get me away from this horrible place. You can't keep me jailed forever."

"Scream away," the doctor said.

There was another squall a moment before Elouise's horrible sound turned into strangled coughing. Nurse Whitley knew the doctor had squirted another tube of medicine down her throat. She would calm down shortly, sleep until morning, and behave herself for a day or two before she pulled the same stunt again. There were times when Nurse Whitley felt sorry for the woman – and times when she didn't. All the time she hated being there, doing what she was doing with a man she wasn't married to, but she knew she wouldn't leave, nor would the doctor send her away. When two desperate, lonely people came together, they clung to each other for dear life.

Doc Robinson stayed with his wife until she fell asleep. He checked her pulse, listened to her breathing, and checked her color before he breathed a sigh of relief. He didn't like doping his wife just to settle her down, but he knew no other way to keep her from driving him crazy. As for her, he hadn't discovered she was already crazy until after they were married. He felt as though he'd been tricked. Cheated from truth. Not one person told him Elouise Blough had been in treatment since she was in the third grade. No one told him her parents had granted her every wish because they felt guilty for their daughter's condition. Her parents were first cousins.

Horse breeders claimed that breeding too closely related horses resulted in one of two things. You got an exceptionally beautiful and intelligent horse, or you got a crazy, uncontrollable horse that should be put down There was no question in Doc Robinson's mind which one of those scenarios fit his wife. Thankfully, people weren't put down. They drew sympathy and were taken care of for the rest of their lives.

He wasn't sure what scenario fit him - - the doctor who tried to keep all people alive. What he knew for a fact was he had been the man who married Elouise Blough, and he had regretted it every moment since. Still, he had committed himself, and he would do his best to honor that commitment.

But . . . but he was not willing to give up his entire life because of her, neither was he willing to deprive himself of what little pleasure he had managed to find with Valarie Whitley. She had been nothing short of a blessing to his miserable life. A doctor saw too much death, too much sadness not to grab onto what little happiness available.

Was there a God up in heaven ready to condemn him to hell-fire and damnation because he chose to take Valarie Whitley to his bed? Was a man who was doomed to a lifetime of misery justified in grabbing hold of a few hours of happiness?

One thing was for sure, he wouldn't be going to the preacher for an answer. He was the doctor who held most everyone's deepest, darkest secrets hidden in his very soul.

Chapter 20

Ida Hadley sat at Beatrice Gidley's table sipping weak coffee and eating flavorless cake.

"The Preacher told me she keeps him as naked as a newly hatched baby blue jay. He's gone to see that man twice, although Doc Robinson told him not to go. He claimed he was trying to keep infections down. If you ask me, Doc didn't want anybody to know that so-called nurse of his keeps poor ole Tucker stark naked and helpless. We don't need that kind of woman around here."

"I never! And to think, I actually allowed her in my home. I'll not do it again, I can tell you that much," Beatrice said as her back straightened and her pointy chin lifted, stretching her turkey waddle.

"Naked, can you believe that? How repulsive! Preacher told me I was being sinful in my thoughts, but the accident couldn't have happened to a more apt person being we all know how sinful he is. God knows, he's nothing but a home wrecker. That liquor he brews has torn up more families than death itself. I can't see there would be much of a loss if Tucker Layman up and died."

"You know what I heard?" Beatrice added to their story. "My Griff was down at the feed and seed store and overheard a bunch of men talkin'. They said that no-account Dobb Simmons hadn't shown up in a coon's age."

"That sounds like a good thing to me."

"Well, yeah, but he had a route he kept to, like clockwork. Some men went looking for him and said they never saw hide nor hair of him. They did say they peeped in the window and saw that little girl sitting in her momma's rocking chair. They said it was cold and there weren't no fire burning," Beatrice continued.

"Dobb Simmons always has been too lazy to chop wood. Sally had to drag in deadfall and chop it herself. He never stayed home either."

"He never missed delivering that sinful liquor to people. Griff said it's been over two months since anybody's seen him."

"Sounds like a good thing to me," Ida said.

"It sure is. It means that girl could be an orphan."

Ida's eyes brightened. "We should get the men together and go after her. They ought to be willing to help us if they think Dobb Simmons is no longer around to shoot them."

"My thoughts exactly. Let's call a meeting with the ladies so they can get their husbands to go with us to get her. We need more children in the orphanage. We really need boys to work the crops, but they're hard to come by. Looks like we'll have to make the girls double up on their chores."

"Don't tell Valarie Whitley about the meeting. We'll vote to blackball her," Ida said. "We simply can't tolerate her kind around decent God-fearing people any longer."

After Ada left Beatrice, she went straight to her husband. "Preacher, we've decided it's best to go back up that mountain and get that poor, little helpless girl. It's nothing short of a sin to leave that poor child all alone on that mountain."

Preacher Hadley gave her a disbelieving look. "Surely you're not serious."

"We are. It's not Christian to leave her up there to starve to death."

"She won't starve. Those mountain folks know how to stay alive by foraging from the time they can walk."

"Nonsense. You know good and well a child can't survive without parents regardless of where they're at."

Preacher Hadley cringed. He had to be careful how he handled this situation – make her think he was not only understanding but also on her side. "She still has a daddy."

"Not according to the talk that's going around. There's talk that Dobb Simmons is long gone."

"Gone where?"

"Who cares where he's gone, or if he's dead or alive. The only important thing is somebody has to save that little girl. You know good and well God has directed us women to do that."

Oh, boy. Preacher Hadley thought. That bunch of women were now trying to use God as being on their side in getting their way. He had to tread carefully if he wanted clean clothes and food that was fit to eat and not burnt to a crisp.

"It's up to the rest of the men. It's too dangerous for one lone man to go on that mountain. There's folks living in those mountains that nobody knows about. Dangerous criminals who are hiding from the law."

Ida smiled. She had prevailed in what she intended. She had no doubt the other women would be persuasive as well.

Ida, Beatrice, Ellie James, and Inez Williams were the four women who were to go with Preacher Hadley, Griff Gidley, and Walt James to rescue Tally. Inez Williams was married once upon a time, fifteen years before, but her husband mysteriously disappeared. Some folks claimed somebody killed his sorry ass, others claimed he ran away to escape living with Inez. Some folks said Inez turned into a bitter woman because of her husband's desertion. Unless her husband was proved dead, she couldn't marry again. She even needed a live husband to get one of those seldom heard of divorces.

They all gathered at the church as soon as there was enough morning light to see, said prayers for success, and crammed themselves into the preacher's car. The preacher, Walt, and Griff Gidley were in the front seat with the four women squeezed together in the back seat. The preacher drove the car as far as the road held up, and then got out to walk the rest of the way. They had planned to arrive at the cabin while Tally was still in bed, but they hadn't realized how slow they had to drive on the muddy road. Recent heavy rains had softened the ground until the tires sunk in the mud of the seldom traveled excuse of a road.

They heard the sound of the branch full and gurgling from spring rains as it rushed down a gully. The morning air was cool enough to tingle their noses. The aroma of damp ground and woods plants was rich and spicy as it reached them. The sun warmed the ground enough to bring the bugs to life. Gnats were biting as the birds squawked and flew from tree limbs in fright as they headed to find a safer place.

Seven people bunched together climbing up the mountain through the heavily wooded forest was enough to put fear in animals, fowl, and humans.

Clancy heard them. He had woken up early, had a breakfast of beans, and headed out to find what had happened to Tally. He planned on checking the cabin first just to make sure she wasn't there, but he never got that far. The early morning breeze was lifting up from the valley the way it often did, bringing sounds up the mountain. Clancy hurried to the rock where the cow died, and Dobb had fallen. It proved the best lookout, but he was too late to see the car coming through the valley. It was chugging its way up the muddy section of the road. He grinned and fumed at the same time. Grinned because those idiots were too lazy to walk far. They were chancing getting stuck just to save a few steps. He fumed because he knew they were on their way to find Tally. They hadn't given up on adding her to their orphanage.

Just to make sure the intruders were who he thought they were, he eased through the woods, hiding in underbrush and behind tree trunks until he could get a good look at them. He fingered Tucker's gun that he carried. It was loaded and he was mighty tempted to take aim and pull the trigger. He figured he could get one or two and no one would ever know he was the one who did the shooting. Dobb Simmons would most likely get the blame.

His mom and dad's Christian raising came to him an instant before he squeezed the trigger. Both anger and relief filled him for not being able to shoot. He took off at a run. He had to beat them to the cabin. He peeked in the window to make sure Tally wasn't there. He didn't see her in the house or anywhere outside. He did see Dobb in the cabin lying on the bed snoring like a fattening hog. Clancy beat on the door hard enough to wake the dead, and then took off at a run to hide behind a rock in the middle of dense undergrowth. A rock was good protection against gun fire.

He could hear the intruders coming through the woods snapping twigs and kicking rocks while thinking they were being sneaky and silent.

"Sheeee, be quiet," one of the women whispered in a high pitch that carried all the way to Clancy. "One of you men go to the window and another to the door. If she tries to run from the cabin, we'll be able to catch her."

He heard movement inside the cabin and figured his knocking had aroused Dobb. Clancy had no idea what would happen next. He flattened out on his belly, sheltering his head behind the rock, to make sure he wasn't in the line of fire if Dobb reacted the way Clancy suspected he would. Clancy held his breath, afraid they could hear him breathing or hear the rapid beating of his heart. To Clancy it sounded as loud as a drum beat.

Sure enough, they circled the cabin, Preacher Hadley halfway squatted against the side of the door jam, reached up his long arm to grab the door handle and yanked the door open. A gun shot sounded from inside the cabin. Preacher Hadley's arm was a moving blur. He grabbed his arm and ran for cover.

"Break into my cabin, damn you!" Dobb yelled at the top of his lungs. "I'll kill every damned one of you." He fired another shot.

Clancy did his best to bury deeper into the ground. He wasn't sure the rock would give him enough cover if Dobb started shooting wildly. He need not have worried. The seven running people made enough noise for Dobb to know exactly which way they were going. Dobb fired, ran after them, continuing to fire. Dobb was slower and had to slow down to reload his gun before he could keep firing. Clancy took his chance on easing up, silently going from tree trunk to tree trunk so he could watch the confrontation.

The seven were running close together instead of scattering. They were screaming and crying out in pain as they reached the car. All seven of them tried to get in the back seat.

"Griff! My arm. I can't drive," Preacher Hadley shouted. "Get in. Go! Get us out of here."

The front windshield shattered as the engine roared to life. Gears groaned and the car shot backward. Another shot got the radiator. The fluid was still hot enough to gurgle and steam. The car kept going backward. One of the front tires blew, and then the other one. Whoever was driving backward didn't stop. They were bumping backward at a fast clip, all the way down the muddy road, the firing of the gun urging them on. Clancy wondered how far they would be able to get before the car stopped altogether.

Dobb let out a long stream of cursing. He called them things Clancy had never heard before. Clancy was surprised Dobb didn't continue after them until he realized Dobb was slowed down by his injured leg and arms. Those seven were still alive because of a broken leg and two broken arms that hadn't completely healed, but they hadn't gotten off uninjured. Clancy watched as Dobb limped his way back to the cabin. He had regretted leaving Dobb's gun behind in the cabin for Tally. He no longer regretted it. Those seven wouldn't be coming back after Tally again. Now, he needed to find where she was hiding.

~~~~

The car had chugged and bumped to the end of the steepest part of mountain before it came to a complete stop as it reached an almost flat spot.

"He's bleeding to death. Somebody, help him!" Ida was screaming.

Walt grabbed hold of Ida's thin jacket and ripped a strip from the front to bind the preacher's injured arm.

"Hell-fire!" Griff yelled. "We're all bleeding. Just look at me."

Everyone looked at themselves, at the specks of blood oozing from wounds where birdshot had entered their flesh. The women started screaming and shaking even worse than before. Those in the back seat were trying to lay down on top of each other, thinking the back of the front seats along with Griff, Walt, and Inez sitting in the front would shelter them from more shots.

"We're sitting ducks," Preacher Hadley said. "We best make a run for it. Get ourselves to the Doc's place afore we bleed to death sitting here."

The women whimpered and huddled down further. Griff and Walt opened the doors and took out running down the muddy excuse of a road, regardless of the openness of the terrain. Preacher Hadley's feet hit the ground next, clutching his injured arm and hand against his chest with his left hand. Ida was running right beside him. Beatrice, Ellie, and Inez had no intention of being left behind. They scrambled over each other trying to get out first, then raced with each other trying not to be the one behind in case they were fired upon again.

Dobb made his way back to the cabin.

Clancy left his hiding place and was on the rock lookout watching those seven running for dear life. Granny Witcher and Tally were hiding near Clancy watching what was going on the best they could. All the shooting got their attention. It was always best to know what was going on.

Suddenly, Tally broke away from Granny Wither and ran to Clancy before Granny Witcher could stop her.

"Clancy," she squealed.

"Sheeee," he tried to hush her as he grabbed her with one arm to clutch her against him, causing him to almost drop the gun he was carrying.

"Come," Granny Witcher whispered as she took hold of both of them and dragged them back into the shelter of the thick underbrush. When she got them far enough away to make sure Dobb couldn't hear their whispers she asked, "What happened?"

Clancy told her. Tally shivered. Granny Witcher only nodded. "They won't get her or you," Granny Witcher told him. "But Dobb caused a big problem. I'm afraid the sheriff will show up if Dobb actually hit somebody instead of just firing a warning shot."

"He got the preacher, maybe some of the others too."

"Ah, law," she grumbled. "If the sheriff shows up to arrest Dobb, they won't stop trying to find Tally. We can't let that happen."

Tally clung to Clancy and looked big eyed toward Granny Witcher.

"I've got an idea," she said. "It's the only thing I can think of for now. Clancy, will you trust me?" she asked.

Clancy didn't know if he could or not, so he didn't answer.

"I trust her. She takes care of me like Momma did," Tally told him.

Clancy looked from Tally to Granny Witcher. "What you got in mind?"

"I want you to take Tally with you and hide somewhere safe. Can you do that?"

Clancy nodded. "Shore I can."

"There's one catch. I'll need to know where you're at, so I can let you know when it's safe to bring her back to me. I can't take a chance on something happening to either one of you."

Clancy shook his head as Tally nodded. "Okay," Tally whispered. "He'll do it," she added.

Granny Witcher nodded. "Give me your word, Clancy, that you won't try to take off with her."

"Do it," Tally said as she looked up at him.

"Okay."

"I'll follow you to where you're going to hide her and yourself. I can't do the job that needs doing until it gets dark."

The three of them took off through the wood. Clancy was going to take them to a cave he sometimes stayed in. A body needed to be like a groundhog. It needed several different holes dug in case it had to escape one of them to hide in another. He had no intention of taking them to his main cave where he had his precious supplies stored.

Granny followed along behind Clancy and Tally. She already knew all the places where Clancy hid out in, or could hide out in, but she had no intention of letting him know. She'd lived in those mountains for over fifty years. She'd hid and helped hide many people many times. She had helped folks much like the way she'd been helped. The difference was that she had stayed in the mountains instead of moving on. She'd had a reason to stay. The man she had fallen in love with was there. Her inside warmed at the memory. Being young and in love was such a wonderful, heaty feeling. That feeling was all-consuming – a young woman's entire world was centered in those feelings.

Now, at her age, much had happened during those years. Lives had begun and lives had ended. Feelings were nothing more than memories – sweet memories.

~~~~

Fury was burning a hole in Dobb's chest. It was more powerful than the pain he was feeling in his arms and legs. The kick from the gun had just about torn his broken arms off. He didn't know for sure who those idiot women were, but he sure enough recognized the men. He knew for a fact they weren't coming after liquor, even though they bought a lot from both

Tucker and him. If women were with them, those better-than-thou were up to no good.

It wasn't exactly like he intended to shoot the preacher. When somebody jerks your door open, you shoot them. It was customary for a buyer of liquor to holler the house to keep from being shot – but this was the preacher and a bunch of women. He'd simply reacted and peppered them with birdshot. He hadn't killed a one of 'em, but that didn't mean they wouldn't claim he attempted murdering them all. The men might not pitch a hissy fit, but he had no doubt those squealing, crazy women would have the sheriff coming after him.

Seemed like he had two choices. Stay there and see what happened, or head out and try to find a place where he could escape, leave those stupid people behind until things cooled down. He had no idea what would happen to him if the sheriff got hold of him. Those women would want to see him strung up to the highest tree. As for the men, hell, they were so pussy-whipped by that bunch of women they would be afraid to go against them, especially if they'd been pricked by a few tiny, harmless birdshot. A few birdshot never killed anybody. It only taught them a bit of respect from sticking their noses in another man's business.

One thing was for sure, if he took off he'd need him some money along with a good supply of liquor to ease his pain. Yep, he decided, that was exactly what he'd do. He'd kill two birds with one stone. He'd get all the liquor he wanted and see if he couldn't find the cash money Tucker kept hid. Dobb knew for a fact that Tucker would never hide his money at his house. He wasn't there enough to watch after it. Money would be much harder to find if it was hidden in the woods near his still or in his shelter. If he couldn't find Tucker's stash, it wouldn't matter. The gun he carried was mighty persuasive. When it came to money or a man's life, there was no question which one he would choose.

Chapter 21

~~Nurse Whitley & Doc Robinson~~

For once, Elouise was sleeping quietly after the doctor sat on the edge of her bed and fed her breakfast – along with giving her medicine. She was taking up as much of his time as he would allow. In the last few weeks, she had progressively gotten more difficult. She would fight them even when she was getting her own way. Elouise thought she was punishing Nurse Whitley by refusing to let her in her bedroom. She didn't realize how happy that made Nurse Whitley. Waiting on that woman was pure hell, to put it mildly.

The doctor thought she was getting worse, but Nurse Whitley disagreed. She was getting much stronger as she flung her arms and kicked her feet. She pointed out to the doctor that she was moving her legs when she had never done that before. The doctor examined her legs and tried to get her to push on his hands with her feet. She would pretend to try as tears filled her eyes. "I can't," she would whimper. "I want to please you, but they won't move. She had never once moved her legs when the doctor was around the way she did was Nurse Whitley was in the room.

Nurse Whitley would turn suddenly and see the intelligence and deviousness flashing in her eyes before she would turn her look into one of helplessness. She had no doubt how much Elouise hated her. To be honest, Nurse Whitley didn't blame her. A woman who had lost her husband's love became bitter. A woman who knew her husband was in love with his wife's nurse became vengeful and dangerous.

The doctor had to use coercion with her. If she didn't take her medicine, he'd leave the room. Most of the time it appeared Elouise hated him, and at the same time, she wanted all his attention. For the last few days, she had been in her irrational mindset. She refused to allow Nurse Whitley to come into her room. If she did, Elouise would start screaming to the top of her lungs. The doctor was giving her more and more laudanum in an effort to keep her calm. It appeared the drug was having less and less effect on her. Thankfully, right now, she was calm.

Nurse Whitley had fixed ham and scrambled eggs for the good doctor and herself. It felt wonderful just to sit across from each other and eat together. The doctor often rushed through a bowl of oatmeal before he attended patients, although he'd checked at daylight to make sure Tucker was still alive. He was the only patient he had in the room he'd started calling his hospital room. Tucker was alive but hadn't come back to himself. He'd fight staying in bed, ripping his stitches out and scraping the scabs off his flesh keeping them bleeding instead of healing. Nurse Whitley had refused to look after him. He was always trying to degrade her with words, or actually trying to physically assault her. When he grabbed the front of her dress ripping the buttons off, the Doc agreed she no longer had to tend to him. Being a nurse didn't mean she had to tolerate being pawed. Doc had been giving him laudanum to keep him quiet instead of so much liquor. The alcohol tended to make him rowdy instead of settling him down.

They heard distant noises they couldn't identify at first. As the noise got louder, it sounded like moaning and crying joined by weak cursing.

"What the . . ." the doctor said as he jumped up and went to the kitchen door. At first, he didn't recognize the group who were hobbling through the yard toward the door of his office.

"Help us! Open the door. We've been shot. Help. Help!"

The doctor forgot all about his food as he and Nurse Whitley rushed through the house to the office room. Doc Robinson didn't believe his eyes. There were seven of them, pushing themselves through the door. The preacher's entire arm was covered in blood. Griff and Walt didn't look to be in too bad condition. He wasn't sure about the women. Their dresses were in rags, their back, hands, and arms speckled with blood. All four women looked like they had been rolled in the damp ground and covered in dirt, leaves, and goodness knew what else.

"He shot us!" Inez was screeching to the top of her lungs.

"Who shot you?" Doc Robinson asked the preacher as he sat him down in the chair. He needed attention far worse than the others.

"Dobb Simmons," the preacher said.

"He tried to kill us all," Ida added.

"Go bring the sheriff," Doc Robinson told Nurse Whitley. "He needs to know what's going on here."

Doc Robinson unwrapped the jacket and strip of material where one of them had tried to bind the preacher's arm and hand. He cut the shirt sleeve from his arm and then used some of Tucker's liquor to rinse some of the blood off, ignoring all the noise coming from the crying women. Griff and Walt stood by silently, watching with their teeth gritted together. He was relieved to find there was more blood than damage. Appeared he'd been shot with number 2 birdshot, which meant there were 87 pellets that could have gone into the preacher's arm. Fortunately, it appeared only a dozen or two hit his arm and hand. The ones that hit his hands were deep. His shirt had provided a little protection but did more harm than good. The pellets had undoubtedly buried bits of material in his flesh. It would take a couple of hours to pick the pellets out and make sure none of the material was left in the holes.

"I'm going to put some salve on your arm and hand to help with the pain, while I check the others out. Who is hurt the worse?"

"Me," Inez jumped in front of the others. "I'm hurting something terrible."

Doc Robinson didn't argue, although he thought she might have been hurt the least according to the blood specks. Her back had taken most of the pellets. Again, there would also be specks of material in her flesh.

"Take off your shirt and I'll start picking the pellets out," Doc Robinson told her.

"Not in front of everybody," she folded her arms across her chest and whimpered.

"Very well. Let me check everyone to make sure all wounds are superficial. Wouldn't want a pellet going into someplace that would kill one of you while I'm working on someone else."

By the time he had checked the other five out, Nurse Whitley had arrived with the sheriff.

All the women started talking to the sheriff at the same time. He held up his hand to silence them.

"Okay. Okay. Hush up. Preacher Hadley, tell me what happened."

The preacher hung his head. "Went to check on the little Simmons girl," he said.

"Why?" the sheriff asked.

"They figured she was left alone up on that mountain since nobody had seen Dobb in a long while."

"And they wanted to put her in their orphanage?" the sheriff asked.

The preacher nodded.

"Then what happened, Walt?"

Walt didn't hesitate. "The women wanted to sneak up on the girl so she couldn't run away. They had the preacher open the door suddenly. When he did, Dobb shot him."

"And the others? How did the rest of you get shot?"

"Runnin' away. He followed us, shooting that double barrel shotgun at us."

"Did any of you holler the house before the preacher opened the door?"

"No. Afraid the girl would run if we did."

"Sounds to me like you rushed in a man's cabin without being invited, or even letting him know who you were, and what you were there for, right?"

Walt nodded.

"He tried to kill us," Beatrice declared. "He chased us through the woods and shot us."

"Anybody tell him who you were."

"Hell no," Griff said. "We were runnin' too fast to stop for small talk."

"Sounds to me like it was your own fault you got shot," the sheriff told them. "You all were not only trespassing on his land, but you also snuck up on his cabin and was breaking in without his permission. Isn't that right."

"No," Ida objected. "That's not true. We wanted to help that pitiful little girl."

"We buried her mother," Beatrice said. "We didn't want to bury her too. Ask the doctor. He can tell you how badly-beaten Sally Simmons was,"

"We couldn't live with ourselves if we didn't rescue that little girl."

"Did you rescue her?"

Beatrice shook her head. "Didn't see her."

"So, all the Good Samaritan trip you women came up with did was to get every last one of your hides filled with what appears to be birdshot. It's a thousand wonders we're not digging seven graves. If he'd used buckshot, we'd have been searching for your bodies."

"But . . ." Inez squawked like a stuck pig.

The sheriff interrupted her. "I've got enough to do without cleaning up the mess you women keep making. Stop it! Leave that little girl alone."

By all the yelling those women did, Doc Robinson thought he might have another man to doctor.

"Preacher, what do you want me to do about this?" the sheriff asked.

Preacher Hadley's face was pale from the loss of blood along with the pain he was feeling. He appeared to be thoughtful for a spell. "Nothing," he finally said. "We had no business barging in there in the first place."

"Appears we got more than we bargained for," Walt added. "Won't make that mistake again. Won't be easy getting the shot up car dragged back here, either."

Talk about angry women, they were cutting a shine.

"Let me know if one of 'um dies," the sheriff told Doc Robinson and went out the door.

"Nurse, gather the supplies and bring them to me. I'll take the preacher into the hospital room to get these pellets out. The others can wait in here."

Doc Robinson took hold of the preacher's uninjured arm and guided him out of the noisy room.

"Women," Doc Robinson mumbled really low like. Love 'em, but they'll be the death of us all."

"Will my arm be normal?" the preacher asked.

"Stiff and painful. Might feel numb for a while, but you don't use it much in preaching. Might need it to fight off Ida and her ideas though."

"Need more than two good arms for that."

"Hang on," Doc Robinson told him. "I need to roll Tucker and his cot out of the room before I start on you. You can lay down on the examining table. Here drink all of this liquor you can get down in case you need the numbing power it gives a man."

"Thanks. Tucker don't look too good."

"Yeah, he's an ugly cuss, all right, but he'll most likely live."

The preacher's brows raised. "He's not dying?"

"Doubt it. Got him doped up so he'll stay still long enough to heal. Got fed up with putting the stitches back in for him to rip them out again."

"Oh," the preacher mumbled. "I ought to say a prayer for Tucker, but right now I'm too busy praying for myself."

"If that no-account sheriff refuses to arrest Dobb Simmons, we'll have to round up some men who have enough guts to take care of him once and for all," Beatrice said.

Nurse Whitley saw Griff and Walt cringe.

"You've got that right. He has to pay for what he's done to us," Ida said. "He could have killed the preacher and us too."

"He danged near killed me," Inez whimpered as though she was the only one who had been injured.

Ellie huddled closer to Walt and never said a word. She was the easiest going of the women and easily led. Beatrice knew Ellie would agree to anything she wanted.

Nurse Whitley left the whimpering and complaining women behind with the men who were trying to sooth their irate wives. They were talking bad of the sheriff for not bringing in Dobb Simmons for a public flogging and then hanging him for trying to murder them. They were claiming they'd see he was not elected again.

Nurse Whitley considered it a blessing not to be elected as sheriff.

Chapter 22

Granny Witcher followed silently behind Dobb Simmons as he limped his way through the woods. Her intent was to remedy the mistake she had made by keeping him alive. It went against her beliefs to take a life, but there were times when it was for the best.

"Sometimes it's necessary for one life to be sacrificed in order for many to live," Lee Gray had told her. "Sometimes it's a necessary occurrence that only I can render."

At first, she wasn't sure where Dobb was going or why. When she realized he was headed toward Tucker's still, she had the answer to why. An alcoholic who had run out of liquor would do just about anything to get it. He had no idea what had happened to Tucker, and probably thought Tucker was still making liquor.

Granny Witcher had not witnessed the donkey dragging Tucker, but she had found the drag trail and figured out what happened. The donkey's hoof prints showed the animal had been running fast. Tucker's body and feet had gouged a streak next to the hoof prints.

She'd even gone so far as to slip jars of salves and bottles of herbs to the doctor's place during the darkest part of night. She'd left the healing medicines on the shelf near where Tucker lay. She had lifted the sheet and examined his injuries. Tucker didn't so much as stir when she poked him with a bony finger. It was evident the doctor was drugging him to keep him from flailing about. She didn't agree with that, although she had done the same with Dobb to keep him still enough for his broken bones to heal. Then again, there were times when not being able to feel pain was more beneficial than anybody ever realized. Too much pain killed.

From what she could tell, Tucker didn't have any broken bones. But she had no say in the care of Tucker. If she was trying to cure him, she would have put him in a tub of Epson salt-water followed up by a good body dusting of sulfur powder, but she wasn't the one who was doctoring him, and she was thankful. She had enough to take care of as things stood.

The big question was what to do about Dobb Simmons. Tally would never be safe with Dobb Simmons living in the cabin. Why hadn't she taken that into more consideration when she was keeping Dobb Simmons alive? She could have allowed him to die much easier than she could kill him now. The only thing Dobb was good for was keeping the selfish women who oversaw the orphanage from coming after Tally. He had done a mighty fine job of it so far. She figured it would be a long time before they came back. Having birdshot picked out of a body's tender flesh stuck in one's memory.

Granny Witcher didn't think the sheriff would take a chance on leaving the safety of the little community to go into the high mountains to arrest Dobb. All he did was pump a little bird shot into people trying to abduct his daughter. There were few and far between people who lived in the mountains. The ones who did live there were the kind you didn't want to mess with, especially when most of them were already hiding out for one reason or another. It was a well-known fact that lawmen who ventured into the mountains, got lost, and were still roaming those mountains trying to find their way out. No one wanted to chance being part of a search party who might never return home.

As for the girl, it would be only a matter of time before Dobb figured out she had Tally at her place. No telling what Dobb would do. He was as sneaky as any wild animal, and far more unpredictable. He had no scruples, no sympathy, no compassion. He thought killing made him superior to what he killed. Like most bullies, he dearly loved to lord it over those more helpless than him.

Dobb went further than that. He longed to destroy everything and anything that crossed him. For years, she had expected Dobb to come after her. Not only had he hated her for giving medicine to Sally, but he also hated her because she existed. So far, Dobb thinking she had some sort of strange powers had kept her safe.

And yet she had saved his life in return for a few gallons of liquor.

Granny Witcher watched as Dobb managed to limp through thick brambles and over and around huge rock cliffs to where Tucker's still was hidden. He searched for a jug of liquor that might have been left behind. He went to a spot in the rocks where Tucker kept a fifth hidden in case it was needed before he got off a run. It was gone. It was the jar Granny Witcher had left at the doctor's place for use on Tucker. She thought it only fitting. When Dobb found there was no reserve supply, he let out a stream of curse words aimed at everyone and everything. He took great offence at not finding what he went after.

His first mistake was kicking the copper pot of the still. It made a loud thumping sound that carried through the woods. Its dull thump echoed from the top of the mountain to down in the gullies. His second mistake was squalling out as he hopped about in pain. The hopping caused his good leg to fly out from under him. He hit the ground and lay there moaning and cursing at the top of his lungs. His third mistake was dropping the gun when he fell and being more concerned with his pain than he was finding the gun and picking it up.

His caterwauling was too loud for him to hear the grunts coming through the woods. Granny Witcher heard them.

"Get up from there," she yelled at Dobb. "Bear's coming!"

He was making too much noise to hear her.

She rushed to where he lay. "Get up! Now! Bear is coming! It'll get here any minute now. Run, run! It's right there behind us."

His cursing increased when he saw her. He picked up a fist size rock and threw at her. It hit her on the arm, doing little harm, but it was enough to aggravate her. She turned and took off at a run as the bear arrived. She'd done her duty by warning him. It wasn't her fault if he didn't listen. She hadn't gotten far when she heard the sound of copper clanging against rocks and roots, more screaming, grunting, and then silence.

She kept on going as fast as she could run. She'd learned years before that a person could not possibly outrun a bear. A person could outrun another person.

She slowed down to a fast walk about halfway from the top of the mountain to Sally's cabin. She'd gone far enough to feel safer, although there was no way to tell what a bear might do. She wasn't afraid of bears or any other wild animal, but she was certainly leery of what they could do to a fragile human. She recalled months of treating Lee Gray from a bear attack before he recovered.

She was breathing hard by the time she reached Sally's cabin, but she couldn't stop to rest. She searched the goat shed until she found a shovel and the ax and started digging a grave beside Sally's in the soft dirt of the garden.

It was almost dark before she was finished digging the grave deep enough for satisfaction. She put the ax and shovel back where she had gotten them from. She made her way to where she had left Clancy and Tally. She wouldn't be at all surprised to find that Clancy had taken Tally elsewhere.

"It's me. Are you in there?" she said a little above a whisper, although she didn't think there would be a hunter or anyone else close enough to hear her.

There were minutes of silence before Clancy appeared without Tally.

"Everything okay?" he asked.

"Bear killed Dobbs," she told him. "Best you and Tally go back to my place. It ain't safe being out here in the open with a mother bear who has just killed a man. She'll be mad at people and might kill again if she comes across another human. That bear found out humans are easy prey."

"What about those church people?"

"I'm taking care of them."

"How?" Clancy demanded.

"I dug a small grave beside Sally's. If that bear leaves any remains behind, I'll bury them in the grave tomorrow along with the girl's clothes. We'll make two crosses with Sally and Tally's names on it. It ought to take care of things, but I don't think those folks will come back, at least not anytime soon. To make sure, we'll roll some big rocks in the road where it starts to climb the mountain. Only hunters will walk that far into the mountain. A bunch of prissy women will be too afraid to walk far. I'll see to it should it become necessary."

Tally moved from the shadows to stand behind Clancy. "Dad is dead?" she questioned in a shaky voice. "You sure?"

"I'm sure," Granny Witcher told her, although she wasn't entirely sure, but from the sounds of his screams until his silence came, it was a safe bet. She would find out for certain come morning. A bear with a full belly would be sleeping it off instead of searching for food. She hoped.

"Take Tally with you. I'll be safe. I've got a gun and ammunition."

"Where did you get a gun and ammunition?"

"Tucker dropped 'em" He wasn't exactly telling a fib. He thought it best not to tell her he'd been to Tucker's place and taken his things. "I figured he wouldn't be needing it as much as I would."

"You know what happened to Tucker?"

He nodded.

"How do you know?" she questioned to see if he'd tell her. She'd seen his tracks along the drag trail, although he'd tried to wipe them out. She ought to take that boy under her wing and teach him how to cover his tracks better, as well as how to appear invisible. Admittedly, he was mighty good for his age, but he was capable of learning more than she had ever come to know.

"Took shelter from the storm and saw the bear scare his donkey and drag him." He saw no reason not to tell her what happened.

"Figured as much," she said. "You covered up the drag trail?"

"Tried."

Tally started to object at Clancy not going with them, but she clamped her teeth together to keep from saying anything. Clancy had been restless, pacing the cave – impatient with her. It was easy to tell he cared about her, but he didn't like the hinderance she caused him. Now that he knew the girl would be safe with Granny Witcher, he had his freedom back.

"Might ought to be extra watchful," Granny Witcher warned him.

"Always watchful," he assured her. "You got a gun?" he questioned. "Can't stop a chargin' bear if you ain't got one."

"I got one." She still had the shotgun Lee Gray gave her years before. She'd never used it, but she kept it oiled up just as he had instructed her to do. She also carried a pistol he'd given her in the waistband of her clothes. She'd had cause to used it a few times.

"Can we stay in the cabin? There is more room than in your place," Tally asked.

Granny Witcher thought about it. "Not tonight," she told her just in case the bear didn't complete the job. "I'll make sure everything is safe tomorrow, and if all is well, you can stay in the cabin."

"By myself?" she asked in a shaky voice.

"I'll be with you," Granny Witcher assured her. "It's best not to leave you alone for a spell"

After Tally had eaten what Granny Witcher had prepared for her, she curled up in the bed and fell asleep right away. It was easy to tell the poor child had been exhausted and afraid. Change was hard on an adult and much worse on a child, but Tally was never a delicate child. In her short life she had learned to survive what landed on her thin little shoulders. A feeling tugged at her that she hadn't felt in years. Granny Witcher had full intention of seeing that girl grow up strong and capable. Something she had not been able to do for her only son.

Granny Witcher longed to go to the still to find out what happened to Dobb, but she hesitated to go out into the dark of night when there was a dangerous mother bear maundering about. The girl should be all right left alone even though she was restless.

No, she couldn't take a chance at this time of going out into the dark of night and leaving the child alone. Finding out what happened to Dobb could wait. What was the hurry anyway? Her knowing wouldn't make a lick of difference to Dobb Simmons. Staying there might make a difference to the girl if she should happen to wake up and find she was alone. She went to the narrow bed and lay down beside her. The even rhythm of the child's breathing and the warmth of her body was a comfort.

Sleep didn't come. Her memory did. The past started rushing back on her when she didn't want it to. She didn't need to remember the past. It was long gone, over and done with. Well, maybe not exactly done with. A woman couldn't change the past regardless of how much she wanted to. Sometimes she couldn't even change the future.

~~~~

Loraine gritted her teeth as Lee Gray rubbed salve on her infected feet. "They're healing," he told her.

"They hurt," she confessed. She wasn't sure how long it had been since they had made it to the cabin. She thought two weeks or more. Her feet had been unbelievably slow to heal. The pain was so bad she hadn't been able to sleep or rest.

"It's to be expected. You're lucky they're not in worse shape considering how infected they had gotten. At least, I think you have a chance to live."

She wasn't entirely sure what to make of his words. She was alive, but how would she live. Her entire life was gone. She could see no future, no happiness, no place for her. As he just said, she was alive for what that was worth. She was beginning to think there were some things worse than death.

"I've been thinking," he said with grave seriousness. "I got a message that I have to go after another runaway, but I don't want to leave you alone. I've arranged for you to stay with some friends of mine."

"A slave?" she questioned. *Runaway* made her think of slavery.

"No. It's been against the law for people to own slaves for many years."

"I know that, but there are such things as free slaves, especially where women are concerned."

"Not a surprise, especially in the more isolated mountains. Stand up. Let's see if you can walk on those feet."

She stood and took a few steps. The pain brought tears to her eyes.

"Not gonna be easy getting you to their place," he told her. "Don't think I can carry you that far. Reckon we'll find out."

Loraine cringed. "I want to stay here," she was surprised at her own words. He didn't seem to be surprised.

"I thought you would, but you can't stay by yourself while I'm gone."

"Why not?"

"It's too dangerous for you to be this isolated in the woods alone. Anything could happen and usually does."

Loraine gave him a bewildered look.

"There's wild animals. Bears, mountain lions, bob cats, and other animals that roam at will. Plus, I have an idea those two men I buried have friends who have discovered their graves by now. Don't know if they'll figure out what happened, but if they do, they might try to find me. Don't want you here alone if they show up."

She didn't want to imagine what would happen if such men were to come upon her again. "Who will I be staying with?"

"Friends," he told her.

"Do they take in runaways?"

"No."

She hated feeling dependent on others, even though she had been totally dependent on her parents as well as Clarence Witcher. Never in her sheltered life had she done anything on her own, unless growing her flowers and making flower arrangements counted. She'd even had help dressing and fixing her hair. She tried to keep emotions from her voice.

"Then why would they be willing to take me in. I have nothing to pay them with." She didn't want to tell him about the few dollars Cooky had given her. It wasn't much, but it might be her salvation someday.

"They owe me,"

She started to ask him what he had done to make them owe him, but he stood up, turned his back on her, and walked out the door.

She sat in the only chair in the tiny, almost empty cabin. There was one chair, a shelf used as a table, a stove, and a narrow bed. So far, she slept on the bed and Lee Gray slept outside. There was one frying pan, one coffee pot, a spoon and a fork whittled out of wood, and a wooden bucket with water in it. As for food, there was a sack of dried beans and a sack of corn meal. He had a smaller sack of salt along with another sack of corn and a tin can of grease with a lid that sealed tight. They had lived on beans and fried corn fritters made from meal and water. Every day, he soaked dried beans in water to soften them up enough to cook fast. He only cooked what they would eat at a sitting. He'd told her the smell of left-over food drew wild animals.

He made a point of bringing foods he'd dug and picked from the woods such as pale, new growth from hemlock trees.

"We need the vitamin c," he told her.

She ate the new growth without hesitation. Its taste wasn't nearly as bad as some of the plants and roots he brought to her. It had a somewhat minty taste to it. He also brought her the bark from willows to chew. He said it would ease her pain, but there was nothing that would ease the hurt inside of her.

"The bark of hemlocks contains a lot of tannin. Comes in handy when tanning animal hides."

Loraine cringed at the thought of animal hides.

"I'm wearing tanned deer hide," he told her. "It makes a soft leather when tanned right. It gives a body more protection than cloth does. Best not to get it wet. It can harden up if you're not watchful."

She didn't want to wear the hides of an animal. She was glad to be wearing the clothes Buck had provided for her. They had been washed in the creek out behind the cabin and dried in the cool mountain air by Lee Gray. Her feet hadn't been in condition for her to stand on them long enough to do much of anything. She had her dress, petticoat and the underwear Cooky called step-ins in her sack. She hadn't worn them.

A week before, he'd brought black cohosh and penny royal herbs and made her a tea to drink. "It'll ease your discomfort," he told her.

At first it hadn't occurred to her that he knew she was having her monthlies. It was the same herbal tea Cooky had made for her, except she had put several spoonsful of honey in the hot tea. Loraine couldn't believe Cooky had thought of her needing such a thing as torn rags during her escape. Loraine wouldn't have thought of such a thing during her rush to save her life. Everything she needed had been provided without thought of where it came from. She had used Cooky's torn rags she kept hidden in her sack.

Lee Gray couldn't have noticed them missing unless he actually searched her sack, which she didn't think he had done.

He must have noticed her reaction to stomach cramping and concluded the cause. But how could he know? He was a man.

It was getting dark by the time he came back. She had already laid down on the narrow bed, but she couldn't fall asleep when he hadn't returned on time.

"Where have you been?" she asked when he came in the door.

"I found someone to take my place," he told her. "Since you won't be able to walk far. I'll forgo this assignment and take the next one."

She wondered where he had gone. She had seen no sign of anyone living close. "Where did you go?" she questioned.

"Over the mountain about fifteen miles from here."

"How?" she questioned. That meant he had traveled thirty miles altogether.

"By foot. I can travel fast when I'm not hindered."

She frowned, not sure she believed him.

"I learned to run fast at an early age. These mountains are crisscrossed with animal trails that are easy to run on if you know where they are. If you don't know these mountains, you can get lost and never be found."

She cringed. The more he told her about the location she was trapped in the more concerned she became. She was in a world she knew nothing about.

"You were a pampered little thing, weren't you?" he said suddenly. "It appears you don't know one single thing about living. Have you ever cooked a meal or washed your own clothes?"

His words almost made her mad, but they were true. "I often watched Cooky do those things. Actually, I was considered well-educated in an intellectual way. We hired others to do the drudgery work."

"Damn. I've been saddled with more of a shrinking violet than I thought. About the only thing you'll ever be able to accomplish is to feed your own face if someone puts the food in front of your nose."

Anger flared in her. Because she had been raised differently from him didn't mean she was not capable of taking care of herself, or at least learning how to do so.

~~~~

A week later her infected feet had healed enough to walk a short distance. She still had salve on her feet and wrapped in rags to keep dirt away from her wounds. She found a broom fashioned out of rough grass tied to a long stick underneath the bed she slept in. She made a point of sweeping the rough-hewed floor, which wasn't an easy or fast job. The moccasins he wore carried a lot of dirt and trash into the cabin even when Lee didn't enter often. She had the feeling he was deliberately staying away from her. The more he was near her, the more he seemed not to like her.

Once she had the floor swept, she decided her feet were good enough for her to take the bucket to the creek to dip up water. She would scrub what few things were in the cabin, and then build a fire in the stove to start the beans cooking. Maybe he wouldn't dislike her so much if she was useful.

Once she had a fire built, which hadn't been easy, she warmed water to bathe and wash her hair in. It had been a long time since she had felt clean. Her body and her hair reminded her of the sweaty smell of Buck's mule she had rode. She had no doubt if Cooky smelled her, she would drag her to the creek behind the cabin and scrub her with sand and then rub her down with mint leaves. Washing in the creek meant being too exposed for her comfort but pushing the table against the door and washing herself felt safe enough. Lee Gray had started leaving the cabin after breakfast and not returning until the evening meal of beans and corn fritters. Oh, how she would love to have a good meal prepared by Cooky, but those days were over. Tears burned her eyes and flooded down her cheeks. Her entire life was as good as over – all because she wasn't able to give Clarence Witcher his much-wanted heir.

When Lee Gray returned to the cabin from wherever he had been, he looked about the cabin seeing all the work she had done. He then looked at her. She had put on clean clothes. She had left her long hair hanging down her back to dry. For a few moments, he simply stared at her until she turned away.

"You've been busy," he finally said as he laid a skinned squirrel down on the shelf that also served as a table. "Boil this until it's tender and then fry it," he told her. "We both need the protein meat provides."

She did her best to prepare the squirrel. She boiled it, put it in a frying pan, and watched him try to eat it. There was no question she hadn't accomplished preparing it correctly.

"You're not eating any?" he questioned.

"I can't." There was no way she could eat one single bite. She kept seeing the skinned, bloody carcass of the poor dead squirrel.

"That's a mistake, but I have to admit I'm finding it difficult myself," he mumbled with a slight shake of his head. "I sacrificed its life for our wellbeing. It would be an abomination not to consume it. You ought to eat some. You'll need strength. We're traveling tomorrow."

"But. . ." she cringed. Her feet were better but not well enough to travel to wherever he was taking her.

"Where to?" she questioned.

"The folks I told you about."

"To the people who owe you."

"Yeah."

"My feet . . ."

"I've made you soft moccasins. You'll be able to walk easier in them."

She doubted it.

The moccasins were soft leather with something fluffy on the inside of them. They were more comfortable than the hard, unforgiving boots Buck had given her to wear, but wearing them was still painful. They pressed on her blisters even when she had put salve on her feet and then wrapped them in rags.

The black sky had lightened to grayness when Lee Gray picked up her sack containing all she owned and placed it beside her. He had wrapped her feet himself and put the moccasins on her feet.

"They fit just about right," he told her. "Day is breaking. Let's get started."

Loraine cringed as she limped out the door. She heard him shut the door behind them. How was she possibly going to be able to climb up a mountain and down the other side to reach their destination? Fifteen miles was a long way, but not nearly as far as she had already traveled. He made a slight noise as he moved away a little ways from her.

"I've got him harnessed and ready to go. He appears right calm." Lee said more to himself than to her.

She heard a dragging sound along with an odd bleating. Only the sky had a little morning light showing. On the ground under the trees it was still pitch dark. She couldn't see what Lee had led beside her.

"Move slow and get on it."

"Get on what?" she questioned.

"The travois. Sit down in the middle and then stretch your legs out. You can sit or lay back. Whichever you find more comfortable."

"What's a travois?" She wasn't about to get on something when she didn't know what it was.

"My people used it for those who were unable to walk, along with carrying heavy loads."

She hesitantly moved a step closer the animal and stopped in her tracks. "It stinks something terrible," she told him. Did he really expect her to sit on that animal?

"You'll get used to the smell – somewhat," he added with a touch of humor.

"Is it dangerous?"

"Not much. I'll be leading him."

She could almost see the darker outline of an animal that stood a little above the man's waist. She took a long, determined breath. She supposed riding anything was better than walking on her tender feet. One thing was for certain, she didn't want her feet to get all that infection in them again.

"How do I get on that animal? Is there a saddle."

"Get on what animal?"

"That stinking travois."

Lee Gray was silent for a minute. A slight chuckle escaped before he silenced it.

"This is Big Bill. He's a billy goat that's been trained to pull a travois. A travois is a kind of sled, but it's made out of thin locust poles and a tanned deer hide. It's light weight and fairly easy to pull. I borrowed the goat and travois last night from Rodney Freeman. Rodney uses him to pull heavy loads he can't carry."

"Oh. Okay," she mumbled, feeling slightly embarrassed and greatly relieved.

"There will be places where you'll have to walk. Big Bill can only pull you where the path is good. He can't pull you over steep rocky ground. He isn't as strong as a donkey, but he is powerful for his size and used to hauling firewood. You'll have to walk over to the travois and sit down on it. If I turn loose of Big Bill, he'll take off running. He doesn't like being away from home."

She walked over to the travois until her leg bumped a pole, did her best to determine the center of it, stepped one foot onto what she thought was the center, and then the other foot. She carefully sat down and placed her hands on each side gripping the poles.

"Scoot up. Your butt is where your feet are supposed to be. A travois is designed for only the tips of the poles to touch the ground. You best save your feet on the down hillslopes. You'll have to walk uphill. Bill won't be able to pull you," he told her again.

She did as she was instructed, not sure about anything – other than she had been foolish to let Cooky and Buck save her life by putting her in this kind of a situation. Surely, she could have disappeared into a more suitable kind of existence, or possibly fed Clarence Witcher a deadly dose of his own poison. Why hadn't she thought of that solution? Being a murderer was more appealing than what she was going through. This was a painful, primitive kind of survival. Never in her wildest dreams would she have believed she would be lying on a deer hide being pulled by a billy goat led by a half-breed Indian.

Lee led the goat forward and the travois bumped along. She felt tears sliding down her cheeks and did her best to stop feeling sorry for herself. Somehow, from somewhere, she would have to find enough grit to continue with whatever life threw at her. It appeared she had no choice if she was to remain alive.

They had traveled for what she thought was an hour or perhaps two, which felt to her more like days than hours. The ground was starting to rise upward slightly, and the goat was straining to pull harder. The sky was now light and the darkness on the ground had faded to blue shadows. Squirrels were chattering and birds flew from tree. Small animals scurried in the undergrowth. The goat snorted, stopped, and reared on his hind legs.

"Should I walk?" she questioned.

"Quiet," he whispered, as his hand tightened on the goat's lead, while he lifted his shotgun with the other hand and looked about.

She was silent, but the goat wasn't. He reared and jerked the travois as he tried to get free from Lee's hold. Lee didn't turn loose, but it was taking all his strength and attention to control Big Bill. She wasn't sure if Lee saw the bear before it charged. It came out of the undergrowth with a raging growl that filled the air a split moment before the shotgun fired one barrel and then the other. The bear lifted up on his hind feet but didn't stop its charge. It slammed its body into Lee. He had turned loose of Big Bill as he along with the bear went down on the ground rolling over and over. The next instant she was tumbling downhill over rocks and brush until she landed against the trunk of a tree. She only heard the sound of Big Bill and the travois going through the underbrush at a fast run.

She clung to the tree as she got to her feet. She didn't know if she should try to climb the tree, run away as fast as she could, or attempt to help Lee. She saw a quart sized rock, grabbed it in her hand and limped toward Lee and the bear. The bear was making a grunting, gurgling sound as all four of its feet jerked and kicked. She threw the rock at it with all her strength, grabbed another rock and threw it.

"Don't bother. It's done for," came breathless words that brought more relief than Loraine thought possible. Lee hadn't been killed.

Loraine saw him crawling away from the bear, making sure he was staying out of the reach of the claws on its jerking feet.

"I killed him, but he was too close for me to dodge its charge. It mauled me some. Got to stop the bleeding long enough for it to clot. Can you rip up your shirt and tie a tourniquet on my arm and leg. We've got to get back to the cabin before my adrenaline wears off and weakness sets in."

She took her shirt off and ripped it into long rags, and then helped him get his leather shirt off.

"Glad it was leather. Helped a little against its claws. See, I told you leather is a good thing. Did you know a bear continues to charge after it is dead? Put the tourniquet above the wound and then wrap the clawed gashes as tight as you can."

She did the best she could with his arm. It slowed the bleeding but didn't stop it.

"Now, for my leg."

She helped him get his injured leg out of the leather britches.

"Your sack," he said, and pointed. "It's over there."

Sure enough, she had been holding her sack of belongings on the travois. It had been thrown off near Lee. She grabbed it and pulled out the rags Cooky had torn for her. They were long enough strips to bind his heavily muscled legs. Thankfully, the gashes weren't as deep as the ones on his arm, but they were bleeding.

He was able to bind and wrap his leg himself with Loraine handing him rags.

"How are we going to get back to the cabin?" she asked him in a trembling voice. "We can't stay here. All the blood could draw more dangerous animals."

"I can still walk. Do you think you can?"

"I think so, but won't walking make you bleed more?"

"Probably, but we don't have a choice. Do you see my shotgun?"

Loraine looked and saw the stock of the gun sticking from under the bear. It's kicking feet had rolled it in the dirt and blood. "It's next to the bear."

"Get it," he told her.

"The bear . . ."

"It is no longer kicking. It won't hurt you."

She limped toward the bear. A fresh layer of sweat broke out on her face and trickled down her neck, but she continued on until she was close enough to grab the gun. She was surprised at how heavy it was as she pulled it away from the bear. The smell of blood and feces were strong enough to make her gag, not to mention the way the dead animal looked laying there in its own pool of blood.

When she got back to Lee, he had his pants and shirt back on and was on his feet with a limb of deadfall in his good hand to use as a cane. There was a look of determination on his face.

"Can you carry the gun? I might ought to load it. Have you ever shot a gun?"

"No."

"I was afraid of that. Oh, well. I've got a loaded pistol. Let's hope it won't be needed. Have to admit I hadn't expected that bear. Hadn't seen any bears in this neck of the woods in a coon's age. Don't know where it came from. Must have been hunters chasing it. Might as well get started."

They both did rather well at walking until they came to where the ground got steep. What was good downhill traveling with the goat and travois turned into uphill misery. Every step they now took sapped a little more of their strength. Lee was growing paler by the minute. The leg of his britches had turned reddish-brown with blood and so had his arm. At least his arm didn't appear to be bleeding as much as his leg even though his arm wounds were deeper. Using his leg was causing it to bleed faster.

"How much blood can you lose without it hurting you?" she asked when they stopped to rest.

"I'm okay," he assured her. "Blood spreads. Looks like I'm losing more than I am."

Sounded good, but she didn't believe him. Even his moccasin had turned red and was squishing as he walked.

"How much farther?" she asked, hoping he would tell her it wasn't far.

"We're about halfway there. Are your feet bothering you?"

"Not much," she lied. The pain was enough to make her want to cry like a baby, but she wasn't about to give in to her pain. She wasn't bleeding to death the way Lee was doing. "Let's go, if you can manage." She had no idea what she would do if something happened to him.

Their progress got slower and slower. She feared Lee was slowing down because of her.

"Got any more clothes in that sack of yours I can tie around my leg? I need to put more pressure on the wound," he asked as he sat down on a log not far from where they had rested before.

She dumped out the contents of her sack and watched as he went through her meager possessions. She cringed when he used her once beautiful dress to bind his leg. It was the last connection she had with her previous life, but what did a dress matter? His very life was draining out of him without her being able to stop it. She made a promise to herself right then, if they survived, she would learn how to save lives instead of being helpless while watching life fade away.

"You be hurt bad?" A man's voice asked only a few feet from them.

Loraine let out a startled sound. A man appeared to separate from the huge trunk of a tree. He was every bit as large as Lee, with black platted hair, deeply tanned skin, and leather clothes almost identical to Lee's. He carried a shotgun in his hand. The barrel rested on his arm and was pointed toward the ground. Lee's hand almost reached for his pistol but stopped, when he saw who it was.

"Bad enough," Lee answered. "Where'd you come from, Rod?"

"Been trackin' a mean bear. Broke into the corn crib and clawed one of my dogs when they tried to run him off. Saw back there where you got him."

"He got me too."

"Yeap, tracked your blood trail." He glanced at Loraine but said nothing to her as he turned to Lee. "Let's have a look at you."

"We bound my leg and arm. Helped the bleedin' some," Lee told him.

"Humph," he grunted as he unwound the dress and stripped the leather britches off Lee's legs. He tied a tourniquet above the gashes on Lee's leg before he unwrapped the rags Cooky had provided. He grunted some more and took a leather pouch from inside his shirt. He sprinkled an abundant mixture of white and grayish-green powder in the leg wounds before he rewrapped them slightly tighter than Loraine and Lee had.

"What did you put on his leg?" Loraine couldn't stop herself from asking. She wanted to know what it took to stop the bleeding.

"It be powdered yarrow, corn starch, baking powder, alum and tads of other stuff. I tote a pouch-full with me just in case. In these woods, a man never knows when he'll need it."

She watched as he packed it on thick and rebound the wounds. He loosened the tourniquet slowly until she saw blood wet the bandages, then he tightened the tourniquet slightly.

"Don't pay to cut all the blood off from a body part for long. Kills it if you do," he told her as he helped Lee get his pants back on. "Let's see to your arm."

"No need. It'll do till we get to the cabin. I'm gettin' right weak."

"I'd say so. Don't reckon I can tote all your weight, but I can take most of it if you're able to hobble." He looked toward Loraine.

"She can't help none," Lee answered his look. "Infected feet. Can hardly walk."

"Where's Big Bill?" he asked as he lifted Lee to his feet.

"Most likely at your place by now. Bear scared the piss outta him."

"Reckon so. Lean all the weight you can on me." He had one arm around Lee's waist and his gun in the other hand. He didn't ask her to carry it as Lee had done. She was beginning to see the necessity of carrying a weapon at all times. Neither Lee nor she would be alive right now if Lee hadn't had his gun at ready.

The sun was going down by the time they reached the cabin. They'd had to stop to rest more times than she could count. She felt fresh tears sting her eyes when she saw the familiar sight, and this time it was from relief instead of pain.

The man laid Lee on the narrow bed and stripped his shirt and britches off. He found a jug on the floor underneath the shelf, uncorked it and held it to Lee's mouth as he helped him to raise up.

"Drink all you can stand. You need it."

Lee drank, coughed, and then drank some more. Rod turned the jug up and soaked the rags wrapping Lee's arm, then did the same to his leg.

"Gotta kill the bad stuff. Bears have lots of bad shit on their claws. If he's lucky, all that bleeding washed the worst of it outta the gouges. Now, let's have a look at your feet. You limped worse than Gray Leaf."

"Gray Leaf?" she questioned.

"Him," he said as he nodded toward Lee.

"Lee?"

"His name's Gray Leaf. Only white folks and strangers call him Lee."

Guess that told her where she stood with him. She was white and a stranger.

"Will he live?"

"Yeap. He's been in a whole lot worse shape. Take off those moccasins."

She hesitated for a moment and then reached for Lee's moccasins.

"Not his. Yourn."

She hesitated for a moment, but finally gritted her teeth and slipped them off her aching feet. Most all the soft stuff Lee had padded her moccasins with was now stuck to her oozing feet. Without saying a word, the man quickly poured the liquor on both her feet.

She let out a yelp as the liquor burned like liquid fire.

"You're a timid thing, all right," he informed her unnecessarily. "Sit down in that chair. I'll hand you salve to rub on 'em. Pick all that cattail fluff off while you're at it."

He turned toward Lee. "I slit that bear's throat to bleed him, but your shotgun blasts oughta done a right good job of it. I'll head back and slice off a ham and tote it back. You'll need some good eatin' to get your strength back."

Lee only grunted.

"Fetch me some water," Lee told her once the man was gone.

She got a dipper of luke-warm water out of the bucket. He lifted his upper body on his elbows as she held the dipper to his mouth.

"More?" she offered after he drank it all.

"No. Don't want it to make me sick. Ought to go slow and easy on most things."

"Are you in much pain?"

"Yeah. You?"

"Me too. Will you die?" She asked what she was fearing. She didn't want him to die any more than she wanted him to leave her with his friends.

"I'm not planning on it. At least not any time soon."

"You look terrible. You've turned white."

"I prefer being a redskin," he tried to smile but failed.

She preferred being who she was as well, and then, a moment later, thought better of it. She certainly didn't want to be Mrs. Clarence Witcher. She wasn't even sure Loraine Carter was who she wanted to be.

Chapter 23

~~Dobb Simmons~~

Dobb Simmons was in a rage when his eyes opened enough to see the witch woman looking down at him. She was yelling things at him in such a fast voice that he couldn't make out her words. Must be some kind of curse. Whatever it was, he wasn't going to let her get away with it. He picked up a rock and flung it at her. She took off running like a scared rabbit.

His hand felt the gun he had dropped, he clutched it as he stumbled to his feet. A noise sounded behind him. He couldn't believe his own eyes. Never, in all his years roaming the woods, had he come face to face with an angry bear. The few he had seen showed him their hind ends in a fast trot to get away. The smell of humans was enough for them to turn tail and make a run for it. As a rule, they were more afraid of people than people were afraid of them. What was it that made this bear different? It was then he saw two cubs climbing a tree. He was too close to the tree for the mother bear's comfort. The she-bear had most likely lit out from a different mountain to protect her cubs. Boar bears were bad to kill cubs in hopes it would cause the females to come back in heat sooner.

What the hell was a crippled man supposed to do? The mother bear had seen him and was standing on her hind feet, grunting her fury at coming upon him. No doubt the smell of mash drew her. He couldn't outrun her or outclimb her. His only choice was to outsmart her or shoot her. He lifted the gun and fired without having time to take aim.

The bear was charging, but not straight on. It charged at an angle causing the pellets to peel streaks of skin and hair off its shoulder instead of penetrating its heart as Dobb had intended.

Pure fear intensified Dobb's vision. The bear was close enough for him to smell the stink and see the hair and flesh that had peeled back as red blood oozed from raw muscles. The bear was now charging straight at him. Dobb screamed in fear, dropped to the ground and rolled toward the still. The bear's charge was spurred onward with such fury and speed only its hind feet clawed Dobb as its tremendous weight caused it to overshoot his body. Dobb rolled with all the strength he had left, hoping he could get under the still before the bear whirled and hit him again.

Bears have excellent sight and can detect the slightest movement. Their sense of smell is more powerful than other animals, plus they can run faster than any horse. Dobb knew he was a dead man as he made his body lodge under the mash pot a moment before the bear whirled and charged again, hitting the pot with four hundred pounds of fury. The pot broke loose and rolled. Dobb rolled with it, screaming at the top of his lungs. The copper coil had wrapped around the bears front leg making the bear stop long enough to fight its legs free instead of going after the rolling pot. By the time the bear had flung the coil loose, the pot had jumped the creek and was tumbling down the hill. Dobb had landed in the middle of the creek. He flattened himself out and hoped the water was deep enough to give him some cover.

It worked. The bear saw the bouncing movement of the pot and heard the noise made by the pot hitting rocks and roots. She went after the tumbling pot instead of going into the water where Dobb was hiding. Dobb had no idea how he managed to get to his feet and make a run for it, but he did. He was running in the opposite direction the bear was going as fast as he could go. He had no idea how much time he had before the bear returned – but return she would. He'd best get a long ways from there in a hurry. Her cubs were up a tree, and he was still alive but in danger for his life. He no longer had his gun or his crutch, but he sure as hell wasn't taking time to search for either. Fear had a way of driving a crippled man onward at an inhuman speed.

He had no idea how long or how far he ran. He'd gone over the crest of the hill and down into a steep gully where he continued to run downhill until he came to another stream of water. He ran into it, tripped on a slick rock, and fell in the water. The cold water felt good on his hot, sweating skin. He lowered his face and swallowed several mouths full of icy water before he heaved in more oxygen in his lungs. He noticed the water flowing around him was an odd color. It had turned a pale shade of red. He been running so fast and hard he hadn't noticed his clothes were covered in blood – his blood. Damned if that bear hadn't mauled him and he hadn't felt a thing.

Chapter 24

~~Dr. Robinson~~Nurse Whitley~~

"It's time to wean him off the pain medication. Liquor is bad enough. Don't need to get him hooked on cocaine too," Dr. Robinson told Nurse Whitley. "It's time for him to get on his feet and move about."

"Fine, but don't expect me to take care of him. I'll not do it regardless of how you try to trick me into it."

"Why not? It's obvious the man adores you."

"Adores isn't the word I'd use. He leers at me. I can't stand it – and …," she added with a firmness Dr. Robinson had learned meant there was no arguing with. "I will not, I repeat, will not be the one to take care of him."

"If you don't take care of him, who will?" Dr. Robinson asked her in hopes she would change her mind, although he knew it was hopeless

"Inez Williams," she said suddenly, surprising herself as well as him.

Dr. Robinson's brows raised in surprise, and then furrowed in consideration. "Why would she do something like that?"

"Money."

"Money?" Dr. Robinson questioned.

"Sure. As much liquor as he sells, he's got to have money. Cash money stashed away somewhere."

Dr. Robinson thought about it for a minute. "It's possible," he concluded. "He sells enough liquor to have a little saved."

"When he comes to himself, ask him if he's willing to pay Inez to take care of him. They said her husband left her years ago, and it's obvious she has a liking for money – as well as

218

other things," Nurse Whitley said snidely, causing the doctor to stifle a grin.

"Other things?" Dr. Robinson couldn't resist questioning, even though he knew what she was referring to.

"You know as well as I do what she does for a living."

"I thought she did it for pleasure," the doctor said with twinkle in his eyes.

Nurse Whitley was obviously irritated at his attempted humor. "I was referring to her bootlegging Tucker's liquor. If he were to die, she would lose one of her sources of making a living."

"I see. So, my dear, you weren't referring to her overtime on the weekends at Ben Orson's feed and seed store."

"No," she told him firmly.

He chuckled softly to himself. Women thought it was their duty to crucify other women for getting paid for doing the same thing a married woman did for free. He supposed it was because married women claimed doing such was their duty, while single women did it for money. As a doctor, he often got to know the entire story including who, why, when and what was going on. One thing was for certain, his nurse shouldn't condemn any woman for such behavior.

He should feel guilty for opening his nurse up to such degradation of character along with opening her up to gossip, but he didn't. He didn't regret one moment of private time he and Valarie spent together. In a world where all he did was listen to the ills and complaints of sick and hypochondriac people, a few minutes of his very own pleasure was what kept him going.

Did he also feel guilty about having an invalid wife in another room while he was making love to a different woman? Perhaps in the beginning, but time had a way of making the most vile of deeds seem normal. His question, and justification, was why did a man have to be punished for the rest of his life because of another person's accident? One he had not been responsible for.

Elouise had always been a hard-headed woman who indulged in exactly what she wanted without regard to anyone else. He had always expected she married him only because he was a doctor. It didn't take him long to discovered Elouise had love only for herself.

"You need to check with Inez about looking after Tucker. It's time for him to be moved to his own home. He'll need someone to look after him for a while," she repeated to make sure the doctor was hearing her.

"You sure you don't want the job? The doctor couldn't resist a final tease, which was something he seldom allowed himself to indulge in.

"Are you suggesting Inez would be more suited to be Elouise's nurse than I am?"

"My dear, I wouldn't trade you as Elouise's nurse for all the gold in California. I wouldn't even trade you for anything or anybody. You've been my salvation and you still are. I'll check with Inez just as soon as Tucker comes around and is willing to pay her."

"I've got an idea," Nurse Whitley said. "Why don't you talk to the preacher. Have him put a bee in Ida's bonnet about getting Inez to care for Tucker. Convince him that Inez needs a decent job and Tucker needs a nursemaid."

"You've got a point there. Those women can be convincing. It could work out for the best."

Dr. Robinson reached out and pulled his nurse to him. She slipped her arms around his waist as his mouth met hers. His mouth tasted like the liquor smelled that she had been pouring over Tucker's wounds. Hers tasted kind of minty, like the peppermint tea she was always drinking. She grew all kinds of herbs as well as flowers in her garden. She'd even started growing her own vegetables instead of using the produce his patients paid him in trade for his services.

"Why do you bother growing your own vegetables when we get more than we can possibly use?" The doctor asked once she took her mouth away from his.

"Remember when I rode with you to deliver the Waltrip woman's twins?"

He did.

"Her husband paid you with vegetables."

"Right."

"I went with him to the garden to hold the sack while he dug potatoes. There were pieces of paper sticking out of the ground everywhere. I could tell the paper was pieces of a Montgomery Ward catalogue. I asked him why those pieces of paper were all through the garden. He told me everybody used the catalogue in their outdoor toilets. He then added every spring, when the toilets were filled up, folks shoveled them out and used the manure to fertilize their gardens."

"Not everyone does such as that," he assured her. "Most folks use it on the field corn they feed to their milk cows."

"And that's why I grow my own vegetables," she told him.

Dr. Robinson was smiling happily as he allowed her to move from his arms. "Want to get away from Tucker's snoring and find us a nice, secluded spot?"

"Where?" she whispered as her lips touched the soft spot in his neck where his beard didn't grow.

"In the storage room. Tucker won't come around for a while."

"I'll lock the doors," she whispered in the tone of voice he loved to hear.

~~~~

Tucker wasn't exactly conscious. He was somewhere way off in his mind. He knew he wasn't awake, and at the same time, he realized he wasn't exactly asleep. He was again hearing the same sounds that haunted his nightmares for the past several years. It was sounds he would never get over hearing regardless how long it had been or how long he lived. It was such nightmare sounds that caused his mind a lot more pain than his body would ever be forced to endure.

The sounds were soft at first, and oh so very familiar. There was heavy breathing, moaning, the rhythmic cadence of grunts and groans. The soft sounds went on for what seemed forever before they grew in intensity. Finally, the sounds reached an almost painful existence. Then came ohhs and awws of relief – of pleasure beyond words.

His drug-induced stupor cast his mind back in time until he once again stood in the doorway long enough to determine where the sounds came from. He ran through the living room to the bedroom door and jerked the door open fearing what he would find.

Sight was worse than sounds.

His mind wasn't prepared for what he saw. The hurt inside him shot upward until it was beyond endurance – beyond every kind of hurt he had ever experienced.

He hadn't expected his own reaction, never thought he had such in him. The calm, easygoing man he'd always been turned into a crazed demon. He hadn't realized he'd moved or grabbed the handle of a dresser drawer, pulling it out, dumping things on the floor. He didn't even realize he'd crossed the bedroom floor until he'd cracked the corner of the wooden dresser drawer against the head that had been lifted to look at him. The surprise of shock at seeing him standing in the bedroom had lasted only a second before his brother rolled off Tucker's wife.

The dresser drawer hadn't stopped its movement, although Tucker had intended it to stop. It hit his wife in the face. Blood squirted from her now broken nose. He drew the drawer back to hit her again.

"No," she screeched. "Stop! Don't kill me."

The crazed demon stopped, frozen, staring at his wife and then at his brother lying on the floor. Tucker was breathing hard, his breath heaving in and out as though he'd run miles without stopping.

"Why?" he whined out. "Why would you do a thing such as this to me?"

He had no idea how long it took – how long he stood there holding the drawer handle as tears ran down his cheeks. It seemed like a lifetime, but it could have only been moments.

His wife had her hand over her bloody nose as she jumped out of bed naked. She stepped over his brother and ran out of the bedroom. Tucker stared at his brother, the man he'd loved almost as much as he'd loved his wife. The brother who surely hated him to do what he had done.

Something happened to Tucker. His entire body trembled and then froze. His teeth were chattering, but thankfully, for some unknown reason, he felt nothing. No hurt; no anger; no hope. He walked out of the bedroom and then out of the house.

The sun had gone down, and the gloaming had set in by the time Tucker came to himself and realized what his brother and wife had been doing - and what he'd done to them because of it. He hadn't planned on attacking the two people he loved, but he had.

He was wet with sweat while he felt freezing cold when the question of what he was going to do about the horrible situation entered his mind. What choices did he have now? What did a man do about a cheating wife and a lowdown, no-account brother?

How could he face the humiliation of having every single person in the area know his own brother had been shucking his corn behind his back? The shame of it hit Tucker hard. He'd rather shoot himself through the heart than have people look at him and know he hadn't been able to keep his wife satisfied. How did a man live after his life's dream had ended?

~~~~

Tucker harnessed his donkey, hooked him to the sled and headed into the woods. He didn't know where he was going or why. He had to go, had to get as far away from his home, his wife, and his brother as he could get. There was nothing on his sled to take to his still and nothing to bring back. His body was simply doing what he had done many times before.

The angry dark sky of night was turning the blood red of morning by the time Tucker led his donkey back to his house. He unhitched his donkey and turned him into the pasture to graze and drink water. He left his sled where it had always been and forced himself to go back inside the house.

The house was empty. Neither his brother nor his wife were there. He couldn't stop himself from going into the bedroom, the room where he and his wife had shared thousands of nights making love. Those times were ruined, destroyed forever. Blood was on the floor where the drawer had split a gash in his brother's head. Blood was on the bed sheets where his wife's nose had bled. He stripped the bed to its springs, including the sagging mattress and took the material outside to his burn pile and struck a match to it. He piled on brush and went back inside. It took all day and gallons of soapy water, rag-mop, and brush to scrub away the blood stains that had sunk into the wood of the floor. He used salt, vinegar, and baking soda in an attempt to scrub away those stains, but the images were forever tattooed in his brain.

The gloaming was setting in again by the time the preacher showed up.

"What're you burning, Tucker? I've smelled your smoke since morning."

"Mattress and bed clothes," he told the truth.

"Why would you do a thing like that?"

"My wife," he stammered as he fought tears. "She left me. No way can I stand to sleep in the bed we shared. It'd hurts too much."

"So, you burned it?" the preacher said as he looked away from Tucker's tortured face. Everybody knew how much Tucker loved that wife of his. He danged near worshiped her, while everybody in the community knew what kind of woman she was, as well as what she did with Tucker's brother when Tucker was doing his thing in the high mountains.

"I burned it," Tucker repeated the words.

It was the preacher who told Ida, and she spread the story about Tucker's wife running off with Tucker's brother.

It went to show because things didn't go the way Tucker planned, didn't mean they hadn't gone the way they should.

~~~~

"Holy shit!" Tucker let out a squall of pain. "Why the hell did you set me on fire?"

"Because you know how to distill damn near 180 proof," Dr. Robinson answered with a grin. "Keeps down infections. Do you remember what happened to you, or did you get what little sense you had knocked out of you when you got that pump knot on your head?"

"Unfortunately, I remember and in a most painful way. And you're not helping the pain go away," Tucker told him, ignoring the doctor's slur without coming back with his usual banter. He wasn't feeling up to it yet. If that pretty little nurse was here instead of the Doc, she would perk him up – make his pain worth bearing.

"Just so you know, I've helped ease your pain a great deal. I saw that you slept for a few days. Sleep cures. Pain kills."

"Where is your pretty little nurse? Life was bearable as long as she was rubbin' salve on me."

"You made too many passes at her."

"I did? Never knew there was such a thing as too many."

"One was too many for her. Now, you're faced with a decision you'll need to make. You can't stay here any longer. I need the space for people worse off than you are. But, if I let you go home, you'll need someone to take care of you for the next week or two while your skin grows back."

"Tell your nurse I won't make too many passes at her from now on."

"Too late. You'll have to lust after someone else."

"Keepin' her for yourself, humm?"

"A man should always keep the best for himself when he can. I was thinking you might hire Inez Williams as a caretaker for the next few days. Do you have enough money to pay her, or do I need to give you a loan until you can get back on your feet and repay me with more of that super one-eighty proof. That stuff can burn hair off a hog's back."

"A little strong for women and children, but just right for a real man," Tucker told him.

"No doubt about that. Now what about Inez?"

"I'll take a loan from you," Tucker was quick to say even though he had the money. If he owed the doctor, he'd work harder to keep him alive. As for Inez, that woman reminded him of the perfect example of a broad-assed witch with a long-hooked nose, but he'd be willing to dance with the devil himself if it meant getting well a day faster.

"I talked it over with the preacher and he put the proposal to Inez. She reluctantly agreed after he upped the price twice."

"Money . . . the real way to a woman's heart," Tucker laughed – and the laugh hurt like the fires of hell.

"Broken ribs hurt, don't they," the Doc said as he saw Tucker's facial expression.

"At least I've still got my good looks," Tucker said.

"Wouldn't go that far."

Chapter 25

~~Granny Witcher~~Tally~~Clancy~~

Tally woke up with a sad look on her face.

"What's ailin' you this morning, chile?" Granny Witcher asked.

"Been dreamin' 'bout Momma."

"Don't fret about her none, chile. Just think how happy she is up in heaven with Billy and her little baby. They've no longer got a troubled moment to live through."

Granny Witcher believed when you dreamed about a dead person it was actually a vision. That person was paying you a visit, but she didn't think it would help telling the girl such as that at this time.

"If Dad was killed by that bear, won't he be up there bothering them?" Tally asked with a deep frown between her brows.

"Nope," Granny Witcher told her firmly. "Don't reckon men such as Dobb Simmons will be going in that direction."

"You don't think God forgave him for being so mean?" Tally asked in a meek voice, her chin trembling slightly.

"Don't think he ever asked God for forgiveness. I'm thinking he liked the way he was and didn't want to change."

Tally frowned. "Is that Momma bear still out there?"

Granny Witcher thought on it a while. "Yeah, I'd say it's still hanging around being it got Tucker some time ago and then got Dobb."

"Would it be safe for us to go make sure he's dead?" Tally asked hesitantly

"No, not for a while yet." She wasn't about to put the girl in danger. She wouldn't be going to search for herbs for a while either.

"Then we won't know for sure, will we?" Tally reasoned beyond a child her age.

"If he don't come back, we'll know." But they wouldn't know for certain without finding his dead body. Granny Witcher figured the bear would move on in time. A wild animal wouldn't like encountering people especially when the safety of her cubs could be at risk. Since Tucker's bear encounter, there wouldn't be any mash to draw the bear, at least not for a while. She wanted to go find out what fate happened to Dobb Simmons for herself, but she didn't dare go during the dark of night while the girl was asleep, and she had no intention of taking the girl with her. It would be too risky.

The girl was a hinderance in Granny Witcher getting out and about, although she was a welcomed hinderance. After years of being able to do exactly what she wanted and going exactly when and where she wanted, she found it necessary to consider the girl and her needs first – but that was as it should be. It was the job of adults to protect and raise children. She'd done that with her boy, and she intended to do it with the girl. The difference was this time she wouldn't make the same mistakes.

Sally and Billy had been living their life and raising their children the way they should until Billy died. Granny Witcher wasn't exactly sure where Dobb Simmons came from. She was now sure he had been the worst thing that could have happened to Sally. If only she had known what Dobb Simmons had been up to before it was too late, she might have stopped a lot of misery and saved Sally's life. Instead, she had left them alone to work out their own lives. She didn't think it was her place to interfere where she wasn't wanted, but it didn't stop her from having harsh unchristian thoughts. Many times, it crossed Granny Witcher's mind how easy it would be to put

Dobb Simmons in a shallow grave, but she'd been unable to take his life, or anyone's life. She wanted to save lives.

She had mistakenly thought Sally needed a man to help with all the work it took to raise a daughter and three boys on the rugged mountain. She knew all too well how difficult it was for a lone woman to survive. During the few times Sally had made contact with Granny Witcher, Sally made sure she didn't let her know how Dobb treated her and the children. In the past few years, Sally had all but stopped seeking any contact with her.

~~~~

Granny Witcher also knew what it would take for a man to survive a bear attack. It wasn't only the deep wounds that ripped the flesh open or the amount of blood loss that was life threatening. It was the infection those dirty claws dumped into the wounds that neither liquor nor herbs could counter their effects. Fortunately, Lee had been a strong and determined man. He had true friends in Rodney and Delia Freeman. They took turns staying with her and Lee for five days. Delia made a point of teaching Loraine Witcher what she thought she needed to know about Cherokee medicine along with what Delia had learned on her own.

"Gray Leaf is a fine man," Delia told her. "He's a tough man, a righteous man." Delia said a lot in a few words. "He risked his life for you. Now, you take care of him."

She intended to take care of him the best way she could. "I don't know what to do," she confessed. "I'm dumb in such matters."

"Not dumb. Unlearned," Delia told her matter of fact. "I'll teach you some of what you'll need to know. When the skin is red and full of puss, make a poultice of lightly-cooked sliced onions. If you don't have onions use wild garlic or ginger root. Come, I'll show you where the wild ginger and garlic grows."

Loraine followed Delia through the woods the best she could as they gathered healing herbs. She watched carefully as Delia prepared the tinctures and poultices, wanting to learn and remember everything.

Delia took her to a willow tree growing near a creek and showed her how to strip the inner bark to boil as a broth. "Drink the liquid and it will take down fever and help with pain, both yours and Gray Leaf's. Use the boiled inner bark as a poultice. It draws out the fever from a wound."

~~~~

Once Delia went back home to do her own work, Loraine was left to care for Gray Leaf by herself. She intended to commit herself to the job of healing his wounds.

"You don't have to hover over me," he told her. "I'm not a dying man."

She hoped he wasn't a dying man, but he certainly was a sick one. When he tried to sit up, he'd break out in a cold sweat. She would put cloths soaked in cold water on his forehead, and fresh bandages she had boiled on his wounds.

"Delia told me to gently bind your gashes. She doesn't want them gaping open or having flies crawl on the open flesh."

"I'm healing just fine," he assured her. "This isn't the first time I've been clawed."

It was the first time she'd taken care of an injured man, and she was determined to do a good job of it. Every night she brewed a tea of willow bark for the man she now thought of as Gray Leaf, as well as herself. It was a bitter brew, but it helped with their pain and enabled them both to sleep easier. The bark she placed on his wounds appeared to be drawing out the redness. It also made her feet feel better when she wrapped them with the bark. She wondered why Gray Leaf hadn't done this for her, but she didn't ask.

She found there was something intimate about rubbing salves on his body. Her hands had never touched her husband the way she was touching this man. The few times she had observed Clarence Witcher's unclothed body, he had a soft body that was as pale and flabby as a wad of the biscuit dough that Cookie prepared each day. Every inch of Gray Leaf's body was solid, corded with muscles and as brown as a well baked biscuit. His flesh felt firm and alive beneath her hands. She wished he would fall asleep as she ran her salve-covered fingers over his wounds. She would have liked to feel more of his muscles than just touching his injuries allowed.

She recalled times when Clarence lifted her petticoat and pulled her bloomers down. She found his humping and grunting repulsive even when she tried not to. Having a husband was nothing like her imagination thought it would be like. Some of the girls she went to school with seemed to be extremely happy with married bliss. Were they pretending or was there something wrong with her? Odd that touching Gray Leaf didn't bring the same feelings as the few times she touched her husband. Could the reason be touching Gray Leaf wouldn't lead to what her husband did?

"What are you thinking about?" Gray Leaf surprised her by asking while his eyes were still closed.

"I'd rather not say."

He opened his eyes and looked at her. "I could feel the sadness in your touch as well as see it in your face. Do you miss the life you left behind?"

"No," she answered, surprising herself. "In a strange sort of way, I'm kind of relieved, and yet I'm also afraid."

"Afraid of what?" he encouraged.

"I don't know how to live this kind of life. I'm afraid I can't survive."

"What was your life like before you had to run away?"

His words *had to run away* hit her hard. Never in her life had she expected such a thing to happen to her. She had been the privileged one. The girl who had it all.

"I was loved and protected by my parents. They thought I would be equally as well cared for as Clarence Witcher's wife."

"Yet he tried to kill you?"

"Yes, he was feeding me poison."

"Why? For money?"

"He needed an heir," she confessed while trying to keep her chin from quivering.

"You are barren?"

"Yes," she whispered.

"Humph," he grunted. "It happens. Sometimes not often enough. A man who is willing to kill his wife should never beget an offspring. He is lower than the belly-crawling serpents of the earth."

"He said I was . . . damaged goods," she said for lack of a better description.

"Damaged?" he questioned.

"By being barren. He claimed he got cheated."

"Our great and wise Creator knows all. He chose not to give your husband an heir, otherwise he would have opened your womb."

Loraine wished he was right, but she couldn't make herself believe it. She tried to hide the inadequate feeling that brought tears to her eyes.

"Come," he said soothingly. "Lay down on the bed beside me, so we can both rest."

"I'll sleep on the floor as I have been doing," she told him. She had slept there since she gave up the bed to him.

"No. We both need the comfort of sleeping in a bed."

She was hesitant as he lifted the blanket and scooted against the wall to make room for her. She eased beside him, surprised that comfort came, and they both slept.

When she woke up, his arm was around her pressing her body to his. His face was buried in her hair with his breath warm on her neck. She had not expected the feelings that took possession of her body. They were feelings she had never gotten from her husband – never. She found herself wanting to stay right there in his arms for the rest of their lives. She felt warm, safe, and perhaps even happy in a way she'd never been happy before.

Odd how living in a shack with no money, no electricity, no maids to clean and cook, no one to do her laundry and help her dress, no fancy dress balls to attend was a far better life than she had ever known.

~~~~

"Will the bear get Clancy?"

Tally's question brought her back to the present with regret. The older she got, the more she found herself wanting to get lost in the memory of Gray Leaf. Oh, if she could only live those years of loving with him over again in real life instead of in her memory.

"Clancy is savvy beyond his years. He knows the ways of a mother bear and how to stay away from her. He'll be alright," Granny Witcher tried to assure her.

"Did Dad not know how to stay away from a mother bear?"

"It appears he didn't."

Dobb Simmons never had enough sense to stay away from anything. He always wanted to conquer everything he came into contact with instead of being smart about things. He used brutality to go after what he wanted and took pleasure in hurting those weaker than him. That was why he hated her. Not that she was physically stronger, which she wasn't. He actually believed her to be a witch with super-human powers she could call down on him at will, and that was something he couldn't destroy.

"Will we be alright?"

"We will," she assured the girl. "If we respect that bear's space, she'll respect ours." At least that was what she hoped.

Chapter 26

~~Tucker~~Inez Williams~~

"Changed my mind. I don't want that Inez messin' with me," Tucker said with disdain. "She's the wicked witch of the west."

"Hiring her to look after you will be a blamed lot cheaper than staying here in my makeshift hospital room. Not to mention all my time you're taking away from other patients."

"What patients?" Tucker demanded.

"The ones I won't allow to come in here to gawk at your skinned-up nakedness."

"Don't want that Inez woman gawking at my skinned-up nakedness ass. Being your nurse has already rubbed her hands all over my body, you hire Inez and I'll take your nurse. I'll pay her double."

Dr. Robinson didn't bother to comment. Tucker knew it wasn't going to happen. He was being difficult; and couldn't blame Doc. Doc wouldn't want Inez either.

"It's stay where you're at and have me knock you out again to save me all the aggravation you cause, or go home and have Inez looking after you. Your choice," Doc told him.

Tucker thought about it. He'd done a little trading with that woman a time or two. He couldn't say it was a pleasure, but she'd been better than nothing. At least she wasn't the kind to expect love and devotion. Liquor and cash were enough for her.

"You still willin' to trade her pay for my next run of one-eighty proof?" Tucker asked.

"I'm willing if you're willing."

"Don't leave me much choice, do you?" Tucker said as though the doctor was taking advantage of him.

"It wasn't exactly easy to get her to agree. Not many women like taking care of another adult, especially when that adult is you. At least she's smart enough to know her income will dry up considerably without you being able to supply men with their much-wanted refreshment."

Tucker ignored the insult part. Such a thing was nothing more to him than water poured on a duck's back. "Yeah," Tucker mumbled. "Most of the men around here couldn't live and survive being sober. Takes a lot of liquor to live with their women."

Doc Robinson was silent, but Tucker had more of a point than most folks realized – or at least wanted to admit, including him.

"When do I have to start enduring my lock-up with Inez?"

"As soon as the preacher, Griff, and Walt arrive to help carry you home."

Before Tucker knew what was happening, Doc had jabbed a needle into his upper arm. "Shit, man," he yelled. "That burns like hell-fire."

"Always burns, but not nearly as much as toting you home while you're conscious will hurt. You'll need to sleep through the move."

"What the hell did you jab into me?" Tucker demanded.

"Same thing I've been jabbing into you for a while." There was nothing like cocaine to keep a man in a coma, not to mention some of the herbs he got from Granny Witcher such as mandrake and other nightshades. It was rather amazing what that old woman knew about using weeds as medicine, but then the natives of Peru had been chewing on coca plants since long before the birth of Christ. Some of the concoctions she came up with were beyond him. Enough worked a miracle, too much killed. He did know that those mountains she gleaned over contained more varieties of plants than any other place on earth. She also knew how to mix them to get the most benefits – something even he didn't know how to do.

Tucker's eyes begin to droop and then closed, but his ears seemed to be working, or he was dreaming one. He felt the Doc rubbed a liberal amount of salve mixed with Vaseline over his body before he wrapped him in a sheet. Tucker heard the door open and the sound of voices.

"You in there, Doc?" Preacher Hadley called out.

"In the back room. Come on it. He's ready."

"Dang. He don't look so good," Griff said.

"He's alright. I gave him a shot to make him sleep while we move him."

"Good idea," the preacher said. "Looking at him makes a man uneasy about what can happen to a body. Who'd have thought a donkey could do that to a man."

The men lifted Tucker off the table to put him onto a stretcher.

"Go easy on him," Doc Robinson told them. "Don't need any of those stitches broken loose."

"He's heavy for such a bony man," Griff grunted as he lifted him by one leg with Walt lifting the other leg. The preacher and Doc Robinson each had an arm. They eased him onto the stretcher, carried him outside and scooted the stretcher into the back of a truck.

"He sure enough looks dead," Walt agreed with Griff

"He'll be okay. He looks bad because I've got him knocked out cold. He'll come around after a while," Doc Robinson assured them again.

~~~~

Inez, along with the women from the church, were already at Tucker's house when Doc Robinson and the men arrived. They had gathered to take over the cleaning and bed making, while having their noses in every crook and cranny as though they were searching for something – or anything. There was nothing more delightful than finding something not previously known about.

"This place is depressing," Inez pointed out. "It's nothing but a pig sty. I'm about to change my mind about taking care of him. I'm not being paid enough to go through this misery."

"You can't do that," Ida was quick to point out. "He needs somebody for at least another a week or two, and you're the only one of us who doesn't have a husband and family to take care of. Besides, we'll have this place spic and span before long. We've already got his bed stripped and cleaned. Good thing the sun was hot enough to dry the sheets Beatrice washed. Ellie hung the quilts over the line to air. They need a good washing, but we don't have time for that right now."

"What about the room where I'm to sleep? Has anybody cleaned it?"

"We left that room for you. We all know how particular you are about things."

The expression on Inez's face said Ida's words were not endearing. "I don't see why we can't all take turns taking care of him," Inez continued to grumble. "That way it won't overtax one person."

Beatrice and Ellie rolled their eyes and remained silent. They knew Inez wanted them to think she wasn't ecstatic about having a good paying job looking after the man who provided most all the liquor in the area. There was no doubt Inez was already imagining how she would be able to profit greatly by the situation. It was obvious they didn't hold Inez in high esteem, but she was one of them and that counted for a lot.

Inez left the women to check out the room that was to be hers. It wasn't nearly as bad as she expected. She smiled to herself pleased with the situation although she had to save face by pretending otherwise. She would get a lot of compassion and help from the church ladies if she claimed she was being put upon; when actually, she was already planning how she could profit beyond what she was being paid. Everyone knew that Tucker should have a huge stash of money hidden away somewhere. He'd been selling liquor for most all his life. The only expense he had were the items required to make his brew. His house and donkey had been paid for a long time ago. He didn't even have a wife to support. According to gossip, she'd run off many years before. Inez could barely remember her.

"That bedroom will have to be scrubbed from floor to ceiling before I'm willing to spend one night in there," she told Beatrice when she returned to where they had gathered.

Chapter 27

Granny Witcher eased out of the narrow bed where she had been sleeping beside Tally. Her shack was so small there wasn't room for two beds. There wasn't even room for a pallet on the floor. It was sleep in the same bed or find a place outside. Her old bones couldn't take the damp, cold, night air that settled in the high mountains each night the way she once could. Every day that passed reminded her of what she was no longer ready to admit. Her time on earth had become mighty limited, which had never bothered her in the past. The only reason it bothered her now was the girl would need her for years to come. It was her duty to raise her, not to mention it was also what her heart wanted. Tally's youth allowed her to sleep soundly, but Granny Witcher's old bones were cramped and miserable. The only solution she could think of was to find out if Dobb Simmons really was dead. It had been several days since Dobb came into contact with the bear. His death would solve two needs. Tally would no longer have to fear her dad, plus the girl would have the cabin to live in.

She slipped out of the shack like a mist into the night. The darkness of early morning didn't bother her eyes nearly as much a bright sunlight did.

Gray Leaf was on her mind. His words came to her as clear as if he was standing beside her.

"A body needs cat eyes. It's easy to see in the dark if you'll take the time to learn how."

Granny Witcher had learned the secret to seeing in the dark was not only how you trained your eyes but paying attention

239

to your surroundings. She knew her mountains, each tree, rock, and path almost as well as she knew her own body.

You taught me well, Granny Witcher's mind spoke silently to Gray Leaf. He remained with her in both his life and his death since the day she left Buck to go with Gray Leaf. She remembered him promising that he would never leave her, and he hadn't – not in spirit. She felt his presence beside her every moment of every day as well as every night. Each year that passed, he felt closer to her. His presence was what kept her going when she no longer wanted to keep going.

"You've not accomplished your purpose on this earth," he would tell her when she grew weary enough to wish she could lay herself down and close her eyes forever. Once her life on earth was over, she and Gray Leaf could be together. The time he spent waiting on her to join him might seem short to him, but to her it was taking an eternity – and eternity of yearning.

"Am I being left here for the girl?" she silently asked Gray Leaf.

"Among other reasons," he spoke gently to her mind. *"The girl needs somebody to save her and you're it"*.

"I couldn't save our son, she reminded him. What makes you think I can save Sally's daughter"

"Our son was a man who became careless. You can't prevent another person's carelessness."

"I'm growing weary," she told him and waited for him to say more, but he didn't. He left her with silence.

Then it came. The lonesome sound of a Whippoorwill calling from higher up the mountain, reminding her that his spirit was still here on earth with her, and yet so very far away. She smiled. He'd told her whenever she heard a Whippoorwill call it would be him reaching out to sooth her troubled soul.

Granny Witcher stopped trying to hold onto Gray Leaf and moved through the darkness, her mind on the girl. There were times when she longed to tell Tally she was Billy Gray's mother, but she knew better than to do a thing such as that. It would be a blight on the girl if anyone knew she had a somewhat connection to the crazy witch woman. Even her own son had refused to acknowledge her as his mother. He feared if people knew he was her son, it would have been more harmful than having people know he was part Indian.

Sadness would almost overcome her from knowing her son was ashamed of her and his heritage. Not only when he returned to the mountains, but when Billy was growing up. When he was a good-sized boy, he began hating his life of living more like an Indian than like the white man. He'd told Gray Leaf he wanted to be sent away. Somehow, Gray Leaf found the money to send him to a private white man's boarding school. Loraine hadn't wanted her son to be sent away from her, but she chose not to stop him. If she had, he would have always blamed her the way so many children blamed their parents for things they railed against.

It didn't take many years for him to realize the white race wasn't as superior as he had imagined it to be. He also realized his heart remained in the high mountains. He returned to a different mountain than the one on which he was born. One he thought he could claim as his own. She had always kept track of their son. Upon his return, she made a point of moving from where she had planned on living the remainder of her life, to be near her son, but she never told anyone who she was or that she had been on that mountain before. She didn't want her beloved son to be ashamed of her or know what had happened to his father. She had always kept her eyes on him simply because she loved him as much as she had loved his father.

It was only a matter of time before he discovered she was near, but never once did he acknowledge her. His refusal to admit she was his mother broke her heart. In a way she understood. In another way she didn't. She hadn't exactly disowned her parents and her previous life, but she had run away in order to remain alive. Perhaps her son had a similar need.

Billy Gray met Sally, married her, and the rest was a sad history.

Except for Sally's girl. She wasn't history.

Granny Witcher forced herself to stop thinking about her beloved husband and son. Even though the white man's law said she was still married to Clarence Witcher, God's law had never made Clarence Witcher her husband. Instead, she relied on God to make her and Gray Leaf united as one. She realized too late that she had only been used in hopes of producing Clarence Witcher an heir. It did her heart good, even now, to know she hadn't been the one who could not have children. She wondered if her replacement reproduced, and if she did, would Clarence Witcher ever know he hadn't fathered an heir?

As she climbed upward, she could feel the night wrapping around her like a damp blanket making her skin prickle even while it gave her the feeling of comfort. She once feared the night, but as time passed, it became her best friend. During the years she had learned to love the solitude of the night woods. It was as though she became a part of the darkness – part of a different kind of life – the difference between day and night. She moved through the trees dodging roots and undergrowth as a feeling of peace took hold.

"I know, Lord. My time to join my beloved Gray Leaf has not yet come. Keep me strong enough to do what has to be done," she whispered a silent prayer. Regardless of how much she wanted to join Gray Leaf, she would have to wait a while. There was a child she was responsible for even though the child was not of her son's blood, she could be considered her grandchild. Regardless of how difficult her existence was becoming, she felt a responsibility for the orphan child, and she was determined to see it through.

As she neared the location of Tucker's still, she heard a faint sound of clanging. She stopped, listened. Could the bear be causing the sound? Was it licking the copper pot? The sound was too soft for a bear to be pawing, and it certainly wasn't the screeching sound a bear scratching the pot would make. She listened more carefully for the sound of grunts or snorting. She didn't hear any sounds that indicated a bear was nearby. She lifted her face to sniff the air. She didn't pick up the stink of bear scat, not even a whiff of the musty odor bears gave off. Instead, her ears picked up the sound of something being dragged.

Was it possible Dobb Simmons was still alive?

Slowly, she eased forward until she was able to see what was going on, making sure she stayed downhill of the wind in case she was mistaken, and the sound was coming from the bear after all. The moon was out enough to see the dark image of a person. A small person not much bigger than her own size. It certainly wasn't the big, bulky form of Dobb Simmons.

She grinned with understanding but with not much surprise. She should have known a boy such as Clancy wouldn't miss out on an opportunity when it was staring him in the face. Since Tucker was out of commission for only the Lord knew how long, Clancy was claiming Tucker's still as his own, one piece at a time. It would be a difficult and heavy task, but she had no doubt Clancy would manage. That boy had never known the word impossible.

He had obviously been at it for some time. There weren't many pieces left. Granny Witcher turned herself around and headed back to her shack. Neither the bear nor Dobb Simmons would be anywhere near or Clancy wouldn't be scavenging Tucker's still. That boy had an uncanny ability similar to hers. Trouble was he still had too much arrogance instead of experience. She'd be willing to guide him along the way if only he'd let her.

"Where have you been?" Tally asked as Granny Witcher opened the door and entered the shack. Her eyes were wide with worry at being left alone.

"You been awake long?" Granny Witcher questioned in a soothing tone of voice.

"A while. I didn't know what happened to you."

"My old bones have a way of waking me up early. Does it most every morning. Why'd you wake up early. Usually sleep sound as a big rock."

"I was dreaming."

"'Bout what?"

"Daddy. He was begging me to keep him from dying. Does that mean I have to help him?"

"How did he think you could help him, much less keep him from dying if his time on this earth is up?"

"I don't know."

"Neither do I. The way I see it, he's either dead or left out of this mountain for good." Which she didn't think he would do, not when he had land, a cabin, and a girl to jump at his every demand.

"I want to know which one," her voice trembled when she said that. "Can we go look for him when it gets daylight?"

Granny Witcher thought about it for a few minutes. She was right sure the bear was long gone, being that Clancy was hauling Tucker's still away. She had no idea what would happen when Tucker got well enough to make the long trip up the mountain to check on his money maker. She did know Tucker wouldn't be a happy man.

It wasn't likely they'd find any sign of Dobb if he'd left the mountain, but it might do the girl good if they made an attempt at looking. What she hoped would not happen was for them to find Dobb injured and alive. If that was the case, would she be willing to keep him alive this time; or do what she should have done when the vicious man had taken over her son's wife and run her son's children off?

"Yeah," Granny Witcher said. "We'll go look for him after a while. It needs to be good and daylight afore we go searching."

She needed to give Clancy time to get everything moved out. How that boy expected to put that still back together and afford parts and ingredients to make a run was beyond her, which he would be bound and determined to do. But then, she'd learned never to underestimate a determined person even when that person was a fourteen-year-old boy.

It would do her mind good to know for sure what happened to Dobb Simmons. Not knowing something when you needed to know was a miserable place to be in.

Chapter 28

Mark it up to the arrogance of youth that kept Clancy from being afraid of the mother bear. He considered himself extra fast and extra smart. Had to be, in order to survive on this mountain for as long as he had. He figured the harshness of survival made a person age before their time. Take the old witch woman. She looked to be over a hundred years old, but she couldn't possibly be that old. She was able to move over the mountains as silently and easily as he could, but then she was one of those Granny Witches who could change her appearance at will. He had read a description of such women in one of his rare books that had once belonged to his mother. It read:

The Granny Witches are the old ones, the original Appalachian queens. They are daughters of the Celts and the offspring of the Durids. The medieval mavens and the natives of the old-world craft. They are all their children – as mysterious as old hills. They still have that Celt and Cherokee elder magic in their bones.

Yep, that was a right good description of the old witch woman. He wasn't sure, but he'd always heard the witch woman had Cherokee blood running in her veins. She certainly knew how to live off the land. Her medicine was powerful, and folks claimed medicine wasn't only what she brewed up in that shack of hers. Her most powerful medicine had to come from the gods themselves. She knew things she couldn't possibly know. It appeared the mountains whispered all their secrets in her ears. It also appeared she controlled every living thing in the mountains including plants and animals. He both feared her and respected her. Might even envied her. At least the girl would be safe now that the witch woman had taken her in. That was unless Dobb Simmons decided otherwise.

He had nailed Dobb in the head with his slingshot out of anger. When the man tumbled down the cliff and lay motionless on the rocky bottom, he was sure that was the end of the cruel man. It wasn't. The man must have nine lives.

From the looks of Tucker's still, it appeared Dobb's nine lives could possibly have come to an end. According to the tracks, the mother bear and Dobb had met up and it didn't appear to be a pleasant meeting. There were strips of Dobb's clothes and a good amount of blood. He had an idea it was Dobb's blood instead of the bears, but he couldn't be sure. He'd also found a considerable amount of hair that came from the bear.

He scanned the area to find out more about what happened. He came across Dobb's gun and picked it up. A smile spread his lips. He was becoming gun-rich, which was a good thing. A man couldn't have too many guns. According to the smell of the gun powder lingering in the barrel, he figured it had been a day or so since it had been fired, which meant the bear was most likely long gone. He followed the blood trail along with the scuffed-up ground where the pot had rolled. It appeared the pot had bounced across a creek. He followed the pot's trail downhill until it landed in a thick patch of rhododendron. It wasn't going to be easy hauling it to his cave, but he would figure out a way to manage.

He stopped, listened, and looked about. There were bear tracks around the pot and a few fresh scratches over the dents the pot got while tumbling. There were no longer signs of the bear, nor signs of Dobb. He didn't think the bear had dragged Dobb's body off, but he couldn't be sure. It would wise to know what had actually happened to the man.

He saw where Dobb had gone into the creek, but not where he had come out. He backtracked to where the pot had jumped the creek and walked along both sides of the water until he found where Dobb had come out of the creek. He followed the tracks, amazed at how far apart the footprints were. For a crippled man who limped, his footprints were nearly five feet apart. The man was running fast. Clancy was beginning to question if the prints belonged to the same man who went into the creek until he started seeing drops of blood. He checked the gun to make sure there was a shell in the chamber. He was more afraid of Dobb than he was the bear – even when Dobb didn't have a gun.

He tracked the footprints over a hill and down into the swag where a good size stream of water ran. Sure enough, he saw a form of something in the creek. He hid behind the trunk of a poplar tree to get a better look. Whatever it was wasn't moving. It didn't appear to be big enough for a bear. Besides, the bear's tracks led in a different direction. What he was seeing had to be Dobb.

Clancy sat down in a clump of undergrowth to wait and watch. One thing he had was patience. When there was no particular place to go, and no hurry to get there, patience came easy enough. "Only a fool rushes into an unknown situation," his dad had always told him. "Better to be slow than sorry."

The sun had traveled a good distance through the sky without Clancy seeing the thing in the creek move. No normal person would lay in a stream of icy-cold water that long without moving unless something was wrong with him. Clancy hid the gun in the bushes in case it was Dobb. He didn't want to give up the gun by having Dobb come up out of the water to overpower him.

He took his slingshot from around his neck, placed a smooth rock in the leather pouch, and eased forward. When he got close enough to tell it was Dobb, he pulled the pouch back and let fire. The rock hit Dobb with a thud. Dobb didn't move, but that didn't mean he was dead. He put another rock in the leather pouch and eased forward.

His guts clenched when he got closer. Dobb was laying on his back, his face toward the sky. White film had clouded over his eyes and his face had turned a pasty color. There was no doubt Dobb Simmons was dead. Silt from the water had gathered on the sunken parts of his body except where the minnows had gathered to nibbled at the torn flesh where the bear's claws had ripped his body and legs. The gashes were long and deep. How Dobb had managed to run this far was beyond belief. It didn't seem possible a man ripped apart by a bear had somehow managed to run for nearly two miles while he was bleeding out.

Fear was a powerful thing.

Chapter 29

~~Tucker~~

Tucker opened his eyes to the smell of coffee perking. For a moment, he felt like a young boy waking up to his mother fixing breakfast. The feeling was good, but it only lasted for a few moments before his aches and pains returned him to reality. He tried to sit up. Pain shot through him. Broken ribs hurt like the fires of hell. He'd be enduring that pain for six to eight weeks. It wasn't his first battle with broken ribs. He'd had them twice before. Once as a boy when his older brother hit him with a homemade ball bat, and once when his wife took a hammer to him while he was passed out drunk.

He couldn't much blame his wife for being mad at her drunk husband. Not only did she pretend to hate liquor, but she was also born as mean as the devil himself. He knew that much about her. She was a challenge in his youth. He was a boy who couldn't resist a challenge.

Marie had reddish auburn colored hair that came out of a bottle, although she claimed it was her natural color. Her waist was thick, her hind end broad, and her chest came close to being as flat as his. He was sure he had to be near passed out drunk when he married the likes of her. He still remembered what his mother had told him when he showed up with Marie.

"Son, you remember Jake Brody who lived up the road, don't you? He was a well-off bachelor with a farm and home, when a conniving woman decided to marry him for what he had. He ought to of known better, but his hormones were pumping hot with want-to. Didn't take long for him to realize what a horrible mistake he'd made. She was as sneaky as an

250

egg-sucking dog, and as un-scruples as the devil himself. Treated him like dog manure on the bottom of her shoes.

"Divorcing her would ruin him. Killing her would put him in jail. He didn't know what to do. Anyway, it just so happened he had a mule as stubborn and hateful as his wife. He wasn't exactly sure what fate came about to put her and his mule in the barn together. He did know she was in the barn gathering eggs when she and that mule got in each other's way. Her temperament wasn't about to tolerate the mule in what she considered her space. She jabbed the mule with the pitchfork, and the mule kicked her in the head. Killing her dead as four o'clock.

"He held a wake and all the neighbors brought food. The preacher watched as Jake stood at the head of his wife's casket greeting people. He noticed Jake would nod his head after each woman spoke with him, but he would shake his head after each man spoke.

"Finally, when all the condolences came to an end, the preacher couldn't contain his curiosity any longer. He went over to Jake as asked, 'what did those women say to you?'

"They said she was a mighty pretty woman, wasn't she? And I nodded."

"And what did the men say?' the preacher then asked.

"They asked if the mule was for sale."

He sure to hell blamed his older brother. There were two and a half years separating him and his brother in age. From the time he was born, his brother hated him, resented sharing anything with him, including his parents' attention. His mother had once told about his brother trying to drag him to the burning fireplace when Tucker was only a few days old. Fortunately, she had heard Tucker crying and came to his rescue.

From that day forward, his brother was determined anything belonging to Tucker should belong to him and he was determined to take it. That included Tucker's wife. In the beginning, Tucker worshiped his wife. He was determined to provide her every desire. If it was impossible for him, she found it elsewhere. Day by day his infatuation wore off until he saw his wife as the kind of woman she was.

What ole brother Joe didn't realize was that he had been welcome to her. It was the way they had gone about it that destroyed Tucker's peace of mind. Even he hadn't expected the rage that filled him at finding them in his bed – doing what Tucker had thought should be his right only.

Now, another woman he despised was in his house – in his kitchen brewing coffee and cooking. He could smell overheated grease. He groaned more from distress at his situation than from pain. He regretted making the sound because it brought Inez from the kitchen.

"I see you've come around," Inez said. "Was hoping you'd stay passed out forever."

He didn't doubt that. At least she was honest enough to say it.

"Get out of my house. I don't need you here."

"Think not? Try getting out of bed and fixing your own breakfast."

He wasn't about to try in front of her. He knew he couldn't do it yet. Not only was the pain too great, his body was too weak. He wasn't sure how long he'd been in this condition, but it seemed like a long time.

"Don't need to get out of bed. If I did, you wouldn't have a job. Dr. Robinson insisted I hire you. Don't know why. But since I made the mistake of doing so, bring my breakfast in here before I fire you. I like my coffee strong and black. Bring my jug too."

"Where is it?"

"In the bottom of the cabinet."

"Already looked under there. There's no jug of liquor."

Tucker gritted his teeth. He ought to have known Inez would steal it.

"The church women cleaned the place before I arrived," she told him. "If they found liquor, they'd pour it out."

Such as that didn't surprise Tucker. They would take his liquor just as fast as Inez would – and it wasn't only the women. He knew for a fact how many of those so-called Godly men guzzled his brew. As for those better-than-thou women, they would be willing to clean a pig sty just to snoop into somebody's else's business. He looked about his bedroom to discover it was the cleanest it had ever been since he lived here – and completely empty of his things.

"Where's my things?" he demanded.

"Ask the preacher and his crew of church women," she snapped as she turned her back and left the bedroom. She returned a few minutes later with a plate of eggs fried to a crisp and coffee that looked like mud in a cup.

"Can you sit up and feed yourself?" she asked.

He tried to lift his hands and his hope sunk. There was no way he would be able to feed himself. Weakness had set in.

"Not only will I have to spoon-feed you, the doc has you wearing something like a diaper. I'll have the disgusting job of washing your hind-end. Good thing it's no broader than a chicken's butt."

Tucker's weakness made him feel like crying. He couldn't stop the tears that came to his eyes.

His weakness seemed to touch a soft spot in the hard-hearted woman.

"You won't be the first man I've spoon-fed or the first hind end I've washed, so don't pretend to be such a victim. You're paying me mighty fine for all the repulsiveness you'll put me through."

He figured that was a fact.

~~~~

Inez was mad at herself for not getting to Tucker's place before the church women did. There was no telling what they found and stashed away for themselves. She didn't see them leaving with anything, but then she wouldn't. Each of those women was smart enough to hide any treasure they found and come back for it later. Cash was a different matter. It could be hidden in clothing. Even religious women might be tempted by cash when they thought its owner might die. If he lived, and their conscience got to them, they could claim they took it for safekeeping. She'd already searched every hiding place she could think to look while Tucker was out cold, and that included the barn and yard. The only place left to search was the woods. She was almost sure the women hadn't gone into the woods to search, but she would.

It was well past midnight when she finally fell asleep. She'd stayed awake trying to think of any place where Tucker would hide cash. She knew he had to have a mighty big stash somewhere.

The next morning, she felt tired and irritable as she built a fire in the wood cook stove to get breakfast. She was hungry.

"Inez," Tucker called out.

"What?" she hollered back.

"Do you know what those women did with my spare gun and ammunition?"

"No," she hollered back.

"Don't hold with them taking my liquor, but my gun and ammunition is a different matter. That's flat out stealing. Go ask 'em where they're at."

Inez didn't mind an excuse to get out of Tucker's house even if it was before she ate breakfast. Beatrice just might be baking something sweet and be willing to share. She took her time walking, enjoying the warmth of the early morning sunshine.

Beatrice must have seen her coming out the kitchen window because she opened the door before Inez had a chance to knock.

"Thought you'd be at Tucker's place," she told her. "Is there a problem already?"

"No more than normal. He insisted I come ask if anybody saw his gun and ammunition when they were cleaning the house. You know how men are – get something on their minds and won't leave it be," she said as she pressed past Beatrice standing in the doorway. Sure enough, it smelled like something had just come out of the oven. A partly-iced cake was sitting on the dining table.

"I didn't see a gun. Don't know about the others. If one was there, most likely one of the men put it up or gave it to the preacher to look after."

Inez pulled out a chair and sat down in front of the cake. "That looks good," she said. "You're the best cook of anyone I know."

Beatrice ignored her hint. "How are you getting along with Tucker? I don't envy you."

"Doc left enough medicine to keep him kind of quiet. He's starting to get difficult when he's awake. Don't know how long I'll be able to take it. Don't let me bother you. Finish icing the cake."

"Need to let it cool some. It's still too warm."

Didn't appear too warm to Inez.

"It's Griff's birthday cake," Beatrice said. "I want it to look perfect for him when he gets home. He's been working mighty hard lately. You ought to go ask the preacher about Tucker's gun. If anybody saw Tucker's gun, it would be one of the men," Beatrice said as though she was trying to get rid of Inez, which she was. None of the women were as nice to her as she thought they ought to be. They treated her almost as bad as they treated Dr. Robinson's so-called nurse.

She knew a lot about every woman far and near. Their men talked way too freely after they had a right smart of liquor in them. Oh, well. She knew better than to mention such if she wanted to keep up doing the things she was doing.

"It sure does smell good," Inez hinted again as she took in a deep breath of the aroma.

"I'll give you my recipe and you can bake one for yourself and Tucker."

"I've tried baking, but my cakes fall flat as a flitter."

"Practice makes perfect," Beatrice told her. "If you hurry, you might be able to catch the preacher. Today is the day he calls on folks."

Inez knew when someone was trying to get rid of her, but it didn't bother her in the least. She'd never cared what anyone thought of her as long as she got what she wanted. Thing was, what she wanted wasn't always the best for her. Maybe it was time for her to change that situation. Once she found Tucker's stash of money she could move to where no one knew her and start all over again. Finding Tucker's money might be her last chance of becoming a high and mighty lady.

All she had to do was work Tucker just right.

~~~~

Talk about the fires of hell, Tucker thought he had been thrown in the furnace to be burned alive, after the Doc insisted he get out of bed and walk. He danged near fell on his butt when he got a good look at what had once been his comfortable home. He might have known those church women would have had a hayday with his place while he was doped out of his mind and flat of his back. The place had been cleaned until it no longer looked or felt like his comfortable home. No telling what they had done with all his things. It wouldn't surprise him to find those women had put silk stockings on his old donkey.

He turned to the doctor. "How about puttin' me back in one of them comas. Don't know how much more of this shit I can take."

"I'm sure Inez would pay me to do just that. However, if you don't want your body to stiffen up to the point where you can't move normally, you've got to start exercising."

"Then you'd better pump me full enough of your pain medicine to numb me all over," Tucker told him as he tried to sit up. "Hell, man, bring me one of my jugs of liquor you screwed me out of."

Dr. Robinson considered it for a moment, nodded, and pulled a flask out of his jacket pocket and handed it to Tucker. "See if you can open that and drink it by yourself."

Tucker was able to hold it in his hands; but screwing the cap off was a different matter. His fingers were stiff and painful. Using his fingers scraped the scabs off causing blood to ooze. He stuck the flask in his mouth, clamped down on the lid with his teeth, and carefully turned the flask until it opened. He spit the lid out, turned the flask up, and drank like a man deprived way too long.

"Easy does it," Dr. Robinson told him.

"Shit man. You didn't have enough in that flask to wet a man's whistle. Give me more."

"Can't. That's all I've got. You've not been able to provide any for a month now. Folks are having to go across the county line for it."

"That's nothin' but radiator acid. It'll kill a man."

"Right. That's why you've got to get back on your feet."

Tucker liked the sound of that, but he didn't like the pain that went with trying. "Say Doc, would you know who got my jug I kept under the sink along with my gun and ammunition? Inez claims my entire house was stripped clean of my things before she arrived. The preacher told her my gun and ammunition weren't in the house when the women got here." He came close to accusing those church women of taking his valuables, but he knew better. They were something else when they got stirred up. He'd listened to their husbands talk enough to know it was a fact.

"Don't know a thing about that," Doc told him.

"My skin cracks and bleeds when I move," Tucker whined. "Does something mighty unpleasant to a man when that happens."

"No doubt," Dr. Robinson said without sympathy. "I'll give Inez some salve to rub on your body. It lubricates and numbs at the same time. Say, how are you getting on with Inez?"

"Humph," Tucker grunted. There were times when she wasn't nearly as bad as he thought she'd be, but he didn't want to admit it to the doctor. Then there were times when he could see the devil shining from the depths her eyes. "Pay you boot if you'll trade your nurse for her."

"Don't think my wife would agree to that." And he wouldn't either. Didn't take long for a man to become addicted to the pleasures the right woman gave him.

Tucker chose not to comment on the doctor's remark, but he and the doctor both knew it was a boldfaced lie. It was a wonder Elouise hadn't forced her crippled body to get up and walk, in order to get rid of the doctor's plaything. Not that he blamed the doctor one little bit. His nurse would tempt the Pope, not to mention a normal man with normal needs. Even Inez was starting to stir up his want-to – when he didn't want her to.

Odd how the woman he despised could touch him just so, smile at him just so, be just so sweet. Her actions were a sight better than he'd ever known her to behave – even the few times he paid her to do it. If he didn't know better, he'd think she'd taken a shine to him. He sure to hell didn't have anything to offer her. His only way of earning money had come to an end, just as his liquor supply had surely ended until he was on his feet again. At least his still would be waiting for him to return. It was that thought that made him ease his pain-ridden body to a sitting position.

"Put your feet on the floor and see if they'll hold your weight," Doc told him.

Even though his boots had protected his feet for a while, they had suffered great damage. It hurt to move his toes.

"How about doing this a little at a time," Tucker said as sweat broke out on his face.

"Right. You've probably done enough for today being there's no hurry for you to get well. I'll give Inez the salve to rub on you twice a day. I'll come back day after tomorrow. Try to sit up on your own between now and then."

*

Inez took her slow time rubbing the salve over Tucker's scabbed-over body. Her fingers were gentle as her hands moved over private places. It made no difference that she hated the man. For years, she'd hated every man her hands touched, and every man who touched her. However, she did what had to be done, just like she was doing now.

She almost smiled. Even a skinned-up man responded favorably to a gentle touch. But then, he'd responded to her touch before. Admittedly, he was always dog drunk when he came to her, and she was always well paid.

"Why did you stop?" Tucker complained.

"I've finished doing what the doctor ordered, which is all you are paying me for. As you well know, anything extra costs extra."

Tucker grinned. Inez said what he expected her to say. It was when people did what he didn't expect that threw him.

Chapter 30

~~Fredrick Dean~~

Valarie Whitley closed her eyes and sank down in a chair at the kitchen table wishing she couldn't hear what was going on in the bedroom. She should go outside to her flower garden. The beauty of flowers could ease her sorrows, at least for a few precious minutes. She needed some time for herself – time to get her mind thinking straight. There were decisions she needed to make – decisions she had never wanted to make.

There was no way she could express how disgusted she was with Elouise Robinson. She'd done everything in her realm of knowledge to help the woman. She'd treated her as tenderly as she would have treated a baby. All she got in return were harsh words, temper tantrums and threats. There was no way of knowing when someone would show up and believe the horrible things the deranged woman was accusing her of doing.

Her and Dr. Robinson's relationship wasn't exactly a secret. The entire community speculated on what Dr. Robinson and she did together. They called her a 'trollop,' a vulgar woman who indulged in unlawful sex.

She called it falling in love.

It was only the community's need of the good doctor that kept the scandal to a minimum. After all, they had never considered her to be *one of them*. Inez Williams was *one of them*, and that was why she got away with what she did – that and the fact none of the women dared admit some of their husbands might have indulged in what Inez represented.

At first, she and the doctor had avoided contact with each other as though they were avoiding the plague. Staying apart caused the need in both of them to grow to the boiling point. It had not been hot, boiling sex they had sought. What it had been was a desperate attempt to ease the unbelievable hurt and loneliness that dwelled in both of them. Sharing love was like taking away the blockage that kept their hurt from flowing away. To her the doctor was a rare man. The kind who was dreamed about and seldom found

As much as she had come to love the good doctor, she'd never been able to confide in him how awful her previous life had been. Her husband had been a brutal man who enjoyed causing pain in others. She had been in her last semester of nursing school when she met him. She graduated, got a job, and became his wife within days of each other.

It took less than a week for her to realize what a mistake she had made by marrying Fredrick Dean. "You've made your own bed, you'll have to lay in it," her mother had told her on her wedding day. "You're not to come running home complaining and expect me to take you in."

Her mother's words hurt her almost as much as the lit cigarettes Fredrick Dean loved to press against her breasts. He laughed when she screamed. Kicked her in the stomach with his boots on when she tried to fight back.

"Fight me," he'd say. "Go at it, you slut. It's invigorates me when you fight back."

Odd how the man you once thought you loved more than life itself turned into the man you hated with your entire being.

The night Fredrick Dean got in a knife fight with another drunk was the best day of her life. There were several witnesses to the fight, encouraging both men to keep at it until their flesh was sliced into ribbons. The loser was the man to hit the ground without getting up. The men put the loser in the bed of a truck and hauled him to the hospital. He lived.

Fredrick Dean was the winner of the fight. He was still standing. He made his way home bleeding like a stuck hog. He stumbled up the steps and fell onto the front porch,

She turned on the porch light and opened the door to see what caused the loud thump. Fredrick lay there in a bloody fetal position. At first, she wasn't sure it was him. Even his head and face were blood-splattered.

"What happened to you?" she asked.

"Help me. Stop the bleeding," he begged.

"What happened?" she asked again, noticing his boots were overflowing with blood.

"Attacked. Knife."

"Why?" she asked.

"Stop the bleeding," he continued to beg. "Hurry. Stop my hurting."

"How does it feel to be weak and helpless? How does it feel to want the hurting to stop?" she asked as she looked down on him.

"Damn it," he'd whispered. "Can't you see I'm dying?"

"Yes, you are dying unless I somehow manage to stop your bleeding."

"Then stop it," he demanded.

"Why should I?" she asked as she unbuttoned the top three buttons of her dress exposing her breasts. She pointed at a raw, oozing burn. "You did that to me last night. Remember?"

He said nothing.

"Remember when you kicked me in the stomach causing me to bleed for two weeks? You wouldn't allow me to go to the doctor. You told everyone I missed work because I had the flu. You said a woman who couldn't survive a little bleeding wasn't fit to live. I miscarried and I was the only one who knew it happened."

"Help me," he pleaded again, ignoring her words.

"A man who can't survive a little bleeding isn't fit to live," she told him similar words that he had said to her. He reacted the way she thought he would.

"Damn it. I'll kill you," he managed to get the words out between gritted teeth.

"I know you will if you survive."

She felt no compassion for him as he lay there on the porch. She wanted him to feel helpless, to hurt, to fear his next breath would be his last. That was the way she had felt many times since their marriage.

It was his turn.

She took her time finding rags to use as tourniquets and alum to pack into his cuts and stab wounds. It wasn't exactly as though she wanted him to die. It was more like she wished he had never existed. She simply wanted him to feel helpless and scared for his life as long as possible. The sooner she tended him, the sooner he would get well.

His breath was still rattling in and out, his chest lifting high with the effort, when she got back to him. His red face had gone pale in the dim porch light. His shirt and pants had been slashed to rags by the other man's knife. She took her time in unbuttoning his blood-soaked shirt. His chest was covered in so much blood it was difficult to tell where the cuts and gashes were. She gagged as she dumped part of the alum on his chest and tried to rub it into his wounds. The blood washed the alum out of all but the deepest stab wounds where a small amount appeared to remain in the muscled flesh.

The copper smell of hot blood was making her feel sicker by the moment. As a nurse, she thought she was immune to the stink of blood, but she'd never encountered this much before. Her hands, arms, and even her clothes were now coated with his blood.

"You ought not to have gotten into a knife fight," she told him. He didn't respond, didn't move.

She ripped open the sleeve of his shirt and tied a rag above the slashed open muscle of his upper arm. The wound was deeper and longer than those on his chest. Alum stayed in the wound as she tried to bind the gash closed by tying one of the rags tight. It must have helped because the blood stopped flowing.

"You're not bleeding as much," she told him before she noticed that his chest wasn't moving. She felt his neck for a pulse. It wasn't there.

She sat beside him on the rough planks of the front porch looking at his pale, blood-splotched face. It didn't seem possible that he was dead. A man as mean as Fredrick Dean lived forever.

She wasn't sure how long she sat there. Her body, her soul, had become something similar to numb, before relief set in.

"You're dead," she whispered. "You are really dead." It had to be the relief that made her start crying. Sweet, pure relief.

Two of the men, who witnessed the fight decided they should follow Fredrick to see if he made it home, They had mistakenly thought her tears came from grief. They told how they had found her kneeling beside her husband, crying. They told how she'd tried to stop his bleeding with tourniquets and alum; then added that he had most likely bled to the point of near death before he fell down on the front porch.

She never told how much she wanted him dead, or how slow she had been to help him. She gathered her meager belongings and left town to search for a job and a new beginning in life. She saw and answered Dr. Joseph Robinson's ad for a nurse. She had no idea the job included taking care of his paralyzed wife – but the job provided room and board. She took the job.

And now all but present time was history.

And present time was the one thing she could no longer allow.

Chapter 31

~~Clancy~~

Clancy didn't know what to do about Dobb Simmons. Bury him was the first thing that came to his mind; but going back to his cave to get a shovel wasn't tempting. Thinking about the work it would take to dig a hole deep enough to bury him was downright appalling, but he was willing to do it if it would be the best for Tally. He wasn't sure what was best, so he eased back into the shelter of the woods and sank down in the shade of the tree he'd hid behind, He needed to think on it a while. How much time he took figuring this out wasn't going to make any difference to Dobb.

Clancy figured Dobb was at Tucker's still for a reason. Most likely he'd been getting ready to run off a batch of liquor himself when the bear showed up. A lot of money could be made right quick when a man had a still. Problem was buying supplies and hauling them all the way up the rugged, high mountains. Dobb was the most likely one to manage such a feat, but the bear's attack kept it from happening.

"Goes to show the best laid out plans of mice and men did go astray," he repeated what he'd often heard his mother say.

Clancy wouldn't mind having a lot of money right quick. As for knowing how to distill the liquor, he figured he could do it as good as anybody else. But it would take him a while to figure out how to get the supplies together. During that time Tucker would get well enough to start up his business. Then it would be too late for Clancy. Of course, he could offer to take Dobb's place helping Tucker with the work. That idea didn't appeal to him. He wasn't and never intended to be a second-fiddle kind of person. He was a do-it-yourself or don't-do-it-at-all kind of person.

He would move Tucker's still to his cave one piece at a time. He intended to keep the still until he was ready to set it up. Tucker would never know it was him who took it. Dobb would get the blame – but not if he was found dead. He could bury Dobb without telling anyone. It might work for a while, but there were men who could read tracks a lot better than he could. Plus, finding a grave this close to where Tucker's still was located wouldn't go well. There would be a lot of questions as to who put the grave there.

During his wanderings, Clancy had come upon one other still a right smart distance away. It was hidden on the far side of another mountain. It was a bigger operation than what Tucker had with several men running it. Those men kept their distance from Tucker, and Tucker kept his distance from them. It was kind of an understanding between moonshiners, each with their own territory. There was also jealousy among moonshiners. Tucker was known to undercut their price, plus his liquor was better quality. The other men had a bad reputation for producing inferior shine. Clancy had heard such talk while his parents were alive.

He was pleased with the idea that came to him. It wouldn't take a genius to make it look as though the other moonshiners had stolen Tucker's still. Plus, he had plenty of time to pull it off before Tucker was in condition to return.

But what was the best solution for Dobb Simmons?

What was the best solution for the pot?

Did he figure out how to drag the pot to his cave first, or take care of Dobb?

Clancy jumped up, went to Dobb and took his boots off, and then searched his pockets, took out a pocketknife, a lighter, and a handful of change. If Dobb had any other money, it wasn't in his pockets. He hid the boots in the undergrowth and pocketed the other things. Relunctly, he lifted Dobb's legs and clamped both stinking feet under each arm. It was a long way to drag a man to Tally's cabin, but there was a grave already dug and empty. He might as well fill it with Dobb.

Clancy hadn't gone far before he regretted his decision. Dragging dead weight was difficult. Dobb weighed almost three times what Clancy weighed. Plus, Dobb's body caught on every rock, root, and clump of undergrowth. Clancy wanted to drop Dobb and leave him behind. Would have if it hadn't been for Tally. The dead man was the poor little girl's daddy. Her mind would rest easier knowing both her parents were in a grave. Knowing his own parents were buried side by side gave him something similar to a kind of comfort. That poor little girl was going to need all the comfort she could get.

Clancy was wet with sweat and mumbling bad words by the time he had dragged Dobb to the empty grave. It had taken hardheaded stubbornness along with a lot of determination. Clancy stopped dozens of times to assure himself he wasn't a quitter. Each time he stopped, he dropped Dobb's bare feet and backtracked picking up bits of clothing as he tried to wipe out the drag tracks with brush. Regardless of what he did he couldn't make the ground look natural. Hopefully, no one would venture that far into the mountains until time and weather could wipe out traces of what had happened.

He rolled Dobb into the grave.

"Shit," he mumbled as he realized he still needed a shovel to fill the grave with dirt. He gathered every loose rock within a hundred-foot radius and tossed them on top of Dobb before he went to search for a shovel.

The day was almost over by the time Dobb's was buried. Clancy considered going to the old woman's shack to tell her and Tally what happened; but getting the still moved to his cave was pressing hard on him. It would be a prize for any of the other moonshiners. It was a prize for him.

Chapter 32

~~Valarie Whitley~~

Valarie Whitley hadn't slept much after the doctor left her bed. She had clung to him longer than usual after they had made love with all the passion she had in her. He was the man she loved. A once-in-a-lifetime love she should have met before they both made a horrible mistake in the people they had married. Sad how the worst mistakes of a lifetime could be made because people were young and stupid. Leave it to the hard knocks of life to wise an older person up. Too bad wisdom didn't arrive with youth. She supposed it was true that a person didn't get to be old and wise without first being young and stupid.

Oh, how that young and stupid could hurt.

Marriage to each other hadn't happened, and the reality was that it never would. Elouise might be a paraplegic, but she was as healthy as the horse that had thrown her. Most likely she would outlive her husband. As for divorcing her, Dr. Robinson had often said he couldn't do it. Neither would his conscience allow him to put her in some kind of home.

So, where did that leave her? Her answer was simple. One she didn't like. *His trollop.*

She could live with that if she were the only one to take into consideration. Gossip hurt, but their love for each other was enduring. She had no doubt it could outlast any gossip. Her love for the good doctor was strong, but not as strong as the love for her unborn child. She couldn't allow her child to grow up in a community that would label it, forever, as a bastard.

She had gotten up with the crack of dawn, pulled her worn suitcase from under her bed where she had stored it when she first arrived. She lay it on the bed, wiped the dust bunnies from it and opened the rusty latch. She stared at the suitcase's emptiness as the stale odor of dust and disillusionment filled her. She longed to snap it back shut, pretend she could leave things as they were, at least for a while longer. Sad moments passed before she started packing her few articles of clothing.

Life was no longer about her. There was someone far more important to take into consideration.

She had considered tossing the old, dilapidated suitcase away several times, but a feeling that she might need it again stopped her. Truth was always in the back of her mind. The truth about the doctor, his wife, and herself.

She hadn't planned on becoming pregnant – never thought it would happen. She figured Fredrick Dean had done so much damage to her that pregnancy would not be possible. What had happened? How could she possibly get with child after all these years?

The why and how of it didn't matter now. What mattered was providing a good life for her baby. One where it wouldn't be known as a bastard.

Thankfully, she'd been able to save almost every dollar Dr. Robinson had paid her. It wasn't a windfall, but it would tide her over for a while if she was extremely careful with every dime. She was not five months along and no longer able to hid her growing stomach. If she didn't leave now, everyone would know.

When she had finished packing her suitcase, she sat down and wrote a letter to the good doctor. She told him she loved him, but she couldn't take being known as his trollop any longer. She wished him luck at finding another nurse – one that his wife might like. *Please don't try to find me,* she added. *I long to live the rest of my life with respect.*

She had no intention of him ever knowing about their baby.

She cried as she slipped the suitcase back under the bed to wait for the perfect time to arrive. She couldn't walk out in the middle of the day when many of the people, plus the doctor, would see her leaving. She wanted to disappear during the dark of night, silently and secretly.

Two days later, her chance arrived. The doctor had given an extremely difficult Elouise a shot to make her sleep during the night when a knock came on the door. She answered it.

"Need the Doc again," Mr. Waltrip said. "My woman's bad off this time. Got here as fast as I could."

"I'll get him," she said as she left him standing at the door with his worn, sweat stained hat in his hands.

"It's Mr. Waltrip," she told the doctor. "He's obviously concerned for his wife. He said she was bad off this time."

Dr. Robinson had been resting in his favorite chair. He needed time to recoup after dealing with his irate wife. Valarie had listened in silence while Elouise was being extremely difficult. Elouise had been even more insistent that he and his nurse planned on killing her. Valarie hated to interrupt his few minutes of peace and quiet, but she also saw the opportunity his absence would provide.

She got his black bag from the cabinet and followed him to the door.

"What about my horse?" Mr. Waltrip was asking after Dr. Robinson told him to get in the car.

"My nurse can unsaddle him and put him in the barn until we return."

"Don't like leavin' my hoss," he said.

"I know, but I might need your help with your wife. It'll take a while for you to ride that horse back home."

"She knows how to care for my hoss?" Mr. Waltrip asked, his forehead wrinkled with another worry.

"She does," the doctor assured him. "Nurse Whitley is an extremely capable woman."

"Okay, then," he agreed hesitantly.

Dr. Robinson took the black bag from his nurse, looked her in the eyes and nodded to her. She longed to tell him good-by and give him one last kiss, but she didn't dare. She closed the door behind him, leaned against it, and listened to the car start and drive away. She hurried to the bedroom, got her suitcase and took out the letter. She carried it to his bedroom and carefully placed on top of his pillow where he would be sure to find it.

She had planned on walking to the next town to catch a bus that would take her anywhere. If she couldn't make it that far during the concealment of night, she'd hide out in the woods until the next night. The horse was an unexpected blessing allowing her to arrive by morning's light. Hopefully, the doctor would not return until the next day. She had no doubt the doctor would find her letter and try to find her. The horse would be the only thing waiting at the next town for him.

~~~~

When Dr. Robinson arrived, he found what he feared. Mrs. Waltrip was miscarrying. Such calamity seemed to be the main thing that took mountain women's lives. A husband had the right to pleasure himself with his wife. Unfortunately, all too often his pleasure ended up killing the woman.

The smell from her discharge was filling the small cabin. From the odor alone, it was easy to tell the fetus had been dead for days. He suspected she had given birth to so many children her womb had gotten to the point where it would no long carry a baby until term. Unfortunately, nature had not aborted it and infection had set in. He would have to go in by hand and remove the dead fetus and afterbirth and then pack her with Sulphur in hopes it would take care of the infection and keep her alive.

"Why don't you take the children outside?" the doctor suggested to Mr. Waltrip. They would surely be scared when they heard their mother start screaming when he stuck his gloved hand inside her. All women screamed even after he gave them a shot like he gave Tucker and his wife. He would also give them some of Tucker's liquor to drink if he could get it down them. Liquor was kind of slow working, but it came near being a miracle for just about everything that ailed a person. Like any good medicine, too much was a killer, but enough did the job.

"Do you think you can get a little liquor down?" Dr. Robinson asked her.

"Don't got none," she told him in a raspy voice that sounded as exhausted as the woman appeared to be.

"I've got some," he assured her.

"Airy thing that'll ease my hurt," she told him.

He opened his bag and took out a plastic cup and his flask of Tucker's finest. He poured a finger's worth, lifted her head and held the cup to her lips. She clutched the cup with trembling hands as she gulped it greedily, obviously well used to drinking such a brew.

He let her head rest back down on the worn mattress that had been covered in oil cloth to keep her bleeding from soaking in.

"I'm going to give you a shot to ease your pain," he told her as he took a syringe out of his black bag.

"Am I dyin'?" she questioned.

"Probably not. Your husband got me here in time."

"Oh," she mumbled. "Death is the only way I'll ever get any rest."

Right, the doctor thought. For some women, the only rest they'll ever get is when they are dead. These mountain women are expected to do nothing other than work from the time they can walk until the day they're laid in the ground. Not only work; they're expected to bear children from puberty until menopause. He knew one woman who bore twenty-two children during her lifetime. A brood horse – a milk cow crossed his mind. What choice did a woman have when they were born in such a place and had no other choice?

He eased the needle into the thickest part of her bony arm and pushed the plunger. She didn't even wince at the sting. When a woman was in as much pain as she was in, a little more hurt didn't matter. He watched her face as the wrinkles of pain eased. Sometimes he felt guilty for keeping women such as Mrs. Waltrip alive. She might be able to lie in bed for a day, maybe two if she was lucky. It was a sure thing that she would be up cooking and taking care of her children and husband before she had adequate strength to do so. Without being given proper healing time, she would spend her days and nights in an exhausted haze, never feeling well, never getting well.

In a year's time or less, Mr. Waltrip would be rushing down the mountain to get him again because his wife would be miscarrying. He might or might not be able to save her another time. If only he had a way to help such women, he'd do it. The only advice he could give was for her to soak a rag in vinegar and insert it inside her right before her husband had his way with her.

Most women looked at him like he'd taken leave of his senses for such a suggestion. They needed convincing it worked. Vinegar killed sperm. He longed to tell them that was what his nurse did to keep from getting pregnant. Instead, he told her only what a doctor had to tell.

He eased his hand inside her, feeling the slickness of blood and slime. She moaned; but did not scream out as he expected. It took a certain amount of strength to scream. This woman no longer had strength and very little will to survive, but she would. A mother didn't allow herself to die when she had a choice along with children who needed her.

What he pulled out was what he expected. A fetus that would fit in the palm of his hand. One that smelled of several days of death. For a moment, he wondered if she had taken something to cause its death? If so, what was it? He quickly put the thought from his mind. A mother always wanted her baby. Odd, how some women had more children than they could take care of, when other women would give just about anything to be able to have one baby.

Mrs. Waltrip was pale and listless. She didn't rally back as fast as he had expected. Her body needed rest, and she was finally getting it thanks to the shot he had given her. He had given her a little more than he should have, considering how weak she was, but she would come around. Still yet, he was afraid to leave her. He stayed by her side as her husband and children came inside the cabin. A least a dozen children climbed into the loft to sleep. Her husband sat on the floor in a corner, his head leaning against the wall as he snored.

He longed for a time when he would no longer care for those in need, but he feared that day would never arrive.

Morning came and Mrs. Waltrip was breathing normally, bleeding only slightly, and alert enough to know what was going on.

"How are you feeling?" the doctor asked.

"Hain't hurtin' much," she mumbled.

Her color was good. He lifted the worn quilt and felt of her stomach. Her womb felt firm enough. She was going to live. What she needed now was rest. He made the decision to give her another shot to make her sleep.

"I don't need 'at," she told him when she saw the syringe.

"Yes, you do," he said as he sunk the needle into the opposite arm he'd given the shot in last night. "You'll rest today and maybe until morning," he told her, and then went to find her husband. He'd gone outside at the crack of dawn. The kids were still asleep in the loft.

He found Mr. Waltrip coming out of the dilapidated barn. "Your wife will live if she stays in bed for the next three days," he told Mr. Waltrip firmly. "Your oldest daughters will have to make do with cooking and things for a while."

"I'll see to it," he assured the doctor.

"She'll sleep the rest of the day and until morning, most likely. If she gets worse, come after me."

"I'll do it. I'll get with you on your payment afore long," he assured the doctor.

The doctor nodded. From what he had observed, the Waltrip's were barely keeping body and soul together. There was no way for them to earn money. They were growing enough food to keep them alive and that was it. He wasn't about to take what they needed, and he didn't. They would be better off if they moved out of the high, rocky mountain and down into the valley where there would be jobs, but he knew Mr. Waltrip would never move away from the place he loved even if it meant an easier life for his wife and children.

"Want to ride back in with me to get your horse?" the doctor asked him.

It was easy to tell Waltrip was torn between getting his horse and looking after his wife.

"I'll walk down the mountain directly," he finally said. "My ole woman needs me here."

Tiredness from lack of sleep took hold as he scattered chickens when he turned his car around in the dirt-swept yard. Who was he to judge a man who did the best he could with the hand that was dealt him? Was he not doing the same exact thing? He had a wife in name only – one that requires constant care. He, and probably Elouise would be better off finding a nursing home of sorts to put her in, but he couldn't bring himself to do it. At least he had a loving nurse to go home to. Without her, he didn't know if he could survive as a man or as a doctor.

What kept him going was knowing he'd arrive home to the tenderhearted woman he loved. She would ease his troubled soul, feed his hunger, and take care of things while he caught up on lost sleep. He parked his car, got out, breathed in the sweet air of relief at finally being home, and walked along the path where her flower garden grew. He smiled at how lovingly she cared for her flowers as well as him. It was his lucky day when she answered his need for a nurse.

His need for life.

Instead of opening the kitchen door and being met with the aroma of coffee brewing and breakfast cooking, he opened the door to hear his wife's irate yelling. The kitchen, the entire house, didn't feel right. The warm home he expected now felt cold, deserted, empty.

He ignored the yells of his wife and rushed into nurse Whitley's bedroom. The room was empty, the bed made, nothing on the dresser. He jerked drawers open.

Nothing!

Only a slight familiar smell of her came out of the drawers to meet him. Fear gripped his chest. Her bedroom couldn't be empty. She couldn't be gone. She would never leave him.

"Valarie!" he yelled, as he rushed through the house. He saw the letter on his pillow.

He grabbed the letter with shaking hands and read it over twice.

Trollop?

Live the rest of her life in respect?

Pain gripped his chest like he had never known.

Chapter 33

~~Preacher Hadley~~

Preacher Hadley had made a point of checking on those in need once a week regardless if they were a member of his church or not. It was part of a preacher's responsibility to keep an eye on the sick and infirm. He was on his way to check on Tucker when he passed by the doctor's house. Elouise's screeching got his attention. Her ranting and raving weren't a new thing. Most everybody in the community had heard her carrying on more times than once. Many had rushed in the house to make sure she was okay, only to be confronted with a rage focused at them. After a while, all their sympathy turned to the doctor. It was obvious the doctor, along with his nurse, were doing everything in their power to keeper Elouise healthy and happy. Her times of pitching screaming fits were nothing anyone could stop.

At first, even he thought she was being illtreated. He had visited her several times until one day she turned on him. She had actually accused him of sexually assaulting her to his face. Fortunately, Dr. Robinson knew such accusations were all in her warped mind. But, what if the doctor along with the people in the community decided to believe her? Such a possibility hit him hard. There were always some folks willing to believe the worse regardless of innocence. His reputation could be ruined by a crazy woman. The doctor needed to put her in some kind of home for his own peace of mind along with everyone's reputation. He made a point of informing the community that Elouise Blough Robinson had crossed over the border line and was now mentally insane. He warned everyone he came into contact with that, for their own safety, it was best to never visit her. Not only did Elouise become irate when she had visitors, it made the good doctor's job of taking care of his deranged wife more difficult.

If the preacher told them such as that, there was little question about it being true.

This morning, preacher Hadley hesitated. Did he dare knock on the door and ask Nurse Whitley if everything was okay? A man had the right to care for his own family without outside interference from other people, and that included a preacher. However, wasn't it a preacher's duty to offer assistance, if and when, it was needed?

He stood there listening. He realized there was no smoke coming from the kitchen chimney. Usually, this time of morning there was always smoke rising, along with the wonderful smell of food cooking. For some reason, the place looked sad, deserted even.

Yeah, he ought to at least knock on the door, see if something was wrong. He wouldn't go inside. He made his way to the door, lifted his hand, and knocked on the kitchen door. No answer. He hesitated, knocked again. Still, no one answered the door.

"Dr. Robinson," he called. No answer. "Nurse Whitley. Are you in there?" Still no answer.

He opened the door. The room was empty. He left the kitchen door open and went to the section of the house where the doctor's office was located. He knocked on the door. Still no doctor or Nurse Whitley answered his knock. It was early, but not that early.

He turned the doorknob knowing the door was never locked, or hardly ever. He entered. There were no patients waiting to see the doctor.

No nurse to run interference if there had been patients.

He opened his mouth to holler the house, but it didn't seem the right thing to do when Elouise was screaming the doctor's name over and over. He gritted his teeth, honed his courage, and walked into the room the doctor used as a hospital room.

Empty.

"Doc?" he called softly. "Are you here somewhere?"

No answer.

He girded his loins, opened the door that led into the private section of the doctor's house, and entered. Elouise's ranting was plainer now, more irritating. A woman who cut such a shine for such a length of time had to be okay.

The sound of sobbing got his attention.

A heart-wrenching sound.

Pure grief.

He followed the sound to the bedroom, debated opening the slightly cracked door. What if he intruded on what another person ought not to witness?

Something that should remain private.

He was a preacher! It was his duty to ease the suffering, wasn't it not?

He silently eased the crack wider and put his eye to the opening. The dependable, strong to the bitter end doctor was lying face down on the bed sobbing like a two-year-old who had cried himself out.

He didn't hesitate.

He crossed the floor to the bed, placed his hand on the doctor's heaving back. "What is it Doc? What's wrong?"

"She's gone," the doctor sobbed. "She left me."

The preacher saw the letter crumpled in his hand. He didn't need to read what had been written, or even ask a question. He knew who had left the Doc.

"Why?" was all the preacher could think of saying.

"Trollop," he sobbed out in agony. "She doesn't want to be known as my trollop."

The preacher could understand that. In the Bible, Mary Magdalene didn't want to be known as a fallen woman, either.

"Bear up, Doc. Taking it this hard won't do you any good," he told the doctor, but he wasn't sure if that was true or not. Sometimes only a flood of tears could ease the pain of a broken heart.

"I'm too weak," he sobbed the words out. "She was my strength, my life. I can't live without her. Don't want to."

"If that's true, grow a pair, get up from there and stop your whining," the preacher shocked him by saying. "Go after her," the preacher said, as though he knew what was the right thing for the doctor to do.

The doctor seemed to come to himself. Never in his life had a preacher told him to grow a pair, much less go after a woman. He suddenly felt ashamed for his weakness. To have Preacher Hadley see him like this was unbearable.

"I'm not myself," he admitted to the preacher as he took a handkerchief from his pocket and wiped his eyes and nose. "I've spent nearly twenty-four hours at the Waltrip place with hardly a wink of sleep. I was counting on my nurse only to find she's left because of vicious gossip."

The preacher noticed that the doctor was getting hold of himself. He was becoming the man he allowed everyone to see instead of a man who had normal weaknesses.

"Why are you here?" the doctor demanded.

"I was on my way to see Tucker. When I passed your place, I heard Elouise carrying on worse than normal. When nobody answered my knock, I figured I ought to check on things."

"Elouise," the doctor said. "What in the world am I to do with her. She needs full-time care and I don't think I can give it to her any longer."

"It's common knowledge that you've done all you can for her. Everybody thinks it's long past time you put her in a home where she'll be able to get whatever kind of help, she needs."

"She's my wife. My responsibility."

"That's right. It's your responsibility. Folks won't condemn you for doing what's best for her and everybody else," he said, as he thought of her accusations toward him. He wondered how many other people she'd accused of wrongdoing. It would be best for everybody if she was committed. It was the doctor who refused to do what was best.

Now that Nurse Whitley was gone, he'd have no choice other than commit his wife to a home far away.

"I best go check on her," Dr. Robinson told him. "I'd say she's hungry and in need of her medication." He downed his head. "Uh, I'd appreciate it if you kept this to yourself."

"I understand. A man, regardless of who he is, has a right to personal weakness, every once in a while."

Preacher Hadley started to leave the doctor to himself, but turned back to him. "If you can't do it, I'll get an ambulance to take her to a home while you go after your nurse," he found himself offering.

"Yes," the doctor surprised them both by saying. "Do that for me if you will. I fear I'm too weak of a man to do it myself."

Preacher Hadley hadn't expected the Doc to agree so quickly, but he'd do what he'd offered.

Instead of continuing his way to visit Tucker, he headed back home. Ida would sure enough be interested in the goings on.

*

Hurt and even anger had filled the doctor to the brim as he went to his wife. She was sitting up in bed, her face red, her hair straggled about her head, her arms waving about as she ranted on about his neglect of her. Odd, how her anger had made her appear to be better than she'd been in years.

He couldn't stomach the sight of her. He'd had all he could take. Instead of calming her down, feeding her, and giving her medication. He left her bedroom, found his black satchel where he left it in the kitchen, and filled a syringe.

The first thing he'd do, after she went to sleep, was find the preacher and have him see to the arrangements.

Then he would be able to find his beloved nurse.

Chapter 34

~~Granny Witcher~~Tally~~

There were no parts of the still left by the time Granny Witcher and Tally got to Tucker's hiding place. Tucker had chosen good. It was just about a perfect spot for a still. It was well hidden in dense woods and surrounded by laurel hells. At the same time, there was a good stream of running cold water coming out of the rocky mountain. Tucker had a metal pipe running from the head of the stream to his still. It was gone. Granny Witcher figured Clancy would have taken the stream of water with him if it had been possible. That boy was worse than a mischief of packrats and a murder of crows put together. Anything left loose and unguarded he claimed as his own and carried it to his hiding place in his cave.

Some parts of the still had to be heavy. She wondered how he had managed until she saw drag tracts of a travois. She had to give the boy credit for figuring out a way to do what he intended. He was as smart as a whip. Had to be to live the way he did. The boy had tried to wipe out the track, doing only half of a job. Sometime, she needed to make a point of showing him how to cover up tracks until they couldn't be easily detected. Once she and Tally found out what had happened to Dobb, she would finish wiping out the tracks, showing the girl how to do a good job of erasing tracks. One never knew when such knowledge would come in handy for Tally. She had a lot to teach the child if Tally was determined to continue living in her mother's cabin.

Granny Witcher hoped she could live long enough to see the girl grown up enough to take care of herself. There was a lot for the child to learn about survival – both physically and mentally. She wasn't sure living on the mountain was the right thing for the girl. It was a hard life but a peaceful one – in most cases. She had both hated and feared the isolated mountains when she first arrived. It was an alien place with no signs of the comforts she had grown up with. It took time along with the love of a good man to show her what she had been missing.

He taught her the pleasure of lying beside a singing stream listening to its song, of lying in contentment beneath a willow tree with its branches caressing the ground. He taught her how to tumble small rocks in a stream until they were smooth enough to make a string of beads. He taught her to love the cardinal's song, and to listen to the haunting honk of migrating geese high in a sky of blue.

Gray Leaf had taught her all about the thing she came to love. He taught her about life.

It was only fitting she pass his teachings on to the girl. Maybe she needed to pass some of his teachings on to the boy as well. *Come time,* she thought. Right now Clancy was in that hopeless teenage stage where he already knew everything far better than any old woman could possibly know.

"I don't like this place," Tally broke through her thoughts. "It feels kinda scary."

"What don't you like about it?" Granny Witcher ask, wanting to know what the girl was feeling.

"It's . . . I don't know. Kinda like something bad happened here."

"It's where the bear and your dad met up."

Tally cringed. Her eyes grew wide as her face paled. "The bear killed him, didn't it?" she asked.

"I figure that's right. Are you sure you're up to finding out for certain?"

"Yeah. I need to know."

Good girl, Granny Witcher thought. "It's always better to know the truth than spent time worrying about things."

"Where's the still?" Tally asked.

"The boy took it."

"Clancy?"

"Yeah."

"Is he gonna make liquor?"

"I doubt it. At least not until a long ways down the road. Come here. See where there's signs of something rolling downhill?"

Tally shook her head. "I don't see nothing."

Granny Witcher moved to a bare spot and showed her how the ground had been raked smooth instead of having piles of dead leaves and twigs in odd places. "When the ground is all level and looks the same, you need to look closer. Look over here near that tree, the ground is the way nature intended. It's not exactly level or smooth."

Tally looked.

"The tracks have been wiped out, but the brush marks are plain as day. You get the same look by takin' a broom and sweepin' a dirty floor."

Tally bent down trying to see and understand everything Granny Witcher was telling her.

"Chile, you're gonna need to pay close attention to the things I aim to teach you. I won't always be here to look after you."

Tally nodded as her chin started trembling slightly. She didn't want to be left all alone. Alone was scary. "What about Dad? Did the bear eat him?"

"Bears don't usually eat people unless they're starving. There's been enough bramble and mass for the bear to forage, not to mention Tucker's mash. We'll follow the brushed-out tracks and see what we find."

Fear came to Tally's eyes as she tried to stop her chin from trembling.

"You don't have to be afraid," Granny Witcher assured her. "I aim to look after you until the whippoorwill calls me home."

Tally gave her a puzzled look; but asked no questions as she watched Granny Witcher wiping out the signs Clancy left behind. The old woman read the signs without telling Tally what she was seeing. No need to scare the child more than was necessary. It was easy to see the places where Clancy had failed to wipe out blood stains. Tracks were one thing, blood stain-soaked ground was another thing. It needed time and a lot of rain not to be visible.

When they reached the creek where Dobb, the pot and the bear had separated company, Granny Witcher figured out what had taken place. It was only reasonable that Dobb would take to the water. The bear would follow the smell of the tumbling pot. She hesitated a moment before following the creek downstream. Would it harm the girl if they came upon Dobb's dead body? After all the things that had gone on, he was her dad.

Oh, well, a person had to learn to deal with death sooner or later. She'd already seen her mother's dead body, plus witnessed her dad dig up her mother's decomposed body and cut out the fetus. She'd already been through worse than seeing Dobb's dead body, regardless of what it looked like after being mauled by a bear.

It was best not to raise a hot-house child who couldn't take the sordid part of living. Children, like plants, needed to be hardened off to life early on. Survive the worst and grow stronger. Be sheltered, and not know how to cope. The hard part was trying to accomplish such without making the child hard and bitter. A child needed a lot of love combined with reality.

Granny Witcher stopped at the edge of the creek where Dobb had bled out. There was a faint coppery scent clinging to mud on the bank. There was also sign where most of the blood-stained dirt had been dug away and replaced with mud and rocks from the creek. Clancy had tried to make the spot look normal. He did a fair job of it. She saw the drag tracks he had tried to wipe out, but he was obviously in a hurry. The grass and weeds were still bent in the direction Dobb had been dragged. She'd have to tell Clancy to always brush in the opposite direction from whatever was being dragged. She took time to help cover up the drag tracks better, but a good rain was needed before they would no longer be as visible.

At first, she was puzzled as to where Clancy was dragging Dobb's body until he made a sharp turn and headed straight for the cabin. It dawned on her that a ready-dug grave was waiting in the garden beside Sally's grave. She wasn't sure if that was a wise decision. If folks saw the two graves, they might come to the right conclusion and realize that Dobb was dead. Those do-gooders would think they had a free shot at capturing Tally.

But, they would be wrong.

Tally was now her sole responsibility, and she was taking it seriously.

Just as she thought, Clancy had taken Dobb's body to the grave and done a fair job of filling the grave in with dirt and rocks.

~~~~

"Let's gather more rocks from the woods and put on top of the grave," she told Tally. She doubted Clancy had dug out the dirt that had fallen back into the hole. She didn't want animals digging the body out.

"Is Dad in there?"

"Yes."

"Are you sure?"

"I'm right certain."

"Should we dig him up to make sure?"

"No. It's best not to disturb the dead. We'll ask Clancy if it's Dobb the next time we see him."

"Is it safe for me to go back home?"

"You'll be safe from Dobb, but I don't about those do-gooders."

Granny Witcher saw the disappointment on the girl's face. Staying in her little shack was miserable for the child. Having her there was miserable for Granny Witcher as well. The cabin had enough room for both of them, along with more space for her herbs and medicines. She hated to give up her own little shack to move into the cabin, but the girl was more important than her privacy.

"Will they get me? Will I need a gun to keep them away?"

"You'll likely need more than a gun."

Tally's chin trembled. "Can you and Clancy stay with me?"

"Don't think it would be a good idea as far as Clancy is concerned. He's the free spirit sort. Don't like having restrictions put on him. I figure on staying with you until you've grown enough to look after yourself." Or until Gray Leaf summoned her to come to him. She tried not to think about what kind of condition her body and mind would be in if she had to stay on this earth for another eight or ten years. Hard living had already taken its toll.

Chapter 35

~~Tucker~~Dr. Robinson~~

Time allowed Tucker's wounds to start healing. But it didn't matter if he was healing or not. It was past time for him to take over his life and get rid of Inez. It had become obvious what she was planning. She was taking way too much time rubbing salve on his scabbed body.

Worse, he was starting to enjoy it.

Inez was the type of woman most men could read like a book. He was certain he knew what was going through her mind. Greedy was the word that best described Inez. Her next step in her plan would be to charge him for pleasure. He knew Inez's kind. Hell, he knew Inez. He'd paid her for pleasure before. Not that he was embarrassed about it. A man needed flesh on flesh, and she was the one available. It wasn't like he was the only man who needed pleasure of the flesh, or the only one who paid Inez to get it. Every man, single or married, wanted to keep such goings on a secret – and was foolish enough to believe he could.

Thing was he didn't want her now. His injuries, plus knowing what she was up to put a damper on his want-to. One thing was for certain, she wasn't the house cleaning type. Yet, she was going through his house with determination.

"I'm cleaning," she insisted. "You've made a pig sty out of this place. "It's obviously not been cleaned since your wife left you."

She could use the excuse of cleaning to search for his hidden supply of money, but she would never find what little he had. He might have tolerated her cleaning streak if she hadn't said those words. For her to bring up his cheating, no-account wife was hitting below the belt. A man never got over knowing he wasn't enough to keep his wife happy, not to mention what his own brother was willing to do to him.

"That's enough," he told her as he pushed her hands away. "From here on out, I can do for myself. It's time for you to go back to your own place."

Inez's eyes widened in surprise. Her hooked nose quivered. It was obvious to Tucker that Inez thought she had him helplessly under her control.

"Don't talk foolishness. It will be weeks until you're able to fend for yourself," she said as her hand move seductively up the calf of his leg.

"Enough is enough," he told her more firmly. "Pack up your things and get out."

"What's gotten into you? How ungrateful can you be? After all the time and work I've put into taking care of you, and you've not paid me a copper yet. I'll leave, but I want my money right now."

"Then you'll have to get it from the Doc."

"What? Get what you owe me from Dr. Robinson? You're the one who's supposed to pay me."

"Doc is holding what little money I've got for me. Didn't want do-gooders to get hold of it after my accident." Which wasn't exactly the truth, but Doc would understand. Tucker didn't tell her Doc traded with him for his deliveries. His liquor was the best disinfectant a doctor could have, but doctoring him after he'd been dragged had most likely taken care of what the doc owed him, and maybe more.

The arrangement worked mighty fine for both of them. Folks paid Tucker cash more often than they paid the doctor cash. Folks knew all too well the doctor was sworn to take care of the infirm and ailing regardless of payment. Tucker was not sworn to give a man free liquor.

Inez looked at him as if she didn't know whether to believe him or not.

"Go on. Get whatever things you've totted over here and get out. I've had enough of you."

Inez's nostrils flared in anger. "Go to Hell," she said, as she slapped him hard in his most tender place. Her back went ramrod straight. She whirled around and marched away.

Tucker considered getting up and following her once his pain had subsided, but she wasn't worth the effort. If she came back to where he was laying on the bed, and got within his reach, he would slap her so hard it would take her a week to find her way back.

~~~~

Unreasonable fury was burning inside Inez. How dare Tucker tell her to leave! After all she'd done for him! Worse was him refusing to pay her. Did he really think she would believe the doctor was the keeper of his money? Everybody knew Tucker was a skinflint who kept his money hidden. He had to have a lot of money considering how much liquor he sold along with what little he spent on things. Even his house was pert near empty of the things a person needed to survive. She'd had to buy food and other supplies from the general store – having the bill put on Tucker's tab.

Inez could barely keep herself from running to the doctor's house. The doctor would prove Tucker was nothing more than a whopping liar. Then, she would deal with Tucker in her own way. Tucker was still weak and bedridden. She was used to dealing with men who were strong as an ox and out of their minds on too much liquor. She could handle Tucker.

What in the world was going on? she wondered as she neared the house. Some woman was screaming her lungs out. Most likely Elouise was having one of her fits. Everyone in the community was well aware of the fits she pulled, but this one was a dilly. Inez was out of breath as she came into the yard where Preacher Hadley, Ida, along with about half of the community's residents were.

"What's going on?" Inez asked as she sidled up to Ida.

"They're taking Elouise to an asylum. Ask me it's way past time. Hadley is an expert on such things, and he says it's definitely long past time she was put somewhere that can help her. Dr. Robinson was too tender-hearted to do it until now. Truth is the doc left it in Hadley's hands. Couldn't stand to see her hauled off."

"Did she get worse or something?"

"Can you believe Nurse Whitley quit because Elouise got too violent to handle? Her leaving forced the doctor to do what he should have done years ago."

"Which is?" Inez questioned.

"I just told you what's going on. She's being put in a straitjacket right now so they can get her into the van to transport her. They say she's strong as an ox and wild as a buck. Crazy people are strong and violent, you know. One of 'em gave her a knock-out shot, but it's not working on her. She almost scratched one of the men's eyes out and bit a mouthful of flesh out of another man's arm. Hadley tried to help them, but she clawed his arms something awful when he tried holding her down."

Inez looked at Preacher Hadley. Sure enough, his shirt sleeves were ripped and streaked with blood. Even the front of his white shirt was hanging open with buttons missing. He was looking miserable and unapproachable to say the least.

"He looks to be on the mad side," Inez made of point of saying.

Ida lifted her chin in irritation. "There's no wonder. He's not liking what's going on with Elouise. He says it was plain derelict not to have sent her off years ago. It would have been best for everyone concerned."

"What about Dr. Robinson. Can't he handle her?"

"I just told you he's not here. Preacher Hadley said he couldn't stand to see them haul her off. He asked the preacher to be here when they came after her. It's a preacher's place to help out where he can. Lord knows he's kept busy doing such as that."

"Where is Dr. Robinson?" Inez demanded. She wanted to find out for sure if Tucker was lying about the doctor having Tucker's money. When they were cleaning Tucker's house, Ida had admitted it was the doctor's idea for her to look after Tucker.

"I'm not supposed to tell, but I know you won't go about spreading gossip. Hadley said Doc has gone off after his nurse. Hadley said the doctor was devastated by her leaving."

"Never thought she'd leave him considering what they've been up to all these years," Inez said.

"Me either," Ida agreed. "They've been thick as thieves for years. It's common knowledge what they've been up to.

"Why do you reckon she took off?"

"If you ask me, it's as plain as the nose on your face. She got fed up with being known as the doctor's trollop. It was high-time she got herself a little pride."

"When will he be back?" Inez demanded.

"How should I know?"

Inez left Ida and went to where the preacher was standing, watching as two men dragged Elouise out of the house. She was wearing a straitjacket, but her feet were dragging the ground.

"Get your hands off me. I'll kill all of you!" Elouise screamed at the top of her lungs. "Get your hands off me!"

She turned her head and her eyes honed-in on Preacher Hadley.

"I see you! You're behind this! You don't want your sorry wife to know what you did to me. I'll tell her right now. You can't stop me. You're a whore monger. You violated me!"

Inez almost forgot why she'd shown up at hearing those words. Unfortunately, the two men dragged Elouise into the back of the van and closed the door before she could scream out more accusations.

Preacher Hadley shook his head. "Poor woman. Her mind deserted her a long time ago. She has no idea what she's saying," the preacher shook his head, as his face showed his pity for Elouise.

Ida gave him a strange look moments before her face became blank. She rushed to her husband's side to show she stood by her husband and was denouncing Elouise's words.

Inez tried to stifle her grin. She knew things about the preacher she'd sworn to never tell. She suspected she knew more secrets about both the men and women in the area than the doctor did.

In Inez's opinion, everyone had a mixture of good and bad within them – even her. The difference in her was that she kept the good hidden instead of hidding the bad.

~~~~

Dr. Robinson drove like a maniac on the rough, dirt road leading to the nearest town. Never had he thought Valarie would leave him. They loved each other beyond life itself. Surely, he hadn't been wrong in those feelings. He would give up his life for her, and he'd thought she felt the same. They had been together for years. From day one, they realized what people would think and say about them, even before they had consummated their love with each other. He loved Valarie more than he cared about his reputation. Valarie continuously told him she felt the same way, so why had she suddenly changed her mind? Why had she up and left him without a word? She had to have a reason, and he didn't think it was because Tucker called her a trollop. Bad words never trumped love.

He didn't think there was anything Elouise could do or say that would force Valarie to leave him. When Elouise became too difficult, Valarie went outside to busy herself in her flower garden. If there had been a problem with her, surely Valarie would have discussed it with him instead of running away during the night leaving nothing other than a letter on his pillow. Valarie had never been a coward. She was one of the most courageous women he knew. There had to be a mighty powerful reason behind her actions.

He was the coward. He couldn't bring himself to put Elouise in an asylum for the deranged, not even in a home for the permanently handicapped. He had focused his responsibility toward his wife, and not the nurse he hired to help take care of her. In hindsight, he had done Valarie a great wrong. He had all but forced her to take care of his wife, while enduring all the insults the people of the community dumped on her. It was true that a woman wasn't allowed to express her desire without being condemned, while a man could get away with such things. After all, men would be men. God made them that way. But a woman always had a target on her back – even when she was doing nothing wrong.

How could loving someone be wrong?

How could comforting someone when they were hurting emotionally be wrong?

How could holding someone in your arms when they had nightmares at night be wrong?

How could pieces of paper supposedly tying people together be more powerful than who God put together?

Dr. Robinson wiped tears off his cheeks. It was true he'd put the wellbeing of every single person in front of Valarie's wellbeing. He had insisted she be a nurse to the people, put them in front of her own wellbeing regardless of how they downgraded her. Why hadn't he realized even a doctor had the responsibility of taking care of his own first. He had considered Elouise as being his own because of a piece of paper. He had put her before himself. Why hadn't he done the same for Valarie?

If he could only get his beloved Valarie back, he would become a different man.

~~~~

Valarie left the horse in a stable and paid for it to be taken care of. She knew Dr. Robinson would rush to the nearest town when he found her gone. But there was no way his conscience would allow Mr. Waltrip to be without his horse. Not when he promised it would be safely waiting for him. The good doctor had a moral compass he lived by.

She also had a moral compass as a woman and a soon-to-be mother. It didn't matter how much a woman loved a man; a mother should love her child more. A man had many options in taking care of himself. A baby only had its mother.

She was a mother now, even though her baby wasn't born. She had become its mother the moment it had been conceived. It was her responsibility to give her baby the best possible life, and she was determined to do just that.

"Where to Ma'am?" the man at the ticket office asked.

She had looked at the bus schedule. One early morning bus was to arrive and leave within the hour. She didn't care where the bus was going. The farther away the better. It would be making several stops along the way. She could get off at any one of them, making it more difficult for the doctor to figure out where she had gone. Not that she thought he would seek to find her. How could he when he had a wife and patients to care for? He wasn't the sort of man who shirked his responsibilities. He only shirked caring for her.

Elouise was his responsibility – not hers. His patients were his responsibility – not hers.

She had accepted that fact before and after she realized she loved the man. She knew what sleeping with the doctor would lead to. Even before they became lovers there was no way to keep the gossip at bay when she'd agreed to become his wife's live-in nurse. She was too young, too pretty to escape gossip. Even if she and the doctor had hated each other, the speculations would have been spread by wagging tongues. The only way to stop the vicious gossip was for her to leave and settle in a place where she wasn't known.

"Where to?" the man repeated.

"Sorry," she was quick to say. "My mind was elsewhere."

The ticket man didn't give her a second glance as she gave him the name of the last place the bus would stop. He quoted her a price which she quickly paid. She was glad the man wasn't paying attention to her. She had feared everyone she came into contact with would be staring at her, speculating why she was getting on the bus. Oddly enough, no one she came into contact with seemed to care.

There were only two men and one other woman buying tickets. She took the men to be salesmen or something of the sort. The other woman was matronly in appearance. She appeared to be happy about the trip she was about to take. There was a smile dimpling her chubby cheeks, and a twinkle in her eyes. Her mop of gray hair was twisted into a knot at the back of her neck. She gave Valarie a once over a moment before she sank her bulk down on the seat across from Valarie.

"Where you headin' honey?" the woman asked right out of the blue, as though she had a friendly right to know.

Valarie resented the intrusion, but she knew it was better to be nice than irritated. Folks remembered uncooperative people.

"Oh, my. You've got a long ways to ride, don't you? I'm not going very far. My only daughter is expecting a baby any day now. It's her first and she's afraid. Wants her momma with her. You got children?"

"No, I'm not married."

"How unusual for a pretty woman like you to not be married. Not many spinsters around these days, especially one as pretty as you."

Valarie didn't know what to say about that remark. She considered telling the woman that she was a widow who had devoted her life to being a nurse, but thought better of doing so. The less information anyone knew about her the better. She simply wanted to disappear – and live comfortably ever after, if not exactly happily.

Chapter 36

Clancy stored Tucker's dismantled still in the very back of the cave, along with his other treasures. He was proud of himself. It hadn't been an easy task to move the heavy parts, but he figured it would be worth the effort come time. He wouldn't be able to set it up for a while, maybe a year or two. He also knew Tucker would be returning just as soon as he was able to get up and walk. Stilling was Tucker's life. He would go plum crazy when he found his still was gone.

Most likely he'd think Dobb Simmons had taken it. But not for long. He'd go straight to Granny Witcher with questions. He'd know she kept eyes on everything that happened on the mountain. He hadn't seen the old woman as he stole the parts, but he knew she would be watching and tracking him. She'd know that the bear had killed Dobb, and that he had buried him in the grave she had dug in the garden beside Sally. What he wasn't sure of was if she'd tell Tucker what happened or play dumb? He was counting on her playing dumb. She seldom told what she knew about things. Knowing nothing paid off. It allowed a person to live in peace.

He wasn't naive enough to think Tucker would let the removal of his still go without reprisal. There was no doubt about it, Tucker would be on a rampage for revenge. Clancy would have to figure out what he could do to put suspicion off himself? Who would he want to get the blame? Clancy grinned. The answer was a simple one. Grubb Claxton and his no-account bunch deserved all the trouble they could get. Their liquor was barely short of straight poison. Folks knew better than to drink it, but when they didn't have enough sense to hold our for the good stuff, they fell back on drinking inferior swill. It would be a blessing if their still got busted up.

Clancy thought about doing it himself, but he wasn't that stupid. He knew he wasn't able to accomplish such a feat at this time unless he could come up with a humdinger of a plan. There were always rough looking men standing guard who were known for their viciousness. What they would do to a boy if caught was just as bad or worse than what they would do to a girl. Even the law feared them enough to stay far away from their still as well as their side of a mountain.

He'd have to do some thinking on a plan between now and when Tucker would be able to make the trip to check on his still. It might be a good idea to mosey down to the valley just to see how Tucker was faring. No telling what was going on down there. Tucker could even be dead, but he didn't think so.

Clancy left his cave carrying a twitch of broomsedge he had gathered to wipe out his tracks. The fluffy, grass-like sedge gave a more natural sweep of the dirt and leaves than switches from trees did. He'd hid in the bushes and watched the granny witch woman using broomsedge to wipe out his tracks where he had dragged the heavy pot from the still. He'd intended to come back and do a better job of wiping out his tracks, but the old woman had gotten to it before he did. That meant she was willing to keep the fact that he had stolen the still a secret. At least for the time being.

He also figured Granny Witcher had found out what had happened to Dobb Simmons. It pleased him to know she had also wiped out the drag tracks of Dobb's body. She and the girl had covered his grave with rocks to keep wild animals from digging him up. She'd also moved the girl back into the cabin, and made sure the girl was with her at all times. However, she hadn't moved anything from her shack to the cabin. Clancy was puzzled why she wouldn't, as the cabin was much larger and more comfortable than her shack. The old woman was plum odd, but he wasn't about to underestimate her on anything. He was confident the girl would be safe as long as the old woman was looking after her. He would also make sure those do-gooder women who gathered children for the orphanage didn't get hold of her. Other than for those women, the girl should be pretty much safe living on the mountain.

Clancy waited until near dark to leave the mountain. He got a shaky kind of feeling when he got close to the valley. It was as though there was some kind of evil spirit hovering over that valley waiting to grab hold of the unsuspecting. He had no reason for the way he felt, yet he felt as though bad things were waiting there for him. The orphanage, the sheriff, the people were more than he wanted to encounter. He felt like a wild animal going into the liar of his enemies, but he needed to know what was going on with Tucker.

What was the worst that could happen to him? Getting caught by the sheriff and not being able to get away from him? That wasn't going to happen. He was still a boy, but the kind of life he lived had made him lean and mean. He also thought the way he had to survive for the past few years had made him smart as the sneaky gray fox.

Once he got near the edge of the woods, he found a creek and rolled in the water wetting himself all over including his face and hair. He then found dry, dusty earth and rolled in it like a horse wallowing in the dirt until he had a good cover of brown. He considered using weeds or twigs of leaves to stick in his clothing, but he didn't want to leave any sign of breakage.

He knew he was being unreasonably careful, but something didn't feel right about the oncoming darkness. Things were too still. Not a leaf was moving. Day birds had gone silent and the night birds hadn't made the first sound. Clancy lifted his head and smelled the air. Storm, he thought. There was a mighty big storm on its way. He best check out Tucker in a hurry and get back to his cave right fast.

Clancy did his best to shrink himself up and become invisible as he sneaked out of the woods, staying in the shadows as much as possible, to Tucker's bedroom window. He hunkered down, looked around. No one was out moving about. The inhabitants of the holler appeared to be as silent as the birds.

Slowly, Clancy stretched his neck until he was peeking in the bedroom window. There was enough light for him to see clearly. Tucker was half-sitting and half-lying on the bed. His attention was focused on something across the room. It was a woman. Inez. She was holding a double-barreled shotgun pointing at Tucker's head.

"Put that thing down," he heard Tucker say. "Afore you hurt yourself."

"You're not going to screw me out of my money. I'm only going to ask you one more time before I pull the trigger. Where have you got your money hidden?"

"Hell-fire, woman, how many times do I have to tell you, I don't have money hidden."

"Liar! You think I won't blow your head off, but I will. I'm gonna count to three and if you don't tell me by then, you're a dead man."

Clancy looked from a very angry Inez to what appeared to be a too calm Tucker.

"One."

"Stop it. I told you the doctor has what little money belonged to me."

"Liar."

"I'm not lying."

"Yes, you are. Dr. Robinson has run off. He's chasing after his whore. Two."

A puzzled look came over Tucker. "What are you talking about?"

"Doc is long gone. If he had your money, it's gone along with him."

"You can't be serious."

"It's a fact. Pay me or you're dead."

"Shoot me and you'll never know if I'm lying or not. The sheriff will get you for murder."

"No, he won't. It's not my gun."

"For the last time, woman. I don't have any money."

"Three," Inez screeched out a few seconds before one of the loudest shotgun blasts Clancy had ever heard.

A powerful force shoved Clancy backward. He hit the ground, felt winded and kind of disoriented. Slowly, he sat up. Glass was scattered all around him. The window had been shot out. Clancy stretched himself up and dared to peek in the broken window again. Inez was lying on her back with Tucker on top of her.

"Damn you!" Tucker yelled, breathless. "You damn near killed me." He grabbed the shotgun up off the floor where Inez had dropped it and hit her dead center between the eyes with the butt of the gun.

So much for her crooked nose, Clancy found himself oddly thinking, as blood bloomed over her face. Evidently, she hadn't planned on how hard a double-barrel shotgun could kick. Plus, it sounded like she pulled both triggers almost at the same time. She couldn't aim worth a shit either, because she shot out the window instead of hitting Tucker. Clancy saw that half the window frame was gone. If she'd aimed a tiny bit different, he'd be without a head. As it was, his ears were ringing, and head felt funny. He was covered in broken glass. He lifted his hand and touched his head. He felt warm liquid. There was blood on his hands when he drew them away.

Had he been the one shot, or was the blood coming from cuts?

"Reckon you hain't goin' nowhere till I get back with the sheriff," Tucker was saying.

Clancy didn't move as he watched Tucker hobble from the house, gun in hand. He was moving slowly and painfully. Clancy knew he had best move too. He had to get to safety before the sheriff arrived.

~~~~

"I've got them shut up nice and safe," Granny Witcher told Tally. "They should be okay."

"Shouldn't we bring them inside with us if it's going to be a bad storm?"

"Would if it was going to be a bad enough, but it hain't. It'll hit hard and fast then be over."

"I don't like storms, and my goat and chickens don't like them either," Tally said with a trembling chin.

"Most things don't, but storms usually clears the air. That's not a bad thing. Eat your supper afore the winds hit. It'll sound worse than it is."

Tally frowned and as Granny Witcher spooned beans and potatoes on two plates. "I'm too afraid to eat."

"Nonsense, child. You've been through a lot of storms afore."

"All of 'em scared me," Tally admitted.

"There's no need to be afraid," Granny Witcher assured her. "Storms come and go and so does the sunshine. A body takes the bad with the good, cause that's how life is."

Tally didn't say anything further as she moved her food around on her plate. She knew she should be hungry, that she needed to eat, but food wasn't what she wanted. She wanted her mother back – her sister and brothers back, but not her dad. She was glad he was in the grave.

The storm hit with a force. First came the wind whipping trees until limbs broke and fell to the ground. Next came the downpour of rain as though the mountains needed flooding. Next came the pounding hail beating on the cabin roof as though it was determined to break the thick beams along with the boards.

At first, Granny Witcher thought the door was being beat open by the storm. She certainly hadn't expected to see Clancy come through the door and fall in the floor. He looked for the world like a pitiful drowned cat – wet and pitiful. By the time she'd forced the door closed again, Clancy's wet clothes were turning pink.

Tally gasped and jumped up so fast she knocked her plate of food in the floor.

"What happened?" Granny Witcher asked as she kneeled on the floor beside him.

"Cut," he mumbled. "Glass broke."

The pink turned to red as his bleeding increased. There were several cuts on his face along with many cuts on his head. His hands were also oozing blood. She ran her hand through his hair, feeling chards of glass sticking out of his scalp.

"Stay still for a minute. I'll fix you up. Don't think you'll die anytime soon," she said as she got up to get a pair of pliers she'd seen on a shelf. "Okay, where did you tangle with all that glass."

"Later," he mumbled. "Gotta catch my breath."

~~~~

"Appears you're tellin' the truth," the sheriff said as he looked down at Inez. You sure enough busted her nose all over her face. She'll be hurting bad when she comes around."

He lifted her hands and smelled for the remains of gun powder.

"Hold out yours," the sheriff told Tucker.

Tucker did. The sheriff smelled Tuckers hands and nodded, satisfied. "Looks like she didn't miss you by much. Blew out the window. Not good with the storm startin' to hit like it is. Ought to nail a board over it."

"Don't think I can manage it. All I could do to get you here. Think I'll have to lay back down. You might ought to take her to the Doc's place."

"Right. You're not looking so good yourself. Doc's not here," the sheriff told him. Reckon she'll have to stay where she is."

So, she might have been telling the truth about Doc. "Nope," Tucker told him firmly. "Have to lock her in your jail. She tried to kill me."

"But she didn't."

"Attempted murder. Arrest her."

"Well now," the sheriff said hesitantly. "I can't carry her. She's a big one. It'll have to wait until she can walk."

"Then you'll have to stay here. I'd hate to have to shoot her once she comes around. Don't think I'm able to fight her off elsewise."

The sheriff grunted. "Me neither."

Chapter 37

~~Valarie Whitley~~Doc Robinson~~

The bus had to make stops letting off and taking on passengers, slowing down travel. Dr. Robinson drove faster than he'd ever driven, taking chances he'd never normally take. Dr. Robinson didn't think Valarie would get off at the first stop. It wouldn't be far enough away. Maybe not even at the second stop, but he had to check those stops out just in case. He was told no woman got off at the first stop. The second stop only one woman got off. She was plump and jolly. Talking to everyone who would listen about her daughter expecting a baby.

Dr. Robinson hurriedly got back in his car and stepped on the gas. Every minute got him closer to catching up with the bus and getting Valarie back. He fully intended to get her back in his arms, in his life. He didn't care what he had to do. He'd stop being a doctor regardless of how much he wanted to take care of people. Nothing mattered more than Valarie. He couldn't live without her – wouldn't want to.

He might have married Elouise in what seemed like a lifetime ago, but he no longer cared for her in the way a man should care for his wife. He'd done everything he could to love and cherish her, but years of her ranting and blaming him for her condition had worn on him until his love had eroded away with each day that passed.

Nothing he did seemed to help. She didn't get better. She got worse and so did his attitude. He came to despise her as well as himself. He no longer lived a happy life. All he was doing was existing to take care of others including his wife.

There was no joy. No laughter. No happiness. He had become a lost man with a lost soul.

And then he hired Valarie. She brought him back to life. He found all the things he'd been missing when he held her in his arms. She brought pleasure back into his bed.

As for Elouise? Nothing he did or didn't do helped her, although he continued to try – out of guilt if not duty. Her body didn't work properly and neither did her mind. She started accusing every man that came into the house of mistreating her in some way or other. She even accused Preacher Hadley of taking sexual advantage of her. Dr. Robinson knew such as that never happened. He had made a point of eavesdropping on every word Elouise and her few visitors exchanged. He needed to know what Elouise was telling people about him. None of it had been good. Some of her stories had ripped at his heart. After a while, the community realized Elouise had lost what little mind she once had.

Elouise claimed every woman who set foot in the house was a woman he was having sexual relationships with. His patients could hear her screaming accusations even though he kept thef   v doors closed. It got to the point where he had to hide his patients from his wife. To do that, he started giving her shots to calm her down and make her sleep.

He'd done everything he knew to do as a doctor and as a husband for Elouise. Now was the time for him to give up on being the one trying to take care of her and send her to a home. He despised himself for leaving the preacher to see that she was sent to a home, but not enough for him to stay instead of going after Valarie.

It was at the third stop that he caught up with the bus. A man got off. Three people got on in front of Dr. Robinson.

"Ha," the bus driver called out. "I need your ticket."

"Hold up, I'm not getting on," Dr. Robinson told him firmly. "I'm getting my woman off."

Valarie was sitting near the back of the bus. Her face pale and her eyes red. She looked shocked, happy, and at the same time sad.

Dr. Robinson made his way down the aisle and stopped in front of Valarie. "Come on," he said.

"No."

"We need to talk."

"No," she repeated.

"Yes. We do. I need to know what's going on."

"I'm leaving you."

"You're not leaving me. You're running away. I want to know why."

"Ha you! Get off this bus," the driver told him.

"I intend to. Give me a couple more minutes," Dr. Robinson said as his eyes looked straight into Valarie's. "I love you, and I have no intention of making you go back. If you're going to leave, then I'm leaving with you."

Valarie's eyes widened. "I don't believe you."

"Have I ever lied to you?"

Suddenly, Valarie became conscious of the people around her. She had run away from people and what they thought and said about her. These people were strangers. She wanted them to know nothing about her. They would know who she was if she stayed. She stood, back straight, chin lifted, face determined, and walked off the bus followed by Dr. Robinson. She refused to get in the car with him.

"I don't trust you," she said, as she hurried to a building and leaned against the outside wall where they could not be overheard.

Dr. Robinson followed with a hurt look brought on by her words. "Why? What have I done?"

"Nothing," she said. "You've done nothing and that is the problem. You did nothing about the gossip or the insults I was forced to endured."

"We knew what we were facing from the beginning. We agreed that our love for each other was strong enough to endure whatever faced us, or have you forgotten?"

"I've forgotten nothing," she told him.

"Nor have I. That's why I did what I've done."

"And what's that?" she demanded.

"I had Elouise put in a home. I've got a packed suitcase and my medical bag in the car. I'm willing to go wherever you want, do whatever you want to do, but I don't intend to lose you. True love is too hard to find to give it up this side of death. Why, Valarie, why are you so willing to give up on us, and don't tell me it's because of gossip."

"You put Elouise in a home? She's your wife," her voice was shock, filled with disbelief.

"She's my wife, but you're my life. That's the difference between day and night. She's my darkness. You're my sunshine. I can't live in darkness any longer – not after I've known what true love is like. So, let's work this out instead of you running away."

"I'm not running away. I'm leaving."

"Then I'm leaving with you."

Chapter 38

~~Granny Witcher~~Clancy~~

Granny Witcher pulled a small flask from her pocket and used a portion of her supply of Tucker's liquor to disinfect Clancy's cuts. He squirmed as he gritted his teeth to keep from crying out at the painful stinging.

"What happened to you?" Granny Witcher asked once Clancy got his breath back.

"Went to check on Tucker."

"And?" Granny Witcher questioned when Clancy stopped talking.

"Inez tried to kill him."

"Tried?"

"She missed."

Granny Witcher frowned. "How? Why?"

"She wanted his money. When he said he didn't have any, she pulled both triggers. She missed, hit the window frame where I was lookin' in."

"I see. What happened then?"

Clancy told her.

"You and Tucker were both riding high on luck."

"Is Clancy going to live?" Tally finally asked. She had been huddled in a corner watching silently.

"He'll live just fine," Granny Witcher assured her. "That is, if he'll learn to mind his own business instead of sticking his nose in everybody else's."

"I don't . . ."

"Poppycock," Granny Witcher waved a hand at him. "Be quiet while I get you some food. Your belly's no farther from

309

your backbone than a spider's string. You need to eat more if you want to grow into a big, strong man."

The look Clancy gave her let her know he already considered himself to be a big, strong man instead of a boy with a chip on his shoulders.

After he had eaten Granny Witcher's share of supper, he fell asleep listening to the roar of the storm passing over the mountain. When his eyes opened again, he was smelling the wonderful aroma of perking coffee and frying eggs. He sat up, mouth all but watering. He'd spent the night warm and comfortable, if he didn't count the pain he was feeling from all his cuts. He sat up – kind of embarrassed at what he considered his weakness by falling asleep when he should have faced the raging storm and left the cabin to make his way to the cave.

He wasn't a wuss. He was strong, capable, needed no one. And yet he had run to Granny Witcher so she could pick the slivers of glass from his painful wounds. He tried to justify his behavior by telling himself it was only a matter of convenience because of the storm – and not because of his pain and exhaustion. He could have done it all by himself. If something ever happened again, he would not give in. He stood, ignoring the wonderful aroma of cooking food as well as his hunger, and left the cabin.

He needed no one.

When Granny Witcher woke Tally up to eat her breakfast, she was obviously disappointed to see that Clancy was gone.

"Where is he?" she asked.

"Ran off to nurse his pride. He'll learn better – come time."

~~~~

Clancy's pride was hurting him bad. Getting cut with glass wasn't his fault, but the fear he felt while bucking the storm to get back to the mountain was. His mother had often told him that fear was only a story you told yourself.

It didn't matter that he was bleeding and hurting, there was no excuse for his weakness. He tried to assure himself he could have picked all the glass out of his flesh, even on his head and back. He now told himself he had become too exhausted combating the storm to think straight. What he wanted was to figure out a way to never get exhausted again. He had to think smarter – be smarter. Such thinking brought him back to Tucker's still.

He was more determined to blame the removal of Tucker's still on Grubb Claxton and his bunch. He needed to accomplish something no one else was man enough to succeed at in order to prove to himself that he was a man.

He considered adding more poison to the amount of poison the liquor already contained, but there was something about killing innocent people that didn't settle well with him. He figured Grubb's men sampled the liquor freely. Poison might get rid of them, but there was no guarantee others wouldn't drink the liquor. As for suffering, folks already did that by drinking Claxton's rot-gut liquor.

What he wanted to do was put Claxton and his bunch out of commission permanently.

How?

He racked his brain for an answer. Maybe he should go check their operation out. See how they operated and where their weaknesses were.

~~~~

Days later Clancy felt he was healed from his glass wounds. As usual, restlessness had taken hold of him. He had to get moving, accomplish something big – like tackling Grubb Claxton's operation. He decided daytime would be the best time for him to slip in. They would be firing their stills during the darkest hours of night. There would be look-outs with guns patrolling the place. The glow of a fire could be seen during darkness, but smoke and heat waves rising into the sky could not. That's why a good thicket of woods and brush was necessary. Best yet was to find a place where huge rock boulders would shield the flames. There was also a need of water and a way to get the liquor hauled out without leaving a trail that could be easily followed.

On one of Clancy's early morning treks, he had wandered near the area where Grubb Claxton's still was located, but he'd never been all the way to it. It was the odor of hot mash that gave the location away. He knew to go no further, but he had no doubt he could find it without much effort.

He stuck the loaded pistol and extra bullets in a pouch he had fashioned out of a skinned rabbit hide he had caught in a deadfall trap. The pouch was well hidden around his waist and covered by worn and ragged bibbed overalls. Clancy was barefoot as usual when he left the cave. Bare feet didn't leave as much of a path as shoes or boots, but he didn't plan on going barefoot long. He made his way to where he had hidden Dobb's boots, put them on, laced the too big boots tight, and headed to the spot where Tucker had his still.

Interesting, he thought, how neat the place looked. He could hardly tell anything had been in that spot. Someone had come behind him and swept the place clean. There had even been leaf mulch scattered around as though it had been there undisturbed for years. No doubt the work of the witch woman. At least she appeared to be on his side instead of condemning his habitual sticky fingers.

Now for him to leave a trail where only a good tracker such as Tucker could follow – a trail with an occasional boot print.

It took longer than he expected for him to reach the far mountain, which was located in another county from Clancy's cave. The county was well known for its illegal brewing of liquor. However, no other stills were located within miles of Grubb Claxton's set-up. It was a known fact that other moonshiners were afraid of Grubb Claxton and his crew. There was nothing too evil for them to indulge in – including the murder of the offender and their love ones. Even the law stayed away from Grubb Claxton's section of the mountain.

Clancy, who had no family, along with blood that was running hot with arrogance, lacked the instinct of self-preservation. He had no doubt he could do what no one else dared tackle. He found a gully where water seeped from under rocks, laid down and rolled in the cold water. Again, he found a rock overhang where the dirt was dry and fine to roll in until he was covered from the top of his head to the bottom of Dobb's boots.

In his mind, he imagined himself to be an Indian sneaking up on the enemy as he crept from tree trunks to clumps of laurel hells. Although he was as skinny as a racer blacksnake, he tried to avoid crawling through branches of the laurel hells. He didn't want to knock off any of the dirt that concealed him.

He was nearing the top of the mountain when the wind changed directions and brought sound with it. His young ears picked up the sound of excited men that wasn't coming from the direction he thought the still was located. Why would men who were getting a still ready to fire come dark be excited? He eased forward, moving slowly, watching where he put the too big boots, trying not to snap a twig. Once he reached the top of the mountain, he eased toward the rock cropping where the voices were coming from. He hunkered down in hip-high brush. He could hear excited voices, but he couldn't see over the laurel hells and rocks. He crab-crawled toward a cluster of white pines that would serve the purpose of concealment. He shimmied up the largest trunk, holding onto limbs, until he was near the thick needles of top branches where he could see where the men were.

What the heck? There was a waist-high circle built of wooden slabs. Eight men were leaning against the outside of the wooden circle hooting encouragement to two roosters fighting in the center of the circle.

Fighting roosters!

These men had an illegal fight going on. He'd heard of dog fighting and even heard of cock fights, but he never thought he'd witness either one. He felt relief that it wasn't dogs pitted against each other. He wasn't fond of a blood sport. Much to his surprise, both rooster heads were bloodied, their necks feathers puffed out and dripping blood. Their viciousness toward each other came as a surprise as they lifted into the air to come down on their opponent's head with long, sharp spears. Their beaks gouged at the skin on tender heads that were missing cones and waddles. Anything that stood up or hung down had obviously been cut off sometime back to keep their opponent from grabbing a hold on.

Clancy clung to the pine branches, back braced against the trunk, and tried not to breathe loud. He didn't know which would get him killed quicker, finding a man's still or coming upon his cockpit. These men appeared far meaner than he had expected. He got the feeling that each and every one of them would not have a second thought about shoving a knife into each other's backs – much less hesitate to gut a mud-covered boy.

One of the roosters got a beak to the eye. It shook its head back and forth as its wings sagged.

"Lookie there. My rooster got him a good one. Told you mine would win," one of the burly men, with a pot-gut hanging over his belt, bragged.

"Hold on, mine's not dead yet," another man sounded hopeful.

"Will be in a minute if you don't pull him out now."

"A one-eyed rooster won't be any good. Might as well let him get finished off," another man spoke up, eagerly wanting to see the bloody death of the other rooster.

"He'll still be good for treading on a hen," the rooster's owner said. Despair sounded in his voice as well as his face.

"Don't want a loser's get."

"Hell, he haint no loser. He's been a reigning champion four damned times in a row," the man said as he straddled over the wooden cockpit wall to grab up his injured rooster. "I done give in to pressure and fought him again too soon," he grumbled as the winning rooster flew up in the air still trying to attack the badly injured rooster.

A man with white hair and long white beard laughed with delight. Clancy judged the man to be in his late fifties or sixty, but he gave off a powerful appearance. Even high up in the pine tree, Clancy could see his broad build along with a pair of mean pig-eyes squinted in a red face. He appeared to be in control of the other men. This had to be Grubb Claxton.

"Okay, It's time for you men to pay up. This here fight is done with. Better luck next time."

After all the men had paid up, some of them walked away from the pit until they were standing underneath the pine tree. Their whispered voices lifted up to Clancy. He could hear them as clearly as if they were sitting on the limb beside him. There were moans and groans along with a lot of cursing. Some of the men were accusing Grubb Claxton of cheating. One man whispered that Claxton had put pepper and other substances in his roosters' feathers to impair their opponents. The grumbling and whispers stopped every time Grubb Claxton's gaze fell on each man.

Clancy watched as the men picked up live and dead roosters and disappeared into the woods going in different directions.

"Need help cleaning up?" One of the remaining men asked Claxton.

"No, get your birds taken care of and be at the still in two hours. It's time to fire up," Claxton said as Clancy watched him stuff money in the chest pocket of his bibbed overalls. A strange kind of feeling came over Clancy that he didn't know how to interpret. It wasn't exactly fear. It was more like being a witness to something that was pure evil. He'd have to think on the feeling a while.

Grubb Claxton stayed behind, cleaning up the area before he picked up a carrier with two live and one dead rooster. He appeared to be a happy man as he also disappeared into the woods. Clancy stayed still, watching and listening for any movement or sound that meant he wasn't alone, or that any of the men might return.

Clancy judged an hour had passed before he dared climb down out of the tree. He started toward the area where he thought the still was located when someone took hold of his arm. He sucked in air as he whirled around, reaching for the pistol he kept close his body.

"Sheee," Granny Witcher hissed in a low-pitched sound. Her lips came within an inch of his ear. "You're getting outta here and never coming back."

"But - -," he started to object when her hand covered his mouth a moment before she gripped his mud-covered arm in an iron grip. She led him away while using a handful of broomsedge to carefully wipe out their tracks. She didn't speak or allow him to do so until they were a good half-mile and a hollow away from the mountain.

"Turn me loose," Clancy whispered.

"Not yet. Don't want you running off and leaving prints that'll be hard to wipe out."

"I hain't gonna run off."

"Give me your word."

"I give it. Did you follow me?"

"You left a trail the blind could follow. Don't talk yet. The wind has changed directions again."

"You're still talkin'."

"My voice is low pitched. Yours hain't."

He remained silent as he watched her walk backward until they came to a creek where she made him walk in the center with her. He'd planned on leaving Dobb's boots in a strategic location, but there was no longer a need. He hadn't figured out a way to destroy their still and blame it on Dobb. He still would, but it wasn't going to be today.

"You're itching to get yourself killed," Granny Witcher told him as though she knew what he was thinking.

"No, I hain't."

"You leave so much as one track and they'll come after you. Especially if you keep behaving like an idiot. These men are no fools. They've lived longer and seen more than you have. You don't know it yet, but those men have deadfall traps set all around their still. Had you gone toward the still instead of toward the cockfight, you'd have been in a shallow grave before nightfall."

Clancy didn't know how to respond, but he knew she was telling the truth. "How do you know?" he asked defensively.

"Not much I don't know about things in these mountains. That includes knowing you'd better get some sense in that head of yours before it's too late. You keep on the way you're going and every man in these parts will be hunting you down like you're a rogue wolf with a bounty on its head."

Clancy gave her one of his hateful looks, not liking what she was telling him.

"Furthermore, you're going to bring every piece of Tucker's still and put it back the same as you found it."

"No, I hain't."

"You best get at it," she ignored his refusal. "Tucker will be making his way up the mountain by the end of the week. He knows about you along with where your cave is located."

"No, he don't."

"Stop your arguing. You think you're the only one who knows things. As for those cockfights, don't expect you to know it, but there's lawmen from at least three counties who indulge in cockfights. Leave them be, Clancy. And for the sake of Tally, don't go stomping around their still especially in Dobb's boots. Like I done told you, if you value your life, stay far away from their mountain. They're a mean bunch, Clancy. A mighty mean bunch."

A mighty mean bunch ran through Granny Witcher's mind over and over. She knew exactly what they could do and had done. The need for revenge still burned inside her. The only thing that stopped her from getting revenge had been her son.

She hadn't wanted the same thing to happen to her son that happened to Gray Leaf. A man couldn't count on luck forever. Bad men got by with far more than a good man ever could.

Now that Billy Gray was dead, and all his children were long gone, it might be time she got the revenge she'd longed for. She'd been praying to Gray Leaf in hopes he'd send her a sign as to what she should do. So far, he hadn't. The only thing she might consider a sign were words from God. *Thou shalt not murder.* What kept puzzling Granny Witcher's mind was exactly what God intended to be murder. Was it the killing of all things, or was it only the killing of humans? Did murder include self-defense or the execution of evil humans?

Did God actually say: *Revenge is mine*?

Did God not also use humans to do his will?

~~~~

"Why do we have to get up this early?" Tally asked as Granny Witcher's bony hand shook her awake.

"Got to gather herbs. Have to make a trip off this mountain soon to get supplies."

"Why can't we do it later in the day?" Tally knew it was useless to argue, but she did it anyway. All of Granny Witcher's scouring the mountains wasn't always to Tally's liking.

"Done told you before, herbs are more potent early in the morning."

Tally couldn't see such as that would make a difference. She yawned and grumbled as she got out of her mother's bed. Granny Witcher had already made up her own bed next to the cook stove. She was too old to climb into the cabin's loft to sleep. She had left her own bed at her little shack and made herself a new one near the stove to keep her aching bones extra warm.

Granny Witcher had traded her healing salves for scrap slabs at a sawmill down in a pine hollow. It had become too difficult to scrounge enough deadfall to keep the cabin warm during the winter months. She believed in preparing ahead of time. She'd also traded herbs for some homespun mattress sacking down in the valley. She'd filled the sacking full of sawdust and a lot of what she called healing herbs. The sawmill men had allowed her to haul off all the sawdust she was able to tote home. Pine sawdust was good to use in the goat stall. It kept the goat from getting her udder dirty from lying in dirt.

Granny Witcher lifted the lid of the stove to poke enough cook-wood in to fix breakfast. A bit of firelight shown a beam onto her pallet bed. A strange look came to her face as she glared at the beam of light.

"That's it," she mumbled. "It's what I've been waiting for."

"What are you mumbling about?" Tally asked.

"A sign. I've finally got it." She continued putting wood in the stove and replaced the lid. She wanted to cook their eggs fast. They had a lot of herbs to gather if she was to fulfil the sign she'd been given.

Granny Witcher left Tally to eat her breakfast as she rushed outside to the pile of ashes that had been piled up through the winter, and spring. Tally hadn't known to work the ashes into her garden soil before it was planted. She put the ashes into a hamper and set the hamper into the wash tub. She toted several buckets of water and poured over the ashes. She'd have to pour the same water over the ashes several time to get good lye water.

After a long day of going against her own advice and gathering more herbs than she'd ever gathered, she lay on her pallet thinking about what she should do now. When she decided Tally was in her time of deep sleep, she left the cabin to make her way to Clancy's cave. She listened for the call of a particular whippoorwill, but all were silent. All she heard were the peaceful sounds of night birds and insects whispering softly in the cool night air. She found a certain kind of peacefulness during the resting time. Sunshine brought energy with it, while nighttime brought contentment to her.

She had to give Clancy credit for keeping the path and the opening well concealed. Even the first twenty feet of the dark cave seemed unoccupied to her now adjusted to the dark eyes. Near the back of the cave things got complicated. There were three different prongs. Two of the prongs were filled to the brim with things Clancy had procured – legally and otherwise.

She found him in a hollowed-out crag on the left side of one of the prongs. He was buried in a pallet made out of several quilts and blankets. His head was resting on a pillow.

"Clancy," she said in a slightly hushed voice, not wanting to startle him awake. "Wake up son. We need to talk."

"Momma?" he mumbled a moment before he came fully awake. When he realized it wasn't his mother talking, he jumped straight up.

"Easy," she soothed. "It's just me."

"What's wrong? What's happened," he demanded.

"Nothing's wrong. I need a favor of you."

"What the hell?" he mumbled, obviously irritated that she was in his cave, not to mention being woken up before he was through sleeping.

"I need you to stay with Tally while I go down into the valley."

"What you goin' there for?"

"Got to trade for supplies and don't want to chance taking Tally with me. Can't chance leaving her alone either. Want me to bring her here."

"No," he was quick to say. He didn't like anybody knowing where his main cave was located – and that included Tally as well as the old witch woman. But then, she knew everything and then some. "When?"

He seemed a little less irritated at the mention of Tally.

"Right now. Left her asleep."

"Don't mind leavin' her alone at night, do you?"

"I mind. Don't have much of a choice at times."

"Don't reckon them folks will chance sneakin' about in these mountains during nighttime."

"There's hunters. Not to mention those no-accounts you paid a visit to. Seems you left broken limbs and scraped bark on that white pine tree you climbed."

"No way," he objected even when he knew it was true. "What're they doin'."

"Grubb and two of his men have been snooping around. They found where Tucker's still had been. Haven't tracked you yet since they're thinking it was Dobb snooping around their place. It's only a matter of time before they realize he's dead. They know what happened to Tucker and that he's not able to get about. Grubb Claxton will figure out it was you and go after you with a vengeance.

"Or go after you," he was quick to say.

"Me and you both. Think what will happen to Tally without us?"

"Let's go," he said as he tossed the blankets, he'd taken from Tucker, aside.

~~~~

Granny Witcher was off the mountain and in the valley while the morning light was still a blue gray. Even the air smelled different down in the valley. It clogged the lungs with what she considered stale, overused air. There was a smell of burned coal, scorched wood, sweat, garbage piles, along with human and animal refuse. Lack of healing air made her want to rush back up into the high mountains where she could breathe the clean, fresh breath of life. But first she had things that needed doing. Going to see Tucker was one of her first stops. Instead of knocking on Tucker's door and hoping he would hear and call out for her to come in, she eased through the unlocked door and made her way to his bedroom.

"Holy shit," Tucker squawked when his eyes opened to see a hunched, dark shadow glaring down on him. "You scared the hell outta me. There for a minute I thought you was the grim reaper standing there in person. What you after?"

"Seeing if you're still alive," she said as her eyes took in his appearance. He was in right good shape considering the shape he'd been in. Still yet, he wasn't ready to do much walking about. Which meant Clancy had a little time left before he had to face the results of his actions. "Why is nobody at the doc's place?"

"Elouise is in the crazy house. The doc ran off with his nurse and hain't showed back up."

"Took long enough."

"Yeah. What're you wantin'? Sneakin' in my bedroom like you've done."

She looked toward the planks someone had nailed over the window proving that Clancy was telling the truth about Inez.

"Grubb Claxton and his men have been snooping about."

"My still?" he asked with obvious concern as he tried to sit up and get out of bed without success.

"Gone." She didn't lie unless not telling the whole story was considered lying.

"Oh, hell! I'm ruined," he moaned in pain as he fell back in bed.

"You got any jugs of liquor left?" she asked.

"Wish I did. I'm in bad need of a jug right now."

"What about the doc? He got any?"

"Don't know about that. If he did, I'd say somebody took it. Most likely his medicine cabinet's plum emptied out by now. Talk's he left in a hurry leaving the preacher seeing to Elouise being dragged off to the crazy house. Why you want to know?"

"I'm in need of a couple of jugs."

"What for?"

"Medicinal use."

"I gave you plenty for lookin' after Dobb. How's he doin'?"

"Not seen him in a while."

"That's odd."

"Nothing Dobb has ever done comes as a surprise unless he'd up and get religion."

"I'm here flat on my back, still hurtin' like the devil shovelin' fire coals over my body, while you're standing beside my bed trying to be being funny. Let's stop the jawin' and you tell me what you're up to?"

"Appears to me you're almost healed."

"Not fast enough for my liking. Stop hem hawing and tell me why you're here. I know you've got liquor stashed somewhere?"

"Just need to set things right."

"What things?"

"I'm old. If I was to die, would you be willing to care for the girl?"

"Uh, what girl?" he asked hesitantly.

"Tally. Dobb's girl."

"Why can't he take care of her?"

"When's he ever taken care of anybody other than himself?"

"That's a fact. We both know what kind of man he is."

"Well then, will you raise her like she was your own?"

"Hell no!" Tucker said. "I hain't fit to take care of myself. Never have been. No way I'm takin' on a little girl to raise. I'm nigh near as bad as Dobb."

"That's not so. You've got a kind heart. Oh, I might add, you'll need to keep your eyes on that boy too. He needs a good influence, a father figure."

Tucker laughed hard and winced at the pain it caused him. "That boy don't need no takin' care of. Never has and never will. He's as wily as a fox and as tough as an anvil. That boy don't need nobody."

Granny Witcher knew better, but she saw no reason to explain further to Tucker."

"You needing anything I can provide?" she asked.

"You want the long list or the short list."

"Short," she told him. "I'm too old for anything that would be long."

Granny Witcher left Tucker with an uneasy feeling gnawing inside her. She hadn't expected Tucker to refuse her request to take care of Tally and Clancy, but she understood his reasoning. Not only was he a moonshiner and an unmarried man; he saw himself as less worthy than other people. He was wrong. It was those who thought themselves superior that were unworthy.

Oddly enough, she did something she hadn't planned on ever doing. Instead of disappearing into the woods to think on what deserved being done, she found herself looking at the tiny, white church not far from Preacher Hadley's place. She didn't want to be seen, but she had a strong urge to walk inside the church. She hadn't been inside a white man's church since she had been known as Clarence Witcher's wife.

A chill crept over her. *Clarence Witcher's wife.* Three of the most despicable words in her existence. Yet, she had a deep curiosity about what had happened to him, his now so-called wife, and what children the wife might have produced. Gray Leaf had once told her he'd talked to Buck who said Clarence Witcher had remarried and the woman gave birth to a son.

As for her parents, Cooky, and Buck, they were older than her and most likely passed on to a better world by now. Bo might still be alive, but she had no idea how to find him – or even if she wanted to. That life was bygone days that were better left far behind. Still, there was no way her history wasn't important. It was a reminder that people existed who couldn't be trusted – even people she loved.

She drew in a determined breath, eased up to the church house, walked up the wooden steps, and touched the doorknob. It turned. The door opened. She looked inside. The wooden floor that led to the pulpit was worn slick by many feet. The pulpit was made of wormy chestnut wood. A black Bible with curled leather binding lay open on top of the pulpit as though it was waiting to be read.

The church seats looked hard and uncomfortable as she turned her gaze from the pulpit to look at their emptiness. She tried to picture what people would sit where. She was disappointed at the feeling that crawled up her spine. She longed for a sense of peace and warmth to come over her, but it didn't. Instead, she got a feeling of cold emptiness, of people who came from custom instead of seeking the love of God. She reached out a bony hand as though beseeching God to lead her inside.

She walked slowly on the worn floor to the pulpit. Her bony hands reached out and caressed the open Bible. The warmth she had been seeking came to her fingertips, up her fingers, into her hands, up her arms and finally reached her heart.

"Trust in the Lord," a silent voice whispered to her. *"Time takes care of all things* – both bad and good. Time does, but maybe not in the way they should be taken care of. Sometimes good people had to speed up before bad things had a chance to happened.

"Forgive me, Lord," she whispered, her thin lips barely moving. "For what I'm about to do."

She moved her hands from the Bible, turned, walked back down the worn floor, and out the door, closing it behind her.

~~~~

"I can't stay inside this cabin any longer. I feel caged inside these walls of logs. I need to breathe air that smells of the earth instead of grease, fried eggs, dust, and body sweat," Clancy told Tally as he rubbed his nose on his shirtsleeve. Smells that he wasn't used to penetrated everything inside the cabin. "How can you stand being inside so much?" he asked Tally.

"Momma is still here," Tally told him. "Sometimes she talks to me."

Clancy shook his head. "No, she don't," he told her firmly. "It's only your imagination."

His words brought tears to Tally's eyes, making him feel guilty, but not guilty enough for him to tell her lies.

"If that's what makes you feel good, go ahead and believe it, but dead people don't talk to nobody."

Tears brimmed over and slid from Tally's eyes and ran down her cheeks. "Why are you being mean to me?" she whined.

"I hain't being mean to you. I aim to tell you the truth about things. Best to face what is real sooner than later. Come on. Let's take to the woods."

"Granny Witcher said for me to stay close to the cabin. She didn't want me running the woods."

"We won't be running the woods. We'll stay close. We can most likely find some berries to eat."

"Okay," Tally brightened a little.

Like most children, she loved all berries and couldn't get enough of them. She also liked being with Clancy. She hadn't had contact with other young people since her siblings had gone away. She longed for the company of someone close her own age and Clancy was it. He made her think about her brother, Jimmy. He was the closest to her own age and the sibling she missed the most. Now that her dad was dead, she wondered if her brothers might come back. She knew her sister never would because she had a husband of her own.

"Do you think we might get married when we get older?" she suddenly asked Clancy.

He looked a bit taken back and then became thoughtful. "Hadn't thought about it but it's possible. I sure hain't seen nobody else I'd want to marry."

"Would we live in Momma's cabin or in your cave?"

"I don't plan on living in a cave forever. By the time I'm a man, I'll have a lot of land and a big house of my own. I aim to be somebody important."

"I don't think I'd want to live in a cave. It's dark in caves, and there's spiders and snakes. I don't like spiders and snakes. I don't like bugs and worms either."

"You'd get use to 'em after a while."

She didn't think so. "Do you think my brothers might come back if they know my dad is dead?" She wanted to find out what he thought about the possibility.

"Depends."

"On what?"

"Where they're at and what they're doin'. If they're happy, they won't want to come back. If they're miserable, they might think life would be better in these mountains now that their tormentor got killed by a bear. Take Granny Witcher, I've heard folks say she could go anywhere she wants, but she stays right here. My folks could never understand why. I understand now. Life here is good because it is what you know, that is if you don't mind hard living, and the everlasting cold winters."

"I don't like being cold," Tally told him. "Was it cold down in the valley where your folks lived?"

"Yeah, it was cold during winter. Reckon it's cold just about everywhere during the winter time. 'Course I've read in Momma's books that there's places where there's no winter. Hain't ever been there. Don't know 'xactly where those places are at. Can you read?" he asked her suddenly.

She shook her head. "Momma was teaching me to read and write. I know my A B C's, and I recognize a few words when I see 'em."

"I can read right good," he bragged. "Momma made me go to school and practice reading and stuff like that every single day, even when school was out. Do you have books, paper and pencil?"

Tally shook her head. "Not anymore. Daddy burned them when he caught Momma teaching me. He slapped her in the face and said women were too stupid to learn stuff. He said all a woman was fit for was to do her husband's bidding. Do you agree with him?"

"No, I don't. Momma could read and write. She said there weren't much difference in men and women and their needs. Do you know why Granny Witcher is going down in the valley?"

"She said she needed supplies for us. That's why we had to gather extra herbs to trade for stuff."

"Do you like living with her?"

"She's okay, but I want my momma."

"Yeah, I want mine too, but neither of us will get what we want. Now, don't you go poutin' up on me and gettin' sad again. Like I done said, we can't change what already is. You know, you ought to ask Granny Witcher to teach you to read and write. I've seen books in her shack."

"You've been in her place?" Tally asked with a bit of surprise.

"Hain't been inside, but I've looked in the window. It pays to keep an eye on things. Let's stop jawin' and get out in the woods."

"Okay," Tally agreed, although she didn't think they should get far from the cabin. She didn't want Granny Witcher to return and find them gone.

"I'm gonna take you around a bit. You need to start learning about things like how these mountains lay, and how to always find your way back home if you get lost. I'll also show you how and where to hide in case someone is about and you don't want to be seen."

"Why? Do you think I'll get lost?"

"It's easy to get lost. Directions can fool you, and things can look alike unless you pay mighty good attention. Even I have to be mighty careful every once in a while."

Clancy took her away from their mountain into a deeply wooded area on the backside of a mountain where Grubb's still was located. It was a secluded area where Clancy hadn't wandered. He wanted to test his own skills as well as teach Tally. On the opposite side of the laurel hell was a dense growth of underbrush above a rock cliff that dropped down into a gully.

Suddenly he put his finger to his lips indicating for Tally to be silent. The wind brought the sound of raised voices to them. He grabbed Tally by the arm as he looked around for a place for them to hide. He pulled her to her knees pulling her behind him through a thick tangle of Laurel limbs. He quickly dug as deep as he could in the leaves and soft dirt and covered them both with leaves and dirt the best he could. He didn't have time to wipe out any of their tracks. The voices were getting louder and closer. Whoever it was would be sure to find their footprint and hiding place if they came their way.

"I'm telling you again, I didn't do anything. I'm being set up. There's no way I'd double-cross you." One of the men was saying. His voice sounded of fear and desperation. Clancy recognized the voice as being one of the men who claimed Grubb was putting stuff in his rooster's feathers.

"It'd take a fool to admit it."

Clancy recognized the gruff voice of Grubb Claxton. Clancy's body tensed. Tally was trembling beside him. Thankfully, she wasn't making a sound. To Clancy's relief, the men walked on the opposite side of the laurel hell from where they had crawled in.

"You've got to listen to me," the man said.

"I've already listened."

A loud thump sounded, followed by a grunt. There were more thumps and sounds that reminded him of the sounds Dobbs made when he tumbled down the cliff where the cow died. Clancy knew better than to lift his head to see what was going on. Tally tried to huddle even closer to him. Neither of them made a sound.

"Good Riddance. Nobody goes against Grubb Claxton and lives."

There was the sound of heavy footsteps slowly walking away,

Clancy had no idea how long they stayed hidden. Each minute seemed like hours. He had listened to the sound of something tumbling down the rock cliff and then someone walking away, but he knew not to leave their hiding place too soon. He knew to be patient enough to make sure they weren't being observed.

~~~~

Granny Witcher didn't get all she had planned to get from down in the valley. She would have to think of what she had intended doing for a while longer. She did get the supplies she needed for the girl. A feeling that she needed to hurry back to the cabin came over her once she'd left the church. She knew something was wrong, she just couldn't pick up on what it was.

When she reached the cabin and found Clancy and Tally gone, she knew her feeling had been right. She dropped her supplies in the middle of the cabin floor and started tracking them.

Gray Leaf had spent months teaching her how to track as well as how to wipe out tracks. At the time, she hadn't thought she would ever put such knowledge to use. She had used both many times over, as well as many other things she had learned from him.

Trusting her instincts had never failed her yet.

She picked up their trail right outside the cabin door, taking time to wipe out her own footprints as well as theirs even though it would take her twice as long to find them. Much to her concern, their footprints were headed in the opposite direction of Clancy's caves. He was headed toward the mountain where Grubb Claxton's still was located. Surely, he wasn't being that stupid. Not only was he putting himself in danger, but he was putting Tally in danger as well. Even Gray Leaf had underestimated the vile cunning of Claxton and his men. There was nothing that man wouldn't and hadn't done.

He was pure evil, a man with no conscience. There wasn't one spark of good inside him.

If those two children came to harm, she was as responsible as they were. For one thing, she had trusted Clancy to be intelligent enough to do as she'd told him. That was her mistake. Hadn't her son, Bill Gray, proved to her that children were determined to go against the wisdom their parents tried to instill in them? She was certain her son's death was an accident. He had gotten careless when cutting a large hemlock tree down. The tree had been shaky. The wood on the inside of the tree was cracked and splintered by strong winds and weather. The tree had come apart before it was completely cut, a section falling on her son. She had checked the tree and surrounding area many times, making sure nobody could have set up the accident. Even Gray Leaf's spirit had assured her it was an accident. What happened to Gray Leaf hadn't been an accident.

She hadn't hammered firmly enough into Clancy's thick head that he should stay away from such an evil man. She'd been afraid he would find him a challenge and try to prove he was smarter than Grubb Claxton and his bunch.

Most important of all was she didn't hold with feuds. All feuding ever accomplished was getting people killed over things that had happened in the past. It seemed Grubb Claxton and his bunch had also let the feud die. That bunch hadn't harmed her son, his wife and children and they hadn't harmed her. Of course, she had to take into consideration they never knew Billy Gray was her and Gray Leaf's son.

Vengeance is mine, sayeth the Lord.

Dark shadows had taken over the woods as the gloaming of night was coming on strong. Granny Witcher was fighting down panic as she got closer to the mountain where Claxton's still was located. No way would Clancy keep Tally out after dark knowing she would disapprove. Something bad had happened. Something she would have to rectify if it wasn't too late. Claxton and his bunch had a way of making people disappear. Even if relatives reported missing people, the law never searched for them. It was a well-known fact a lot of the law was in cahoots with Claxton.

Often, Granny Witcher stopped to listen for sounds carried on the wind. The night birds had started calling and insects were chirping throughout the woods. Their footprints had become hard to distinguish in the darkness even for her, but she was slowly managing to stay on their trail being her eyes had already adjusted to seeing in the dark. The woods had become a continuous darkness until there were no longer shadows being cast. The birds stopped calling and the insects grew silent moments before sounds reached her ears. It was the sound of something or someone rushing through the woods, tripping over roots, and bumping into undergrowth as they tried to hurry without making noise.

Granny Witcher silently stepped behind a large tree trunk in order to remained hidden in case it wasn't Tally and Clancy. Her body was as slender as a bent twig, her clothes always dark, which made her almost invisible when she chose. Relief filled her in waves. It was the children. Perhaps they had gotten lost and was trying to find their way home. Hope this assumption was right fell when she saw that Clancy was walking backward with slender branches in his hands as he tried to wipe out their footprints.

Both children gasped with horror as she stepped out from behind the tree trunk. Clancy grabbed at his clothing. Pulling out a pistol with shaking hands.

"Easy. It's me," Granny Witcher said in a low voice she hoped wouldn't carry.

Relief showed on their faces as Clancy lifted his finger to his lips to indicate for her to be silent. She nodded, took the branches from Clancy's hands to wipe out their tracks. She motioned for them to continue on their way. Clancy was walking in almost the same places she had tracked them. He obviously hadn't been lost, but she sensed the fear that was coming from them in waves.

Neither of them spoke until they were inside the cabin. Tally burst into tears as she threw her arms around Granny Witcher in a near death grip. Granny held her close as she glared at Clancy in the darkness of the cabin.

"What happened?" she demanded.

"I was teaching Tally how to find her way home," he said defensively. "I had no idea we'd cross paths with Grubb Claxton and the other man." Clancy drew in a deep breath to calm himself and then told her the rest of what happened.

"Are you sure Claxton didn't see you."

"Yeah, I made sure he was long gone before we came out of hiding. That's why it got dark on us."

"And the other man?"

"I left Tally hiding and crawled out of the laurel hell to check on the man and make sure nobody was about. The man was only a twisted-up speck at the bottom of the ravine."

"Are you sure he wasn't alive."

"Positive."

Granny Witcher believed him. Her flesh grew goose bumps. She had found Gray Leaf at the bottom of the same ravine. Grubb Claxton was at it again – getting rid of anybody who opposed him. She'd been unable to get Gray Leaf's body out of the ravine. It was all she could do to get herself down and up the sheer rock walls. She had dragged Gray Leaf to the most sheltered place she could find, dug a shallow grave in the rocky ground and covered it with rocks. She'd sat on the grave for days, not eating or drinking, as she mourned the loss of the man she loved.

She and Gray Leaf did not live in this mountain range at the time. Gray Leaf and Rod Freeman had gone after the young Claxton and his bunch after they had brutally attacked Rod and Delila's daughter and left her for dead. When Gray Leaf and Rod didn't return, she had taken it upon herself to track her husband until she found him. To this day, she hadn't discovered what happened to Rod. He never showed up again.

She stayed in the area for a while because it was where her beloved's spirit remained. Finally, out of desperation and the hopes she could ease her hurt, she went back to her home.

She found it odd that her son had chosen the mountain near where Claxton's still was located to live. He had no idea that was where his father was murdered.

From that day to this day, she had longed for revenge. And done nothing.

Revenge is mine, sayeth the Lord.

"You'll have to spend the night here. Best you not go to your cave just yet. You can sleep in the loft. I'll build a fire and fix you both something to eat."

"I'll be okay going to my place," Clancy objected.

"No," she told him firmly. "There are reasons for you to stay here." The way she said that let Clancy know she had something in mind. He argued no further.

~~~~

There was a time and a season for everything. Clancy's snooping behavior had made sure the time had come for her to do something. Once Tally's fear had eased and she had fallen asleep, she turned to Clancy.

"I want your word of honor that you will stay here and not leave this cabin unless you are sure there is an extreme danger for Tally and you. If you become afraid, take Tally to your cave and stay there until I come for her."

"Why?" Clancy demanded.

"I've told you all you need to know. Do I have your word of honor?"

"Yeah," he said a little too quickly.

"Tell me you give me your word of honor on the grave of your mother."

Clancy looked stunned. Her words let him know she planned something big. "I give you my word of honor," he finally told her. "But what if you don't come back?"

"Then I'll have to trust Tally into your care."

Clancy swallowed hard and looked into her wizened face. "You best come back," he told her.

"Lock the door and keep your gun handy. If Claxton shows up, shoot him," she told clancy as she eased out the door.

She went to the goat lot and took two jugs of liquor she'd hidden out of the hamper of sawdust. This wasn't what she'd planned on doing when she left the cabin that morning, but it was the way things stood now.

She carried the jugs to her shack, hoping Claxton and his bunch hadn't been there. They hadn't. Her shack and supply of herbs were exactly as she'd left them. She lifted a plank in the floor and took out a bottle of liquid she'd prepared a few days before just in case the time came when she'd need it. The time had come.

There was no way she could wipe out all the evidence Clancy and Tally had left behind. She had no doubt Claxton would discover the children had witnessed what he had done. He was a smart enough man to check things out in a day or two to make sure all was well. A hard rain might help to wipe out their trail, but there was no assurance of rain for at least a week.

"Am I doing what ought to be done," she whispered, and listened for a sign. Sure enough, on the far mountain came the faint call of the whippoorwill. Gray Leaf was sending her a sign. "Talk to me?" she added silently, but he had no words for her. No other sign if what she was about to do was right or wrong. It was her choice.

Poison hemlock is a dark green plant with lacy, fern like leaves. In May through August, it bloomed white and was easily confused with plants that did not contain poison. Its blooms were two to three inches across. Its stems were hollow, ridged, and hairless with purplish blotches. Every part of the plant was deadly. She knew to be extra careful not to get it on her clothes or bare hands when she gathered it. She had used both the juice pressed from the stems and roots as well as all dried parts of the plants. She poured the contents of the bottles into both jugs.

She headed toward the far mountain saying a prayer that God would stop her if she was doing something that ought not be done. If it was God's will, she prayed for his guidance and help in not harming those who should not be harmed. She strained her ears to hear any sound a whippoorwill might make. All was silent. She continued on.

She smelled the familiar scent of mash and sweating men before she got close enough to see them. She moved into the shadows knowing the fire would serve to blind the men from seeing farther that the light cast by the fire.

Just as she'd expected, Claxton and his bunch were running off a batch of shine. They were putting it directly into jugs to be sold to pitiful men who didn't think they could live without being soused out of their minds. They had a wooden sled hooked up to a red mule and were putting the jugs in the sled with cardboard and rags around each glass jug to keep them from breaking when they were hauled off the mountain.

Granny Witcher waited, counting the jugs it would take to fill the sled. She had been there watching them many times before. She made a point of knowing what the men who had killed her beloved husband did. She'd watched them grow old, their hair go gray, their faces red, and livers shot. She had seen their bellies grow fat until their pants would no longer fit over their bellies. She had watched and done nothing – until now.

Claxton always kept jugs of Tucker's liquor for him and the men to drink as a reward after each run was secured in the sled. No way was he or one of his bunch willing to drink what they run off. They knew better. Two of Tucker's jugs were sitting off in the shadows near where she hid. Those men had set the jugs aside to make sure they didn't get mixed up with their own brew. The jugs and lids were made slightly different.

When her chance arrived, she eased forward and switched the jugs with the two she brought containing the poison hemlock and carried Tucker's jugs of liquor into the woods with her. Claxton and three of his bunch grumbled with relief as they pulled dirty red and blue handkerchiefs from their hind pockets and wiped sweat from their faces.

"Damned if I'm not ready for some shine afore we head off this mountain with Big Red. That mule gets more contrary with each breath it draws," Grubb Claxton said. "I'd put a bullet between his eyes if I had another one trained to take his place."

"Have to admit ole Tucker does brew some good stuff," one of the men said.

"Fool," another man said. "Go broke running off good liquor the way he does. Ought to figured that out by now."

"Went by his still a while ago. It was gone. Figured that crazy witch woman hauled it off somewhere. She has a way of making tracks disappear – as well as other things."

"She puts the hee bee gee bees in me," another man said.

"Best to leave that witch be."

"Did Tucker die?" another man asked.

"Hain't heard if he did," Claxton answered. "How about you, Bub? You ought to know being you spent some of your cut last week on visiting that Inez woman."

"He's still alive," Bub chuckled. "No thanks to Inez. She tried to shoot his head off but missed. Goes to show a woman can't shoot worth shit."

"Hain't you afraid to poke that woman? I heard she has a bad case of the clap," another man said.

"I don't do no pokin' on her. Know better. She's got a mouth that could suck a river dry."

"And you admit it?"

"Hell, yeah, I admit it. You men ought to give it a try if you hain't already."

"My wife's not a nasty woman."

"Mine either."

"Shit then. You don't know what you're missing."

"Talk is she learned how to do that from siphoning gas during the middle of the night. You teach her how to do that, Bub?"

Bub cursed as the men laughed like it was the funniest joke they'd ever heard.

Granny Witcher stayed hidden as she watched Grubb Claxton go to the jugs and take them to the men. She watched as the men took turns drinking the liquor from both jugs.

"Man, that's good stuff," one of the men said. "It's the best I've ever put in my mouth," he said as he handed the jug to Bub. "What do you think."

Bub drank, coughed, and drank some more. "Yep, it's mighty fine. Tastes a little different than usual. Kinda makes me think of parsnips my old woman is always cooking," he said as he took a seat near the sled.

Claxton was drinking heavily on the other jug. He never shared until he'd had his fill. He pulled the jug away from his mouth, smacked his lips, and sat down beside Bub. "Does have a slight twang to it. Wonder what Tucker done different with this run."

Another man took the jug from Bub and drank, coughed, drank, and then held the jug under his nose. "Shit. I ought to have had my turn afore Bub. "His mouth made it smell like rat piss. I'd say he returned the favor to Inez."

"Hell-fire, I never done that. Know better," Bub said.

All four of the men laughed and kept on drinking.

Granny Witcher leaned against the tree and waited. Poison hemlock usually worked fast. They had drunk so much liquor she doubted they would puke up any of the poison before it had a chance to work. She didn't think the alcohol would alter the poison. She used liquor to preserve the power of the herbs she used. They should start feeling the effects soon. In three hours, it would be too late for them.

It didn't take long until the men started grumbling about their bellies hurting. Next came trembling and jerking. Claxton tried to stand, but his legs gave out. "So...om... wro...ng." he managed to get out. The other three men were withering on the ground, huffing to get enough oxygen in their lungs without success. Claxton appeared to realize what had happened, but it was too late to do anything about it.

Granny Witcher ignored the urge to go over to them, tell them this was payback for what they'd done to Gray Leaf and all the others. She didn't give in to her urge.

The sky was lightening up a bit by the time by the time she finally walked over to where the men lay. They were no longer moving, no longer breathing.

She took both jugs, walked over to the still and poured out what liquid was left on the still. She sat the jugs down, went to the sled and took two jugs, poured out the liquor on the spot where she'd poured the other liquor. She took the empty jugs to where the men lay, put them down and walked back to the still, gathered a hand full of dry leaves, put them under the still and struck a match. Flames flared up with a woosh.

She took the two poison jugs of liquor and made her way off the mountain to the place where Clancy and Tally had hidden. She went to the edge of the rock cliff and tossed Tucker's empty jugs into the ravine where they busted into many shards.

"Is it time?" she questioned and then listened for the call of the whippoorwill she'd been waiting for. It didn't come. But she heard his voice in her mind.

"Not yet. You have two children to raise before we can cross over."

Chapter 39

Ten years later Tally got her wish. She and Clancy married after he had built his nice house on the very top of the mountain near his cave. Granny Witcher had forced him to return Tucker's still, but Tucker never got it into operation again. Tucker got a job with the new lady doctor who moved into Doctor Robinson's house and took over his practice of taking care of the people in the valley. She told Tucker she'd bought the house from Doctor Robinson and his wife. He told her he never planned on practicing medicine again and didn't want his two sons to become doctors.

When Clancy was sixteen, he had started off-bearing at the sawmill down near the pine woods. He saved ever dime until he was able to buy the sawmill, build his house, and marry Tally. Granny Witcher had enough strength to hobble down the wooded aisle in order to give Tally away. They had gotten married in God's church. It was a beautiful spot filled with spring flowers growing next to her mother's and baby brother's grave. It was also near her dad's grave, but regardless of how many flowers Tally planted, none would grow on his grave. It remained a dirt mound covered with scattered rocks.

There was a young preacher who married them by the name of Jim Gray. He was the only one of Granny Witcher and Gray Leaf's grandchildren who had returned to the mountains. He'd returned to rescue Tally and ended up staying in the cabin with her. Granny Witcher had moved back to her shack and listened for the whippoorwill to call for the very last time.

After the wedding was over and the newlyweds went to their new home, Granny Witcher wandered into the woods alone. The gloaming came on slow and beautiful as she made her way back to her shack. The sky in the west was a mixture of pale pink and gold before it turned a blue gray as night silently came on.

She wasn't surprised in the least when she heard the whippoorwill call. "Is it finally time?" she asked.

"It's time," Gray Leaf answered.

She took her special elixir and hoard of matches down from a shelf, struck a match and held it to her herb filled mattress. She backed out the door as flames flared up. She stood back from the heat watching her shack turn into ashes within minutes. Once she was sure the fire was out, she drank her elixir and turned away from what had been for so many years,

Relief filled her as she held out a bony claw of a hand. Another hand seemed to take hold of it as she was guided through the woods. She knew where Gray Leaf was taking her, and she was alright with their destination.

The time had finally arrived.

www.ingramcontent.com/pod-product-compliance
Lightning Source LLC
Chambersburg PA
CBHW031057260626
47172CB00001B/115